D0522390

Born in Karachi, Pakistan in 1975, **Khurrum Rahman** moved to England when he was one. He is a West London boy and now lives in Berkshire with his wife and two sons.

Khurrum is currently working as a Senior IT Officer but his real love is writing. He has a screenplay, which has been optioned by a Danish TV producer, but is now concentrating on novels. *East of Hounslow* is his debut.

East of Hounslow

Khurrum Rahman

ONE PLACE. MANY STORIES

HQ
An imprint of HarperCollins*Publishers* Ltd
1 London Bridge Street
London SE1 9GF

This paperback edition 2018

1

First published in Great Britain by
HQ, an imprint of HarperCollins*Publishers* Ltd 2017

ISBN: 978-0-00-826209-9

MIX
Paper from
responsible sources
FSC
www.fsc.org
FSC™ C007454

This book is produced from independently certified FSC™ paper to ensure responsible forest management.

For more information visit: www.harpercollins.co.uk/green

Printed and bound in Great Britain by
CPI Group (UK) Ltd, Croydon, CR0 4YY

To my two beautiful boys.

This is for you. This is because of you.

Part One

An eye for an eye only ends up making the whole world blind.

– Mahatma Gandhi

1

My name is Javid Qasim. I am a Muslim, a British-born Muslim.

Do you know how many times I have been pulled over by the police since 9/11? Once. And that was because I was nonchalantly jumping lanes without indicating my intentions to my fellow drivers. I got a ticking off from the fuzz, who were quite happy to forego the paperwork and give me a friendly warning. They didn't even search my car, even though the stench of skunk was unmistakeable. To this day I am proud to say that I have never had my fingerprints taken.

Do you know how many times I have been racially abused since 7/7? Not even once. I get called Paki every day, but not in the *what the fuck did you call me?* way. In my circle it's a term of endearment. You see, we know who we are. And what some may see as an insult, we see as a badge of fuckin' honour. The word Pak means pure and the word Pak means clean. And if you didn't know that, then consider yourself educated.

I'm not stupid or naïve. I am aware of exactly what is happening around me but you've got to play the game, otherwise you might as well carry a big fat *kick me* sign on your back. Don't walk around wearing a sodding shalwar and kameez with a great big dopey beard and drive around in a fuckin' Honda. That's when you get pulled over and that's when you get racially abused. But not me. Why? Cos I play the game.

I know the plight of my Brothers and I know the struggle of my Sisters and I feel for them, every fuckin' one of them. *But what do you want me to do about it?* No, man. It's not my war. Call it religion or call it politics or call it greed. It all amounts to the same thing: bloodshed, devastation and broken homes. Why would I want to get my head into something like that? Especially since my life has basically been one sweet ride – not too different from my latest acquisition, a black BMW 5 series. It's only two years old, less than thirty on the clock and it's comfortable as fuck, which is essential in my line of work, as I spend a helluva lot of time in my car. It's my mobile office. I picked it up for a cool twenty G. I paid over the odds but fuck it, I could afford it as business was ticking.

I was sitting in my ride at the back of Homebase car park in Isleworth, West London, waiting on a customer. He was late, which would normally piss me off but I was otherwise distracted by all the shiny buttons and gadgets on my new whip. The speakers sounded sik and my nigga 'Pac never sounded so good as he rapped about dying young. I clocked my patron approaching and I couldn't help but frown. This was exactly what I was talking about. He's wearing a plain white suit shirt tucked into his tracksuit bottoms, finished off with a pair of Bata flip-flops, looking like he just stepped off the fucking boat. I know for a fact that he's forever being targeted because he looks like a fucking freshy. No one likes a freshy.

He looked around the car park and I realised I hadn't told him that I'd replaced my Nova. I flashed my lights at him and his smile widened at the sight of my Beemer. He approached and walked around it, whistling appreciatively, taking special notice of my customised rims. I slid my window down and told him to get the fuck in. He did and he slammed the door, hard. I bit my tongue.

'Salaam, Brother.'

'You're late,' I said.

'Sorry, Brother, I just came straight from the Masjid. Didn't see you there. Then I remembered it's only Thursday. You only ever come for Friday prayers, Javid,' he said, laughing at the unfunny observation.

We shook hands and the deal was done. He left with a fistful of Hounslow's premium and I with a fistful of dollars. He slammed my door and toddled off in his ridiculous outfit. I hate that fuckin' sanctimonious prick. In the space of a minute he vexed me twice. Firstly, he took a swipe at me because I don't go the Masjid day in, day out. It doesn't make me any less of a Muslim than he is. So what if he decides to grow a beard and I decide to grow marijuana? I'm still a Muslim. I couldn't care less if you sit in Aladdin's eating your Halal Inferno Burger whilst I sit in Burger King eating a Whopper. I am still a Muslim. I'll drink when I want, I'll curse and I'll fuck and I'll gamble and I'll get high. So what?! Read my lips. I. Am. Still. A. Muslim. I believe in Allah and only He can judge me. Not you. Or anyone else who walks this land.

Secondly, he called me Javid. No one, but no one, calls me Javid, not even my mum. No self-respecting drug dealer is called Javid. No playa is called Javid. Girls don't wanna be giving out their phone number to a guy called Javid.

Seriously.

Call me Jay.

2

I woke up in my own sweet time. I rubbed the shit out of my eyes as I ran my tongue over my pearly whites, which were anything but. It was Friday. Day of worship, day off from my daily dealing. On Friday I should be clean and my thoughts should be pure, which is not easy especially as Katrina Kaif, Bollywood sex siren, was staring down at me, wearing a sheer sari, which had obviously been soaked whilst she was out singing and dancing in the heavy downpour. Her sari clung to her every arc and her smile was greeting me with more than just a good morning. I resisted the urge, instead averting my eyes to Malcolm X, looking dapper in his black suit. The quote emblazoned at the foot of the poster read: *If you're not careful, the newspapers will have you hating the people who are being oppressed, and loving the people who are doing the oppressing.* Boom. There you have it. What a fucking line. I don't know much about Malcolm X, but he was a Muslim and made shit happen *and* he was friends with Muhammad Ali. I mean, how many cool points is that? I had a couple of books on his life knocking around somewhere, which I hadn't got around to reading, but I have seen the movie a couple of times. Denzel Washington's portrayal was on the button.

Prayers were at one. Sutton mosque was only a mile away but I still had to allow myself at least half an hour travel time because Friday prayers are always packed and there's always traffic as Hondas and Nissans jostle for parking spots. I stayed in bed for a touch longer and browsed through my phone, hungry customers requiring merchandise. *Sorry, not today. Hit me up tomorrow* was my token reply. There was a text message from my mum, asking me if I wanted eggs for breakfast, sunny side up? *Oh yes please* was my response. She came back with: *Well you better go to the shops and buy some eggs.* I could just picture her downstairs in the living room, chuckling to herself whilst watching Phil and Holly. My mum is pretty cool; she ain't like the other Asian parents where it's all *education, education, education.*

We've lived in the same house, just the two of us, all my life. I'd be hitting thirty in a couple of years but I had no intention of moving out. Have you seen the house prices? Fucking obscene! No shame living at home with your mum, especially if you're Asian. It's the norm. I may not be where I expected to be by this stage of my life, but, you know... Fuck it! Got my health, a few quid in my pocket. Life ain't so bad. Well-doers telling me to knock dealing on the head, find a real job, *get out of my comfort zone* – the fuck I want to do that?

My old man died in a motorbike accident whilst I was still warm and developing inside Mum, so I never actually got to see him – so it's not like I lost him because, really, I never had him. They had an arranged marriage and the accident occurred within the first year. Mum wasn't too cut up about it either, as she once told me that she *hadn't got around to loving him yet.* Anyway, Dad died. The world spun along and Mum and I spun along with it.

Mum doesn't treat me like a child, but on the flip side she doesn't treat me like a man either. To her, I'm somewhere in-between. I realise that she dates and isn't averse to a night out, and I know she knows that I'm out there getting up to all sorts, but as long as I'm not bringing the police to the door, and she's not bringing guys home for me to call *Dad*, then it's all good in the hood. We keep out of each other's business, adhering to our unsaid rules.

*

In preparation for prayers, I took a thorough shower, the water hot enough to cleanse away all of my bodily sins. I rubbed and I scrubbed to compensate for my colourful lifestyle. I didn't drink the night before because I did not want to be hungover at prayers, but I did party hard and I did toke hard and at the end of play, in the back of my Beemer, I spent some quality time with a half 'n' half girl, christening my new car whilst listening to fuckin' Beyonce, who, by the way, I can't stand, but the chicks seem to like all that girl empowerment crap. I'm all for it. What do I care?

I brushed my whites twice in the shower and tried to get rid of the lingering taste of her in my mouth, concentrating in particular on my tongue, which felt like it was about to fall out of my mouth. My final act was to go to town down below – I have to be free from any sins. Have to be Pak.

It's only on Fridays, when the Shaitan – *Satan* – is banished from my thoughts and replaced by Farishta – *Angels* – that I seem to spend all day feeling guilty. I put on my cleanest clothes: loose dark blue jeans with a plain black T-shirt. The tee has to be plain – no depiction of any unbelievers. That's what Mr Prizada, the guy who runs the newsagents and after-school Islam Studies, used to tell me back in the day. I selected my aftershave carefully, ensuring that there was no alcohol present. I chose my rattiest, tattiest, vagabond sneakers, as they would be off and shelved as soon as I entered the mosque. Muslim or no Muslim, a thief is a thief is a thief, and I've had a pair of Nike Air Jordan's Limited Edition liberated from me in the past and I ain't walking home in my socks again. Lesson learned.

I was clean. I was dressed. But not quite ready. Even though I had showered and scrubbed to within an inch of my life, I had yet to perform Wudu – *Ablution*. Running order goes like this: wash hands and arms up to my elbow, three times. Rinse out my mouth, three times. Wash my face, three times. Wet my hands and run them from my forehead to the back of my head. Clean behind and in the grooves of my ears. Finally, wash each foot, three times. All this had to be carried out with the right hand where possible. Now, between Wudu and the end of prayer, if I have to visit the toilet for a number one or, indeed, a two, the Wudu is broken and has to be carried out again. If I happen to pass gas from behind, Wudu is broken. If I fall asleep, fall unconscious, bleed or vomit, Wudu is broken. Honestly, I find it tough, and I only do this once a week for Friday prayers. Others… Well, they do this five times a day, seven days a week.

I gave Mum a kiss and walked out of the house into the cold sunshine, my trusty rucksack tight against my back. I passed my old Vauxhall Nova and gave it a loving pat on the roof. It was my first car and it did me proud. It was going to kill me to sell it. With a press of a button the boot of my Beemer flipped open and I stashed the rucksack, rammed full of bags of skunk and bundles

14

of cash, inside. Even though I don't deal on Fridays, I still had to have the bag nearby at all times, and that particular night I had to drop off the cash to Silas, my supplier, and pick up my cut, and he'd decide whether to send me back with the leftover gear or replenish. I started the car and the air conditioning took mere seconds to kick in. I switched from CD to radio, as I couldn't have rap music and all the profanities and sexualisation that comes with it polluting my pure mind, and I headed for Sutton mosque.

*

I saw a handful of parking spaces directly outside the mosque. I double-checked the time, just in case I had turned up an hour early, and I wondered if the clocks had gone back and I was still on yesterday's time. The mosque was normally rocking around this time, with wall to wall Pakis lining the streets. Instead, it was quiet.

With difficulty, I parallel parked in a tight spot directly outside the mosque. There were other, bigger spaces but I wanted everybody to see my ride. It took me a few attempts but I finally managed to squeeze in. As soon as I turned off the engine I realised that I couldn't leave my car here, not with weed and unscrupulously collected money in the boot, so close to the House of God.

I whispered *Bismillah* to myself as I stepped into the near-empty mosque. The first person I saw was Kevin the Convert, who was stood near the shoe rack, which, like the mosque itself, was near empty. Kevin was speaking animatedly to Mr Hamza the Cleric.

'A crime reference number,' Kevin said incredulously, waving a piece of paper in his hand. 'And what? You think that is *enough*?' Kevin scrunched up the paper and looked as though he was about to throw it to the floor in disgust, but thought better of it and handed it back to Mr Hamza.

'Brother Kevin, we must stay strong,' Mr Hamza said in that same deadpan tone that we were accustomed to when he led Friday prayers. He flattened and neatly folded the piece of paper and put it into the side pocket of his kameez. 'This is a time to

15

keep your head and have faith. I know, just like you know, just like everybody knows, the police will not help.'

'So why call them?'

Mr Hamza smiled, revealing a gap in his teeth that, as kids, we used to rip the piss out of. 'A crime has been committed, Brother. The police have to be called. Even though it is to give us a meaningless number, we must still adhere to the law of the land that we have chosen to reside in, otherwise we are just as wrong as the sinners around us.'

I removed my shoes and placed them on the shelf. I kept my head down and walked past them into the main prayer hall.

What I saw made me sick.

Illustrated on the far wall, just above where the Imam led prayers, was spray-painted a crude drawing of two pigs. From the mouth of one, a speech bubble read: *eat me or get the fuck out of my country.* The second drawing was another pig adorned with explosives, with the caption: *BOOM.* I averted my eyes and looked up at the heavens and at the large, beautiful chandelier that had only just been purchased and installed after a whip around. Hanging from it were ladies' undergarments. With shaky legs I walked around the prayer hall, taking in the scene. Holy literature had been removed from the large bookshelf and thrown to the floor, replaced by printed images of naked women and homosexuals harshly tacked to the bookshelf. The prayer rug had been removed – offensive graffiti had been sprawled across it, I later learned – and I found myself standing on a hard, cold floor.

What should have been a house full of Muslims standing side by side, praying in harmony and perfect synchronisation to Allah, was replaced by a dozen or so Brothers cleaning.

I glanced around the Prayer Hall. I watched one of the bearded regulars bring in a ladder and hold it under the chandelier, but as there was no wall nearby he had nowhere to lean it. He shook his head in frustration as he laid the ladder down. I looked on as another regular placed a table directly underneath the chandelier and then a chair on top of the table to give enough height. Between the two of them, one secured the chair and the other climbed onto the table and then comically and dangerously scaled up onto the chair. They removed the ladies, undergarments, holding them with just their fingertips, and then swiftly disposed of them into a black bin liner.

I looked around for a familiar face and I spotted Parvez, who lived across the road from me. Parvez is by far the most infuriating guy I know and, bizarrely, also the nicest. We had history. He would hover around me like an irritating mosquito, always popping around my house unannounced. He would go on about Fear of Allah, Judgement Day, Taqwa and Hadith, amongst other teachings. He was harmless, though, and despite my efforts I couldn't not like him.

Parvez was knelt down, picking up broken prayer beads and books, and not quite knowing what to do with them. I stooped down on the floor next to him and immediately started to help out. Parvez looked at me with glistening eyes and, just like that, I felt my own eyes spiking with tears. I blinked them away and placed my hands on his shoulders.

'They've stained our home,' he said. 'We must get the Masjid back to a state of cleanliness.'

'Parvez. What the f— What happened?' I said, watching my language. 'I... I don't understand. What happened?'

'Kafirs,' Parvez said, by way of explanation. 'Kafirs is what happened, Brother.'

'But, how? There's someone here at all times.'

Parvez shook his head and wiped away his tears. 'Everything will come to light in due course, Inshallah, and we will act accordingly.'

I nodded in agreement, even though I didn't quite know what I was agreeing to.

3

I left the mosque feeling pretty good about myself. My initial anger had melted away and was replaced by something similar to... I don't know what. *Faith? Respect? Solidarity?* There were initially only about a dozen of us cleaning the mosque. Word had spread fast via social media and old-fashioned word of mouth that Sutton mosque had taken a beating. I wasn't surprised that word hadn't reached me; I didn't move in those circles. The regulars were redirected to attend neighbouring mosques for the all-important Friday prayers, but as soon as prayers were over and the clock hit two, Pakis turned up like they were giving away free samosas.

No word of a lie, about two hundred of them all bearing the necessary tools: bleach, rubber gloves, tins of white paint and paint brushes, mops, refreshments and, of course, some of the finest home-cooked, butter-infested, blazing hot, heart-attack-inducing food. I watched as they made a social event of the whole scene. There was the sound of laughter bouncing off the walls, there were tears and embraces. The hall was treated to a brand new paint job and a local Sikh businessman – *a Sikh, the old enemy!* – who owned Punjabi Carpets, graciously donated a variety of new carpets and rugs until the prayer mats were replaced.

We turned that place inside out, leaving it looking brand new, and we left feeling holier than thou.

Those stupid fucking two-bit vandalising motherfuckers didn't know the first thing about Islam and about our strength within. Attack us again. Go on, I fucking dare you.

My phone rang as I approached my Beemer. Before answering, first things first, I checked the boot and made sure that the gear and the bills hadn't been jacked. Satisfied, I checked my caller display. It was Parvez. *What's he want?* I had just spent the best part of the day with him, helping to clear up the mosque. I hoped he wasn't taking the time we'd spent together to be some sort of bonding session, and he now wanted to hang out with the cool kids. He was a good guy, but well and truly part of the God Squad, and I think he'd always seen me as some sort of project. Parvez the Preacher, we called him. I ignored the call and pocketed my phone.

I closed my boot and over the roof of my car I saw the cops walking towards me. Just one copper, actually. He wasn't in uniform but I have a sixth sense when it comes to picking out the fuzz from a line-up.

And besides, this particular copper happened to be my best friend, Idris Zaidi.

I would never tell him this but Idris is one cool motherfucker, and the reason I would never tell him this is because *he knows* he's one cool motherfucker and I don't feel the need to indulge his already inflated ego. We go back to day dot, born within a day of each other. Our mums became friends in the maternity ward at West Mid Hospital. Aunty actually helped Mum a lot during that period, as my old man was busy decomposing. They were like sisters, and we like brothers. We were at nursery together, and then we hit junior school hard, making the right noises and earning respect at the grand old age of nine or whatever the fuck it was. Right little tearaways. But it was secondary school when things turned somewhat. Idris showed more of an interest in his studies and I showed the same commitment towards having a good time. The amateur shrinks amongst you would probably put that down to the lack of a father figure, but I was too busy having a good time to give it thought. So, soon-to-be PC Plod plodded off to university, and did pretty well too, according to the Masters degree hanging askew over his fireplace. He became a cop and I became a robber. Or, to put it more accurately, he a detective and I a dealer.

As Idris approached I surreptitiously checked him out. A dark blue casual blazer, with a crisp blue shirt. Wrapped around his neck in a loose knot was a lightweight black-and-white polka-dot scarf designed for design rather than to serve a purpose. A pair of tight skinny grey trousers, which made me wonder how the fuck he was going to give chase if the occasion occurred. Nice shoes, though – black suede Fila hi-tops.

We shook hands and I nodded for him to jump in. I waited nonchalantly for him to acknowledge my new whip.

'Nice,' Idris said, smirking at me knowingly. Always knowingly.

'Yeah, it's all right. Gets me from A to B.'

'Look at you trying to act cool with your new ride. You crack me up.'

'So, what's the latest? You don't call, you don't write. Bad guys keeping you busy?'

'Yeah.' He smiled. 'Something like that. Keeps me in a job.'

My phone rang again. I looked at the display and frowned. 'Shit. Parvez!'

'The Preacher? That Parvez?' Idris asked.

'Yep. One and the same,' I said, weighing up whether to answer it or not. 'I better get it. It's the second time he's called in the space of a minute. Hang on.'

'He loves you, you know that, right?' Idris said, poking me in the ribs. 'He lurves you!'

'Fuck off.' I swiped my screen and answered. 'Yeah, Parvez. 'Sup?'

'Aslamalykum, Brother,' Parvez said. 'Thanks for helping out today.' *Helping out?* I didn't like the way he said that. He didn't mean to say it in that way, but it came across as a touch patronising and it wound me the fuck up.

'Of course.' I said. 'Thank *you* for helping out today.' Yeah, that's right! How you like me now? Two can play that game.

Parvez comes back with, 'Please, Brother. It was my duty, my Farz.'

Oh, I give up. He played the Farz card. Fine. Whatever. You're a better Muslim than me. Sanctimony is not becoming. I inserted the key into the ignition and the Bluetooth immediately kicked in and the technology gave me a small thrill as I placed my phone down on the centre console. However, my thrill was short-lived as Parvez's voice was now emanating through my Blaupunkt speakers, sounding twice as annoying.

'Am... am I on speaker?' Parvez asked, at the change in transmission.

'Yeah… So, what's going on?'

'Right. So some of the Brothers are assembling at Ali's Diner at eight tonight.'

'And?'

'We need to talk about what happened at the Masjid. Discuss best way forward. Security and that. You know?'

'Yeah, I know,' I sighed. I looked at Idris, who was predictably shaking his head at me. I turned away from him. 'What time?'

'Eight, Brother. I'll see you there, yes?'

'Yeah, cool. In a bit.' I ended the call.

'*Really*, Jay?' Idris exclaimed.

'Uh… did you not hear what happened at the mosque?' I asked, sounding defensive. 'I've just come from there. It was a state. I helped with the cleaning. Man, we turned that place inside out.'

'So, you helped out, right?'

'Yeah, course. I was there most of the day. I don't recall seeing you there.'

'I was at work, you twat. What I'm saying is, you've done your bit. What is there left to do?'

I shrugged. I was an accomplished shrugger. I had a shrug for every occasion. This one was slight, barely a movement, a little lift of the shoulders. A shrug that said: *maybe something, maybe nothing.*

'Are you going to track them down with the rest of the *Brothers*?' he said, and I could just feel the cynicism dripping in his tone. 'And then what – you going to give them a good beating? Maybe someone would be kind enough to stab one of them, so this will never happen again.'

'Look, calm down, Detective Inspector! Chill, man. Take your copper's hat off for a minute and put on your Paki hat and see it from our point of view. Something like this happens, people just need to vent and be around others akin to them.'

I hadn't realised until I'd finished that I'd raised my voice.

Idris looked at me with elevated eyebrows. 'Akin?'

'Yeah, fucking akin. I can throw down an akin when the moment takes me. Or do I need a diploma?'

'All I'm saying, Jay… Find another way to help. Sitting in a room full of angry Muslims isn't healthy. You want to help, do it another way.'

'What other way?'

'I don't know, Jay. Just another way.'

'I'm not you, Idris,' I said.

He looked out of the passenger window. I fiddled with the temperature controls on my dash. Silence filled the car. It wasn't awkward. We were tight enough not to feel the need to fill the airwaves with inane chatter. Silence sat comfortably with us. After a spell I broke it.

'Is there any heat on me?'

'No, Jay. Not heard any whispers. Just keep discreet and don't make any stupid moves,' Idris said, eyes roving all over my car.

'It's under Mum's name. Asian parents are always buying cars for their kids, right?'

'Yeah, maybe,' he said.

'What?'

'What? Nothing!'

'I know you wanna say something. Say it.'

Idris sighed. Then he shrugged. His shrug wasn't as good as mine. It was exaggerated, shoulders touching his ears. Then he sighed some more.

'Fuck's sake. *What*, Idris?'

'Jay. We go back a long way, right? Me and you, we're like brothers. Fuck that, we are brothers and I know you better than you know yourself.'

'Yeah. And?'

'So, I know that you can't be happy with what you're doing. You're smart, Jay. You're one of the most creative guys I know. You can do better than this. Yes, you're making *some* money, but is this what it's going to be like for the rest of your life? You're not on our radar because you're low level, but inevitably—'

'I can't be doing a Dolly Parton, Idris. Starters, I got no qualifications. So what are my options? Burger King, security guard, baggage handler? Nah, you're all right, mate. Not for me.'

'Start a business… A legit business.'

I wasn't about to tell him about the rented one-bedroom flat in Cranford. Fluorescent lamps, bags of skunk seeds and soil, the fucking lot. It was a rash decision, a moment of grand delusions, one I realised that I could not have gone through with. I planned to clear it out at my first opportunity.

'You must have some savings by now,' he continued. 'You've been doing this forever.'

I shook my head.

'What? *Nothing*?'

'You're sitting in it,' I said, sheepishly.

'You spent it all on the car?' He sounded incredulous. I felt stupid. He smiled at me.

A smile laced with sympathy.

4

Kingsley Parker sat alone in a large conference room at the head of the table. He twirled aimlessly in his chair and wondered how many decisions had been made in this very room? How many lives saved and how many lives destroyed? Which number was greater? Parker looked up at the clock and then at his phone, which was sitting face-up on the huge table. It rang, as he knew it would. He answered on the first ring.

'Tell me,' Kingsley Parker said. 'How's our boy?'

*

At Thames House, 12 Milbank, MI5, his colleagues referred to him as Chalk. Parker had earned the nickname in 2003 when he was part of – in his view – the huge joke that was the invasion of Iraq and the search for weapons of mass destruction. *A joke with a devastating punchline.*

He had been travelling late one night or early in the morning, by himself, against orders, in search of some company. It was a road often travelled by others within his regiment, soldiers who missed the touch of a loved one. But it was also a road that, at this time of the night, was deemed too dangerous to travel. There had been sightings of Iraqi insurgents, various reports of kidnappings, some which led to the beheadings that were broadcast by the local news stations and online across the world.

It didn't matter to Parker. He was so strung out from battle that he welcomed the risk. Craved it. He told himself it wasn't just the sex but the need to be held tight, to be embraced, and to alleviate the frustration and anger and guilt that consumed him at having to fight such a shitty war.

Parker had drunk deeply but hadn't quite arrived at drunk. He was singing along to Elvis Costello when his headlights picked out the body of a young girl lying across the road. He smiled to himself as he slowed down. The girl looked to be no older than seven or eight but it was hard to establish as she was curled up into a ball with her back to him. Never had he seen such an obvious set-up, the body placed just *too* perfectly. He stopped the car forty yards short and pulled the freshly cleaned Browning handgun from his shoulder holster.

He watched the shadows on either side of the road and from his combats he slipped out a flask and took a generous sip. Parker knew he could continue driving; there was enough room either side of the girl to manoeuvre through. But he was tired. Tired of fucking Iraq. Tired of being part of something that had such sharp teeth but no intelligence. The loss of so many homes and lives. The women and the children and the livelihoods. Tired of the trigger he himself often had to pull. Parker knew he had taken out important high-value targets, but at what fucking cost? His sleep was punctuated with nightmares and a recurring dream of a nameless, faceless boy watching his father mowed down, his mother obliterated and his home redecorated. It was waking from that nightmare that had propelled him into a government-issued vehicle, down a dangerous track, in search of the warm embrace of a warm body.

Parker switched the headlights off and disabled the interior lights, which would have illuminated him when he opened the door. Even half-cut he wasn't going to be anyone's target. He rolled out of the vehicle and as soon as his boots found purchase on the floor his adrenaline kicked in. He spun away from the vehicle into the dense shadows at the side of the road, cocooned by darkness. In his fast-beating heart he knew that this could be the time and place where it all ended for him, but maybe that's the way it had to be. God's will. Parker was not a religious man but too often recently he had woken petrified that when the time came he really would be cast down into the dark depths of a volcanic hell, because he hadn't used his own God-given mind, and instead had just followed orders. The orders that left him looking at shattered bodies.

There was no easy way to do this so he just walked confidently towards the girl. His eyes adjusted to the starry night, and with the light of a quarter moon he could see the girl's shoulders rise and fall ever so slightly. The way she was laid looked as though she had been placed comfortably in bed and had drifted off to sleep, after her father had told her a sweet bedtime story, about how he would protect her from all the evil soldiers.

Any small doubt that Parker might have had about this being a set-up vanished. Any thoughts he had about this girl being genuinely injured vanished.

Parker closed his eyes and said a simple prayer. Not a rehearsed prayer, ripped out of a book, but a genuinely heartfelt prayer. He asked to be forgiven. He asked for his family to be protected. But most of all he asked for peace. Parker opened his eyes.

The body had gone.

The girl was now standing on the side of the road, glaring victoriously at him. He smiled warmly at her and nodded, and then he turned his attention to the three men who were standing in front of him.

The first thing he noticed was that they were all carrying Kalashnikov automatic rifles, but it wasn't this that disturbed him. It was their footwear. They were all wearing US military-issue heavy-duty desert boots. *Trophies. Were they stolen or crudely removed from a still-warm body?* Parker's eyes travelled up away from the boots and to the bright white cotton shalwar and kameez speckled in fresh dirt that they would have picked up as they lay on their stomachs in the grass, hiding and waiting for him to step out of the jeep. Each face was covered tightly with red and white chequered ghutrah scarves.

Three sets of nervous eyes accosted him. Angry, accusing, reckless. One of them spoke. Parker couldn't tell which one as the mouth was trapped behind the ghutrah and the sound came out muffled but unmistakeably audible.

'Put your hands up... Now! Hands in the air.' The accent heavy and guttural.

Parker slowly put his hands up in the air, bent at the elbows. Okay. So this is what death's door looked like. His life didn't flash before his eyes; instead he thought with regret that he wished he wasn't wearing his military fatigues. If he'd had a choice he would have wanted to die clean, and not covered head to toe in the clothes in which he had shed so much blood.

'Throw your weapon to the ground. Slowly… Do it now!' another voice, younger, instructed.

Rather than do as instructed, Parker reached down with his right hand and removed the Browning from the small of his back and brought it down to his side. Gun pointing to the floor, his finger caressing the trigger. Three pairs of eyes widened, their plan to take him hostage and execute him on film no longer an option. Kalashnikovs moved into shooting position, the safety switch notoriously cumbersome to operate.

Kingsley Parker lifted his holding arm and shot the one to his left in the neck and blood sprayed out towards Parker's face, but before the blood had reached him, Parker had put a bullet between the eyes of the man in the middle. A burst of fire came from the last man standing but Parker was already moving. He dropped low, and as he rolled away his left hand joined his right and steadied the Browning. A quick double tap to the chest dropped the third man.

Parker swung left and trained his gun at the girl. Only her eyes were on him. No risk there. He swivelled back to the men just as they were falling, bodies overlapping and twitching momentarily. At first glance it was impossible to establish who the tangled limbs belonged to. Parker covered them with his gun but they were no longer a threat. Just dead men. Fighting a cause.

Somebody's husband… Somebody's brother… Somebody's father.

The fight went out of Parker as quickly as it had arrived. He turned his attention back to the girl. She took a tentative step towards him, and another, moving faster with each step, almost running towards him. Parker holstered his piece and opened his arms, knowing she needed him and he needed to hug her, that this was the embrace he had been craving, the embrace which just for a minute would make him forget where and who he was, and would dispel the nightmares.

He felt tears spike his eyes. The little girl ran towards him and, with as much force as a child could muster, kicked him in the shin and continued running. It was bloody agony and Parker hopped on one leg, trying to hold his shin, and then stumbled onto the ground on his back.

He laid in the dust and laughed loudly, and didn't care who heard him, didn't care about the fact that there were three dead bodies alongside him with their eyes open, staring up into the beautiful night.

It turned out one of the men that he had killed was a high-value target, according to the deck of playing cards he carried with him at all times. Nine of clubs. Mahmud Al-Aziz. When this story did the rounds back at headquarters, how he took out three Kalashnikov-carrying Iraqi insurgents with only a Browning, his nickname was born. Quick on the draw. Chalk.

That was the last time Kingsley 'Chalk' Parker had fired a weapon in anger.

*

A little over a decade later, after heavy counselling, and after resigning his commission, Parker found himself working for MI5.

Demons compartmentalised.

It was due largely to the one man who Parker trusted without question that he had allowed himself back into an ongoing war. Major General Sinclair Stewart had played a big role in convincing Parker and, in some part, convincing the Director of Counter Terrorism at MI5 that Parker would be key in locating and capturing The Teacher, their highest target and the leader of the terrorist group Ghurfat-al-Mudarris.

Not much had been known about The Teacher, but he was assumed to be responsible for a number of attacks that had taken place, solely against the West. Many of those who worked under his command, who were involved directly in the attacks, were British Muslims, based in Luton, Blackburn, Coventry and London. Some died in the name of religion, others were detained. But none spoke. That was the respect that The Teacher commanded from his pupils.

'Some activity, sir,' said the voice on the phone. His name was Teddy Lawrence. He was new to the job and already pissed off with the bullshit of the no-value, no-purpose surveillance he was tasked with. 'You know about the attack on Sutton mosque?'

'I do,' said Parker. 'Our boy was there?'

'That's affirmative. For almost five hours. Cleaning operation – started small but escalated quickly.'

'I can imagine… Who do we like for it?'

'I'm not sure, sir. It's being looked into. Just vandals, I guess, sir.'

'This is more than that, Lawrence. This could get nasty. It *will* get nasty. The Muslim community will, without doubt, take action.'

'I agree, but whatever happens will be domestic. It's not our place… Not yet.'

'Anything else?' Parker asked.

'There's a meet tonight at twenty-hundred hours at Ali's Diner in Cranford, West London. Not far from Heathrow Airport.'

'Keep eyes on our boy. He may make an appearance.'

Hesitation. A barely heard sigh. 'Yes, sir.'

'What is it?' Parker asked.

'We've been on him for twenty-one days. He's low-key. Just another dealer. I don't know what to tell you. Nothing to reports; nothing sticks out.'

'Stay on him,' Parker instructed. 'He's the one.'

5

Ali's Diner is a place where everyone knows your name. And your business. It's not often that you see an unfamiliar face in there. Mosque-goers, students, Aunty-Jis and Uncle-Ji's, the Somalis, the small Irish contingent that operate out of the neighbouring estate agents, all frequent visitors. There are other eateries close by, but between Ali's famous Volcano Burger and the Tawa Chicken Wrap, they have no chance of long-term survival.

Shishas, normally lined up against every wall, had been removed and replaced by more chairs and tables. Ali knew it was going to be a busy one, and Ali wasn't one to miss a trick.

He was right: the place was rocking. Packed to the rafters. Ali usually flies solo but that day he had a small team of three assisting him. The stench of grease and meat attacked my senses and put me off my fried chicken. It hadn't even turned eight and there we all were. United. And evidently hungry. The door opened with a jaunty chime, all eyes moved in sync towards it and the draught blew in the self-titled badass that is Khan Abdul. He was flanked by two equally mean-looking characters known as The Twins. They weren't actually twins. In fact, they couldn't have looked more different. It was just a moniker that sounded vaguely cool based on the fact that they did everything together. Khan stood at the door and waited for everyone to take him in. Some of the older lot got up and heartily shook his hand, and the younger lot looked up at him in awe, not yet having earned the respect to approach him.

Personally, I thought he was a twat. I wanted to share that thought with Parvez, who was sat opposite me, but with the way his mouth was open and his eyes twinkled, it was as if a Paki Father Christmas had just walked in.

Khan approached the counter and Ali greeted him with a masala chai. He took it in his meaty hand and sipped from it, scoping the room over the rim, ready to address his audience. The three of them were dressed almost identically: black baggy clique jeans and market-bought black leather jackets. There was enough leather to offend the Hindus and embarrass McDonalds. They looked like they had just stepped out of the nineties. That was my problem with Khan. He had never quite left that era; he had never quite grown up.

Around maybe the mid-nineties, Khan Abdul was part of the SL1 Crew. A gang mainly comprised of Muslim youths, some students and others on the dole. They operated out of Langley, Slough. The Holy Smokes and the Tooti Nungs, who ran Southall at that time, were comprised mainly of Sikhs and Hindus. So, not to be outdone, some dumb Pakis formed the SL1 Crew and, like some fucked up Robin Hood and his Muslim Men, they got up to all sorts. But unlike the Smokes and the Nungs, they had no agenda. Well, no, that's not true. The SL1 Crew did have an agenda: trouble and strife.

Local Muslim business encounters non-Muslim competition.

They stepped in.

Mixed relationship between a Muslim and a non-Muslim.

They stepped in.

Racially motivated attacks, protection rackets, joyriding, stabbings. You name it, they indulged in it. With pride.

Almost twenty years later, in his late forties, married with kids, Khan is still at it, desperately trying to hold on to his reputation. The SL1 Crew had long been forgotten about, but Khan still waved the flag for thug mentality. Idiot.

The only reason why Khan is still respected, and will be until his days end, is because he stabbed the leader of a rival gang who had raped a Muslim girl. Instant fucking hero status. It came to light after that it was actually consensual, and she only cried rape because she didn't want her parents to find out. But that's just details.

I watched him as he stood in front of the counter at Ali's Diner, larger than life and twice as ugly. Ready to hold court.

'Brothers,' Khan started, and the room was excited.

'Soldiers,' he continued, and the room just about exploded.

I scoped the room and all around me people were hyper, some on their feet, thumping their chests with their fists, others thumping the table. Parvez shouted, '*Allah hu Akbar*' and that just seem to rile them even further, and it was continuously repeated and echoed off the walls. This was the kind of reaction you would expect at the end of a decent speech, not after two words. I could tell Khan was trying his hardest not to display a shit-eating grin. With open hands he requested for the room to quieten.

'Our way of life has been compromised. Our religion has been attacked,' Khan said, clearly pleased with his obviously rehearsed opening gambit. He scratched the side of his stubbled face. 'So, what do we do?' Khan looked around the room, milking it. The question was clearly rhetorical, so no suggestions were forthcoming but the anticipation was palpable. 'Do we continue our peaceful existence and hope that it doesn't happen again? Or do we send a message out, loud and clear? All we want is to abide by the five pillars of Islam. We don't want any trouble, we don't want to bother you. We just want peace.'

What the fuck did Khan know about the five pillars of Islam? I bet he couldn't name them. The closest Khan had ever got to Mecca was driving past the Mecca Bingo Hall in Hounslow High Street. I wanted to stand up and challenge him. Embarrass him. But I didn't because I had grown fond of my teeth.

Idris was right: I should have stayed away. I looked at Parvez, who was hanging onto every word, every letter that was coming out of Khan's mouth. I looked at my watch, aware that I had to see Silas in a few hours. With time to kill, I sighed to myself and sloped down in my seat as Khan continued.

'It wasn't us that flew into the Twin Towers. We were sitting at home watching *Jeremy Kyle* or whatever when that shit happened. But yet they continue to blame anyone of colour. *That* is our bleak future and *that* is now. This will never end. We must stand together side by side, hand in hand and build an unbreakable chain. The power of Allah reigning through us, and if any of those fucking pig-lovers try to penetrate us, we will drop them where they stand. Without fear and without consequence, because we are protected by the Almighty. No one can touch us. We will no longer be governed by rules and by laws, which are designed by the Kafir for the Kafir... So my message to them is simply this: You touch us... We'll touch you back.'

I could sense that the room was about to overreact again and explode into madness. Khan was counting on it with his whole plastic prophet speech, wanting to add another notch to his legacy. But before anyone had a chance to react, Shariff, a local community worker, stood up and, much to Khan's annoyance, turned his back to him and addressed the room.

'Brothers, I would just like to say that today I am proud to be a Muslim. The support and unity was evident at the clean-up at the Masjid... And look! Look around you right now. Taking time out of your busy lives to help find a better way. But... this is not it. We must use our heads, Brothers, and find a peaceful way forward. Violence does not resolve violence.'

'Oi, Gandhi, sit the fuck back down,' Khan countered, but for the first time the dynamic of the room altered. Partly because Khan spoke rudely to a valued member of the community, and partly because of what Shariff had said – *find a peaceful way forward*. People started to fidget in their chairs as silence descended. Shariff turned to face Khan, staring at him challengingly. One of The Twins stepped forward with intent, but Khan held him back.

'You make a good point, Brother...' Khan said.

'Shariff.'

'Shariff, right,' Khan said, making a mental note. It was clear that Shariff wasn't going to be on Khan's Eid card list. 'We have tried and failed to find a peaceful way forward.'

Shariff snorted. 'Khan, don't be a fool.' I swear the whole room took a sharp intake of breath as that word bounced around from ear to ear until it reached Khan and verbally slapped him in the face. 'There is not a peaceful bone in your body. You came here only because you saw an opportunity. What is it with you? Why are you trying to corrupt our minds with revenge and violence? Is there not enough of that already? Like so many of us, you are a husband and you are a father. Think about our families, think about how they would cope if something happened to us... to you. And for what? Huh, for what? We attack them, then what happens? I'll tell you what happens: a white version of you will give a similar speech to attack us right back, and round and round we go, never able to break out of this deathly circle. And I don't say that lightly, because there *will* be death. Eventually and inevitably. Is that what you want on your conscience, Khan?'

Khan's smile didn't wane but there was no mirth in it. He just nodded, with calculated eyes. 'Brother Shariff. You have your way and I have mine. There is one jungle and one lion,' Khan continued. Left Twin narrowed his eyes in confusion as to where Khan was going with this off-script jungle/lion metaphor. 'And when the lion is cornered he attacks with everything he has. That's what we are. Lions!'

'We are not animals, Khan. We are—'

'Enough,' Khan shouted, loud enough for everyone's Wudu to be broken. 'This meeting is over,' he declared. As he looked around the room, his eyes stopped briefly on me before flitting away. 'If you want to go against me then go home and put on your lipstick and bangles. Whoever is with me, meet me outside.' He inhaled through his nose, nostrils flared, and then with a puff of his chest Khan declared, 'Tonight... we are soldiers.'

Unlike the last time when he'd referred to us as soldiers, and the room went fucking mental, this time, not a murmur. I could see the look on his face: he wore a crazy expression. Nothing good had ever come out of that expression.

Khan tried again. This time thumping his chest with his fist. 'Soldiers of Islam...' Again, nothing. No reaction, or at least not the one he was hoping for. 'Soldiers of Allah!' Man, he was getting desperate. I noticed Parvez, battling with himself, squirming in his chair. Parvez had always hero-worshipped Khan ever since I could remember, and now I could see his eyes siding with Khan. He started to rise from his chair; I grabbed his elbow and tried to force him back down.

'Parvez. Don't be a sap. Sit down,' I pleaded. But he wrenched his arm away from my grip and stood up. He looked adoringly towards Khan and thumped his puny chest.

'Brother Khan,' he said, his little voice carried comfortably across the room. 'I am a soldier of Allah.'

'Good man,' Khan said. 'What's your name, Brother?'

Ouch. I could see a glimpse of hurt in Parvez's eyes. Last year when Khan had been in trouble with the police for scratching cars with private number plates and needed an alibi or something, I don't know the whole story, but Parvez sorted him right out. So for Khan not to remember his name must have really, *really* upset him... But he didn't let it show.

'Parvez,' said Parvez.

Khan nodded, some distinct acknowledgement, but not much.

'Parvez, and anybody else who wants to join me – I'll be outside.' And with that and a scowl, Khan stomped out of Ali's Diner.

6

Let me tell you something about Muslims. And I'm talking about the majority here. Despite the contrary belief, we are a patient, tolerant and sincere bunch. We integrate with those around us. Really, we don't care if you're black, white, Jew, Christian, straight, gay, or a pre-op drag queen; we will sit with you and break bread with you. On Christmas Day we'll eat a halal chicken with all the trimmings whilst watching the Queen's Speech, and we'll overdose on chocolate eggs at Easter. Some places in England don't fully celebrate St George's Day because it may offend Muslims. That is the biggest load of bullshit I have ever heard. You don't see us backing away when it comes to celebrating Eid, or the Hindus secretly cowering away in the corner when it's Diwali. No, we give it full throttle and we go at it with gusto. The trouble is, it's always the minority opinion that makes the waves. That's what is printed and spewed out on the news, with bells and whistles added for effect, with talking heads, fucking so-called experts, adding to the propaganda. It's sensationally sensationalised sensationalism.

Truly, most of us, we don't care. Celebrate away. Fly that flag.

That is exactly what happened at Ali's Diner. Yes, we were angry. But actually going out there and carrying out the revenge, the act, it's not going to happen, not by the majority, anyway. But there are always one or two or three, and it's these idiots that will make the news, fuel the gossip and form public opinion, putting us back to square one where we have to keep explaining ourselves – *we're not all like that, it's the fucking minority!*

It's by this token, you shouldn't be surprised to hear, that Khan and Parvez were standing outside Ali's Diner, in the biting cold, planning and plotting revenge. The rest of them stayed in the warmth and listened as Shariff collectively and peacefully tried to find a way to put a foot forward. I had other things on my mind. I had to get back to my car and make sure all the money I'd collected was collated in rubber bands just as Silas liked. I thought maybe I would take a walk after, as the fried chicken was sitting heavy on my heart. I just didn't want to be sitting in Ali's anymore. I walked out and Khan and Parvez turned expectantly. I greeted them with raised eyebrows.

'Anybody else coming?' Parvez asked.

'No, man. They're all inside. Shariff is holding court. Ain't no one coming,' I said. 'Where are The Twins?'

'Gone. Early start tomorrow,' Khan said. 'They both have job interviews in the morning.'

'Oh. Right. So that's that then,' I said, with an air of what I hoped was finality. Parvez looked hopefully at Khan and I could just picture the chimps in Khan's head trying to come to a decision.

'No,' Khan said. 'That's not that. Fuck The Twins and fuck the weak-ass Pakis in there. We don't need them. It's just us... The three of us.'

Khan and Parvez bumped fists.

'Hang on a minute! No fucking way, man. You both do whatever the hell you want. Don't get me involved.'

Khan zipped up his nineties leather jacket with a disappointed shake of his head. I watched it slide over his growing belly.

'Come on, Brother,' Parvez said to me. 'We can't let this go unpunished. We're relying on you.' He had this determined look in his eyes, a look that was new to me. It didn't suit him. I was concerned that Khan was going to get him beaten up, or worse. 'They disrespected the Masjid, Jay. We can't let them get away with that. Right, Khan?'

'Leave it out, Parvez. He ain't coming,' Khan said. 'Bunch of pussy holes, that's what your generation is.'

'Parvez, a word, please,' I requested.

'Anything you want to say, Brother, you can say—'

'Fuck's sake, Parvez. Come here for a minute.'

Parvez looked to Khan for instruction and Khan, after giving me an arrogant smile, nodded acquiescently. I moved a few steps away and waited under a dimly lit lamppost. Parvez followed suit and stood in front of me. No, stood is wrong. He was excitedly, or nervously – probably the former – hopping around from one foot to the other. He either wanted to go toilet or he was just hyped up – probably the latter.

'Parvez. Are you sure about this? This is not you, man.'

'No, *this is me*, Jay, and this is you. This is all of us. I am sick and tired of being targeted. Personally and as a religion. Allah knows I try to be patient, bite my tongue and curb my anger. But with Khan behind me, I know we can hit them. *Hard*. Send a message, yes?'

Parvez the Preacher. Parvez the Pacifist. Now Parvez the Psycho. Drunk on a few meaningless words from a meaningless thug who he fucking idolised. I wanted to grab him by his Primark shirt lapels and shake the dumb out of him, but I knew that would not make a touch of difference.

'You're sure about this?' I asked.

He stopped hopping for a moment and looked me right in the eyes. 'I'm sure, Brother,' he said. 'C'mon, Jay. Let's do this. We have to be proactive in the war against terror. They think that they can—'

'Parvez, shut up for a second,' I interrupted. I had never heard the phrase *war against terror* used in the reverse context. It made me wonder. 'And can you stop fucking hopping around for a minute and let me think?'

'But Jay, we—'

'Let's go, Parvez.' This time the interruption came from Khan. Parvez looked at me with expectant eyes.

I expelled air and said, 'I'm coming too.'

7

The sight of Khan approaching my car with a cross spanner, a metal bar and a cricket bat made me want to run him over. He got in and dumped the makeshift weaponry in the back seat and I watched Parvez weigh them up. At Khan's request, we stopped at Parvez's house first for a change of clothes. He now had on a topi and a lightweight, beige shalwar and kameez, over which he had on a bloody black leather jacket. He looked like an idiot. Or a target.

I drove at low speeds because I didn't want to be pulled over with bats and bars in the back seat and weed and cash in the boot. My palms felt sweaty and I wiped them on my jeans. I flicked the radio on and tuned it to Sunshine Radio, an Asian community station, which operated out of the heavily Asian-populated town of Southall. I heard the unmistakeable voice of the resident DJ, Tony Virdi.

'*New reports are coming in thick and fast. It seems that further attacks have taken place around the Ashford area. Five Asian youths were seen running from St Mary's Church, which had its windows smashed and was broken into. Also some local shops have been vandalised on the Ashford High Street and a local pharmacy has been set alight. It is not confirmed yet whether this is retaliation but the signs do not look good. After the commercials we are joined by Dr Riaz Ikram, the author of the best seller,* War, What Isn't it Good For? *But please, for your own safety, stay at home tonight, folks. This is Tony Virdi reporting—*'

I killed the radio.

'Looks like Ashford's taken care of, eh, lads?' Khan said to no response. 'Yeah, Staines is the place to be. Especially Elmsleigh car park... You got any battle tunes, Jay?'

The last thing I wanted to do was put on some gangsta rap; it would only serve to make Khan more volatile. I looked in the rear-view and Parvez was looking out of the window blankly.

'Parvez. You all right, mate?' I asked.

'Course he's all right. He's a fuckin' soldier. Ain't that right, Parvez?'

'Yes. I'm fine,' Parvez said. His words a stark contrast to his tone. 'Soldier of Islam.'

'Why Elmsleigh, Khan?' I asked.

'Elmsleigh car park is Kafir city. The place is full of good-for-nothing white boys. Doggers, slags, dealers, chavs, fuckin' name it. Place is filth. They deserve to be hit.'

'But what've they got to do with the attack on the mosque? Why are we moving on them?'

'*We* won't be the ones making the first move.' Khan said, inclining his head towards Parvez and smirking conspiratorially at me.

8

I pulled up around a hundred metres away and looked towards Elmsleigh car park, and it looked back at me with bad intentions. Harsh orange lighting seeped through the slits between the three storeys, lending to its menace. The car park just seemed to breathe and pulsate wicked energy. From what I remembered from my one and only visit, there were badly designed, narrow bays and ticket machines that never worked, broken CCTV and the strong smell of piss. A haven for junkies and pissheads. Sexual activity of all kinds was reserved for the middle level, and the floors were littered with used condoms and joint butts. I scrunched my face at the thought of wheeling my Beemer in there.

'Lose the leather,' Khan said to Parvez.

'Have a heart, Khan,' I said, as Parvez slipped his jacket off. 'At least let him keep his jacket on. It's freezing out there.'

'It is okay, Brother,' Parvez said, placing his hand on my shoulder before stepping out of the car in only his shalwar, kameez and prayer hat. We watched him make his way to the car park on foot. *God help him.* Dressed like that it wasn't just the cold that was going to get him.

Khan reached in the back seat and grabbed a cricket bat and a small metal bar.

'Take your pick. Or there's the cross spanner if you prefer. But not easy to conceal.' *As if a cricket bat was!* I took the cold metal bar. 'Good choice. When it kicks off, strike to the head. Do not pull your arm all the way back – they'll see it coming a mile off. Short, sharp bursts. Boom, boom, boom, and then on to the next one. Got it?'

I nodded, I had no intention of striking anybody in the head. I was only there out of some misguided notion of loyalty for

Parvez. If anything happened to him, his mum would destroy me.

'Okay. Drive. Slowly.'

I pulled in and it was immediately clear that we would be outnumbered.

'More Kafirs than I thought there'd be,' he said helpfully.

'Can we go now, Khan? *Please.*' I was coming across like a coward but I couldn't care less. 'Let's just grab Parvez and go. This is ridiculous – we're so fucking outnumbered.'

Khan reached inside his jacket and pulled *his* weapon. The blade alone was twelve inches long and it looked to be at least half that across. I couldn't tell you if it was a knife, a meat cleaver or a machete. But it was shiny and jagged and I could see in the reflection the fear etched on my face.

'This should even things up, eh?' Khan said, as he pressed his finger on the tip of the blade and drew blood, which he then proceeded to calmly lick off.

Parvez had clocked us drive in and positioned himself where we could see him, leaning against a pillar situated outside the lift about ten metres to my top right. To my left, eight hostiles, all white, a mixture of baseball caps, hoodies and skinny jeans. Not the culprits, but in Khan's eyes, as close as fucking possible. They were curiously watching Parvez with a measurement of suspicion, wanting to react but uncertain in their approach. In fact, by their bemused expressions, *they* seemed more worried about him. There was muted conversation and puzzled looks. One guy, a grey hoody pulled tightly over his head, shouted something across to him. Parvez put a finger innocently to his chest in a *sorry, are you talking to me?* gesture. I slid my window halfway down and wrinkled my nose as the stench of urine crept into my car. The guy shouted louder this time, loud enough for me to hear.

'What'd he say?' Khan asked.

'He's asking *what have you got underneath your shirt*?'

'Ha! Does he think all Pakis walk around strapped with explosives?' Khan said, as he typed out and sent a text message on his phone. 'Sorted!' he said quietly to himself.

Parvez patted his chest and stomach to prove that he didn't have anything underneath his kameez, and they all took a tentative step back as though he was about to detonate.

Grey Hoody leaned into the VW Beetle that he was standing next to and whispered something to the passengers. Two doors flew open and two guys stepped out, two seats were folded down and two girls stepped out from the back dressed in cheap tracksuits, one in blue shell and the other in sickly purple velour. They confidently strutted towards Parvez, who had now pushed himself off the pillar. I watched him straighten his topi. There were about a dozen guys who had now gathered around the Beetle, watching carefully, feet shuffling, a bundle of nerves and anticipation. Velour spoke first.

'So… what?' she said. 'You some kind of pervert?'

'*No!*' Parvez replied, horrified.

'Hoping to get your rocks off peeping into cars, are ya?' Velour continued.

'I am not a pervert,' Parvez said, eyes darting towards us and quickly away again.

'Well, what are ya, then? You look like a cunt terrorist,' screeched Shellsuit.

'You fuckin' do as well. You got big balls coming in here dressed like that,' Velour said, and then she moved with her hand, as if she was about to grab Parvez by the testicles. Parvez flinched and clumsily took a step back into the pillar. The girls laughed at his predicament.

'Did you have anything to do with the attack on St Mary's Church? Was that you and your Paki mates?' Velour asked animatedly.

Parvez opened his mouth to respond but before the words could leave his mouth Shellsuit spat in his face and Velour ripped the topi clean off his head and turned towards the baying crowd and waved the topi in the air like some sort of fucking trophy.

My fingers were wrapped around the door handle. I turned to Khan. 'Now?'

'No. Wait!'

There were shouts of encouragement and sounds of laughter. With the back of his arm Parvez wiped the gob off his face and unexpectedly and viciously wrenched the ponytail of Velour, pulling her back towards him and snatching the topi back from her hand. She let out a high-pitched, earth-shattering scream.

And that's when it all kicked off.

Parvez's eyes widened and he ran, hat in hand, towards the stairs to the upper levels. The hostiles pelted after him, disappearing up the stairs to a chorus of *Paki* and *Wog* and the like. I gripped the metal bar and flung my door open. Khan did the same and we ran across the car park to the door leading to the stairs. I could hear my shoes in my ears pounding on the floor and I wished I had my Nikes on instead of my crappy mosque shoes.

After quickly checking the first two floors, we flew through the door of the third. I came through first, with Khan just a fraction behind me. They all had their backs to us in a semi-circle. Through a small gap I saw a flash of cheap beige cotton in the foetal position, as Velour and Shellsuit rained brutal kicks into Parvez's back and ribs and the guys cheered them on. Behind me, a guttural, feral sound, a fucking *ROAR* emanated from Khan, which stopped the proceedings sharpish. All heads turned. Their focus was now on Khan as they first walked and then ran towards him. But they stopped short as Khan, bent at the knees, pulled out his blade with a smile.

'*C'mon then!*' Khan growled. 'Who wants to take a ride in an ambulance?' He waved the blade around in small circles in front of him, like a sparkler. I ran to Parvez and helped him to his feet.

'Shit, Parvez, you all right?' I asked, knowing what a stupid question it was.

'Yes. I'm fine,' Parvez said. I took him limping and hobbling to the far wall. He looked down over it, as if jumping three storeys down was our only way out.

'Jay, look,' he said, pointing down towards the ground. 'There's more cars coming in.'

There was nothing I could do about that. Ten against three or thirty against three, what's the difference? Either way we were getting fucked. Our best hope was to leave this place with most of our organs intact.

Khan was now surrounded in a tight circle, holding the hostiles at arm's length, fiercely arcing and poking the blade towards anybody who tried to cover ground. There was a serene look on his face, a look of contentment. This was Khan and this was his element. If he died, I believed he would die doing what he loved most. One brave soul came at him from behind, pulled

44

his arm tightly around Khan's thick neck. Khan dealt with that with a forceful backwards head-butt, breaking his nose. He then spun on his heel to face him and brought the butt of the blade down, striking him again on his already busted nose. Blood and mucus fountained out as the chump fell to his knees. But this gave the others a small window to step in closer, and they took it. I saw a beer bottle bounce brutally off Khan's head and it threw him off balance. His legs wobbled but he turned towards his attacker and gave a back-handed slap that lifted the guy off his feet and onto his backside. But then a flurry of strikes rained down, and Khan fell to one knee, and I could see him desperately trying to muster up some strength, but he didn't have the time or the space and, all too easily, the mob swallowed him up whole.

My mind whirled and span as fight or flight kicked in, and I blindly went in, knowing full well what would happen to me. I dragged one guy off and laid into him with the bar. The bar that I never intended to use. Striking him hard and quick on the side of the head, and then as he fell to the floor I continued to lay blows on his back until I heard the sickening sound of something shatter within him. I stopped. Before I could contemplate my next move a knuckle duster hit the side of my head, sending me sprawling, the bar slipped out of my hand and clattered somewhere around me. I was seeing stars. I shook my head to clear my thoughts and from a distance I could just about make out Khan getting the same treatment that Parvez had got from the two girls. But these weren't girls, these were big guys, with big boots and big fists, stomping and pounding into his flesh. Grey Hoody was standing over me, smirking. My eyes had not yet cleared after that knuckle-duster blow, and all I could see were two yellow eyes and the Devil's smile. In his hand he held my metal bar, and just as he positioned himself to strike me, the screech of tyres and the high beam of headlights deafened and blinded me further. Three cars haphazardly halted, doors flung open and feet hitting the ground. All I saw were chequered ghutrah scarves bound tightly across faces. The cavalry had arrived.

The game had just evened itself out.

9

After Khan's back-up arrived, the scene became a blur. I couldn't tell you who was winning, who was losing, whose blood was lining the tarmac or whose tooth had just flown past my head. There were punches and kicks and bars and blows and knives and fucking Khan, who looked as happy as a child at Disneyland. Someone was laying face down on the ground. He wasn't moving and it frightened the hell out of me. That feeling intensified when I realised it was the same guy I had viciously and repeatedly swiped with the bar. A short while ago I'd wanted to hurt him with everything I had. Now, worried that I could have fucking killed him, I just wanted to help.

I shook him by his shoulder gently and then again, a little firmer. Still no movement.

How much jail time am I looking at? Am I going to get raped in prison? Am I going to rape in prison? Mum is going to be so disappointed in me. I blinked away my thoughts as I saw movement. Relief washed over me as he stirred and lifted his head and took in the surroundings. I followed his train of thought as he concluded that he was better off staying put and playing dead.

Relieved, I left him to it. I jogged over to Parvez, who was slumped along the back wall. I helped him to his feet and he winced, as if his body had just recalled the kicking that the two girls had inflicted. I made a mental note to take the piss out of him about that at some point. He put his arm around my shoulders as we gingerly moved across the car park and down three flights of stairs. I pushed open the door and looked at the empty parking bay where, once upon a time, my car had been parked.

My beautiful BMW. The beautiful black leather bucket seats that I had set just so. The crystal-clear six-by-nine Blaupunkt speakers. The Pioneer stereo that I'd just had fitted, and all my burned MP3 CDs, for which I had spent hours painstakingly selecting just the right songs.

Gone.

My trusty rucksack containing the remainder of Silas' gear.

Gone.

Seven grand of Silas' money.

Gone.

10

I was sat at the back on the top deck of an almost empty one-eleven bus on my way to see Silas. I spent the journey nursing a cut above my right ear with a used tissue, trying to piece together the blur of stupidity that had just taken place. I cleared the condensation on the window with my sleeve and looked outside. I was three more stops from Silas, my supplier and employer and all-round fucking psychopath.

There is only one way to describe Silas. And that's in detail.

At first glance you would not know how to pigeonhole Silas. He dressed preppy, which suited his slight frame, but lived gangster. Thin-framed, black, half-moon reading glasses usually hung down from around his pigeon neck on a thin gold chain. Silas had a penchant for V-neck sweaters in vibrant colours, always worn over a crisp white shirt with his initials embroidered on the collar. His short dark hair was always neatly side-parted, and you would never notice a difference in growth. His trousers were relaxed and patterned, the type that wouldn't look out of place hitting balls on the green. On his feet you would find delicate suede slip-ons with tassels. He lived in a house. A very big house. In the suburbs. Double-fronted with enough space in his drive to comfortably park five cars, which was just as well as he owned five cars. He lived alone. Just him and his cook and his security and his hairdresser. There were always girls hanging around too. He clearly had a type. Tall, Amazonian, muscular-looking girls, tottering around in impossibly high heels and little more. Rumour had it that Silas had his own private strip club in the basement. It was the closest thing I'd seen to the Playboy mansion. But Hugh Hefner he was not. Silas looked expensive and Silas smelled expensive and he drove and he lived expensive. He was polite and well-spoken and he controlled, what? Maybe sixty per cent of any narcotic sold in West London. It all went through him: weed, skunk, coke, H, uppers, downers, lefties, righties, Viagra, Valium and any other mind-bending, thought-invoking, impotence-zapping substance that you could think of. Also, and this was just whispers, but I'd heard that he had a small arsenal tucked away somewhere. And when I say small, I mean huge. Enough to make Rambo blush.

I peered out of the bus window as the Odeon on the high street slipped past me. The so-called revenge attacks didn't seem to have hit Kingston. There were clubbers and night-goers and general happiness in full effect.

I was relieved to be away from Khan and Parvez and into relative peace. Fucking jokers with their fucking half-arsed plan. And who suffered? Me, that's who. And if I didn't have my story straight then there was a whole lot more suffering coming my way. If Silas so much as had an inkling that I was blagging, then I guess I would soon be able to confirm whether he did indeed have a huge arsenal, as it would be pointing at my fucking head. So bullshit to one side, I decided to come clean.

The bus stopped. It had to – it was the last stop. End of its journey, and quite possibly the end of mine.

11

Big, burly and black is how I would describe Staples, the sentry that stood guard outside Silas' place. He'd earned his nickname for his penchant for using a stapler in a somewhat unorthodox manner – eyes, mouth, ears, nostrils and any other orifice that needed stapling shut. He was a tough motherfucker. Tough enough to scare away any would-be chancers, and tough enough not to think a jacket necessary, even though, through his tight T-shirt, his nipples told a different story.

'Staples,' I said, smiling brightly. 'I'm getting cold just looking at you.' He smirked at me and we carried out a complicated handshake.

'You're late, Jay,' Staples said. 'Gaffer been waiting for you for time.'

I checked the time on my phone. Past midnight, just. I looked up at Staples and tried to gauge Silas' mood through him.

'Car trouble, man,' I said, and shrugged nonchalantly.

'The fuck happened to your face?' I touched the side of my head and felt blood seeping from it, and instantly felt light-headed. 'I hope you haven't been dripping claret all over the fucking drive, Jay.' I took out the already bloody tissue from my pocket and held it to my head. 'That's disgusting, Jay. Hang on.' He took out a bulky walkie-talkie from his back pocket and spoke into it. 'Serenity. Get your beautiful behind into the hallway and bring your first-aid kit.' Staples moved his bulk away from the door and let me into the hallway. 'Wait here. Serenity will see to you… And Jay?'

'What?'

'Smarten the fuck up next time. You're bringing down the house prices.'

I was sat in the most supremely comfortable grand armchair. Somewhere in the background Sinatra was telling me that he did it his way. Two perfectly formed, cosmetically enhanced breasts hovered precariously, inches away from my face, with a thin silver chain and pendant that read *Serenity* nestled between them. The keeper of the breasts fussed around my wound as she gently and expertly applied a small bandage to it.

'There,' she said, admiring her handiwork. 'Try not to touch it; you don't want to infect it now.' She strutted away and my eyes tracked her until she tottered out of view.

'Isn't she just a peach?'

I followed the voice and realised that Silas was sitting directly opposite me in an even grander and more ostentatious armchair than mine. He was in a black robe with a gold trim, parted just enough that I could see his hairless bird chest. One leg was up on the chair, with his bare foot planted on a velvet cushion as he cleaned out his toes with the blade of a nail cutter. Once satisfied, he blew the top of the blade towards me and dropped his leg to the floor, his foot finding comfort in a blue suede loafer. He crossed his legs and his silk maroon pyjamas rode up to reveal a pale white ankle.

'Silas. Sorry, I didn't notice you,' I said, and instantly regretted it.

'I don't blame you, Jay. Serenity has that effect. As beautiful as she is caring,' Silas said fondly. If he was offended, he didn't show it. My finger reached for the side of my head. 'Don't mess with it. Let it heal naturally. You do not want to get on Serenity's bad side.'

I put my hand down on my lap and tried to look comfortable.

'I met her when I was getting my appendix taken out,' Silas continued. 'As I was lying on the hospital bed coming to, there she was, standing over me. Larger than life and as beautiful as the Devil could have made her.' Silas' gaze flitted away from me, lost somewhere in the distance. 'Naturally I offered her a job and I provided her with a cute little uniform and all the kit a nurse could require. Her husband decided to demonstrate his displeasure one night by turning up here, unannounced. Unfortunately at the time she was going way beyond the call of duty. Staples did what Staples does best, and he left with his eyes and mouth stapled shut.'

Silas smiled.

I smiled back.

'Jay,' he said.

'Yes,' I said.

'Where the fuck is my money?'

Here we go.

Even though I was planning to go with the truth, I had rehearsed it in a manner that would buy me some sympathy. A ticking off, maybe, but ultimately a *shit happens* response from him.

'Now, I'm no Sherlock Holmes,' Silas said. 'Shit, Jay, I'm not even Watson. But I didn't see you pull up in your car and I don't see a bag. I'm pretty sure that you haven't got my cash *or* my gear in your pockets. So I surmise – no, I *deduce* – that you are empty-handed. Feel free to correct me.'

I just sat there. I was speechless. I was without the power of speech. *Elmsleigh car park. There was a brawl. Khan and Parvez dragged me there. No, no, start with the mosque. There was an attack at my local mosque and...*

'Speak, motherfucker!' Silas said, shattering my reverie.

'My car... It... It got jacked,' I stuttered, well aware of the spittle flying out of my mouth.

'So? What does that have to do with the price of tea in China?' He uncrossed his legs and leaned forward closer to me, resting his elbows on his knees. He smelled good. Expensive. 'Unless, of course, you left my shit in your car, unattended.'

Unattended? Yeah. Doors open? Yeah. Keys in the ignition? Oh yeah.

My silence said all that had to be said. Silas watched me, amusement in his eyes, waiting for me to respond.

I opened my mouth to apologise. Silas narrowed his eyes in anticipation.

I thought better and closed my mouth. Silas clenched his jaw in irritation.

He looked above and behind me. I turned my head a touch to the side and I could feel the presence of Staples, standing directly behind my armchair.

'How much?' Silas asked, just above a whisper, loaded with understated menace.

'All of it,' I said, my voice feeble.

'Cash? Gear?'

'Both.' His eyebrows told me to elaborate. 'Seven grand in cash and about two grand worth of green.'

'Ten grand?'

'Nine,' I said, correcting him.

'Ten grand,' Silas said. 'Would you like me to get you a calculator?'

'Ten grand,' I said, defeated.

Sinatra had given up the ghost and the room was filled with an eerie hiss. Silas stood up and tightened the belt to his robe, accentuating his non-existent waist. He paced up and down in front of me, four steps one way, then four steps the other, hands knotted behind his back, his suede loafers padding softly on the carpet.

'The thing is, Jay, I like you. Always have. You've been a good servant to me.'

Servant!

'But I just can't let this go. Do you know *why* I can't let this go?' Silas asked.

'Principles.'

'Jackpot, Jay... Principles. The cornerstone of every successful business.'

'I'll pay you back, Silas. I just need time. If you just give me some more gear, I'll have the ten back to you and then some in no time.'

Silas, still pacing in front of me, shook his head, barely a movement, but it was clear I wasn't leaving there with fresh supplies.

'Okay, fine. That's fair,' I said, to appease. 'I'll find another way.' There was no other way. I had nothing. I couldn't even sell my car and I couldn't wait for the insurance money to come through because I hadn't got around to insuring it. 'I just need time, Silas,' I repeated. 'I can get a job and pay you in instalments.'

Silas grinned. I caught a flash of his too-white teeth. 'Instalments?'

'Yeah. I can sort you out a G a month, every month, without fail.'

'So… A grand a month.' Silas counted ten on his fingers. 'For ten months and we'll be square? Is that what you're proposing?' A twinkle in his eye. Hope in mine.

I nodded. Even if he agreed, it was going to be impossible to come up with that kind of loot without dealing.

'I tell you what, Jay.' I heard nasty phlegm rattling around as he cleared his throat. 'You have until next Friday. Midnight.'

That's when I fucked up.

'C'mon, Silas, be fair.'

Silas stopped pacing sharply. He turned on his heel and faced me. My words seemed to echo around the room.

Silas took his eyes off me and glanced behind me, and before I had a chance to turn, I was being lifted off my seat by my hair, pulled sideways over the arm of the chair. I scrunched my face in pain as Staples tightened his grip. I could feel cold metal around my ear as a stapler was clamped around it. Before I could react, Silas was on top of me, straddling me, laughing manically. He had the blade of the nail clippers in my nose, stretching my nostril. I stopped wriggling and froze. I didn't want my ear pierced or my nose sliced.

'What did you say to me, boy?' Silas hissed.

'Nothing,' I said, as the stench of toenail clippings reached my brain and his erection dug into my chest. I wanted to vomit.

'That's what I thought,' Silas said, as he dismounted. Staples released the grip on my hair and moved the stapler away.

I was breathing hard. Silas took his seat opposite me.

'Why are you still here?'

12

Kingsley Parker walked out of his apartment for the third time in a matter of minutes. He had got to the end of the quiet, leafy road, which he hated, when he realised that he'd forgotten his phone and had to turn back. With his phone in his possession, Parker had got as far as South Kensington tube station, when he once again had to turn back, having realised that the details of his destination, haphazardly scribbled down on a scrap piece of paper, were still sitting on his bedside table, under the year-old bottle of vodka, seal unbroken, that acted as his security blanket. More time wasted. Parker was going to be late.

The Tube journey was uneventful and he bided his time eyeing up passengers for signs of sinister nervousness. It wasn't his intention; it was his training. His knee jackhammered and his stall-bought coffee threatened to spill as he questioned himself and his ability to carry out his job. The same thoughts as yesterday. The same thoughts as every day.

Parker arrived at Church House Conference Centre to find Dr Thomas Gladstone sitting in a booth in the canteen reading a file. He cleared his throat and the doctor looked up.

'Hello, Chalky,' Gladstone said. They shook hands and Parker slid into the seat opposite him. Parker squirmed at the mere mention of his nickname. Gladstone picked up on this immediately, and gave the slightest nod of acknowledgement.

'I am sorry that you've had to meet me here but I have lectures all week. Needs must, hey? Shall I be mother?' he said, pouring the tea for them. 'Drop or an ocean?' he asked, holding up a small jug of milk.

'Somewhere in between. Thanks.' Parker watched him pour. He had to force his knee to stop hammering.

Gladstone brought the cup to his lips and blew the steam away as he eyed Parker. 'Are you all right?'

'Yeah, I'm fine,' Parker lied, shrinking under Gladstone's gaze. Gladstone let it slide.

'So? Small talk or shall we get straight to it?' Gladstone asked, trying to lighten the mood.

Parker said nothing.

'Straight to it it is, then,' Gladstone said, as he placed the file on the table and put his hands over it. 'Why him?'

'We've had watch on a few candidates but there's something about him. He seems as comfortable on the streets as he does in the mosque, able to change his dynamic as required.'

'I see you haven't lost the old instincts.'

Parker shrugged. Unwilling to commit.

'Do you not think that one of our own would be more suitable?' Gladstone asked.

'No. I don't. He is well known in the community and he has ties to Sutton mosque. I think the risk factor of him getting made is slim.'

'Whereas our guys may stick out?'

'It wouldn't be the first time.' Parker nodded towards the file. 'What did you think? I realise that you've only had a few hours to look at the file, but what are your impressions?'

'It doesn't matter. A few hours or a few days, my reading would be the same.'

Parker waited for Gladstone to elaborate. He didn't.

'And?' Parker was getting tired of prompting him.

'He's perfect,' Gladstone exclaimed. 'Or he's all wrong.'

What the bloody hell does that mean? Parker thought, and he gave Gladstone a look that said exactly that.

'You want to use him as an asset, but will he play ball? Lord knows you have enough on him to persuade him. Trousers well and truly around his ankles, *and* with his fingers in the cookie jar,' Gladstone said. 'He is impressionable and, if handled correctly, he can be willing. But therein lies the problem.'

'How so?' Parker asked, rubbing his temples. This was not what he wanted to hear.

'Willing and impressionable. Two very significant words. Given the right environment he can be willed and impressed upon in the other direction. Take him, or any young man for that matter, and put him in a hostile situation. Training camps, lectures, Imams, weapons, jihadists. Bonds are formed, lessons are learned and seeds are planted. How do we know that he won't deviate?'

'With all due respect, Dr Gladstone, that's what I'm asking you. It's your area of expertise. Do you think that he could double-cross?' Parker said, the hint of desperation in his voice evident, and he hated himself for it.

Gladstone smiled passively. 'Look, Parker. I have successfully profiled rapists, serial killers and paedophiles, and had a direct hand in their capture. But this… This is different. It's grey. What we know about extremists is that we don't know very much. Not really. Especially not enough to profile them. They can come from any background. A diverse bunch. Only a few months ago we have had a high-flying, suit-wearing, secretary-shagging lawyer blow himself and everything around him up outside the American Embassy in Turkey. In the last twelve months we've seen scholars, junkies, alcoholics, bin men, the unemployed, all turn. It doesn't matter. *Status does not matter.* The popular, the loner, even the *non-religious.*'

'Yes. Okay. I get the picture,' Parker said. Not rudely, though that's how it sounded.

'They do not fit a single demographic profile and they all have different views and assumed paths. Drawn in for reasons political, personal, religious or otherwise. They don't wear a uniform and they don't play by any particular rules. So you tell me: how do we know? How can they be profiled?'

Parker nodded thoughtfully. Gladstone was right. How *do* we know?

Parker took a sip of tea. Gladstone did the same.

'It's a judgement call, Parker.'

13

I had killed thirteen prostitutes, sent a missile into a cop car and accidentally shot my best friend in the head. In the process I'd made almost a half a mill and that figure was rapidly rising. But it wasn't the kind of money that would impress Silas, and hiding in bed for two days straight, playing *Grand Theft Auto*, was not going to solve my problem.

I was fully aware of the deep shit I was in, but I needed time to think. And the result of all my thinking? Not a goddamn thing. I would have to resort to asking Mum. There was nothing to be ashamed of in asking a parent for help. It's my right to ask and it's her right to provide.

I pushed myself out of bed and I padded my way downstairs. Halfway down I heard an unfamiliar voice.

A male voice.

I pushed open the kitchen door just as said voice uttered something so fucking hilarious that it made Mum throw herself onto his lap. My presence soon put a stop to their laughter and they both smiled nervously at me as they took in my evident bedhead and my Batman onesie. Mum had the good grace to detach herself from him. She walked over to me and planted one on my cheek. I sat down opposite whoever the fuck he was and Mum slid into the seat closest to him – even though the seat next to me was available!

'This is, um, Andrew. Andrew Bishop,' Mum said, by way of introduction. 'Andrew, this is my son, Jay.'

He put his right hand out; I put my right hand out too but it didn't make contact. Instead I reached past his hand and, in a pathetic act of rebellion, I grabbed his coffee and took a sip of it whilst eyeballing him from over the rim.

One–nil to me.

He took his left hand into his right and shook his own hand at some attempt at humour, and it made my mum unsuccessfully stifle a laugh.

One–one.

We sat in awkward silence for a few seconds as I finished off Andrew's coffee, daring him to say something to me in *my* domain. I checked him out. Dark, wavy, presidential hair dropping effortlessly over his big forehead. A nose that can only be described as prominent and dark eyes that held mine without hesitation. Stripy shirt with a loose brown blazer, with patches on the elbow and a jaunty novelty tie that sat askew. Looking for all the world like a geography teacher.

Andrew glanced at his watch. 'Oh, look at that. Must dash.'

Yeah, on your bike, mate. Dash away!

'Andrew,' Mum said, 'teaches at Heston Primary.'

I knew it.

I shrugged. Big and exaggerated. The kind of shrug that did not require decrypting. Andrew and Mum stood up in tandem. Mum stepped to him, straightened his tie and then tiptoed and kissed him on the face. *On the fucking face!* They smiled stupidly at each other for a second, and then they walked out of the kitchen and into the hallway. I heard the front door open but not close. I walked out of the kitchen and into the hallway and made myself into a sixth toe. I watched them carefully talking in hushed tones. I sniffed loudly. I cleared my throat. I forced a cough until finally he got the message and walked out.

Mum gave him a cheery wave and said, 'Good luck!' She hesitantly shut the door after Andrew was out of sight, and I made my way back into the kitchen for some Coco Pops.

Mum walked in as I was slamming the kitchen cabinet shut. She slapped me on the back of the head.

'What the fu—'

'Excuse me?'

'What was that for?' I asked, rubbing the back of my head.

'Calm down, Jay. You've made your point,' Mum said.

I finished preparing my cereal and sat at the table whilst she loaded the dishwasher. This clearly was not the right time to ask for ten large.

So instead I asked, 'Good luck for what?'

Mum didn't answer me straight away. She took off her marigolds and pulled up a chair opposite me. Her features softened, her earlier annoyance with me no longer visible.

'It's Andrew's last day at school.'

'How sweet. Are all the kids going to sign his shirt and flour-bomb him?' I said, through a mouthful.

Ignoring my sarcasm, Mum placed both her hands out invitingly onto the middle of the table. I looked at her curiously as I crunched loudly on my cereal. I slowly put the spoon back in the bowl and my hands reached out to hers.

'Jay... We need to talk.'

I swallowed. Never had she said that to me before. Yeah, we talk, but we don't *talk*.

'What is it, Mum?'

I could see her trying to piece together the words in her head, which just added to my already increasing anxiety. Different scenarios ran through my mind, none of them pleasant.

'*Mum! What?*' I said, and it came out like a high-pitched squawk. My hands had tensed and tightened around Mum's.

'Andrew and I... We, um... Well, we... I don't know quite how to say this.'

Okay, so they had been seeing each other. No big deal. I wasn't that naïve to think that Mum was still pottering around the house, pining for a good Muslim man to make an honest woman of her. I released my hands from hers. It's wasn't like she was dying, or anything that would warrant holding hands. For a second there, just for a *minute*, she had frightened me.

'Yeah, yeah, Mum. You don't have to spell it out.' I aimed for and hit nonchalance. 'So you're seeing this Andrew character. I get it. So what we looking at? Marriage? Is he moving in? Gonna live in sin, are we?' I said, with a wink. I leaned back in my chair and continued to devour my Coco Pops.

Silence for a moment. Then, 'We *are* going to live together... In Qatar.'

I stopped eating. 'Where?'

'Qatar. It's in the—'

'Yeah, I know where Qatar is,' I said, unnecessarily raising my voice. 'When?' I asked, a little softer.

'Soon... Wednesday.'

'Wednesday? *This* Wednesday? As in the day after tomorrow? *That Wednesday?*' I said incredulously. Even as I was saying this my mind was in overdrive. *This could be my way out. Yeah, Wednesday. I can be out of here before my Friday midnight deadline and not have to worry about Silas. This could work!*

'I know what you're thinking, Jay.'

You have no idea what I'm thinking.

'But Andrew has been offered a teaching job in Doha and he asked me to go with him.'

I didn't say anything. Thinking, thinking, thinking.

'I kept declining,' she continued. 'I must have said no a hundred times. I kept wondering how it would affect you. But then I thought... I'm not such a bad mum. I've done a pretty good job raising you on my own. A beautiful boy to a handsome young man.'

She kept on going. I tuned out.

My mind was made up. In the last few seconds I had planned out my next few days. I had to see Idris... And I guess I should probably see that annoying twerp Parvez. Say my farewells. *Goodbye lads, I am off to pastures new. Hot and exotic. I'll send you a postcard. Goodbye, Silas, I'll definitely send you a postcard. Maybe a picture of me on a sunbed, browning myself with a margarita in hand.* Oh yeah, the ultimate fuck you.

I tuned back into the conversation, feeling elated.

'You'll never know how proud I am when I'm with you... But it's time to think about myself. I know you'll be all right, Jay...' She wiped her tears. I hadn't even realised that she had been crying. She cleared her throat. 'I'll leave everything documented for you: service providers and any important phone numbers.'

What? Where is she going with this?

'I'm confident, in fact I'm certain, that you can run things around here.'

That's when it hit me. Late to the party as always.

'Am I not coming with you, Mum?' I said, my voice only just above a whisper.

'Oh, Jay,' Mum said.

She stood up and walked around the table and held my head tightly to her chest. I sat frozen, listening to her heartbeat. It took all my effort not to cry. I closed my eyes tightly and deeply inhaled her scent, the realisation hitting me that from here on, my problems were mine alone. I got myself into this mess. I had to get myself out.

If Mum believed that I was ready to be a man then, fuck it, I was ready to be a man. I detached myself from her and emerged with a smile that told her exactly that.

14

Hounslow High Street hustled and bristled with every type of religion, culture and colour. Ten different languages could be heard in a two-minute walk. All walks of life, from the prim to the pauper. Students, couples, doddery old dears, shoppers looking for their Pound Shop fix mingling with the shoplifters, chancers, dealers and thugs that kept Hounslow police station one of the busiest nicks in West London. In keeping with the rest of Hounslow, the police station was a nondescript, brown, square building, dull and dated. Scaffolding had covered the side of it for as long as anyone could remember, and the enquiries desk had been moved to a shoddy Portakabin plonked directly outside, with an ever-present queue.

As per usual, Idris Zaidi walked past the Portakabin at the start of his shift with a disappointed shake of the head, and as per usual, Idris Zaidi promised himself he would work on his transfer out of Hounslow. A transfer to neighbouring and upmarket Chiswick would be nice. A better class of criminal. It was that fantasy that was ringing around his head as he carelessly brushed into the oncoming Chief Superintendent Penelope Wakefield.

'Ma'am,' Idris said. 'My apologies.'

Wakefield mumbled something incoherent, until she realised who it was and her eyes widened.

'Zaidi. My office in ten.'

'Yes, ma'am,' Idris replied, and stood straight to attention, noticing the man who was accompanying the Chief. He was dressed in a shoddy old ill-fitting pea coat, with a woolly hat pulled down low. Idris acknowledged him with a tight smile. The man stared back at Idris with such intensity it felt as if he was trying to see into his soul.

*

Idris stood in front of the large pine desk. Files and documents were stacked neatly in the corner. The half-eaten remnants of a breakfast bar and a sealed fruit yoghurt sat in a small Tupperware box. A computer whirred breathlessly, as if exhausted by the punishment it had to endure. The Chief's eyes were on him. Idris glanced down at the empty chair next to him, waiting to be asked to occupy it. Her phone had the audacity to ring and, without taking her eyes off him, she answered it before the first ring had faded. She greeted the caller with a stern '*Not now!*' and the phone was back safely in its cradle. It would be a very long time before that caller tried to ring again.

Idris was not about to play a game of who blinks first.

'Ma'am?'

Wakefield inhaled through her nose and then expelled air through her mouth. 'We have shown a great deal of faith in you, Zaidi.'

'Yes, ma'am.'

'You got a first in Law from Queen Mary University.' It wasn't a question, so he didn't answer. 'We saw the potential in you from very early on and we admitted you in the Fast Track Promotion and Development Programme, a decision that was not roundly popular amongst your peers, especially those senior to you. The Fast Track Programme duration is three years.' She squinted at him. 'You completed it in two.'

'Yes, ma'am.' What else was there to say? Idris wondered why his CV was being regurgitated at him.

'You were out of uniform, sub-heading and then heading teams in a remarkably short space of time. Your record speaks for itself.'

'Yes, ma'am. Thank you, ma'am.' Idris felt like he'd said too much even though he had hardly said anything.

'With your law degree you chose to uphold the law rather than stand in a court and pick holes in it.'

Idris chose to say nothing.

'So, my question to you is this: why *did* you choose to become a police officer?'

Idris cleared his throat. He knew the answer to this. It wasn't the first time he'd been asked this very question. In fact, he remembered smashing this very question when he'd first been interviewed for the Met.

'I was attracted to the diversity of the role. Every new day brings a new challenge, which I thrive on both mentally and physically. The opportunity to help people make better choices and the opportunity to save lives. Being able to lead a—'

'Stop. Start again. This time *you* tell me. I don't want hear extracts from a handbook.'

Idris swallowed. His throat was dry, his palms sweaty. His pupils floated to the far right of his eyes as he tried to recall the real reason that made him apply for a life in the force when he had other, easier and certainly more lucrative options.

'My father, actually,' Idris said, smiling at the memory. 'Yes, my father. He would say to me time and time again: *Son, there is too much violence and evil in this world, which we cannot control. But we can control what is happening on our doorstep.* It's funny but I've never told anybody that before.' Idris looked at the Chief for some sign of softness or emotion. There was none. Wakefield's eyes were steady and steely.

'We grew up in a bad neighbourhood. My dad wanted to be part of the force but all he could manage was a job as a security guard. A job that he took very seriously. Sometimes to a fault.' Idris shrugged. 'And I wanted to emulate that attitude, that mentality. One day I'm going to have kids and I want them to grow up in a safe environment, which I know is probably just a pipe dream. But I have to try, and it's not just for my children, it's for everyone who cannot protect themselves. I want to protect them as my father protected me. I am sick and tired of the scum that litter our streets.'

Wakefield smashed the palm of her hands on the table. The sound reverberated around the room. The neatly stacked pile of documents shuddered and dislodged, the top sheet deciding to make a break for it and lazily arcing through the air before landing itself in the bin. The shudder also disturbed the mouse and the PC monitor came to life, lending a harsh glow to Wakefield's face.

'So why is it that you have been seen on many occasions with a known drug dealer?'

There it was.

Jay.

Wakefield calmly tucked a stray hair behind her ear, which had become loose during her outburst. A feminine gesture that seemed out of character.

'What's happened?' Idris asked in a low, measured tone.

'Do you know how it would look for you, *for us*, if word got out that one of our own has been associating with a drug dealer?'

Without taking her eyes off him, Wakefield opened up the top drawer to her right and picked out a brown envelope. She threw it down on the desk.

Idris picked it up and slipped out several photographs printed on 7 x 5 glossy card. There were three photos, all taken within a very short period. Minutes.

The first was of Idris and Jay in a Vauxhall Nova, Jay's arm hanging out of the window with a dubious roll-up in his hand. The second appeared to show a third person peering through the driver's window, seemingly in conversation with Jay.

The third photo showed a clear exchange of currency and a small package.

Idris calmly slid the photos back into the envelope and placed it back on the desk.

'He's a friend,' Idris said quietly and clenched his jaw, waiting for the onslaught.

'You stupid boy. The front page of every bloody tabloid, if this gets out. I can see it as clear as day. What do you think is going to happen to you, Zaidi? Hmm? Sitting in the bloody car with a criminal whilst a drug deal takes place right under your bloody nose.'

'With all due respect, ma'am,' Idris countered, 'he's a low-level juggler. He only deals to mates. It's not like we're looking at him.' Idris' eyes fell on the envelope. 'Why are we looking at him?'

'*We're* not,' Wakefield said. A small change in her expression led Idris to believe that she had given away far more than she wanted to.

'I haven't done anything wrong, ma'am.'

'You have a bright future ahead of you, Zaidi, and you are in real danger of jeopardising all that you have worked towards, and all the trust we have placed in you… Am I making myself clear, Zaidi?'

Idris gritted his teeth and held his tongue.

'I insist that you cut off ties with Javid Qasim.'

'Ma'am?'

'You are not to see him again.'

Idris knew how this was going to sound but he said it anyway. 'He's my friend.'

'Make a choice, *Detective Inspector*,' Wakefield said, emphasising his title to hammer home the point.

'This is bullshit,' Idris muttered under his breath, purposely loud enough for the Chief to hear. Wakefield let it slide as she replaced the envelope back in the top drawer.

'Dismissed.'

Idris stood his ground for a moment; his blood bubbled and threatened to spill over. He eyed the Chief momentarily before turning on his heel and walking towards the door. He placed his hand on the door handle but didn't turn it. A question had been burning through his mind as soon as he had seen the photographs. He looked down at his hand and his knuckles had turned white. He released it and turned to face the Chief.

'Who was that man you were talking to outside?'

'I said you're dismissed,' Wakefield said, her head down, avoiding eye contact.

Idris couldn't let it go. 'Is this anything to do with him?'

This time Wakefield's head snapped up and her eyes locked onto his.

'Get out of my office, now!'

15

Major General Stewart Sinclair sat in Boardroom 3 alongside John Robinson, Assistant Director of Counter Terrorism Operations. Boardroom 3 was the smallest boardroom in the Security Service building, however it remained a popular choice due to the breathtaking and calming views of the River Thames. On the table in front of them was a printed photo of Javid Qasim. Teddy Lawrence, the young officer, sat across the desk from them and was on his second exaggerated glance at his watch.

Kingsley Parker walked through the door, removed his pea coat and hung it on the back of his chair. As he sat down next to Lawrence, his coat slipped to the floor. Lawrence suppressed a smile. A smile that did not go unnoticed. Parker picked up the coat and looked around the room for a coat stand. Unable to locate one he folded the coat and placed it on the chair next to him.

'Traffic bad, Parker?' Lawrence asked.

Parker ignored him.

'Right. Let's get started, shall we?' Sinclair announced. His authoritative manner was such that anything he said sounded like an announcement. Every word enunciated and boomed, ensuring that there could be no mistakes as to what had been said or heard. The Major General had previously been in the army and he still used his rank. 'Parker, you attended two meetings,' Sinclair looked down at his notes, 'with our very own Dr Thomas Gladstone and Chief Superintendent Penelope Wakefield of Hounslow Met.' Sinclair didn't wait for a response. 'Would you like to brief us?'

Parker fidgeted slightly in his chair. His woolly jumper had started to itch and he had to make a concerted effort not reach around and scratch his back. He started slowly, tripping over words, but he eventually found some rhythm as he filled them in. From his peripheral vision he could see the obvious glee emanating from Lawrence.

'Well,' Sinclair said, 'the good doctor, as always, at his elusive best. He is right, though. It is very much a judgement call. What's your take on it, Parker?'

'The ease in which he can adapt to his environment could see him as an invaluable asset. It wouldn't take much for him to get noticed by the radicals who attend Sutton mosque. Already he's shown his commitment to the community with helping out at the mosque and then the subsequent revenge attack at the car park in Staines. No question, news of his action would have been noticed.'

'And we've got him by the balls!' Lawrence chimed in.

Sinclair looked at Lawrence calmly, with an amused look on his face. 'We'll come to you in a moment, son. Please continue, Parker. How did it go with Wakefield? Will she bend?'

'She isn't best pleased with our proposition. Given the time frame, she feels that she is being rushed into a decision that she doesn't want to make. They have invested a lot of time and resources targeting the upper-echelon drug dealers. One particular big fish, actually.' Parker reached across to his coat and dug around awkwardly from pocket to pocket, and eventually removed a crumpled photograph and placed it on the table next to the photograph of Javid Qasim.

'Who are we looking at?' Sinclair asked.

'This is Silas Drakos, AKA The Drake, AKA The Count. We believe he is responsible for a high percentage of the drugs that flow through West London. He is also believed to be involved in the buying and selling of some very heavy artillery.'

'Drakos is not our problem.' Robinson finally broke his silence and a waft of his lunch emanated. 'Wakefield *has* to cooperate or we go over her head.'

Parker carefully eyeballed Robinson. Robinson was exactly the kind of guy that Parker hated. The type that he had reported to throughout his career.

'Wakefield has expressed concern that if they were to pick up Javid Qasim, Silas may go to ground.'

Robinson looked at each face around the table. 'Somebody care to tell me how a bloody drug baron is taking precedence over national security? I don't care if he's Pablo *bloody* Escobar.' Robinson jabbed a nicotine-stained finger onto the crumpled photograph. 'Silas Drakos is not a priority!'

Silence descended. Parker put his hand on his knee before it started to hammer and counted to ten in his head. He took a breath and in a calm, measured voice he said, 'There is a way to appease both—'

'*Appease?*' Robinson shouted, as though he and that word had shared some dark history. He stood up and walked over to the water cooler. 'Let me tell you something, gentlemen – we are currently watching eight Muslim clerics, in London alone, who are openly spreading hate and inciting violence. These clerics attract a big audience, and make no mistake that audience is growing by the day. It is clear as crystal what their agenda is, but can we kick them out? No, we bloody can't. Because our government and our laws and our policies are in place to *bloody appease!*'

Robinson came back to the table. His face had reddened and he was slightly out of breath. He drank his water greedily.

'Please, Parker,' Sinclair said, ignoring the outburst. 'You were saying.'

'We have gathered enough evidence for Javid to be convicted. That evidence falls into the hands of Wakefield. They bring him in and he gives a statement pointing to Silas.'

Sinclair rubbed his chin as he visualised how this would play out.

'So, Silas is arrested and we have Qasim in our pocket,' Sinclair clarified. He looked across at Robinson. Robinson hesitantly acquiesced with a gentle nod. 'Only question now is, will Qasim play ball? We have him for dealing and assault – he's looking at a short spell inside. Is there a chance that he'll keep quiet and take the hit?'

Sinclair turned to Lawrence, who looked about ready to burst if he didn't have his say soon. 'Lawrence, anything you would like to add?'

Lawrence sat up straight, cleared his throat and held strong eye contact.

'Yes, sir. We have Javid Qasim's car in our hold. In the boot of his BMW we found a rucksack containing seven thousand pounds in cash and just under a pound of high-potency skunk weed, both of which we believe are the property of Silas Drakos. Regardless of who they belong to, the possession charge alone is going see Qasim receive a significant sentence. On top of which, it's reasonable to assume that Drakos would not have been happy that his drugs and money have gone missing – and that's putting it mildly, given his violent reputation. For both of these reasons I think Qasim has no choice *but* to sing.'

Sinclair nodded and his eyes momentarily flitted to Parker.

'It was the wrong move,' Parker said.

'With all due respect, sir,' Lawrence continued, 'we have invested a lot of time and manpower scoping Qasim. *I* saw an opportunity and *I* took the initiative. And as a result we now have enough on Qasim to mould him as we please. We'd still be watching him now if I hadn't—'

'You've made your point, Lawrence,' Sinclair said.

'Well, I think that shows a lot of enterprise,' Robinson piped up, happy to recognise a kindred spirit. 'What did you say your name is?'

'Lawrence, sir,' he said. 'Teddy Lawrence.'

*

In the corridor outside, Sinclair indicated for Parker to hold back as they watched Robinson and Lawrence walk cosily away.

'They may as well hold bloody hands,' Sinclair said. He turned and faced Parker. 'It's done. You don't have to say it.'

'Sir?' Parker said.

'Lawrence… He's not your responsibility anymore. I'm going to ensure that he is moved somewhere better suited. His enthusiasm may impress some but moving forward we need discipline and a clear line of command.' Parker nodded as Sinclair continued. 'Get Wakefield on board. She has no reason to decline. Qasim can give her Drakos on a platter… And listen, I think we should have first crack at the boy. This whole Drakos subject is a by-product. Qasim has to agree terms with us first. And then – and only then – can he give a statement pointing at Silas. It has to be in that order.'

'Yes, sir,' Parker agreed.

'Get a couple of our guys to pick him up, arrange it so the boys in blue tag along too. But before he sees the inside of that police station – he's yours.'

'Mine, sir?'

'I want you to handle him from here onwards, Parker.'

*

Parker had already decided that he was not going to mention the rucksack or the BMW to Qasim. If he was going to have a relationship with him, it was imperative that it was built on trust. Revealing that they had his car and gear would be the wrong move. He was Qasim's handler; he would handle him how he saw fit.

Parker needed to freshen up. He walked into the toilet and looked into the mirror. His tired eyes stared back at him. He reached up to his face and touched the pound-coin-shaped gap in his stubble, the result of alopecia brought on by stress. The cubicle door opened and Lawrence walked out. Parker dropped his hand from his face. They stood next to each other as Lawrence washed his hands.

'No hard feelings, eh?' Lawrence said, through the mirror. 'I did what I had to do.'

Parker rolled and cracked his shoulders and turned on the tap.

'You have to admit: taking his car was the icing on the cake.'

'You went against my order,' Parker said quietly as he slowly rolled up his sleeves.

'Not really. You weren't exactly giving out any orders to go *against*.'

'Rule number one: follow orders,' Parker said, as if rolling out an age-old mantra.

Lawrence noisily squirted soap onto his hands.

'Still a bit sore about what happened in the meeting?' Lawrence asked, smiling arrogantly. He turned off the tap and shook his hands dry, droplets of water splashing Parker. 'What happened to you? Huh? Where's this Chalk I keep hearing about? No offense, but you walk around looking like you don't know what day it is.'

The speed and ferocity with which Parker gripped his right ear dropped Lawrence to one knee. The soft flesh burned and threatened to tear within Parker's large hand. Lawrence, his face scrunched in pain, used both hands to try to pry away Parker's grip from his ear. When that failed, Lawrence punched him with all the power he could muster in the ribs. From his position on one knee he had the perfect angle to cause some damage. Two punches in quick succession, hard and fast. Parker's body didn't react, and his grip didn't waver. Instead it tightened and he viciously twisted Lawrence's ear so it was almost positioned upside down.

'Okay,' Lawrence screamed. 'Fucking okay!' Then quietly he hissed, '*Please*.'

Parker released his ear just as quickly as he had grabbed it. He turned to the sink and calmly washed his face. He dried off using the paper towels and walked out of the toilet without giving Lawrence a second look.

16

The minicab pulled up outside our house, or, I should say, my house, about mid-morning. I started to lug Mum's suitcases into the boot as she rushed around the house, room to room, saying goodbye to all the furniture and all the things she held dear. I slammed the boot shut and the cabbie gave me a deathly stare. I put up an apologetic hand to him, just as Idris walked around the corner.

'Don't you check your fucking voicemail?' Idris barked before he had even reached me.

'The fuck is your problem?' I said, matching profanity for profanity.

Idris and I had only ever argued the one time, when a chilli-eating competition got out of hand. But if he wanted an argument now, then I was ready to give him one.

'I've been trying to reach you, Jay,' he said as he got closer. He noticed the minicab. 'What's going on? Where you going?'

'To the airport. Mum's leaving today.'

'Oh shit!' Idris exclaimed. 'That's today? I knew that. I fucking knew that. Mum did tell me.'

I had never seen Idris so rattled, as though all his cool had left him. Mum walked out of the house looking like a seventies Bollywood starlet: white flared trouser suit teamed with huge oversized dark sunglasses, holding a midsize black leather travel bag.

'Why don't you come along? See Mum off,' I asked. 'And then maybe you can tell me what's on your mind.'

Idris looked towards Mum, who was waving happily at him, and it seemed like his brain had just rebooted as he walked over to her. He gave her a customary peck on the cheek, effortlessly liberated the travel bag and linked arms with her as he escorted her, smiling, to the waiting minicab.

Okay, so maybe not *all* his cool had left him.

*

We were sat at a Sports Bar in Terminal 2 at Heathrow, Idris opposite me as we waited in silence for our lunch to arrive. Mum and Andrew were now airside, no doubt stocking up on duty-free goods. It was, as expected, an emotional farewell. Mum's white suit had ended up stained with a mixture of her mascara, my snot and both of our tears. I hadn't felt any shame sobbing my heart out in front of Idris, who had just about managed to hold it together himself.

'So, what do you think of Andrew?' I asked.

'Yeah, he's all right,' Idris answered, absentminded, his eyes flitting all over the place before landing on mine. 'They seem good together.'

An Arab couple walked into the Sports Bar, the wife covered from head to toe in a Burka. In a heartbeat, the tension in the room become palpable and the din died down for a millisecond and then started up again.

'Poor bastards,' I said. 'Do you reckon they ever get used to that?'

Idris didn't seem to hear me. The food arrived, a full English breakfast, minus the scum. I tucked straight into it.

'Jay?' Idris said, ignoring his food.

'Yeah,' I said, with a mouthful of hash brown.

'Look, I don't want to freak you out.'

'Well, don't then.'

I smiled. He smiled. But only briefly before his expression turned to dour again.

'I'm serious, Jay.'

I looked at my meal longingly, and then hesitantly I put down my knife and fork. I took a sip of my orange juice and placed my glass down on the table.

'What's bothering you?'

'I think they're coming for you,' Idris said, rubbing his forehead.

75

'Why do you say that?' I asked, as controlled as I could, when everything in me wanted to scream a thousand questions.

'It's just something that happened at work.'

'Like what?'

'My chief had me in her office.'

'Oh, did she now?'

'She showed me some photos of us together in your car,' he said, rightly ignoring my childish remark.

'In my Beemer?'

'No, your Nova.'

'So?' I said, trying to remember anything untoward that had happened in my Nova that would have cause to be flagged.

'You were doing a deal.'

'Yeah, I remember that. A few weeks back, yeah?' I said, and then realisation hit me. 'And you were in the car with me?' Idris nodded. 'Oh, shit! Did you get fucked? Is that what this is about?'

'Yeah, I did, but—'

'God. I'm sorry, man. I didn't fucking know. How much trouble are you in? Can they prove that it was a deal? I could have been passing anything.'

'No, Jay, shut up for a second. This isn't about me getting the hairdryer.' Idris leaned in and lowered his voice. 'It's about them *watching you*.'

'What do you mean *watching me*? I haven't done anything wrong! Nothing that warrants surveillance, anyway.'

'I know that, Jay. If they were going to arrest you for your nickel-and-dime bullshit dealing they would have pulled you over, searched your car and hauled your ass down the station. This is something else.'

I looked down at my food. It didn't look too appetising anymore. 'Idris,' I said tentatively. 'The attack on the mosque. Last Friday. Do you remember?'

'Yeah, course.'

'Do you remember I told you about that meeting at Ali's?'

'Yeah,' Idris said, his eyes narrowed, as he tried to follow my thought process.

'Do you remember—'

'Can you stop saying that, for God's sake. I'm not fucking *senile*,' Idris said, loud enough for a few patrons to crane their heads in our direction. 'Go on.' He lowered his voice. 'You were in Ali's. So? What happened?'

'I ended up with Parvez and Khan.'

'*Khan?*' Idris said, rubbing his face again. 'What the hell were you thinking?'

'All right, calm down, man. You're getting loud again.'

Idris sat back in his chair, crossed him arms and motioned for me to carry on.

'We got into a dust-up with some white boys in Staines. I tooled one of them... Pretty fucking badly. But he was all right... I think,' I said, sheepishly. 'Do you reckon that's what it's about?'

'No... I don't know... It could be.'

'Yeah, well, thanks for clearing that up, Detective.'

'Look. What do we know for a fact? They've been watching you for at least a few weeks, right?'

'So they can't be after me because of the fight. That only happened last week.'

I cracked my knuckles. A nervous trait that hadn't been evident in a very long time.

'Unless.... Unless...' Idris said.

'What? Unless what?'

'Unless they were *waiting* for you to screw up.'

17

We decided to take the bus home rather than fork out for another minicab. We sat up on the top deck, right at the very back. Me at one window, Idris at the far other. A big gap between us, just like we did a thousand times back in the day on the way to school. That back seat belonged to us, and even though there was a huge gap between us, everyone knew better than to occupy it.

This felt like that, but at the same time it didn't.

My stop arrived first. We made rushed plans to see each other soon, to shoot some pool, but I think somehow we both knew that would never happen. It felt very much like the next time we saw each other everything would have changed.

As I put the key in the front door of my empty house I heard a car pull up behind me. I turned to face a silver Ford Mondeo haphazardly parked halfway across my drive, inches from my Nova. I'd already lost one car recently; I wasn't about to lose my fucking Nova too. I glared through the windscreen, ready to give the driver a piece of my mind, but first I wanted to get a good look just in case he was bigger than me. There were two of them, both white, one male and one female, and they were releasing their seatbelts, eyeballs fixed on me. I instinctively knew who they were, even before the second car pulled up directly behind them. This car was a white Vauxhall Astra with blue lights attached to the roof and the word POLICE written back to front on the bonnet.

The hairs at the back of my neck stood to attention and I broke into a cold sweat. Four doors opened in tandem as the couple from the first car stepped out, and two uniforms got out of the police car and stood behind them. They stood in the middle of my driveway, watching me carefully to see if I would make a move.

I looked down the road to my left and then I looked down the road to my right. Escape was not an option. Mexico was a long fucking way away. Across the road curtains twitched and I knew what my nosy neighbours were thinking. *His mum has only been gone five minutes and look...*

I coolly turned back towards my front door and looked at the key still swinging in the lock. I turned it and opened the door.

I walked into my house and shut the door in all their fucking faces.

18

I think it was due. It had to be. I'd been on easy street for as long as I could remember. Even back at school I did pretty much whatever the fuck I wanted to, and I never ever found myself in detention or in the headmaster's office. I don't know why that was. I think maybe I had some charm, or an innocent face or whatever, but shit never seemed to stick to me. Teachers left me alone, bullies didn't target me, and to an extent Mum let me be too. I just never got busted. Until now.

The four little pigs knocked on my door and I answered it, nonchalantly eating a Twix. They didn't seem too chuffed at having the door shut in their faces. A uniform reached across with handcuffs. I still had one full stick of Twix remaining so I clamped it between my teeth as they secured my wrists behind me.

I was escorted out the front door and the twitching curtains had progressed to some of my neighbours standing out on their front porches, gawping.

I think maybe it's the rap music or the too many viewings of *Scarface*, but I acted like a man without a care in the world. I walked confidently with my chest out, the Twix hanging from my mouth like a Cuban cigar, my steps measured and my gait straight-up gangster.

Better that than the world seeing me cry.

*

With my hands cuffed behind me, I was sliding all over the place on the leather seat every time we took a turning. We reached a junction and stopped at the traffic lights, and it took me a moment to realise that we were in the wrong lane. Hounslow police station was to the right but we were out in the left lane.

I shifted around in my seat and looked out of the rear window, just as the patrol car left its position as sentry and manoeuvred next to us in the correct lane. I noticed my driver give the uniform the slightest of nods as the traffic lights turned green and the patrol car turned towards the police station. And we went in the opposite direction.

I waited a minute, thinking maybe there was another car park for unmarked police cars. When that didn't materialise my mind went into overdrive. I couldn't think of *one* rational reason why they wouldn't have taken me to Hounslow nick, and then with a jolt I realised that when they had arrested me, they hadn't read out my rights or my charges.

I started to see signs for Isleworth and then Brentford, and the next thing I knew we were on the fucking motorway.

'Where we going?' I was frightened as to what the response might be. And they gave me the most unnerving response possible.

Silence.

I looked at the back of their heads. I could see their side profiles and they carried no-nonsense, business-like expressions on their faces.

They definitely weren't the police and this was definitely not an arrest.

Was I getting kidnapped? I know how that sounded, but I couldn't think of any other explanation. Could this be Silas' doing? He had always been one for the dramatics but I still had two days left before my deadline.

I positioned myself so I had my back towards the door and I could just about grip the handle. But then what? Even if they hadn't locked me in, what was I going to do? Jump out onto the motorway with the car doing north of seventy? I glanced around the car, desperately searching for other options. A boot to the side of the driver's face would cause the car to veer, leading to a possible distraction. But at this speed, on the motorway, with a heavy goods vehicle in the next lane, there was every chance that I could end up in a far worse situation than I was in already.

My shoulders ached because of the unnatural position my chained hands were in. If shit kicked off and I had to defend myself, I would have no chance with my hands trapped behind my back. I had to try and bring them to my front. I pushed my shoulders back as far as they could go and tried to slide my hands from underneath. It was a tricky manoeuvre and I almost popped my shoulder at one point. Hollywood made everything look so easy. I was seriously out of breath and my hands were now trapped under my arse. Every muscle in my upper body screamed to give up. So I did.

The car started to slow down without any obvious reason – there was no traffic for as far as I could see and there wasn't an exit for them to take. The driver indicated left and pulled over onto the hard shoulder.

That really threw me. Were they going to beat me, or worse, right there on the hard shoulder, with hundreds of witnesses driving past? This was bordering on the bizarre and if it wasn't for the pain racing through my shoulder, I would have had this down as some sort of cheese-induced dream.

I heard the loud growl of an engine and I turned back to see a serious-looking black motorbike pull up a few feet behind us. The rider walked towards the car. He was still wearing his helmet and in his other hand he held another. The couple opened their doors and got out of the car. They stood in a tight triangle by the side of the car. The rider handed the woman the spare helmet, and I saw him reach up and take his own helmet off and hand that to the man, as well as the keys to the bike. I couldn't see his face but he was tall and powerfully built. I watched as the couple mounted the motorbike and rode off. The driver's side door opened and the rider climbed in.

He turned and faced me, and his dark, dead eyes seemed to look right through me.

You know when you give somebody cut-eyes. *That* look, *that* glare. The one that says in no uncertain terms: *I am not scared of you. You should be scared of me.* In my world that look is second nature. It took me a while to perfect it, and I used it as a weapon. I could tell you about any number of occasions when I've got out of scrapes and misunderstandings just by shutting somebody down with *that* look. Eyes slightly narrowed, grinding teeth, jaw clamped tight. Measured and menacing. I had it down to a fine art.

But this guy… Forget about it.

He looked at me as if I wasn't there. His eyelids drooped in a way that cried out for sleep. The whites of his eyes were tinged with yellow and his pupils were two black holes. His face made him look older than his body would have you believe. I couldn't compete and I dropped eye contact almost immediately.

'Javid Qasim.' Not a question. He knew me.

'Yeah,' I said, without sound. I swallowed and said it again, with as much confidence as I could. 'Yeah.'

He reached into the pocket of his trampy pea coat.

'Turn around.'

'Fuck you,' I hissed. False bravado making an appearance.

He pulled his hand from his pocket and I recoiled. He was holding up a small key. 'Turn around.' This time I did and he removed my handcuffs.

'Thanks.' I muttered, as I twisted my wrists, trying to get the blood circulating back into them.

He turned away from me and faced front. He adjusted the rear-view mirror until he had a good visual of me.

'My name is Kingsley Parker. And right now I'm the only friend you've got.'

19

Friend?

Like buddies? Like Best Friends Forever? Like, let's go for a pint and try our luck with the local talent?

I don't think so.

Parker passed me a deck of B&H over his shoulder. I took one out and slipped it between my lips. I lit it using the car lighter, whilst he watched me through the rear-view mirror. I pocketed his deck.

'Javid Qasim,' Parker said, and continued monotonously. 'Jay, to your friends. You've lived all your life in Hounslow with your mum, Afeesa Qasim, who just this morning flew from Heathrow to Doha, Qatar, with one Andrew Bishop. You were there to see her off, along with your childhood friend, and now Detective Inspector, Idris Zaidi.' He waited a beat. I let it sink in. He continued. 'You are not averse to a drink, most usually a pint of San Miguel at your local pub, the Rising Sun, and you like to have the odd gamble, which you carry out online on your phone, which by the way is a Samsung Galaxy S8.' He turned his head slightly over his shoulder towards me. 'You haven't had much luck recently. Maybe gambling isn't your thing.'

'Kane missed that penalty in the last minute. Would have been quids in otherwise,' I said, as though this was a casual fucking conversation.

He turned back and continued to address me through the mirror. 'You attend Sutton mosque every Friday for prayers and you helped with the clean-up and restoration of the mosque after it was attacked.'

'All right, mate. Stop right there. Wanna tell me what you want?'

'We've been watching you, Javid.'

'*No! Really?*' I said. 'And call me Jay.'

He nodded.

I put out my cigarette in the small ashtray and clumsily climbed into the front seat. The sudden movement caused Parker to swiftly pull his arms up at chest height in a defensive stance, fists tight and ready. In doing so his elbow hit the wiper switch. I sat next to him, showing the palms of my hands in a placatory gesture. He relaxed and dropped his hands onto his lap. We both looked ahead in awkward silence and watched the wipers redundantly judder against the dry windscreen.

'Look, I know you ain't the fuzz,' I said, reaching across and turning off the wipers. 'So… who or what are you then?'

'I work for the government, son.'

A cold shiver ran down my spine. He had already mentioned my affiliation with Sutton mosque. Had they put two and two together and got twenty-two? 'I'm not a terrorist, I swear.'

'No. I know that.'

I waited for him to elaborate. He didn't.

'What the fuck, man? Can we stop playing twenty questions?'

It was clear that Parker was uncertain where to begin. I wondered if maybe the guy who was originally supposed to be here had called in sick, and they'd had to draft in this clueless lump to take his place.

'Jay, we are in the process of recruitment and development. Part of the reason for the surveillance was to establish personality. You, Jay, fit the profile and we would like you to come and work with us at MI5.'

'MI5!? Get the fuck outta here.' I snorted, looking around the car for hidden cameras. It had to be a joke, an elaborate set-up. 'Who put you up to this? Is this gonna be on YouTube?'

'You are young, capable and, according to your medical records, you are fit and healthy. You would make a fantastic addition to the team. A real asset… We think you can make a difference. I am offering you a job, son.'

The way he said that left me with no doubt that he was telling me the truth. And I hate to admit it but it excited me.

'But…' he said. And left it there.

'Oh, here we go. But what?'

'You're in deep with Silas Drakos. You owe him some money and, from what I've been told, not only is it a substantial amount, but you haven't got a hope in hell of paying him back. Now, unless you've got that kind of cash stashed somewhere we haven't been able to find, I think you're about to be on the back end of a lashing. And given Drakos' history, it's not going to end well for you, son.'

Not that I was counting, but that was the third time that he had called me 'son'. I didn't mind it. It felt strangely comforting.

'You're in a whole lot of trouble.' Parker turned to face me just in time to see me shrug.

'You don't know the half of it,' I said, under my breath.

'No, *you* don't know the half of it.'

'That supposed mean?' I asked. His agitation fed mine.

'Aside from Silas, the police have evidence to make a very strong case against you. The way things are looking, you could be doing some hard time. They know about the flat in Cranford.'

That shook me. They fucking had me.

'It looks very much like it's set up for growing some serious cannabis, judging by the fluorescent lamps and the bags of soil, not to mention the packets of feminised skunk seeds.'

'I was going to give that flat up. I swear. It was a dumb idea. I could never have made it work,' I said, trying to keep the desperation from my voice.

'Regardless. Coupled with the fact that you are a drug dealer, albeit a low-level one, it doesn't look good for you.'

'How long am I looking at?' That whole venture with the flat was going to put me away, and I wasn't ever really going to go through with it. I could not believe my shitty luck.

'Wait.' He held up a big hand. 'There's more... Eugene Milford is currently in hospital with severe concussion.'

'Eugene who?' Then it hit me. 'Shit!' I said, sliding down in my seat, the beginnings of a headache looming. 'Elmsleigh car park.'

'When Eugene got home that night, after suffering a heavy blow to the head, he collapsed outside his house. His father found him and called for an ambulance.'

'How is he?' I asked, feeling very fucking small.

'Hard to say with a head injury... But signs are promising. However, Milford Senior insists that Milford Junior presses charges.'

I closed my eyes. 'How long?' I asked again.

Parker expelled air. 'If you get yourself a top lawyer, you're looking at three years, and if you keep your head down inside, you'll be out in two.'

'I can't afford a top lawyer.'

'Then you'll be provided with one.'

'A crappy one, though.'

Parker nodded. 'Yes... A crappy one.'

I couldn't go to jail; there was not a chance in hell I would survive three months, let alone three years. Yeah, I can handle myself, but that's because I pick my battles carefully. In there I wouldn't have that luxury. I closed my eyes, but behind my eyelids my eyes were dancing with harrowing visions of getting daily beatings in the morning, getting my food thieved in the afternoon, and getting royally shafted in the evening.

As though he'd read my mind, Parker said, 'We can make all this go away.'

'What are you proposing?'

'A two-tier agreement.'

I had a strong feeling I knew what one of those two was, and I had a fair idea what the other one could be. But I asked anyway.

'What's the first?'

'Silas Drakos. He's part of a large ongoing investigation, and with your help they can put him away for a very long time.'

'He's going to kill me,' I reasoned. Truth was, if I didn't get my hands on 10K pretty fucking sharpish, he was going to kill me anyway.

'He won't know it's you,' Parker said, not quite reassuring me. 'Tomorrow you give a statement down at Hounslow police station. Tell them whatever you know about Drakos, and I have it on good authority that he will be picked up that very same day.'

No Silas, *no debt, no threat hanging over me.* But could I do it? Could I break the oldest rule of the streets? *Could I grass?*

'I need to think about it.'

'That's fine. You have twenty-four hours, otherwise you will be arrested, and this time it will be for real.'

I nodded wearily.

'The second condition is that—'

'I come work for you,' I said, interrupting him. 'At *MI5*.' I let out a small, incredulous nasal laugh at the absurdity of it.

'Yes, Jay.'

'And you want me because I fit the profile, right? I could make a difference. Something along those lines?'

I turned and faced him. He pursed his lips and I noticed his knee hammering. He knew what was coming.

'Or is it because I'm a Muslim?'

20

Teddy Lawrence sat waiting outside Robinson's office, surreptitiously eyeing up the PA. He had been shopping in preparation for his new role at MI5, a role more suited to his talents. Jeans, trainers and sweatshirts were off the menu. Now it was all about sharp, fitted suits and crisp shirts with polished black Oxfords. A proper uniform. No longer would he be the skivvy that carried out long, boring surveillance work, on his stomach in the dirt, armed with a camera and cheap coffee. And no longer would he be working for that has-been, Parker. Lawrence had already disliked Parker, but that had been a professional aversion. Now, with his ear still throbbing, Lawrence hated him with a passion.

Parker had made it personal.

Let's see where we both are in twelve months' time. Lawrence smiled at the thought as he continued to check out Robinson's PA, wondering if Lucy or Laura or whatever her name was had noticed his dark blue suit, cut by the hands of Cad & the Dandy, Savile Row.

The door to Robinson's office opened and Major General Sinclair stormed out, carrying a scowl, his red ruddy cheeks redder and ruddier than ever. He glared at Lawrence.

'You can go in,' said Laura or Lucy.

Assistant Director of Counter Terrorism Operations John Robinson was not one for appearances. Showering, it appeared, was not a high priority, and underarm sweat patches were evident not only through his shirt but also through his crumpled blazer. On occasion he had food stuck between his teeth, and his breath always smelled sickly sweet. His office, though, told another story altogether. Bright natural light flooded through the floor-to-ceiling glass windows, overlooking some of London's most treasured structures. There wasn't a desk or computer in sight; instead there were two black leather three-seater sofas, facing each other with a tinted glass coffee table in-between, littered with high-end glossy magazines and newspapers and a Cisco conference phone.

Robinson always enjoyed the look of surprise when somebody entered his office for the first time. He sat down and motioned for Lawrence to take a seat opposite him.

'Nice suit,' Robinson said.

'Thanks,' Lawrence replied. 'Nice office.'

'It'll do,' Robinson said, as he looked around the office. 'For the time being.' Robinson crossed his legs and considered Lawrence as a small victory. 'Welcome on board.'

'Thank you, sir. I appreciate being given the chance.'

'You were wasted there, Lawrence.' Robinson ran his tongue across his front two teeth. Satisfied that part of his lunch wasn't lodged there, he continued. 'I just had a very interesting meeting with Sinclair.'

'Yes, sir. I just saw him leave. He didn't seem too happy.'

'We had a disagreement... Regarding you, actually.'

'Sir?'

'It seems that he wasn't impressed by the role we have offered you.'

Lawrence shifted uncomfortably in his seat.

'Sinclair was...' Robinson continued, searching for the right word, '*adamant* that you are to have no part in this ongoing operation. He wanted to have you removed from Kingsley Parker's orbit. In part, I agreed. You and Parker are not compatible.' Lawrence absentmindedly touched his ear. 'But that doesn't mean to say that, going forward, you would not be of any value. You've already shown yourself to have some grit, and it's thanks to you that we have full control over Javid Qasim.'

Lawrence nodded. Robinson stood up and walked over to a large mahogany cabinet and opened it. He picked out two whisky glasses, holding them in one hand with his thumb and forefinger, and in the other hand he brandished a bottle of Scotch. Robinson placed the bottle and glasses on the coffee table and proceeded to pour a decent shot into each glass.

'Cheers,' Robinson said, as they clinked glasses. 'I am not interested in what Sinclair feels. You are still very much involved in this operation. But now you work directly under me: you report to me and you answer to me.'

'Yes, sir,' Lawrence said. He felt a touch light-headed as the trail of whisky burned through his chest. But more than anything he felt the adrenaline start to rush through him.

'Now,' Robinson said. 'Let's discuss your first task.'

21

The sky was dark and the moon was full, which made it feel later than it actually was when I eventually got home. From Parvez's house, from across the road, he had a direct view of my front door, and I hoped he hadn't seen me earlier, being handcuffed away. The last thing I needed was for him to pop round with his words of fucking wisdom. I walked in and the house was freezing. I blasted the heating and kept my jacket on until the house warmed up. I ran upstairs and went straight to the secret hiding place where I kept all my stash that I didn't want Mum to see – a red Nike shoe box. I flipped open the lid and took out a half-empty bottle of Smirnoff vodka and a ready-rolled joint. I went back downstairs, slumped on an armchair, turned on the box and channel-hopped without paying any attention. I drank greedily from the bottle and puffed mercifully, holding every pull deep in my lungs before exhaling. The combination of the two, along with an empty stomach, took effect in no time at all.

I logged onto my banking app and checked my bank balance, hoping for a miracle, a bank error to the tune of ten thousand. It showed £500, five hundred more than yesterday, transferred by Mum as she said she would, with the same amount to be deposited regularly over the next few months, on the promise that I would double my efforts and look for a job. Well, *about that, Mum*, I had just had a very interesting job interview on the hard shoulder of the M4 for the Security Service!

Parker was right: I didn't have a hope in hell repaying my debt. It seemed I had few options: grass up Silas and then join MI5 as the token Paki; or get banged up; or get killed.

Apart from the recent incident with Silas, he'd always been good to me, but I guess that's because I'd always been good to him. I'd always been on time with my drop-offs, every other

Friday without fail, and I took my cut without counting it. Any gear I had left over I knew I could shift the next time, especially as there were always a lot of student parties at the local college. A couple of times after I'd made a drop, Silas wouldn't let me go home, instead making me stay for hours into the night, watching back to back nineties movies whilst getting wasted. There was one particular time, when we were both smashed on tequila shots and some very fine Blue Cheese skunk, that he insisted that he show me something. He took me up to the converted loft space. Outside a heavy-duty door there was a small, numerical keypad. He clumsily entered the pin incorrectly and, just as he was about to try again, he paused. His hand hovered over the keypad and I could see him calculating through his high, as he tried to come to a decision. Slowly Silas dropped his hand to his side and turned to me. 'It's not meant to be,' he said simply.

I didn't push him, even though I was curious as George. We went back downstairs and he indicated to me that the night was over.

He came *this close* to showing me *something*.

I had a good idea what was behind that door, and I knew if I put pen to paper it could put him away for a long time.

*

Three hard knocks on my front door made me jump out of my skin. After the day I'd had I thought it would be wise to clock who it was first through the living room curtains. I tutted loudly to myself when I saw that it was one of my freshy neighbours.

'Jay, Beta, I knocking on door for long time,' Aunty Rashida said in broken, heavily accented English. 'I saw you come home and then I thought something bad happened to you when you not answer.' She wasn't a real aunt but everyone of a certain age and colour on my street was a fucking uncle or aunty.

'Salaam, Aunty,' I said, mirroring her clumsy inflection. 'Sorry, I was busy, I didn't hear you. Sorry.' I wasn't taking the piss; I always talked like that to my elders whose first language wasn't the Queen's. It was patronising, I know, but also the most effective way to communicate. 'How are you?' I said, eyeing up the Tupperware in her hand

'Fine, Beta. How is Ami? Has she landed safely and soundly?' she asked, wrinkling her nose. I knew she could smell the drink on my breath.

'Not sure,' I said, through the side of my mouth. 'I'm just waiting for her to phone.' I knew why she was here, and it wasn't to ask about my mum. I also knew that like most *Aunty-Jis* she didn't have any tact.

'I saw lots of policeman take you today,' she said. Straight for the jugular.

I cursed under my breath. 'Not to worry, Aunty,' I said. 'Misunderstanding.'

She looked at me with a confused expression as she tried to decipher *misunderstanding*.

'*Mistake*. Big mistake,' I said, making it a little easier for her. The smell from the Tupperware was now making its way into my house and my stomach rumbled, and at that moment I missed my mum so much.

'But they put...' She couldn't find the right word, so, balancing the container in one hand, she put her wrists together.

'Handcuffs,' I said and she nodded excitedly at the new word that she had learned. 'No. Aunty. It was nothing. Just a mistake, big mistake. Please don't worry.'

We stood there for a moment, aimlessly nodding at each other. My mouth had started to water as I recognised the smell. Lamb biryani!

'Is that for me?' I said, pointing at the container.

'Yes, yes. For you.' A smile flashed across her face. 'I come in? Warm up for you?'

Yeah, right. More like fish for more juicy details to go and tell the rest of the neighbourhood watch committee.

'Sorry, Aunty. I really am very busy right now.'

I smiled sweetly, liberated the container from her and shut the door, just as she opened her mouth to say something.

*

I had my tray set up with my spoon and fork, some mango pickle and a cold glass of lemonade. The microwave pinged and the lamb biryani looked picture-perfect. The sweet smell rose up into my nose and attacked my senses, almost sending me delirious.

Then there was another hard rap on my front door. *What the fuck, man?* I placed the plate on the tray and looked longingly at it. I stomped to the door in frustration and, without checking who it was through the front window, I opened the door, ready to give my nosy neighbours a piece of my mind.

I hadn't realised that I'd been punched square on the nose until I was on my backside in my hallway holding it. Two pairs of Timberlands walked into my house and shut the door behind them.

22

Through watery eyes I looked up and Staples and another guy, who I had not yet had the pleasure of being introduced to, were towering over me.

'What's that smell?' Staples said, as his nostrils flared. 'That smells fucking divine.' He turned his attention to his comrade. 'Ben, take Jay into the living room, will ya? I'll be back in a tick.'

I was lifted onto my feet, dragged into the living room and thrown down onto my armchair by not-so-gentle Ben. He stood smirking in front of me, proudly showing off every one of his gold teeth. Staples walked into the living room with my plate of lamb biryani in hand. He pulled up a chair and sat adjacent to me as he tucked into my supper, making all the appreciative sounds that I should have been making.

'You want some, mate?' Staples said to Ben.

'Nah, you're all right. Indian food gives me the runs,' Ben said. 'I'll get some KFC later.'

My head was spinning from the drink, my senses were numb from the skunk and my eyes were still watering due to my bloody nose. I could sense Staples eyeing me over the plate but I didn't dare give it back. Instead I turned my attention to the TV. Through my blurred vision I could see a red ticker tape scrolling across the bottom of Sky News, but I couldn't make out what it read and the volume was too low to hear.

'What are these little black things?' Staples said, picking out a whole pepper from the biryani and holding it up between his thumb and forefinger.

'What?' I said.

Staples threw it at me and it bounced harmlessly off my head. I didn't even have the energy to flinch.

'Kali mirch,' I said wearily. 'Whole pepper, in English, I think they're called.'

'Are they edible or are they put in for the aroma so it—'

'What do you want, Staples?' I interrupted.

'Did it sound like I'd finished talking, motherfucker?' Staples hissed at me. 'Interrupt me again and it will be the last time you do, you get me?'

I just nodded, unsure whether he had finished talking.

'Now, as you're in such a hurry for me to get to the point, I will.' Staples eyes fell on the now empty bottle of vodka, which I did not remember finishing, and the butt of my joint sitting, without a care in the world, in my ashtray. 'I just dropped in for a friendly visit, is all. Just to make sure that you're getting Silas' money together.'

'I've still got two days left,' I said. I rubbed my eyes and my vision started to clear. From the corner of my eye on the TV I could see an aerial view, but it was hard to determine what the view was of because a thick spiral of black smoke was obstructing whatever it was that they were trying to show. The information bar at the bottom of the screen stated that it was *Breaking News*: *Edmonton, Canada*.

'I'm not one to judge a book by its cover, Jay,' Staples said. 'But it looks very much to me like you are drinking your problems away. Hmm? Looking for an answer at the bottom of a bottle.'

I had no answer so I gave him my default response. A shrug.

'Well?' Staples asked.

'I still got two days,' I repeated. 'We had a deal.'

Staples laughed. 'We're just here to see how you're getting along.'

Staples kept talking, but my attention was fully on Sky News. They were now showing a different angle where the middle of a large building had collapsed, and was billowing black smoke. Men and women were running and staggering out of the building and gathering in the car park. Others were being carried. The feed zoomed in and to my horror I realised that that they weren't men and women. They were boys and girls.

They were children. And the building was a school.

Staples had stopped talking now and Ben had taken a break from giving me menacing stares. Their attention turned towards the news and they quietly watched the horrific events that had taken place.

It was harrowing. And I silently prayed to whoever was listening: *Please don't let it be us responsible.*

But I knew better.

*

We watched in grim silence as the children and teachers held each other, sobbing their fucking hearts out. Medics were on the scene treating those who were still treatable. The press swarmed, taking morbid pictures, and police milled around uselessly, unsure of the correct procedure.

'Turn that shit up,' Staples said. A sign flashed up: *Warning. Graphic Images.* I located the remote control and cranked the volume right up and, just as I did, at that very moment, there was a loud blast that tore through the surround-sound speakers, filling my living room. The unmistakeable sound of death.

The remote control dropped from my hands and I leaned back hard in my armchair, as if trying to get as far from the TV as possible. The echo of the explosion was still ringing in my ears. Staples was up on his feet like a shot. In doing so he knocked the plate; rice and succulent pieces of lamb scattered on the floor. Ben dropped down onto his haunches and held his head in his hand, mumbling random expletives to himself.

A black swirl covered every inch of my 50-inch plasma as smoke billowed around, looking for a direction to head towards. Behind the smoke, there were earth-shattering, ear-piercing screams. The feed cut to a different camera, showing the grounds of the car park, which was carpeted with a sick concoction of bodies, limbs and internal organs.

The bastards. The fucking hateful bastards. They had waited for everyone to escape from the building after the first attack, and gather in the car park. *As they knew they would.* Then a second bomb had detonated right there in the fucking car park, taking out all of those children who were fortunate enough to have survived the first attack.

The feed then mercifully cut to the Sky News desk. The newsreaders were as white as ghosts. The man put a finger to his ear and listened into his earpiece. He nodded solemnly to himself.

'*We have confirmed reports coming in from various sources that Al-Jazeera have just aired a video tape. The tape appears to show a group of three armed masked men claiming responsibility for the atrocities that took place earlier today. They declared that they belong to a group called Al-Aqab.*'

Ben got up from his haunches and turned to face me, his expression masked with rage. 'That's your fuckin' fault,' he spat. 'You hear me?'

I did hear him. My blood boiled and my breathing deepened.

'Ben...' Staples said, turning from aggressor to pacifier.

'No, fuck that,' Ben continued. 'It *is* his fault. Him and his so-called fucking Paki brothers.' Ben took a long stride towards me and lifted me by my jacket. His face an inch from mine, his breath like an old suitcase. 'Does this shit make you happy, bitch? You going to have a good laugh about this with your *Brothers*?'

The impact of the ashtray smashing against the side of his face sent Ben sprawling to the floor. I stood over him and glared, knowing what was to come.

*

Staples and Ben left soon after. I took a good kicking and I took it well. They couldn't do much damage as I still had a debt to pay. I was laid out on my back on the living room carpet, directly underneath the TV. From my view the picture was upside down. There were two photos on the screen of my so called 'Paki brothers'. They had been teachers at the school. One had detonated the explosive in the school canteen, and the other from his car in the car park. They would have known the emergency meeting point in the car park, and planned accordingly.

I got to my knees and touched the side of my body. My ribs ached, but from my limited medical knowledge they didn't seem cracked. I gingerly got to my feet and stood in front of the television. My finger was on the power button but I was unable to switch it off.

They replayed the harrowing scenes from earlier. On the third floor, above the devastated school canteen, a small girl in a black blazer, a few sizes too big for her, appeared at a smashed window. She looked over her shoulder, and whatever hellish nightmare she saw must have been worse than the thought of jumping out to her certain death. She stepped forward and dropped.

I put my hands on the top of the TV and slowly tilted it towards me. I let it tilt until it was at the point of no return, and I watched it slowly drop to the floor. The carpet broke its fall as it landed face down. Still intact. So I stamped on it. Once, twice, three fucking times, until I had crushed it and it stopped talking to me.

Silence enveloped and suffocated me.

I walked around the living room and trashed everything I could get my hands on. Photo frames were smashed. My armchair overturned. The remote control took flight straight into the large mirror that hung above my sofa. I kicked the shit out of the plant pots and broke a leg off the coffee table.

Out of breath, I made my way upstairs to my room and collapsed on my bed. My final thought, before sleep mercifully found me, was: *Maybe I can help. Maybe I can make a difference.*

Part Two

*I never switched sides,
I just switched lanes.*

– Anonymous

23

I couldn't remember the last time I had slept so well; it was a slumber like no other. I found myself in the exact same position that I'd been in when my head literally hit the pillow. My eyelids fluttered but did not open. I heard car doors closing and engines starting up. The world outside my window, on its way to what a new day could bring but most likely wouldn't. I didn't want to open my eyes, not yet anyway. Because once they were open I would have to face things that I didn't want to face.

I stretched and tried to crack my back but my movement was restricted as I hadn't bothered to take my jacket off the night before, or my shoes for that matter, which may have explained the excessive sweating, but then I had also forgotten to switch off the heating. *Yeah, Mum, you shoot off, I'll be fine. Right as fucking rain!*

A dark shadow blocked the daylight that was seeping through my eyelids and I finally opened my eyes to determine the offending item. Parvez was stood at the side of my bed, bearing down on me with a concerned look on his face. In his hand was my Italia '90 mug. It was steaming and it smelled very much like coffee. He gave me a tight smile that begged a question or two.

I closed my eyes and he disappeared.

'I made you coffee, Brother.'

Shit, he was still there!

I shuffled up on my bed, resting back against the headboard, coffee in hand. I took a sip and made a face. It was too strong for my liking and way too milky, but it was much needed and much appreciated. Not that I would tell Parvez that. I grunted my appreciation. Over the rim of my mug I watched him walk around my room and I struggled to recall his last unwelcome visit here. At one period of my life, it had seemed that he was a permanent fixture, coming and going as he pleased. Which begged the question:

'How did you get in, Parvez?' I asked, to no response. He was hypnotised by the Katrina Kaif, Bollywood sex-siren poster. Not his fault. It had that effect. 'Hey! Yo?'

He tore his eyes away from the poster. 'The front door was open.'

'Oh,' I said. And just like that, it all came rushing back to me.

Parvez sat down on the edge of my single bed, not close enough to be touching but close enough. His eyes moved over my sorry state.

'Did you sleep with your jacket on?'

I shrugged.

'And your shoes?'

I shrugged again. He nodded.

'Did you forget to shut your front door?'

A third shrug would have just been rude, and he had just made me coffee, so I dignified his question with an answer, of sorts.

'Um...'

'Were you... You know?' Parvez asked, and he made a face full of unbridled disgust, and just like that Parvez the Preacher was back in town.

'Yeah, Parvez. I was drinking. *And* I was puffing.' I looked at him, daring him to challenge me. He didn't. 'But I wasn't drunk, or high.'

'So, what then?'

'It wasn't me that left the door open. I had some visitors, all right, and they probably left it open on the way out... Shit, man. Why do you ask so many questions?'

'I'm just asking because—'

'Because what?' I snapped. 'Look, Parvez, I've got a long list of things to do today and you're not on it. I haven't got the time or the patience for one of your patronising, self-righteous, bullshit lectures.'

'You were burgled last night,' Parvez said, and stood up in a huff. After all these years he had finally got offended. I could hear him trudge slowly down the stairs, each heavy footstep serving to make a point. I heard the front door open.

'Parvez,' I shouted, half out of my bed. 'I wasn't burgled.'

The front door closed softly. So much for storming out.

I put my coffee down on the bedside table and jumped out of bed. I was feeling uncharacteristically guilty for the way that I'd spoken to him. I skipped downstairs two steps at a time and jumped the last four. I landed flush in the hallway and as I hurried past the living room I quickly glanced inside. What I saw stopped me in my tracks. I doubled back and stood at the entrance of the living room.

Parvez had cleaned up *my* mess.

It was spotless.

The remains of the smashed television had been removed, as had the broken mirror and the photo frames. My armchair had been picked up and set back in its correct position. The table leg had been, somewhat crudely, spliced back into its position and the table sat proudly yet pathetically wonky in the middle of the room. But what really killed me was the dust pan in the corner of the room, with the remains of the soil that had fallen from the plant pot. Even though the vacuum cleaner was in plain sight in the hallway, and an easier option, he'd decided against using it. Why? Because knowing him, and knowing how his tiny brain worked, he wouldn't have wanted to disturb me with the racket the vacuum would have made whilst I slept. So he opted for the quieter option, the broom. Who does that? Really, who the fuck *sweeps* a carpet? Only the stupid and the naïve. And the loving.

I walked out of the house and stood in my driveway, looking towards his house. He had just about reached his front door when he turned around and looked at me. I put up my hand and smiled at him. He ignored the gesture and went inside.

I never really had considered Parvez a friend. Because he was more than that. He was an agitator, an annoying little brother, and I knew that he would be a part of my life, forever.

I switched the crappy 17-inch TV in my bedroom on and watched the aftermath of the horrific events from the night before. Edmonton, Canada. I'd never heard of it. Geography was not my strong point. According to the reports, it was the fifth-largest municipality.

I took out my mobile phone and googled *municipality* with one eye still on the TV. Two photos of the bombers appeared. Their names were Mushtaq Khan and Abdul Ali. Twenty-seven and thirty-one years old. They looked for all the world like two regular Joes. Both clean-shaven and bright-eyed. They had kind expressions, the type you would associate with a teacher children enjoyed being taught by. A bit like Andrew. The programme flipped back to the sullen-looking newsreader, reeling off deathly numbers.

My mind was made up.

24

A man determined, I walked with confidence towards the entrance of Hounslow police station. From my peripheral vision I saw a figure appear at the second-floor window. I peered up but couldn't work out who it was through the reflection on the glass, until he opened the window and popped his head out. He wore a perplexed look and gestured for me to wait there.

I sighed. The last person I wanted to see was Idris.

I stood just outside the entrance and waited, some of my earlier confidence starting to wane at the thought of trying to explain myself to Idris. I sparked up to calm my nerves.

Idris walked out and, without breaking stride, grabbed me by the arm and took me along for the ride. I stumbled but managed to recover my footing. I wrenched my arm back and stood my ground.

'The fuck you doing, man?' I said.

Idris stood in front of me and hissed, 'What the fuck am *I* doing? What the fuck are *you* doing?'

I straightened out the crease he had left on the arm of my jacket.

'You should have called me first, Jay. You know I can't be seen here with you. We have to wait for this… whatever this is, to blow over,' he said, his arms animatedly flaying all over the place. 'You can't just toddle on down whenever you want to see me. If the Chief sees us together I am—'

'All right, *all right*. Calm down, will you?' I decided to put him out of his misery before he spontaneously combusted. 'I'm not here to see you, mate. Don't flatter yourself.'

Idris' eyes narrowed as he processed the information. 'Then what?'

'Look, I can't chat at the minute. Link me later, and I'll fill you in.'

'Is this about... you know? What we talked about?'

'Idris. Seriously, man. We'll chat later, yeah?' I said, not willing to give anything away. He nodded and I could see concern etched on his face.

We bumped fists.

'In a bit, yeah?'

'Yeah. In a bit,' I said, and he disappeared inside. I took a deep breath, composed myself and followed suit.

*

I was directed to a waiting area by a rotund, grubby-looking copper, whose not-so-white shirt was untucked from the back of his too-tight trousers. He made a note of my name and left me to it. I whiled away the time deleting text messages on my phone from customers wanting to be hit up. I started to calculate in my head roughly how much I would have made if I'd still been dealing, when an altogether smarter-looking copper appeared and asked me to walk with him. He took me down a narrow hallway and we stood outside a room. Attached to the door was a gold-plated sign that read *Chief Superintendent*. He knocked on the door. A stern female voice informed us to enter. He opened the door and let me go through into the dimly lit office.

She was sat behind a desk and eyed me with interest. There was a guy sat opposite her in a sharp, dark blue suit. He also gave me the eyes, but his carried something warmer, more friendly. It put me a little at ease.

'I am Chief Superintendent Wakefield,' she said, all matter-of-factly. 'We've been expecting you.'

I nodded. Sharp suit stood and put a hand out to me. I took it and shook it. His grip was stronger than mine, his palms drier.

'Nice to finally meet you, Javid. My name is Lawrence. Teddy Lawrence.'

We sat in a triangle with the desk separating us from Wakefield. This Lawrence character seemed very eager to make me comfortable. He offered me a drink and he offered me a croissant. Never one to turn down a freebie I said yes and yes, much to Wakefield's obvious disdain. For whatever reason, she didn't take to me but I didn't really care; I wasn't there to make friends. I just wanted to give my statement and get the hell outta dodge. I waited for them to take me to one of those bright white interrogation rooms with the tape recorder and the pretend mirror that was really one-way glass, but that didn't happen.

Wakefield picked up the phone, pressed a single button and in that clipped manner of hers that I was now beginning to adjust to, said, 'Three coffees.'

'Javid, I believe that you have been briefed and that you are fully aware why you are here?'

'You can call me Jay.' She looked at me as though she had a bad taste in her mouth. 'But yeah, I am fully aware. I met with Kingsley Parker and he, you know, *briefed me*.'

'Very well,' Wakefield said. 'Mr Lawrence, here, is a colleague of Mr Parker and he is here in the capacity of...' She struggled to find the right word.

'Let's just say I'm here to oversee,' Lawrence said. 'Supervise.'

'You know Parker?' I said, turning to him.

'Oh, yes,' he said. 'I know Parker.'

'So, moving forward,' Wakefield said. 'The subject is Silas Drakos. You are to give a written and signed statement. It will take place in this room, at this desk, on your own. Do give as much detail as possible but only what you know. Only facts. You have as much time as you require. Clear?'

I nodded.

'Is that *clear*, Javid?'

'Yeah, it's clear.'

'On completion, pick up the phone, dial one and ask for me. We will go over the statement together and once we are all satisfied, then we will require your signature. Any questions?'

'No, that's fine. I understand.'

Wakefield gave me a pen and a pad of paper and stomped across the office to the door and held it open for Lawrence. He got up from his chair and bent down, his face next to my ear.

'Don't worry about her,' he whispered. 'Best of luck with the statement. Make sure you bury this clown.' I nodded. 'And Jay... Welcome to MI5.'

The hairs on the back of my neck stood to attention.

Welcome to MI5.

*

It felt strange picking up a pen and putting it to paper. I kept getting cramp in my hand and my handwriting was not how I had remembered it to be. But once I got flowing I was on a roll. It took me the best part of three hours and three sheets, front and back, to complete the statement. I threw everything at it, providing dates and times of pick-ups, drop-offs and amounts in cash and in weight. I named as many of his accomplices as I could, including that fucking thug Staples. Despite Wakefield insisting that I deal only in facts, I thought that it would only help if I mentioned the room. *The mystery room*. The lock-up that Silas had once taken me up to but changed his mind and denied me entry. I had a strong feeling that that room was housing some seriously heavy fucking artillery. If that was the case, then it would only serve to add to the time that Silas was looking at serving.

I didn't feel guilty. Not for a second.

When I had finished, I picked up the phone and dialled one and asked for Wakefield. She was back in her office before I even had the chance to put the phone back in its cradle. She sat, straight-backed, and read the statement, twice. After the first time, she made me sign every correction that I had made.

Seemingly satisfied and, from the looks of it, quite impressed with the level of detail, she asked me to sign it.

'Excellent,' she said, more to herself.

Taking that as my cue, I stood up and stretched my neck and flexed my fingers.

'What happens now?' I asked.

'Mr Lawrence is waiting for you. He is responsible for you now.'

'I mean, with Silas? He... He won't know that... You know?'

She peered at me over my statement. 'No,' she said. 'He won't know.'

25

I walked out of Chief Superintendent Penelope Wakefield's office a changed man. It's funny, I'd never before referred to myself as a man, but that's how I felt. A real man, with a real purpose in life. I had taken the first step towards my new life, into a world that I knew had changed. A surge of adrenaline coursed through my body. I switched my phone on and immediately it vibrated in my hand. I looked at the text message from an unknown number. It read:

Visitors Car Park, Grey Volkswagen Passat

I walked through the station quickly with my head down, wanting to avoid Idris. I stepped out and the sun was shining on me. I saw Lawrence before I saw the Passat. He was leaning against the driver's side door, speaking with a pretty Indian copper in uniform. She was smiling and playing with her hair. If Parvez had witnessed that, he would have been furious. He hated seeing white guys with Asian girls.

I hung back whilst he said a few words to her. She slipped him a card and a smile, and walked away. He looked over at me and gestured with his head for me to join him as he got into the driver's seat. I approached and jumped in the passenger's seat. I smiled at him like a long-lost cousin and he nodded coolly at me.

'You can't beat the German manufacturing, right?' I said, babbling small talk as I took in the interior. 'I drive German, too. Black BMW 5 series. Actually, scratch that. I *used* to drive a black BMW 5 series. It got jacked!'

Something crossed his face and his head dipped slightly.

'Did you report it stolen?' he asked.

'Yeah. But what's the point?' I said, shaking my head. 'They're not going to do a damn thing. Too busy pulling over Pakis.'

Lawrence shook his head a little, as though he agreed, but he seemed keen to move on.

'First opportunity, we'll get you to sign all the necessary documents.'

'Secrets Act?' I said, showing off what little knowledge I had gathered through a cursory Google search earlier.

'That's right, Jay. The Official Secrets Act. You will be entrusted with classified information and covert tasks. It is imperative that all information stays with you. Your role centrally is to help us with the targeting process, using your intelligence to map out what we can about the terrorist network.'

There you have it. That word. I nodded it away casually, even though my stomach was twisting.

'Don't worry, Jay,' he said, reading me correctly. 'Your approach will be tailored to your skillset.'

It made me uncomfortable. What skillset? The skillset of being a Muslim, that fucking skillset?

'I trust your meeting went well with Chalk?' Lawrence continued.

'Chalk?'

'Parker, sorry. We all know him as Chalk.'

'Right,' I said, storing away that bit of information. 'So, you guys working together?'

'Not quite,' he was quick to point out. 'I work directly with Counter Terrorism Operations.'

'Okay,' I said, noncommittally, not quite knowing if I should be impressed.

'Parker is our man on the ground. I am overseeing it all,' he said. Maybe I should be impressed.

'Where do I fit in? Who do I report to?'

'To Parker. He's handling you.'

I must have displayed a little bemusement because he went on to explain what *handling* meant.

'So, a handler is somebody who is appointed to you. He is your first point of contact, whether it's to provide information, or if you have any issues. A handler will help you to make the transition from a... civilian to a spy.'

'A spy?'

'Yes. That's your primary role in the project. If you do, however, have any issues with your handler, you contact me directly and I will act accordingly.'

I shrugged.

'*Do* you have any issues with Parker, Jay?'

'Not really... He's just not what I expected from an MI5 agent.'

'As opposed to me?'

He smiled. He was fishing for a compliment and unwittingly revealing a little about himself. I got the impression the two of them did not get along. When I'd met Parker, there was something about him, like a vibe that came off him, as though he'd been damaged. I believed him when he spoke. This guy, shielded behind his expensive suit and his smug smile, I wasn't so sure about.

I, inexplicably, felt the need to defend Parker.

'But I guess that's a good thing, right?' I said. 'You don't want to be walking round with a sign around your neck telling the whole world that you're MI5, right? Parker's got that whole drifter look down to a tee. He's all right, man. He's cool.'

Lawrence's smile stayed on his lips but drained from his eyes.

26

I didn't want to go home. The day was too nice to be cooped up alone in my room, with only my thoughts for company, so I hit the Rising Sun. A worse-for-wear Khan was propping up the bar and by the state of him he looked like he needed the bar for physical support. I ordered myself half a pint of San Miguel and moved to a corner table.

My phone beeped. A message from Idris. He wanted to meet. I had to face him sooner or later; may as well do it over a drink. I texted back my location, then bided my time wasting gold coins on the fruit machines.

I heard my name being called from the bar. Khan had been replaced by Idris, who was gesturing with his hand to ask if I would like another drink. I showed him my glass to indicate that I was good. Idris approached and placed his red wine on the table just as Khan walked out of the gents. He swaggered over to our table and before Idris had a chance to sit down, Khan was all up in his face.

'Looky, look, look,' Khan said. Idris swayed his head back slightly at Khan's beer breath. 'We have a constable in our midst.' The two of them had never gotten along. Khan had always demanded respect, which he received from the majority, but Idris was firmly in the minority.

'Go away, Khan,' Idris said, calmly.

'You don't tell *me* what to do, Constable.'

'It's Detective Inspector.'

'Ooh. *Detective Inspector.*' Khan was all over the place. Drunk as a skunk and as smelly as one. 'I'll tell you what you are.' He jabbed a podgy finger on Idris' chest. 'A fucking shell-out coconut!'

I was pretty sure that he meant *sell-out*. I took a firm hold of my beer and sat back in my seat. If they were going to go at it, there was no need for my drink to spill.

'Why don't you find a corner somewhere and sober up, eh?' Idris said.

'What you going to do? Arrest me?' Khan said, loud enough for the few patrons to sit up and take notice.

'Arrest you? No. Unfortunately, being a first-class twat is not yet considered a crime. But when it is, I'll be coming for you.'

Khan's eyes narrowed and he stared at Idris with intent. I watched from the safety of my seat and nursed my drink. I wasn't going to get involved unless it kicked off. Then, and only then, would I have to join forces with the coconut.

'You sold your soul to the Devil,' Khan spat, regaining momentum. 'You know why?'

'This I would love to hear.'

'All right, Detective. I'll tell you. We need Pakis like you and me and Jay to start fighting, to make our voices heard, to show the world that we are not afraid,' Khan said, with surprising clarity considering his state. 'We need to stick together and give it to them. We have every right to walk this land how we see fit, *we* have every right to knock a few white heads if we see a Brother in distress. If we want to govern our countries with our rules, who the fuck are the government to send in soldiers to tell us any different? It's people like you who decide to join the fight, but end up picking the wrong side.'

'You don't know what you're talking about, mate.' I could see from Idris' expression that Khan's words had affected him.

'The fucking police,' Khan spat, literally. 'You've joined the most racist institution in the country. You have no idea, *mate*! Harassing Pakis on nothing more than a whim. Feeding the media with bullshit propaganda. Your fucking white commissioner, sitting there in front of the world's cameras, telling them about the *Muslim* sex ring in Birmingham or whatever other crime, making the rest of the world hate us that little bit more. And then they question our retaliation!'

'Hold on. The police would never say that it was *Muslims* behind it. That's all on the media.'

'You thick cunt,' Khan said, sadly. 'Who do you think it is that leaks that information to the media? You ever think about that? It's you. It's fucking you.'

Idris all of a sudden looked exhausted. He stepped back away from Khan and sat down opposite me. We made the briefest of eye contact and before he broke it I saw something I couldn't quite figure out in his eyes, something I had never seen before. *Guilt. Remorse. Defeat. The truth.* I stood up. It was time to quash this. I walked to Khan and put my arm around him and slowly guided him away from us.

'I'm right, aren't I, Jay?' Khan said softly. 'He knows I'm right.'

I asked him about his wife and kids, trying desperately to change the subject. I sat him down at a table at the far end of the pub and he rested his head on his arms. I mouthed *water* to the barman and left Khan to it. I walked back and took my seat opposite Idris.

'That was some entrance, Idris,' I said, trying to lighten the mood.

'I was having a good day until then,' Idris mumbled.

'Yeah?'

'Yeah!'

'Well, are you going to tell me about it?'

'I've been offered a promotion,' he said flatly.

'Oh, you gangster. That's fantastic news,' I said. I thought about clinking glasses but for some reason it didn't seem appropriate. 'What post?'

'It's not confirmed yet. But if it goes ahead I'll be heading a small team of my choosing. Working directly with the Met Drugs Directorate.'

'Sounds, uh, cool,' I said, acutely aware of my own drug-dealing past.

We sat in a rare moment of awkward silence.

'So, I guess you want to know what happened to me today,' I said, trying to get together in my head what and what not to feed him.

'No. Don't tell me. I don't want to know, not anymore. I can't...'

'You can't what?'

'I can't get involved.'

'With me.' It wasn't a question. He nodded anyway.

'Sorry, Jay. But this is a very big deal for me. We can't be seen together, not for a while, anyway. They're going to be watching me closely for the next few months. I can't afford to slip up. When all this shit dies down, we'll—'

'We'll fucking what?' I snapped. Maybe I was being unreasonable; it *was* his precious career in question, but maybe I didn't give a fuck. Our paths had always moved in different directions but it was always the strength in our friendship that allowed us to share space and time. We were like brothers, and for him to even suggest... No. No fucking way. At that moment I could not handle it. I was still really feeling the loss of my mum, and now Idris too! Well, Idris could fuck right off.

'Congratu-fuckin-lations, *mate*!' I said. His untouched red wine sat on the table and I clinked it deliberately hard with my glass, watched it topple over and spill all over his trousers. He was up like a shot, dabbing at the wet patch with his hands.

I took a sip of my beer and watched him. The sip turned into a gulp as I knocked back my drink and stood up.

'Khan was right. You *are* a fucking sell-out.'

'Grow up, Jay. Just fucking grow up!'

I've known for a long time that those words were never far from his lips. I *had* finally grown up; it was just a shame that he would never know just how much.

I stormed through the pub and out into the rain.

I walked to my Nova, unlocked it and opened the door. Before getting in I glanced behind me, towards the pub, expecting Idris to come rushing out, trying to make amends.

He didn't.

27

I spent the rest of the day in my bedroom. I had the run of the whole house but I didn't want to set foot into the living room. I was still feeling a little guilty that Parvez had cleaned it after I'd massacred it.

Every so often, actually almost every minute or so, I would check my phone. Just in case Idris had left a message of apology. He fucking owed me one. I repeatedly checked the signal on my phone, and made sure that the volume was up high, and each time I did I felt like an idiot for doing so, and cursed myself. And then I cursed Idris. And then I checked my phone to see if he'd texted.

On a whim and after boredom had set in, I decided to go into the loft. I convinced myself it was to just have a nosey around, see if I could find anything of interest, but I knew deep down that I was looking for something specific. Something that had been on my mind lately.

My dad.

It was rare that I'd give him any thought. Odd occasions when I was younger, maybe, father's day, I guess, and sports day, watching all the other kids busting a gut trying to impress their dad. I got through all that shit with my mum, I didn't let his absence shape me, but... I think it may have. And now I'm alone, in need of some fucking guidance, there he is, uselessly popping back into my head again.

I flicked on the light in the loft and got started. I rooted through boxes and found some old school stuff. Runner-up or third-place medals, never a winner. School reports damning me and breaking Mum's heart. I found an old broken lawnmower and tried to figure out how it got up there. It hit me with a certain sadness that Mum would have lugged it up there by herself. The Dad-shaped hole in her life evident in mundane everyday chores.

I went through every box, through every folder and every photo album but I couldn't find a single photo or reference to my old man. It was like he'd never existed. Although I did find, rubber-banded, a load of old bank paying-in books that belonged to Mum. I picked one at random and flicked through it. On every page, on every stub, dated a month apart, there was a payment for £3,000. I looked through another, this one years old, 1990. The same entries: three grand, every month.

Mum only ever worked part-time, so it wasn't like she was bringing in that kind of figure, and shamelessly I hardly ever contributed. So where was this money coming from? I wondered about the house we lived in, the area. It wasn't bad. Even though we were in less than glamorous Hounslow, we still had a decent house on a decent street. We had a big-screen Plasma, surround sound, games consoles, nice clothes, and always good food on the table. Growing up I don't think Mum had ever said, *That's too expensive*, *Jay* or *Not this month*, *Jay*. I used to have the baddest BMX bike. I remember it getting stolen when I was ten and bawling my eyes out. It was replaced within days. It had never even occurred to me how we were actually able to afford these things. How we never went without.

Now I knew.

Well, actually, no, I didn't. I knew somebody was helping us. Though I could not work out who.

A spider scuttled across somewhere in my eyeline, making me jump. I knew that my time in the loft was nearing an end, so I got out of there before the spiders put their heads together and formulated a plan of attack. I dusted myself off, returned to my bedroom and glanced at the phone. No messages. Then it rang. A number I didn't recognise. But I knew by the odd formation of the numbers who it was and my heart beat that little bit faster. I answered it.

'Mum?'

I stood stock-still. There was no way I was risking losing phone signal.

'Can you hear me?' Mum asked.

'Yeah, Mum, I can hear you, clearly,' I said, loudly.

'Jay, Beta,' she gushed.

'It's so good to hear from you, Mum.'

'Sorry it took so long to call. It's been hectic. How are you?'

'I'm fine, Mum. Really. All good over here. Don't worry about me, tell me how you are?'

'We are good, Jay. We've been in a hotel for the last couple of days, but just today we've been given the keys to our new place.'

Our new place. Not mine.

'Sounds exciting. Have you unpacked?'

'Not yet. Today we're going to be rebels and hit the beach, and leave the grown-up stuff until later on,' Mum said, laughing. It sounded beautiful, a proper happy laugh.

'I'm so glad, Mum. Listen, give Andrew my best and go out and enjoy the sun, yeah?'

'Hang on just a minute, can't I talk to my son for a while?'

We talked for a bit longer. I could hear Andrew in the background and Mum laughing at him. We covered the standard stuff – the weather (hot, apparently), and what side of the road that they drove on in Qatar (right side, apparently). We talked about nothing really, and then we were saying our goodbyes.

'Okay, Jay. Keep in touch, you have all my contact details.'

'Yeah, will do, Mum. Enjoy it. We'll talk soon. But not *too* soon.'

We said goodbye to each other, like five times. I took the phone away from my ear and I was just about to kill the call when I remembered I wanted to ask her something. I quickly put the phone back to my ear.

'Mum, *Mum.* You still there?'

'Yes, Jay, I'm still here.'

I almost bottled it. The last thing I wanted her to think about in her new life was Dad.

'I, um, actually, it doesn't matter.'

'No, Jay. Come on now, tell me. You know you can tell me anything.'

'Honestly, Mum, really it's nothing.'

'*Jay!*'

'It's just, I was in the loft.'

'You, in the loft? That's a first. Did you get over your fear of spiders?'

'Ha. Yeah. No. Just having a nose around. Thought I would look through some old photos,' I said. 'I couldn't find any. I found some but none of… you know?'

120

Silence on the other end for a beat, then she said quietly, 'Yes, I know.'

Silence on my end for a beat, then I said quietly, 'Do we have any?'

'Are you missing him?' she asked for the first time ever.

I laughed without expression. 'Missing him?' *How can I miss someone who I've never met? Who I can't remember what he fucking looks like?* 'No, I was just curious, just killing some time.'

'Oh, okay.' Her voice sounded distant.

A noisy silence, then she said, so gently, 'Are you missing me?'

I gripped the phone so tightly that I thought that it would crush in my hands. I looked around my room and knew that it would never again magically tidy itself up. That she would never again text me to come downstairs. I knew with certainty that I would never hear her movement around the house or her gentle rhythmic snoring at night, which never failed to help me sleep. The false bravado came rushing back.

'Nah, Mum. You've only been gone five minutes. I'm having the time of my life. Nightly house parties, girlfriends coming and going, you know how I do it.'

She wasn't buying it. 'Do you want me to come home?'

'*What?* No, Mum! It's cool. I'm cool.'

Everything is just fucking cool.

'Jay?'

'Don't stress. I was just curious, all right. No big deal. Go get some suntan lotion on and have a drink on me. Make sure Andrew doesn't burn.'

She *still* wasn't buying it. But she let it go.

After the call had ended, I realised that I was still gripping the phone to my ear. I placed it on the table in front of me and just stared at it.

Enough of this moping around bullshit. I had to get myself together.

28

I showered and I shaved and I put on some clean clothes. Maybe Idris wasn't going to call to apologise. But the least I could do was call and apologise to Parvez.

I looked out of the window towards his house. The front door opened and out he stepped. I picked up my phone and dialled his number. I watched him root through his pockets for his phone. He slipped it out and looked at it, as if trying to weigh up whether or not to answer. The cheeky fucker ignored it and pocketed the phone. It was hard to discern if he was still angry at me or just busy. The thing was, Parvez was never busy. A busy-body, yeah, but not regular busy. He always seemed to have all the time in the world, especially for me. So he must have still been pissed at me for snapping at him. I suddenly felt bad for him all over again, going about his business with my shit hanging over him. It would have been hard for him; he wasn't as strong as me.

I was still a little disturbed at how he'd acted during the aftermath of the attack on Sutton mosque. It made me realise that I didn't know him as well as I once had. His thirst for revenge had surprised me and, fuelled too easily by Khan, could have seen him hurt or worse.

I watched him jump into his mum's Paki-Mobile – a Honda – and start the engine. With fuck all else to do, an idea started to formulate. I thought it would be interesting to follow him in my car, see what he's up to. Eventually I'd surprise him and then I would apologise for the way I'd treated him.

Before I knew it I was running down the stairs. From the hallway table I scooped up my sunglasses and the keys to my Nova without breaking stride. I opened my front door and slowly peered my head out. He was still reversing out of his drive like a pensioner. I waited for him to complete the manoeuvre. In truth, I could have had a cup of tea and a couple of samosas in that time. Finally, he was out. I unlocked my Nova and jumped in.

I needed to manoeuvre out arse first, too, but I waited for another car to pass and sit between my Nova and his Honda. No cars seemed to be coming, and I worried I would lose him. But then a Ford Capri cruised past, and as soon as it did I dropped it into reverse and backed out onto the road, spinning the car like Steve McQueen.

And then I stalled it!

I stuck it in neutral, restarted it, threw it straight into second and I was away. I flicked the radio off as I wanted to concentrate on the target.

I had a good view of the Honda from behind the Capri. I noticed its left indicator come on, even though there was no left turn for a good thirty metres. Parvez – ever the considerate driver. After what felt like an age, the Honda turned. Thankfully the Capri turned the same way and I followed suit. Straight into traffic! As I sat stationary, in what was turning out to be the world's worst car chase, I started to feel a bit stupid. I didn't quite know what I was trying to prove.

Cars crawled slowly and eventually the Capri turned off and I was directly behind Parvez. He didn't seem to notice. I followed him, now half-heartedly, and soon the traffic opened up and Parvez put his foot down and drove like a madman at twenty-five miles an hour! Mercifully the journey wasn't long, and Parvez eventually pulled up outside a house in neighbouring Osterley. I parked a few cars back and watched him.

He stepped out of his car and surreptitiously looked around, as if he was on a mission of his very own. He loitered for a minute and when he was content with whatever he was looking for, or hiding from, he crossed the road. He approached a detached house, the door opened and he entered. He didn't even have to lift his hand to knock!

Somebody was expecting him.

I had nothing better to do that day so I decided to complete my mock mission. It kept me busy, and it had stopped me from thinking about Mum and Idris. And Dad. Also, I was quite curious to see what Parvez was up to. I switched my radio on and waited.

It was tuned into the Asian station, Sunshine Radio. I didn't change it, it was just nice to have some background noise.

I didn't have to wait long for action. A bus pulled up at the bus stop about fifty metres from where I was parked, and two Pakis stepped off and walked towards the house. They didn't talk or even acknowledge each other, just walked side by side. Eyes furtive. As soon as they were at the door, it opened and they entered without breaking stride. Again, no knocking necessary.

I took out my phone and opened up the notepad app. I made a note of the door number. *Number fifteen.* I made a note of the street name. *Jersey Way.* I made a note of the two guys that walked in after Parvez. *Two Pakis, medium height. Dark hair.*

Parker or Lawrence still hadn't contacted or instructed me. I was doing this all off my own bat, so when I did eventually start I would have had some surveillance experience. What started off as creeping behind Parvez out of curiosity seemed to be taking a strange turn. Not quite bizarre, but definitely in the neighbourhood.

What happened next?

I fell in love. Right there and then.

She wore a pair of blue faded skinny jeans, not tight, but tight enough. A white loose blouse, not low-cut, but low enough. Her hair was down but as she walked she was in the process of effortlessly tying it into a ponytail, revealing more of her face. *Oh, man! Her face.* Her features were soft but her eyes determined. Her nose button-like and her lips parted and curled upwards as if she was aggrieved about something and about to let loose. A slow romantic Indian song started playing through my head and I immediately switched the radio off. As she neared number fifteen she delved into her bag and pulled out a black shawl. With a flick of a slender wrist she unwrapped it with a flourish and covered her head. She didn't stop at the door and I was certain that she was going to walk past it. But the door opened and she stepped right in.

No knocking required!

I made a note.

29

I stayed put in my car. I was curious to know what was going on behind that door. I was slouched low in my seat and I still had my shades on, even though the sun had deserted me. I would cast quick glances at the door and the windows for any further activity. There was some twitching coming from the upstairs window, but it was impossible to establish who the twitcher was. Nobody else had entered the house. It was just the four of them, plus whoever had been in there before. I waited as long as I could until I lost interest. I'd run out of things to keep my attention. I didn't even have sugary treats or coffee to keep me alert. I added another note on my phone for future reference. *Bring coffee and donuts.* It was time to go. That was enough surveillance experience for one day, and I had no idea when Parvez would come out. I would catch up and apologise to him another time. I straightened up in my seat and removed my shades. I started my car and indicated my intention to pull out.

Then the door to number fifteen opened.

I quickly killed the indicator, slouched back down in my seat and hurriedly slipped my sunglasses back on.

Pakis one and two walked out. From their purposeful strides, they seemed... not angry, but riled up. Their short walk back to the bus stop was determined. A minute or so later, Parvez and The Girl walked out of the house. Once again, I couldn't quite see who was behind the door as it swiftly shut.

They both crossed the road, bearing the same purposeful look as the bus-stop Pakis. Determined. *Riled up.* It was the exact look that I had first seen on Parvez during the Elmsleigh car park dust-up. I remembered how easily he had been led by Khan, so whatever was taking place behind the doors of number fifteen concerned me; somebody as naïve as Parvez could easily be led into something far worse.

They stood outside Parvez's mum's Honda and talked. I obviously couldn't hear a word, but I could tell that Parvez was a little nervous – it wasn't often that he was in the company of a beautiful woman. She removed the shawl from her head and placed it back in her bag. She undid her ponytail and, like a shampoo commercial, her hair came tumbling down. I could see Parvez looking around everywhere but at her. I laughed out loud to myself. Man, Parvez is such a chump. He had a stunning girl in front of him and he was trying so hard not to look at her. If I was stood out there in front of her I would have, by now, had her digits or been rejected.

She was gesticulating with her hand, as if trying to communicate directions. He looked towards where she was pointing and frowned. He pointed in the opposite direction. It looked, judging by the body language, that she was asking him for a ride and trying to explain where she wanted to go, whereas Parvez appeared to be telling this incredibly beautiful girl that he was going the opposite way. I shook my head in disappointment. I threw caution to the wind and decided to abort the mission. There was nothing else left to gain from it, I had what I needed. And besides, there was this heavenly creature that I had to be near.

I checked myself out in the rear-view mirror, stepped out of the car and casually walked the short distance towards them. Parvez did a double take when he saw me approach and I saw him mouth something unintelligible.

'Parvez, mate!' I said. 'Fancy seeing you here.'

He looked nervous. 'Jay... What are you doing here?' He frowned.

'Now is that any way to greet an old friend?' I was purposely ignoring the girl because I had read somewhere that beautiful women respond to being ignored.

Parvez composed himself and shook my hand. 'Sorry, I was just surprised at seeing you here, that's all... Aslamalykum, how are you?'

'I'm all right, I was just driving by when I realised I needed some cigarettes, and I knew there had to be a Patel's around here somewhere.' I risked a quick glance at the girl to see if she liked my *Patel* reference. She wasn't even looking in my direction. I thought *I* was the one ignoring *her*. It was time to take it up a notch. I cleared my throat.

'So,' I said. 'Are you going to introduce us?'

'This is Sister Amirah.'

'I didn't know you had a sister, Parvez,' I said, nudging him. They didn't laugh at that. My material was weak that day.

She looked up and I put my hand out. She reluctantly placed hers in mine. It was the softest hand in the world. Probably.

'It's a pleasure to meet you, Amirah,' I said, with my best, all-conquering smile. All toothy and wide.

Amirah just nodded at me with bored eyes and released her hand from mine.

'What you guys up to?' I asked.

'Not giving me a ride home is what we are up to!' she said, breaking her silence. Her voice was just as I had imagined it to be. Pissed off!

Parvez looked down at his Crocs.

'Where do you want to go?' I asked. 'I can—'

'No!'

'No, what?'

'No, I don't want you to give me a ride home. I'll walk,' Amirah said huffily, and before I could respond she turned on the heel of her sneakers and walked away.

What's that line from that movie? *I hate to see her go, but I love to watch her leave.* Parvez nudged me out of my trance.

'What the hell is wrong with you, man?' I asked. 'You should have given her a ride home.'

'You wouldn't understand.'

'Try me.'

'There's no way I could do that. Can you imagine if one of the elders saw us? It'll get back to my mum and she'll be on the phone to *her* mum arranging wedding dates.'

'Wedding dates?' I said, my eyebrows taking flight.

'You know what I mean.'

'You're serious? This isn't the dark ages anymore, Parvez. Dinosaurs have stopped roaming the earth. I'd be more concerned about being spotted driving around in a Honda.'

He looked at me to display just how serious he was. I decided that it was time to change the subject. I leaned against the Honda and asked him nonchalantly, 'So, what are you up to?'

I saw his head start to turn towards the house but he thought better of it and turned back towards me.

'Nothing. You know... Nothing.'

'It's just when I was parking my car I saw you leave that house,' I said, inclining my head towards number 15.

'Jay, do I have to tell you everything I'm doing? And besides, I thought you were *busy*. You didn't have time for me earlier. What was it that you said? Something about a list and me not being on it!' he said, expertly changing the subject back to me. His face dropped a little and I remembered that I owed him an apology.

'Yeah, Parvez. I'm sorry, truly. I shouldn't have spoken to you like that. I fucked up, man.'

'Can you not swear around me? I've just done Wudu. Now I'm going to have to do it again.'

'Sorry.'

'My ears are not a toilet.'

'Sorry,' I said, laughing, which in turn made him smile.

We stood around for a moment, getting the awkwardness of the apology out of the way.

'Did you go to the police?'

How could he know that?

'What? What do you mean?'

'The burglary at your house.'

'Nah, that weren't no burglary. It was just a... mishap. Thanks for tidying up, though. But, for future reference, don't tidy up after an actual burglary.'

Parvez thought about that for a second. 'Because it's a crime scene.'

'That's right, Parvez. Because it's a crime scene,' I said, looking up at number fifteen. The curtains in the upstairs window were in full twitch. 'I think one of your mates is watching us.'

'I should go. I shouldn't be standing around here.'

'Why?'

'Just...' he said as he opened his car door.

'Yeah, all right... So what is it then, some sort of Islamic Studies?' I asked, refusing to take the hint.

'Um, yes. Kind of. Look, Brother, I really must go.' He got into his car, started the engine and drove off.

As I watched him go, I knew that something was amiss.

Because Parvez did not put his seatbelt on!

30

I drove home in something of a daze. Questions led to more questions and raced through my mind. Parvez, number fifteen and Amirah took up the bulk of my thoughts, so I wasn't paying much attention to the road or my surroundings. A motorbike zoomed rudely past my driver's side, breaking my broken musings. It slowed down a touch in front of me, and came to a stop at the traffic lights. I stopped behind him and I had an inkling of who it could be from his wide back and his tall frame. I could see him looking back at me through the side mirror on the bike. I stared back and he lifted the visor to reveal his face.

Yeah, Parker.

He flicked the visor back down and the lights flicked to amber and he was gone. I guessed he wanted me to follow.

My heart picked up speed as my Nova did. I followed Parker around the houses, down back roads that I recognised, and then out through to roads that I did not. We ended up on a dual carriageway taking us well out of Hounslow and towards Hammersmith.

We pulled up outside a set of crappy garages, not dissimilar to those you see in crappy housing estates. He got off the bike and walked towards one of the garages, gesturing that I should follow. My imagination was running wild as to what might be behind the door of such a non-descript garage. I pictured state-of-the-art technology, huge screens mounted on the walls with visuals of every CCTV camera in London. Or maybe at the press of a cleverly concealed button we would be transported to an underground command centre. Maybe I was getting carried away, but it did feel electric to not know where my new life could take me.

Until I got in.

It was as crap on the inside as it was from the outside. A hastily built makeshift kitchen, with a long wooden worktop on either side, a dirty white Butler sink and electrical points that would have failed every safety test. The cupboards above had doors hanging precariously from their hinges. The walls were peeling paint and were covered in ripped pictures of Page 3 girls. Most bizarrely, there was a female mannequin, without a stich of clothing, provocatively bent over a table in the middle of the room, staring blankly at me.

The whole set-up was quite far removed from my perception of all things MI5.

Parker mumbled his dissatisfaction and removed the mannequin from the table, replacing it with two chairs. I brushed down the seat of the chair with my sleeve and sat down. Parker shifted through some boxes and pulled out a dirty-looking kettle. He turned the tap on and it spluttered noisily before exploding to life.

Eventually, he placed what looked like a cup of tea in front of me and sat down opposite me as I took in my surroundings.

'What is this place?'

'This...' he said. 'I don't know what this is. It's just somewhere out of the way. It serves a purpose.' I wrinkled my nose. 'How did it go today?' he asked.

'Yeah, went well, I think. I gave a statement about... you know?'

'I do.'

'Has he,' I whispered unnecessarily, 'been arrested?'

He nodded.

'*Has he?*' I screeched.

'About an hour after you gave the statement, the police assembled and scrambled a ten-man team to his location. Approximately an hour after that, Silas Drakos was sitting in a cell waiting for counsel. The last word was that he was to be moved to another location and charged officially... He won't be going anywhere for a long time.'

'Did they search his house?'

'Yes, they found what they were hoping for... And more.'

'The lock-up?'

'That's right. The lock-up. It was being used to house some very serious weaponry. I haven't got all the details but I believe it was vast. All in all, there were over a hundred pieces... But as I said, I don't have all the details.'

I let out a barely audible whistle.

'It's all down to you, son. You did well.' He said it like he meant it.

Pride swelled in me. I felt like a huge burden had been lifted off my shoulders and I felt like I was walking on air.

'Now, we have to forget about that. It's a victory, but it's not our victory,' he said. 'It was and remains a Met operation; our involvement is no longer required. We walk away, clean, and move on to our own agenda.'

'Which is what, exactly?'

He sighed. I could sense him weighing up the words in his head.

'Right. First of all, welcome on board,' he said. I nodded and thanked him. 'Now, your role is very simple. It's not designed to stretch you. I largely want you to be yourself. So I don't want to give you any training, because it would only serve to change your mindset and muddy the waters. Which we don't want.'

'That makes sense, I guess.' I was gutted. I'd been looking forward to being a fully trained badass MI5 agent. 'Then what?' I asked.

'I know you have ties with Sutton mosque, and you are a well-known and liked member of the Muslim community within Hounslow. Currently, you only attend the mosque once a week, on a Friday. But it is very normal for someone of your age to start to attend more often, especially as you are at a crossroads in your life.'

'Crossroads... Is that where I am?'

'You're not dealing anymore, you haven't got a job, and your mother has left the country. It's only natural for you to fill that gap with something. Let it be religion. That gives you the perfect in. So, yes, attend more often, try and stay behind for any lectures or classes. Move around and talk to people. You seem quite sociable, so that shouldn't surprise anyone. Just keep your ears and eyes open. Try to remember any new faces and anything that sticks out.'

'How do I report back to you?'

'I'll write my number down on a piece of paper; it is imperative that you memorise it and lose that paper.'

'Okay. Get in, mingle, look out for anything untoward. Be myself,' I summarised.

'The only difference is that you have an increased interest in your religion.'

'Like finding myself?'

'Yes.' He eyed me with curiosity. 'Like finding yourself.'

I sat back in my chair and contemplated what he'd said. There was a lot to take in, but broken down it was manageable. I could do it, easily. But I didn't *get it*. I mean, what are the odds of me bumping into a fucking terrorist or whatever in the mosque and then said terrorist *or whatever* spilling his guts to me? It was a one-in-a-million shot.

'Parker, I, um... Is this the best way forward?' I asked, carefully. Already questioning. I didn't want to be *that* guy that undermines, but neither did I want to be the guy who nods stupidly like a Churchill dog, either.

'How do you mean?' he asked.

'I mean, what are the chances of running into someone... *report-worthy*? I've been going there for years and I've never seen or heard of anything out of the ordinary. Look, you've gone to a lot of trouble to get me in but it seems like, with all due respect, you don't quite know how to best use me... Not all mosques house terrorists, you know?'

Parker blinked. His lips tighened. His cheeks reddened.

'Sorry,' I said, not quite knowing what I was apologising for.

'No,' he said softly. 'Don't be. We are facing an enemy that fights without fear or consequence, an enemy that could present itself in any form. Organisations like us around the world are fighting a losing battle. To a certain extent, we have been successful, particularly in this country, and that's solely down to gathering intelligence. Our agents are everywhere, tapping phones, checking emails, dissecting inflammatory websites and yes, looking at mosques. Most of the time it's a needle in a giant haystack. But on that occasion, that one occasion where we can establish a connection, gather enough evidence to keep one step ahead, then we can move when necessary to stop an attack and save lives. That's the objective. It's not straightforward and it doesn't always produce results but... knowledge can only be seen as power.'

I bit my tongue at my immediate response and sipped my tea. I pulled out my phone and looked at the notes I had made earlier.

Maybe something, maybe nothing.

I put my phone on the table, facing up so that Parker could see. He took his sweet time reading my notes, considering that there wasn't that much to read. He read it silently and then re-read it back to me in a monotonous tone.

'Number fifteen Jersey Way – Two Pakis – Medium Build – Dark Hair – Hot chick – No knocking required – Bring coffee and donuts.' Parker looked up at me, not quite following. It seemed my notes didn't have enough meat. I had to quickly get better at this spying lark. 'What is this?' he asked.

I explained.

Parker listened to me. At first it seemed like he was humouring me, but when I explained my curiosity and the way that it went down, he seemed to be slowly but surely taking me seriously. I told him about the way they each nervously looked around on approach to number fifteen, and how there was someone on sentry behind the upstairs window, constantly looking through the net curtains and obviously signalling for someone to open the door for a quick entrance. All of which giving me the impression that they did not want to attract attention.

I didn't mention Parvez by name, but I alluded to him.

'I know somebody who can maybe get me in,' I said cautiously, and then followed it quickly with, 'but I can't say who.'

Parker nodded and, to his credit, didn't push for a name. He scratched his face for longer than necessary.

And then we worked out a plan.

Throughout the whole meeting I had been dying to say something to him, something light-hearted in what was otherwise quite a heavy situation. Hoping that it would make me feel like part of the team. I had played around with it in my head, tried, unsuccessfully, to work it into conversation. But as we parted ways, I decided to say it.

'Nice one, *Chalk*.'

It didn't receive the reaction that I had expected.

'What did you say?' Parker asked, not quite aggressively, but close.

'What? Nothing. Just, Lawrence said that...' I left it at that, because, by then, from the mere mention of his name, Parker had flicked down his visor and zoomed off.

31

Oh-Seven-Five-Two-Two, Two-Three-Seven, Two-Two-Six.

Is that right? Sounds right.

I sneaked a peek at the bit of paper that Parker had given me with his scribbled mobile number. I closed my eyes tightly as I laid on my bed, arms behind my head, and ran the number through my head again.

It had been a couple of weeks, give or take, since my meeting with Parker. He hadn't been in touch and I hadn't expected him to, and I was still feeling a bit funny about the way he had reacted at the mention of Lawrence's name. It was, to say the least, an overreaction. Strange old character, that Parker. Not quite sure how I felt about him being my handler. I decided it was time to make contact. I dialled his number from memory and as soon as I heard his monotone greeting, I tore up the bit of paper and updated him on the last couple of weeks. Starting with the first visit, in my new role, to Sutton mosque.

I think it was a Tuesday.

Familiar faces, who I would normally see on a Friday, surreptitiously stole glances at me, and if I happened to make eye contact, they would smile curiously.

Jay? At the Masjid? On a Tuesday?

Most part they left me alone and let me get on with it, which suited me fine. It was all about appearances at the beginning. The day after that, Wednesday, Kevin the Convert approached me after Maghrib prayers, and shook my hand.

'It's good to see you again, Brother,' he said.

'Yeah,' I said, and added a shrug for good measure.

'Everything all right, yes?'

'Yeah, everything's fine, man.'

He didn't press me; it wasn't exactly odd seeing a Paki in a mosque, even a puffing, drug-dealing, drinking, layabout kind of Paki.

I saw Parvez a couple of times from across the prayer hall, and he would acknowledge me with the most brilliant, bemused expression. We didn't really talk; he would just say his prayers and leave.

By Thursday, I was walking into the mosque and shaking hands with a fair few. Elders, who had normally avoided eye contact with me, due to my reputation, were now patting me on the back and some even embracing me. I took it all in my stride, keeping my eyes open at all times.

Friday prayers, as always, the place was heaving.

From a MI5 point of view, I knew I had a specific role to fulfil under the guise of finding Islam, turning to Allah at the *crossroads* of my life. But, it came so easy to me. It didn't feel like a guise at all. It felt like the most natural thing in the world. Like I was supposed to be here.

All I knew was that when the *Azaan* – call for prayers – rang out, I stood there, with my head bowed down to the Almighty, my hands crossed just under my chest, standing with a Brother to my left and a Brother to my right and Brothers behind me and Brothers in front of me, it gave me a feeling that I had never ever experienced: total serenity, calm. My mind was clear and my shoulders weightless. The only thing that mattered was my direct link to Allah.

It was divine. Truly.

Yeah, I know how that sounds.

The weekend came and went and I was in. No one thought twice about my sudden interest in the God Squad. Some of the regulars would even say to me, 'See you tomorrow.' It wasn't a question, it was expected. I was one of them. I actually *was* one of them.

Week two, I stepped it up a notch. Kevin and I became closer. Not quite friends but just two guys who would meet in the mosque. We would sit at the back of the prayer hall in between prayers, drinking mango juice and snacking on dates. Just talking. Sometimes chit-chat, other times deeper. I told him a bit about my situation and asked him about his.

'It's quite an achievement,' I said. 'Converting to Islam. Especially in this day and age.'

Kevin nodded thoughtfully. He was a peculiar-looking guy, tall and wiry, with small eyes. He always wore a topi on his head, even outside of the mosque, as if to say to the world: *I'm white, I converted. Is there a problem?*

'We all have to find a path, Jay. I found mine at a time when I was losing in this game called life.' He rolled up the sleeve of his shirt and showed me his forearm. It told a faded story of drug abuse and suicide attempts. I turned away after a moment and he pulled down his sleeve.

'Why Islam?' I asked, genuinely curious.

'It was kismet, as they say. See, I never quite understood it... Islam, that is. With most religions you have a gist of what they are about, right? But all I knew about Islam was that it was a very angry religion. My downstairs neighbour, at the time, he was a Muslim. Hamza.'

'As in Mr Hamza, the cleric? From here?'

'Yes, one and the same.' He nodded. 'In all the years living so close to each other, we had never spoken, not even a neighbourly exchange or an acknowledgement. One night, he was praying at home, and pinkish water was dripping from his ceiling onto his prayer mat. He came up to my flat to investigate. He let himself in as I was in no state to answer. He found me in my bathtub, drowning in my own blood and dirt.' Kevin turned towards me and expelled air, as though parting with that information had tired him. 'If the water hadn't filled up and leaked through his ceiling...' He stared dramatically past me over my shoulder, his eyes moist. 'I would have died.'

I nodded solemnly. I didn't say anything. I sensed there was more to come.

Kevin blinked away the moisture in his eyes and continued. 'An episode like that really makes you sit up and reflect. Anyway, after a stint in the hospital, Hamza checked up on me every day. Cooked for me, shopped for basics, that sort of thing. He threw out all my booze and gear and replaced them with healthy foods and books. One thing led to another and before I knew it, I attended the Masjid with him, just to observe, more out of curiosity than anything else. I wanted to know what it

138

was about Islam that gave Hamza so much peace. I sat at the back, just like we are now, and I watched hundreds of people in perfect synchronisation, both physically and mentally, give themselves wholly to Allah. I don't know what it was. I *still* don't know. It was as though a serene sensation had enveloped me, like I was floating. It was a high that no drug or drink could give me. And at that moment I knew, I was *certain*, that I wanted that, I *needed* that... That was it for me. No AA meetings or rehab. Islam saved me and I owe my life to it.'

I wanted to say *Fuck*! I nearly did say it. The story warranted it, but I was aware that I was sat in a mosque, so instead I said, '*Damn*.' Stretching the word out past its one syllable.

Kevin grimaced. 'You shouldn't use that kind of language in a Masjid, Brother.'

Better than the alternative, mate.

He continued talking and I hate to say this, especially as he had just laid out his soul to me, but he did start to bore me a bit. He was talking about the five pillars and how he hoped to fulfil them. Then he went on about the importance of investments in mosques and other Islamic institutions, and I was all but tuned out. I think at one point he spotted me looking at the clock.

Then he said something that caught my attention.

'You just have to look at what happened in Edmonton to realise what we are going through.'

I switched back on.

'Sorry... What did you say?' I asked.

'Edmonton, Canada. The terrorist attack on the school a couple of weeks back.'

'What about it?'

'I agree fully with the intention, the *reason*, but targeting a school? No, no, no, that is beyond barbaric. A child has no bearing in our war. A child has no influence in the decisions that their parents make, who they vote for and the government they put into power. All those young lives lost in a heartbeat, giving the world, the bigots and the racists even more reason to attack us.'

Adrenaline swam through my body. *What are you saying?* I wanted to ask. But I couldn't work out if it was the right move. I decided to take a risk and just come out with it, when

I noticed him looking over my shoulder again. This time he wasn't staring thoughtfully into the distance. He was looking at somebody.

I turned my head and Parvez was stood behind me. He looked down at me and I acknowledged him with a nod. His timing could not have been worse.

'What are you doing, Jay?' he asked.

'Parvez, can we chat in a bit?' I said, as always, trying to get rid of him.

'Brother Parvez. Aslamalykum.' Kevin stood up and shook hands with him. 'I better be on my way. I must get to Tesco before prayers. They have a fantastic halal section.'

I stood up too. I didn't want him to go just yet. Stupid Parvez with his stupid timing!

'Do you have to leave now? I was really interested in what you had to say. Don't mind Parvez, he was just going.'

'No I wasn't,' Parvez said, his arms crossed defensively over his chest.

Kevin put a hand on Parvez's shoulders. 'There is nothing I could say that Parvez doesn't already know about. He's one of the good guys.' A knowing look passed between them as he said his goodbyes and left, leaving me alone with Parvez the Preacher. We stared at each other like two old gunslingers, mentally sizing each other up.

'Let's go for a walk, get some fresh air,' Parvez suggested, without warmth. Just like a Mafia hitman would.

'Why? Are you going to whack me?' I said, trying to lift the mood.

'I don't know what you mean,' he said, deadpan.

Exactly as a Mafia hitman would.

32

We had been walking for a few minutes in an uncomfortable silence. We passed a few mosque-goers, who acknowledged us with a token 'Salaam'. One stopped and chatted to us, just small talk really, but I could see that it was annoying the hell out of Parvez. He didn't seem to like the fact that members of the mosque were treating me like one of their own. Which was fucking ironic considering that he had spent a helluva lot of time trying to push me into this life.

'Well, this is nice, Parvez,' I said, breaking the silence. We had taken a random turn into an alleyway behind the mosque. 'Perfect evening for a romantic stroll down a grim alley. Now, are you going to tell me what your problem is or am I going to have to buy you dinner first?'

He stopped in his tracks, his head down, looking at his stupid Crocs. He muttered something. I couldn't work out what he was saying. I sighed and leaned back against the wall.

'Parvez, can you talk to me and not at your shoes?' I said, not snapping at him – which would normally have been my first reaction. Something was obviously bothering him.

'What are you doing, Jay?' he said, leaning against the wall opposite me.

'What do you mean? I'm not doing anything! What're you chatting about, Parvez?'

'Why are you always at the mosque? I don't understand.'

'What is there to understand? Why are *you* always at the mosque?' I said defensively and regretted it immediately. 'Look, man, I'm just going through something at the moment, that's all, and coming to the mosque, you know, it helps, gives me some peace, some time to think and work things through.'

'What?' Parvez asked. 'What are you going through?'

I remembered Parker's advice, to keep as close to the truth as possible.

'It's just a combination of things, really,' I said, rubbing my head, as though I was stressed out. 'After Mum left, I don't know, there was a big hole in my life.'

Parvez nodded in agreement. 'Yes, I know how close you were. It's just a shame that she chose to spend her life with a Kafir rather than with her son,' he said, not maliciously, but still.

I really had to dig deep down and shut down all my natural instincts, otherwise I swear to God I would have knocked his head clean off for talking like that about my mum.

'How do you feel about that?' Parvez asked.

'Andrew's all right and I know he will make her happy but, yes, you're right, she should never have started a new life with a, you know... a Kafir.'

'Maybe she'll convert him.'

Yeah, right.

I decided to change tack and move away from my mother's perceived shortcomings.

'That's not the only reason... I gave up dealing too.'

'*No!*' Parvez's eyes lit up, and a smile that had been long missing appeared. 'Brother, that is the best news I have ever heard.'

Really? The best?

'I couldn't do it any longer. I just woke up one day and decided to be a grown up.' I laughed. He laughed louder. He moved in towards me and gave me a really nice but slightly awkward embrace. Maybe it *was* the best news that he had ever heard!

'So, what are you going to do for money?' he asked, letting go of me.

My mind flashed back to the paying-in books that I had found in the loft. Three grand a month income from our mystery contributor.

'I have a bit saved up, enough to get me through.' I shrugged, nonchalantly.

'I can't tell you how happy that makes me, Jay,' he said. 'That's Allah's will, Brother.'

'Yeah, it is. It really is Allah's will.' I wasn't about to tell him that it was actually Silas' will.

142

'So I guess that explains why you're always at the mosque,' he said, in a eureka moment.

'Yeah, man. As I said, it's a combination of things. Mum chipped, I knocked dealing on the head and...'

This was it, this is where I had planned for the conversation to lead. I composed myself and took an internal breath.

'And what?' he asked.

'The attacks in Canada,' I said, in a hushed tone. 'It got me thinking, man. You know? It's bad what's happening to us. Islam is being blackened. I want to help those people, somehow.'

My hand was rubbing the back of my head, perfecting that stressed-out look.

Parvez instinctively took a step back, the heel of his Crocs hitting the wall behind him. His mood changed and he looked nervously around over his shoulders. Then in a meek voice he said, 'What do you mean? Help how?'

'Just, you know. There is a right way of doing things... And a wrong way. Take the attack on the mosque a few weeks back. Remember how we retaliated? I mean, I was dead against that shit, but now, in retrospect, I think we did the right thing. We sent a message out to those bastards. Yeah, it wasn't the actual guys that vandalised the mosque but that's not the point, you know. The point is *we* didn't stand back and let it happen. We did something. An eye for an eye, right?'

I think I went too far, judging by the way Parvez was looking at me. Questions and curiosity etched over his face, none of which he expressed vocally.

I was tempted to say more, entice something out of him. I had a feeling that something was going on with him, something related to number fifteen. At that moment I wasn't doing it for MI5; I just wanted to find out the extent of his involvement and get him as far away from there as possible. Because that boy is as naïve as they come and that naïvety could well see him strapped to an explosive vest.

Anyway, I had put the seed out there; it was up to the weather to determine how it flourished.

'Can I ask you something, Parvez?'

'Yes,' he said, but he was still a bit spooked.

'Why have you been ignoring me at the mosque the last week or so? It seemed like you were pissed off with me. Like, it wasn't my place to be there.'

'It's not that.'

'I mean, you've been trying to get me on the straight and narrow for as long as I can remember. It's partly down to you that I started to look at my life and started to think about the afterlife. How I would answer to Allah.' I sighed theatrically, took a breath, and continued. 'I've known you all my life, man, and it saddened me that you, *you* of all people, wasn't sharing and rejoicing in... in... whatever this is!'

'You'll never know how happy I am for you, Brother,' he said. 'You have chosen the right path and I am guaranteed a place in paradise for helping you see that path.'

'Then, what? Why the cold shoulder?'

Parvez looked up into the clear sky; the moon was out in its full glory. A tell-tale sign that it was time for prayers. Then, tearing his eyes away from the night and landing on mine, he said, 'Because... I think that you are being watched.'

33

Robinson was sitting cross-legged, one arm draped across the back of the three-seater sofa. A jug of water and one glass sat in front of him. His eyes flitted between the clock and the door, waiting for the knock. He had already visualised how he would greet them all; no need to get up and shake hands when a curt nod would suffice. The speaker on the table buzzed. He acknowledged it and smiled to himself. He heard the knock on the door, counted ten seconds in his head and then barked 'Enter'.

Sinclair, Lawrence and Parker walked into the office. In that order. Robinson gave the rehearsed curt nod to Sinclair, who returned one of his own and sat down opposite. Lawrence sat down next to Sinclair and crossed his legs, letting his designer socks come into view. Robinson watched with amusement as Parker looked around for somewhere to sit. Robinson could have moved to one end of the sofa but he didn't want to. In the end, Parker decided to just stand by the tall window.

Sinclair started, without preamble. 'There has been a development, which I would like to inform you of. I don't know how it will change things. But first,' he addressed Parker, 'I would like an update on Javid Qasim. How's our boy getting along?'

'Well. Very well indeed. He's surprised me. Jay has leaped into his role, he's enthusiastic and has contributed ideas of his own. I think he is going to be a real asset to the team.'

'That's all very well, Parker.' Robinson smiled, a little mocking. 'But would you mind telling us what he is *actually* doing.' He caught Lawrence's eye and saw amusement in it reflecting his own.

'He is keeping as close to his own life as possible. The only thing that has changed is that he is visiting Sutton mosque more often and keeping his eyes and ears open.'

'Is that it?' Lawrence said. 'No intel?'

'No, Lawrence. That is not it,' Parker said. 'There is a house in Osterley, number fifteen Jersey Way. Supposedly it is used for Islamic Studies, but the whole set-up suggests otherwise. There has been some suspicious activity, which Jay would like to further investigate. It may well prove that this address is being used to potentially groom young Muslims. He has a friend who is involved and through this friend he will try to infiltrate.'

'Who is this friend?' Sinclair asked. 'Do we have a name?'

'Negative, sir. Jay is hesitant to reveal the identity and I haven't pushed for it. Not yet, not until necessary.'

'We need a name, Parker,' Robinson said. 'Jay isn't in a position to be calling the shots. You're his handler. Handle him!'

Parker opened his mouth to respond, but Lawrence beat him to it.

'Parvez Ahmed.' Lawrence felt every eye shoot towards him and he loved it. Seemingly from thin air, he pulled out an iPad and placed it on the table. He opened up the photos app and slowly scrolled through several photos of Parvez. 'A childhood friend of Javid Qasim. He was present with Qasim at the riot at Elmsleigh car park, the night after Sutton mosque was vandalised.' Lawrence looked at each person in turn, just to ensure that he had everyone's attention and continued. 'He is a regular at said mosque, attends daily, at least three times a day, five times on a Friday. He is currently unemployed and living with his parents in Hounslow, across the road from Qasim. No priors, but he has travelled to Islamabad on two occasions. I've requested a background check.'

Parker looked intently at the image of Parvez until the power save kicked in and the screen went blank. He looked up to find that Sinclair was staring at him.

'Bravo, Lawrence,' Robinson said, somewhat unnecessarily. Lawrence just nodded coolly, but his insides were having a party. 'Job well done. Anything to add, Parker?'

'Jay has also become close to another regular at the mosque, who may be of interest. His name is Kevin.' Parker knew what question was coming next and he hated himself for not knowing the answer.

'Do we have a surname?' Sinclair asked, hopefully.

'No, sir,' Parker said.

'Lawrence?' Robinson prompted.

'I'm on it. Shouldn't be too difficult. He's obviously a convert. I'll have his full name by end of play,' Lawrence said, making a note on his iPad.

'Right. Well. If there's nothing else to add on Qasim, Sinclair can update us on the new development,' Robinson said, giving the floor to the Major General.

'At nine a.m. this morning,' Sinclair announced, 'Silas Drakos was released from custody.'

34

Sinclair waited for the news to sink in before he continued.

'Drakos' counsel managed to cut a deal.'

'*Deal?* What the bloody hell are you talking about? We gave them Drakos on a goddamn plate in return for Javid Qasim's safety,' Robinson raged, his face scrunched so all his features were touching. 'That was the fucking *deal*!'

Parker stood at the window, his hands tightly clasped behind his back, looking out at the London skyline. He was certain where this was heading, and he was certain what the outcome would be. It was an outcome he would not agree to.

'Is this confirmed information?' Lawrence asked.

'I got word from Chief Superintendent Wakefield this morning.'

'Drakos is, without question, the biggest drug dealer in West London,' Robinson said. 'We have a written statement from Qasim pointing a finger at him. From what I understand they found significant quantities of narcotics and weapons at his house, and more at a second location. The Met have enough on him to put him away for a very long time. So, Major General, I ask you again, what the *bloody* hell are you talking about?'

'The guns,' Parker said quietly. 'This is about the guns.'

Sinclair nodded. 'That's right. Drakos has agreed to give up his supplier. A Simon Pratchett, currently based in Manchester.'

'Is that name supposed to mean something to me?' Robinson asked.

'Simon Pratchett was arrested in 2012 trying to supply eight thousand AK-47's and thirty-six million rounds of ammunition to a terrorist cell in Darfur, Sudan. The hearing was delayed until 2014, and ultimately thrown out of court. Pratchett went underground. However, rumours and chat circulated that he was still dealing in arms but on a smaller scale. Mainly keeping his business afloat on our shores.'

'That's where Drakos comes in,' Lawrence chimed.

Sinclair nodded.

'Bigger picture?' Robinson asked. 'How does this affect us?'

'It won't take long for Drakos to work out who was responsible for seeing him put away, if he hasn't already. One moment Qasim owes him ten thousand and the next he's in handcuffs. Drakos is many things, but stupid isn't one of them.'

'How about if Qasim pays the debt? Would that make a difference?' Lawrence asked.

'Silas Drakos is as crazy as they come,' Sinclair said. 'How do you second-guess a bloody madman?'

'Bloody hypocrite.' Lawrence stood up abruptly, shaking his head in disbelief. 'Correct me if I am wrong, but didn't *Drakos* just grass to get *himself* out of trouble?'

'Short-term.' Robinson held out his hand, indicating that a decision had been made. 'Let's arrange eyes on Drakos. Qasim is to go nowhere near him. You understand me? Not until we see this thing through.'

Lawrence sat back down and nodded.

Sinclair didn't respond but his silence was one of agreement.

Parker, still at the window, his back to them all, listened to the reasoning and the inevitable result of it. There was not a thing he could say that would make a difference.

But he said it anyway.

'We have to get him out.'

'Don't be absurd, Parker,' Robinson snorted. 'What do you expect? Witness protection, relocation, a new bloody identity?'

'He can't be part of this anymore.' Parker turned to face Robinson. 'His life is in danger.'

'Not going to happen.' Robinson dismissed it with a flick of the wrist.

Before anybody could react, Parker had cut the distance between them in one stride and was towering over Robinson, his fists balled. His face screwed up in wrath.

'*His life is in danger!*' Spittle flew from Parker's mouth.

'*Parker!*' Sinclair was on his feet, his hand firmly on Parker's shoulder. 'Stand down.'

Parker walked out of the office before being ordered out. He wouldn't give them the satisfaction. He waited outside for Sinclair, pacing, burning a hole in the carpet. He knew, he *knew*, they were dead-on. It was the right move, the only move. But it was a nightmare scenario. Jay was potentially the key, the missing piece of the jigsaw that could provide a breakthrough and lead them to their number one target, The Teacher.

The office door opened and Sinclair stomped out. He did not appear impressed as he walked towards and then past Parker. 'Walk with me.'

In Sinclair's altogether more humble office, Parker stood silently in front of his desk.

'You are not a damn soldier anymore, Parker.'

Parker said nothing.

'This is not the barracks or the bloody mess hall.'

No, Parker thought, *it's not.*

'I shudder to think what would have transpired if I hadn't been there.'

Parker knew what would have happened. It replayed over and over in his mind, each time increasing in violence.

'I've vouched for you from day one, when all I heard was opposition. I have spent the last thirty minutes trying to convince Robinson not to have you relieved of your duties.' Sinclair exhaled through his nose. His toned softened, to one that he wasn't comfortable with. 'Parker... It's the only solution, and I know that you know that it's the only solution. It's bloody crap, but it's the right bloody move. We have a very big player in our sights and the safety of one man cannot jeopardise that.'

What could Parker say?

'So, going forward.' Sinclair's tone back to business. 'Eyeballs on Drakos to be organised. But Qasim continues. He's doing a good job, which in my books means that you are too.'

Parker dismissed the compliment without any thought of entertaining it. He knew when he was being pacified.

'It is imperative that he is not informed of this development.'

Parker nodded. Just about.

Sinclair eyed him momentarily, until he was satisfied that the message had sunk in, and then dismissed him.

Parker left the room without having said a word.

35

So *they* were watching me. When Parvez told me that, I freaked a little. Worried that my cover had been blown. That, in my eagerness, I had somehow given the game away, talked to too many people, asked too many questions. Painted a target on my back.

But it wasn't that. Not at all.

They *were* looking at me. But in a completely different way. Parvez went on to explain that they noticed a change in my prayer patterns. The heavy attendance. The new leaf being turned over.

Hounslow has a large Muslim community, but like all communities everybody seemed to know everybody else's business. They knew that my mum had left me on my own. They knew that I had stopped dealing and assumed I had no job, no income. They knew about my involvement in the fracas at Elmsleigh car park. I was viewed as one who was vulnerable. A young Muslim who was at a crossroads in his life, trying to determine which path to take. They wanted to help me choose a path.

They saw me as a potential recruit.

Now all I had to find out was who the fuck *they* were.

Parvez wasn't about to divulge that information. He would just say that my name had come up on occasion, that questions had been asked. He warned me to keep a low profile and that I shouldn't get involved.

The problem was that I wasn't sure *how* to get involved. So I continued in the same vein. I started to attend Basic Islamic Studies within the mosque, led by our cleric, Mr Hamza, in the hope that whoever was watching would notice.

The classes took place once a week in a small back room at the mosque. The attendees ranged from the very young – I'm talking four-year-olds – to the very old. The lessons themselves were pretty tame. Knowing the difference between good and bad.

Respecting your parents and elders. Charity, five pillars, reciting the Quran, etcetera. We sat uncomfortably on the carpeted hard floor and listened intently to Mr Hamza, whilst we chorused *Inshallahs*, *Mashallahs* and *Alhamdulillahs*.

In one session, Kevin joined us. He looked around the class until he spotted somewhere suitable to sit, which just happened to be next to me. Other spaces were available. Mr Hamza was telling us a story about a Chinese man who, after a failed suicide attempt, woke from a coma. Due to the brain trauma, he didn't recognise his wife or his kids. Although somehow he knew all the words of the Quran from memory. A man who had never ever picked up the holy book, never showed any interest in Islam.

'It's a miracle!' exclaimed Mr Hamza.

I wasn't quite sure his wife and kids saw it that way.

'I haven't been to this class in years,' Kevin whispered to me, as he tried to get comfortable on the floor.

'Yeah? I would have thought this would be right up your street,' I whispered back.

'Yes, it was. But these classes have a cycle. After a few sessions, they become repetitive. Take this story, for example, about the Chinese guy. I have heard it on many occasions.'

'Is it true?' I asked.

'Until you see something with your own eyes, what is true and what isn't?' he answered, somewhat cryptically.

'Right. So maybe I should look elsewhere. You know, to further my learning on Islam.'

'Don't get me wrong, it is about Islam and living your life cleanly. Perfect for somebody like yourself who is relatively new to this,' he replied. 'It also educates you on the meaning of jihad. It really is interesting how—'

He was interrupted by a piece of chalk bouncing off his shoulder.

'If you have something to say, please join me at the front and share it with the class,' Mr Hamza said, looking pleased with his aim.

'I was just telling our Brother here about jihad.'

'Ah, yes, Brother Kevin. A noble and worthy subject. Please,' he said, waving Kevin forward. 'Join me. Share with the rest of the group.'

Kevin joined Mr Hamza at the front and stood facing the class. Mr Hamza nodded for him to proceed. 'Aslamalykum, young Brothers. For those of you that do not know me, my name is Kevin.'

'Aslamalykum, Brother Kevin,' was the enthusiastic joint reply.

'I know what you are all thinking. What kind of terrible name that is for a Muslim? You would be right. It's awful.' Some of the kids giggled. 'The Quran states that a convert is not obliged to change his name. It's a personal choice. If I am honest, I just cannot be bothered having to change my name on every piece of documentation.' Cue more laughs, some elders joining in. Mr Hamza smiled broadly. Kevin continued. 'So, where was I? Yes. *Jihad*. I was just starting to explain to Brother Jay the true meaning of the word. Does anybody here know what *jihad* means?' He looked at the kids.

The children all looked to each other, daring the other to answer. One skinny little boy, probably about seven, spoke up.

'Fighting,' he said. 'It means fighting.'

'Fighting, you say?' Kevin said, nodding, stroking his chin. 'Fighting against who?'

'Against the Kafirs.'

'What's your name, young Brother?'

'My name is Sami.' He grinned around at his friends, happy to be the centre of attention.

'Well, Sami, if I was to Google *jihad*,' Kevin said, with air quotes, 'it would define it just as you have told me. *A war or struggle amongst Muslims against unbelievers.*' Kevin looked around the room at all the young faces, adding a touch of theatre to the proceedings. 'In fact, that definition is identical to the one that can also be found in the *Oxford Dictionary*. And we all know that the *Oxford Dictionary* cannot be wrong.' Again, more air quotes. 'Well, I am here to tell you, kids, and excuse my language, but it's all poo-poo.'

The younger kids exploded into laughter.

Kevin was enjoying his moment up on centre stage. He motioned for everyone to calm down and continued. 'I'm sorry, Sami, but that is not the correct meaning of jihad, that is what the newspapers and television want you to believe.' Sami's face fell. 'But it's not your fault, it's a very common mistake, even for Muslims to make. Would you all like to hear the real meaning, the *true* meaning?'

The kids all chorused a big fat 'Yes'.

'*Jihad* does indeed mean to fight, but it is the fight that Muslims have internally. Within themselves. Striving to become a good Muslim, not giving into temptation, leading a clean life, as is written in the words of the Quran.'

'*Mashallah*, Brother Kevin,' Mr Hamza said, patting Kevin on the back and pushing him back to his place. The kids clapped him off and Kevin plonked himself down next to me as Mr Hamza took questions from the floor.

'Well said, Kevin. I did not know that.'

Kevin turned to me, his demeanour a little darker. 'That was for the benefit of the class. That boy, Sami... He was right.'

'What?' I said, somewhat confused.

Kevin stood up, but before reaching full height, with his mouth close to my ear, he whispered, 'Come and find me in the car park after class finishes. It's time we talked.'

36

It was the second time Kevin had said something peculiar and walked away without giving me a chance to counter. I had a feeling that he was the one watching me. *Or at least he was one of them.* I had told him about my life and I was sure he saw me as one who required direction.

I hurried through the mosque towards the car park. He was waiting for me just outside the shoe rack.

'Let's go,' he said. 'We'll take my car. There's somebody I want you to meet.'

*

En route, Kevin seemed fidgety, which was out of character. He was normally calm, subdued.

'What did you mean by saying Sami was right?' I said, looking out of the window, mentally trying to remember the route we were taking. 'Right about what?'

'He was right, Brother. Do you not see? He was spot on. The definition of *jihad* has, over the years, become convoluted. Yes, it is a struggle within one's self, in a way that *Kafirs* will never understand. They take each day with selfish attitudes. Damaging their bodies with alcohol and drugs and polluting their mind with filth. We have been given this gift of life by the highest of powers and it is our duty to live as clean and pure as possible. *That's* the fight, *that* is the jihad.' He stopped to take a breath. 'But like the boy said, jihad is also a fight against non-believers.'

He pulled up outside a small shisha bar called the Purple Rain.

'Go inside,' he said.

'Are you not coming?'

'No, Brother, I am not.'

'Hang on. Where are you going? Who's in there? I thought *we* were going to talk,' I babbled.

'Do you trust me, Brother?' he asked.

'Yeah, I trust you,' I said. 'But—'

'Then walk inside with Allah in your heart. It's going to be okay. It's just a meeting.'

37

Predictably the walls were painted purple, but that's not what I noticed first. There were no chairs, just big, comfortable velvet cushions on the floor, placed around low tables. But again, that's not what I noticed first. A waiter approached me and asked me something but I ignored him. My eyes were transfixed on what lay straight ahead of me.

Through the cloud of lazily swirling shisha smoke there was a figure sitting, eyeing me curiously. I was hypnotised as I walked in the straightest of lines, ignoring my surroundings, tunnel vision in full effect, and sat down opposite Amirah.

'Um... Hi.' It was the best I could come up with. She put the pipe to her lips and inhaled generously before expelling it through her nose. It smelled of apple and tobacco.

'What would sir like?' asked the waiter, who was suddenly looming over me.

'Same as the lady... Apple and tobacco,' I said, smoothly and confidently, eyes attached to hers, giving her what I hoped was a winning smile.

'The lady is having double menthol and vanilla extracts, sir.'

'Right,' I said, my smile frozen in place. 'I'll have that then.'

'So,' I said to Amirah. 'This is a nice surprise.'

'Surprise? Tell me about it. It came as a big surprise when I found out it was *you*.'

'Not sure I know what you mean.'

The waiter came back with a shisha and placed it in front of me. Never had I hit one of these things before but it couldn't be that hard. I'd been puffing on joints for years, so what's the difference? She pulled the pipe to her lips, took a long pull and I followed suit. She removed the pipe, tightened her jaw and expertly let out cute little smoke rings. I removed the pipe from my mouth and tried to emulate her. I coughed and spluttered and the waiter rushed over and rubbed my back like a mother would a child.

I still got it!

I poured myself a glass of water, sipped greedily, and recovered quickly. 'You were saying,' I said, my voice a little hoarse.

'I've been hearing some good things about you.'

'Yeah? From who? Parvez? I wouldn't take much notice of him.'

'No, not Parvez. And no, I don't take much notice of him.'

'So, who has been saying these so-called good things about me? I'd like to buy them a drink.'

'That's not important right now. What is important is that your work has been acknowledged... And appreciated.'

That threw me a bit. *What work?* I didn't know how to respond, so I took another hit of the shisha and waited for her to continue.

'The spirit you showed after Sutton Masjid was vandalised.'

'Oh right, I see. With the clean up and restoration? That wasn't no big deal, I was one of many. It was my *Farz*. My duty!'

'Yeah, I know what Farz means,' she said, dropping the warmth before quickly recovering. 'But not only the clean up, but the way you handled yourself afterwards. You didn't sit on your hands; you were proactive in your actions. You took the fight directly to the Kafirs. You sent out a message.'

I looked around the room, trying to buy time. I had to respond carefully. I finally took in the purple garish décor, the sumptuous oversized velvet cushions, and the beautiful girl sitting in front of me, who was eyeing me up, taking my measure, establishing if I was the right kind of person.

'I did what I thought was just,' I said, in a low, measured tone. I wasn't about to tell her that I was only there to keep Parvez out of trouble.

Amirah nodded and then, with a smile playing on her face, she said, 'Well, you fucking rocked it.'

The mouth on her! Could she be the perfect girl?

'Um, yeah. I guess I did.'

She tapped a perfectly manicured finger on her lips. Apparently I wasn't the only one who needed to think carefully about what came out of my mouth. She obviously did not want to give too much away but she needed to know if I was willing. She chose her words carefully.

'Remember where you first met me?' she asked.

'How could I forget?' I replied, smiling.

'There are a few of us—'

'Us?'

Her eyes told me not to interrupt her again.

'There are a few of us who attend classes, twice a week at that house in Osterley. I would like to see you there.'

'You would?' I said, giving her a knowing smile.

'Will you fucking grow up?'

'All right. God! All right.' I threw my hands up in the air. 'I'm only playing. What are these classes, anyway? And what time? I don't want to miss prayers.'

'You can pray at the house. The classes are designed to further your knowledge.'

'On what?'

'On Islam.'

'I'm already taking weekly classes at the mosque. In fact, I was just there today. Is this something similar?'

'No. What you're taking is basic education designed for five-year-olds.'

'There are elders present too,' I said.

'Those lazy old farts are just killing time in between prayers and they can't be arsed to go back home to their nagging wives. Trust me, those classes are for children. Are you a child?'

'No,' I said childishly.

'Well, that's settled then. Okay?'

'No. Not okay.' I sat back. I didn't want to make myself look like an easy target, jumping in with both feet and my tongue hanging out.

'Do you not care?' she said.

'About what exactly?'

'You, your people, those close to you and those around the world. What they are going through. Surely you must feel something,' she said, a pinched, pained expression on her face.

'Yes. Of course I care. You know I do. But I've got too much on my plate right now. And besides, no white man has ever stepped to me. The cops leave me alone and nobody be calling me a Paki. Look, I'm going to tell you how I see it: Muslims in this country, they're not getting a hard time. Not really. Not unless you're spouting off or inciting violence. You think the average Joe gives a crap about how you dress? Nobody cares if you're covered from head to toe or wearing a shalwar and kameez. Yeah, you get the odd idiot shouting the odds, but it's a rarity. It's certainly not enough to start a fucking war.'

Amirah sat back against her cushion, her eyes burning into mine, arms crossed over her chest. I stood up.

'I'm going out for a cigarette,' I said quietly. Leaving her to mull things over whilst I did a bit of mulling of my own.

I stepped out of the shisha bar and lit up, smoking it like it was the last fag on earth.

What the fuck had I just done? There she was, handing me an in, and I gave her reason to doubt me. I don't know why I did that. Well, maybe I do. I was scared, all right? I was scared that if I showed eagerness it would look too obvious. If I had said to Amirah, *Yeah, sure, sweetheart, lead the way, let me just tape a wire to my chest!* then questions would be considered and asked. I had to be clever. Start taking things slowly. The last thing I needed was to be at the back end of a waterboarding.

I finished my smoke and peeked inside. Amirah was on the phone. I had a feeling that the topic of conversation was yours truly. I gave her some time and sparked up another. Halfway through my smoke she came out and joined me. Without asking, she took the cigarette from my hands and put it to her lips. I thought it was an intimate gesture. But maybe she just wanted a smoke.

'You've been in Hounslow most of your life, right?' Her voice was softer, more appeasing than before.

'All my life,' I said, as though it was something to be proud of.

'And you've never suffered any form of racism or attack against you?'

'No. Never.'

'You live in a heavily populated Asian area with a high percentage of Muslims. You have mainly Muslim friends and you hardly ever set foot out of Hounslow.'

'How do you know that?'

'I don't.' She smiled. 'I just guessed. It wasn't difficult. See, Jay, do not take this the wrong way, but you live a sheltered life, protected by your environment, and as a result you have become blind to what is happening under your nose.' She threw the cigarette down. 'These classes will help you see things that you have never considered.'

I shrugged a *whatever* at her.

'I can see in you what you cannot yet. I want to help open your eyes.'

'Open my eyes?' I snorted. 'How?'

'Outside of your cosy little community, Muslims are being attacked without reason,' she said, and I felt a lecture coming. 'Forget what is happening around the world. Here, right here, in jolly old England, we are being attacked. I don't necessarily mean physically attacked in the streets, spat at or beaten. I mean the small things that have a big impact. A look, or a whispered insult. Making us feel like we don't deserve to tread the same path as them, because of our beliefs, or the way we carry out our lives in the way that we see fit. Pick up a newspaper or read a fucking Twitter feed. It's filth, how they see us and what they say about us. It's easy to ignore once, twice, three times. But it never stops. It's relentless. And just because *you* haven't seen it yourself, it doesn't mean it is not happening.'

She was beautiful.

'So what are you suggesting?' I asked, allowing her to see that I was slightly interested. She pulled on her bottom lip for a moment, knowing that a little more push was required.

'I want you to visit a café and after that you can decide.'

'That's it? What's that going to prove?'

'Just do it. Sit there for about half an hour, treat yourself to a cup of tea and a sandwich.'

'And what?'

'And observe.'

38

It was a rundown café in a rundown part of South London. From where I had sat, at the back, right next to the stinking toilets, it looked as if the customers were also rundown by whatever life chose to throw at them. All white, of the trashy variety. The type that whined about lack of employment, thanks to all the *foreigners* taking all *their* jobs.

You know the tune.

As soon as I set foot into the joint, people's eyes flickered over me, glances that did not seem to relent throughout my stay. Telling looks that implied a sense of xenophobia. Maybe the attacks in Canada were still fresh in their minds.

A family of three, in particular, seemed to be paying me the most attention. The dad, or whoever the fuck he was, with his black eye and cut just under it, kept his eyes locked on me, as he was being whispered to or egged on by his wife, or whoever the fuck she was. The snotty young child, who couldn't have been more than ten, and looked like he hadn't showered since his last birthday, also stared at me as if he had wanted to ram his Power Ranger figure down my throat.

I took a sip of my tea and looked elsewhere, not looking for trouble. My eyes landed on a leaflet on the table. I picked it up.

SAVE BRITAIN. VOTE UKIP.

I turned it over and read the back.

KEEP CALM AND VOTE UKIP.

I looked around the other tables and there were similar leaflets planted on all of them.

It was obvious why Amirah had chosen this location. Even someone like me, who liked to think of himself as immune to the anti-Islamic brigade, could be a possible target. Well played, Amirah. She was well on the way to proving her point. I knocked back my cuppa and started to make tracks, before I got my head kicked in by a ten-year-old and a Power Ranger. I pushed my chair back and got to my feet, ready to walk out with my eyes firmly fixed to the ground, then the door chimed and somebody walked in.

I couldn't leave, not anymore. I couldn't leave her alone. Not here.

I sat back down, knowing that whatever potential grievances they had with me were about to be transferred to a new target. And they were about to be multiplied... And then fucking squared!

She must have been lost or ill-advised, or just looking for a place to sit down with her baby. I watched as, with difficulty, she pushed open the door with her elbow, and then twisted her body so that she could reverse herself and the pushchair in. Nobody got up to help. By the time I was on my feet and approaching her, she had made it in. I sat back down at my table and waited for the inevitable to unfold.

She was covered head to toe in a Burka. Head covered, face covered, everything covered. Even the baby in the pushchair was hidden behind a muslin cloth. She approached the counter, seemingly casual, as if she was a regular. Her head lifted towards the menu board and she took her time selecting what to order. The grubby-looking woman behind the counter, with a grubby-looking apron, which appeared to have the contents of the menu splattered all over it, and a name tag that read *Jo*, watched her.

Burka pointed at the menu board and, judging by her head movement, seemed to be ordering.

'You're gonna have to speak up louder, love. Can't 'ear ya under all that material,' Jo said. I noticed her look at one of her customers and shake her head in disbelief.

Burka repeated her order and Jo looked at her with a grimace on her face. 'The All-Day Breakfast, without sausages?' Jo asked. Burka nodded, enthusiastically. 'It's still gonna cost the same with or without, you might as well 'ave the sausages. More for your money, eh, love?' A stifled giggle from somewhere in the café. Burka waved her open hands at her, indicating no.

'Suit yourself. Take a seat wherever. I'll bring it across.'

Burka looked around. There were plenty of empty tables and available seats. She made eye contact with me – well, I think she did, anyway – and wheeled her pushchair, weaving clumsily, knocking into chairs and tables. A few tuts rang out around her. Her destination seemed to be towards me. Yeah, great. Nice one, Sister!

She stumbled forward slightly and then she seemed to be stuck, held back. She looked behind her towards the floor. Black Eye had his foot on the hem of the Burka.

Shit. I'm going to have to get up and do something here. But before that thought could come to pass, she had, with some force, tugged it free and continued towards me. She parallel parked the pushchair on the side of the table, pulled out a chair opposite me and carefully sat down.

Then she said something that made an already bizarre situation even more so.

'What a stupid fucking bitch!'

I looked up at her in bemusement. Had I heard her wrong? Or did she, under her Burka, shielding her modesty from the world, have a mouth on her?

'Excuse me?' I said, my eyes almost popping out of my head.

'You heard me.'

I should have known as soon as she entered the café. Only she would have the balls to pull a stunt like that.

'Amirah. What the fuck are you playing at?' I looked towards the pushchair. I could just about make out the watermelon-shaped head through the muslin cloth covering it. 'And whose baby have you stolen?'

She discreetly lifted the muslin off the pushchair, revealing the baby, except it wasn't a baby, it was, *actually*, a fucking watermelon. She replaced the muslin over the fruit and I just knew that she was smirking under her veil.

'Look at them,' she said, purposefully loud. Louder than I would have liked. 'It's like we're from a different planet.' She folded the UKIP leaflet into a paper airplane and flew it at me.

'Will you stop fucking around? You're going to get us murdered.'

'Sitting there drinking their coffee,' she continued. 'If it wasn't for Muslims they wouldn't have fucking coffee… or chess… or shampoo. Although I can't see this sorry lot taking advantage of any of those.'

'I don't care if we invented Sky Plus. Can you keep your voice down?' I hissed.

She turned her attention fully to me and asked, 'So, what did we learn today, Jay?'

I looked around the room, and the room looked back at me with menace. I turned my head back quickly to Amirah. 'Yeah, all right, you made your point. Can we go?'

'It doesn't matter if I am dressed in a burka, or that you're dressed in jeans and a T-shirt, and walk and talk like they do – you'll never be one of them.'

'I get it. Okay, I fucking get it. Now can we get out of here? You win, all right?'

'I always win, Jay. It's just something that you're going to have to get used to,' she said, clearly enjoying proving her point. 'Besides, I'm waiting for my meal. I am famished.'

And just on cue, her plate arrived and was placed on the table. We both looked down at it and then at each other. And then at Grubby Jo, who stood above us, smirking for a moment before returning to her station. I knew right then that shit was going to hit the fan, and most of it was going to land on me.

'Hmm,' Amirah said, looking at her All-Day Breakfast, with two sausages staring back at her. 'This is not what I ordered. Must have been a terrible mix-up,' she said. 'Never mind. I seem to have lost my appetite.'

I could feel every eye, every whisper and muffled laugh directed at us, waiting for us to make a move. Our move should have been: lesson learned, let's get the fuck out of here. Instead, Amirah slid her chair back, the legs scraping noisily on the floor, and lifted up her plate, balancing it on the palm of her hand.

'Where are you going?'

'I'm going to return my meal and leave.'

'What about the…' I looked at the pushchair. *Baby?*

'Leave it here.'

She walked towards the counter, where Jo stood defiantly, with her arms crossed over her chest.

And then Amirah launched the plate.

I watched open-mouthed as the plate flew perfectly over the counter, with Jo taking a sideways dive. It landed plum on the menu board and smashed on impact. Beans, hash brown, grilled tomato, eggs, sunny side up, and two sausages stuck briefly to the board before lazily descending.

The door chimed and Amirah had left the building.

Grubby Jo did not get up, she stayed cowering behind the counter. But the rest of the friendly patrons were up on their feet, eyes at the door. And then eyes on me!

Fuck's sake!

I was up like a shot, not giving the pushchair another thought, pushing past stubborn bodies and out into the fresh air. Amirah, now disrobed of the Burka, stood across the dual carriageway, smiling at me. I ran across two lanes one way and then two lanes the other, almost getting hit by a cyclist in the process, and stood next to her, out of breath, with my hands on my knees.

'What the fuck, man?' I said. She started to laugh. I couldn't help it, I joined her. 'Now can we go?

'Not quite yet,' she said, mischief dancing in her eyes. 'The best is yet to come.'

We waited a few minutes before the door to the café opened and everyone bolted out, trying to outdo each other, pushing and barging. It didn't take long for me to work out what had happened.

'The pushchair, they think... they think it's a bomb.'

'How's that for narrow-mindedness?' she said, as the customers and Grubby Jo quickly made their way to the end of the street, most of them with phones attached to their ears.

'Amirah, you *can't* do that.'

'Do what? I haven't done a thing. I just broke a plate. Hardly terrorism, is it?'

'I'm going in to get it. Look at them, they're scared out of their minds.'

'Leave it in there, they deserve it.'

Ignoring her, I ran back across the road and into the café. I retrieved the pushchair and calmly wheeled out the fucking watermelon. I made sure that I was seen by the customers. I gave them an *Oops, we seem to have left our baby behind* look.

I looked across the road and Amirah was gone. My phone beeped, informing me of a text message.

Now your eyes are open. Call me if you are interested.

39

To: John Robinson, Stewart Sinclair
Cc: Kingsley Parker
From: Teddy Lawrence
Subject: Kevin Strauss/Parvez Ahmed
Attachments: PA1.jpeg, PA2.jpeg, KS1.jpeg, KS2.jpeg, KS3.pdf

FYI

Parvez Ahmed – age 27. Based in Heston and living at home with his parents and brother. Currently unemployed and regularly receiving benefits. Affiliated with Sutton mosque, Heathrow mosque and Cranford Islamic centre. Regularly attends 15 Jersey Way, twice a week, Tuesdays and Thursdays at 2 p.m. Two recent trips to Pakistan: 10–24 October 2014 and 9–27 January 2015. Each time landing in Islamabad and each time citing a family wedding as reason of visit. His family in Pakistan are located in Karachi, which is 1447 km south from Islamabad.

No previous.

(See attached photos PA1 and PA2)

Kevin Strauss – age 36. Based in Hounslow West. Lives alone. Parents currently live in Australia. No known partner. Assumed to have converted to Islam in 2009. Works from home as a freelance web designer. He is also the author of many inflammatory websites, which incite hate against the West and organise and populate protests. Affiliated with Sutton mosque,

Ealing mosque and regularly gives lectures at Cranford Islamic centre. He is also a regular attendee at 15 Jersey Way.

Two trips to Jalalabad, Afghanistan: 11–23 March and 17–27 June 2012. Two trips to Islamabad, Pakistan: 10–24 October 2014 and 9–27 January 2015. For all four trips, reason cited as Business.

(See attached photos KS1 and KS2)

(See attached files KS3 for arrest sheet)

Regards
Teddy Lawrence

The email, Parker thought, had an underlying hint of smugness. He could picture Lawrence sitting hunched over his laptop with a triumphant smile on his face. Establishing pertinent information that Parker himself could and should have provided. It infuriated him that Lawrence chose to 'cc' him into the email, as if he was just a voyeur watching from behind the curtains, rather than include him in the 'To' column.

The hard copy of the email had arrived to Parker at his home by MI5 courier, with strict instructions that Parker had to sign for it. It was common knowledge that he didn't regularly check his emails, so it had to be this way.

As he read through the printed email again, he tried to determine how much of this information he should pass on to Jay. It was imperative that Jay keep his mind clear of everything but the task ahead; this information would only serve to cloud his judgement. Sometimes knowledge is not power, it's a noose around your neck. If Jay were to learn this information then it would have to come from Parvez or Kevin, and then his reaction would be natural. Genuine.

What was clear from the email was the fact that Parvez and Kevin were going far beyond the duties of a typical practising Muslim. It was obvious that the reasons they had given when travelling were a cover and, in the case of Parvez, not a very clever cover. It was also telling that they had both visited Islamabad twice, on the same dates for the same duration.

There are a lot of mountains and privacy around those parts, and it would be easy to assume the obvious reason for the visit. Kevin's other two trips to Jalalabad also raised some concern, as that particular location is known for its many training facilities.

Parker placed the hard copy of the email to one side and flicked through the printed attachments. Two images of Parvez, both with effortless clarity. One image was of him outside fifteen Jersey Way, looking over his shoulder with one foot in the door. The second image was as though Parvez had posed for it: stood outside the mosque, leaning casually against a lamppost and looking straight down the throat of the lens.

One image of Kevin was just as clear. Smiling, he was stood by a Range Rover outside a church, stone in hand, looking as though he was about to apply a deep scratch to the paint work of the car door. The second image, not as clear, was of him at a protest, sitting on somebody's shoulders, his face masked with rage as he held aloft a burning Bible like a trophy. It was a look that Parker had seen many times in his life.

Unbridled passion and hatred.

40

One by one they walked in. The instructions were clear. On approach the door will be opened for you to enter. If the door is closed do not knock or ring the bell, do not look up at the window or wait. If the door is closed, continue walking.

The door was open.

They climbed up the narrow stairs, past the chintzy wallpaper and the stair-lift chair. They made their way into the back bedroom, and sat on the floor and waited. There were some hushed whispers as there always was, some nervous energy and quick glances at the door, waiting for it to open and the class to begin. Though they had been coming to these classes for a long while, the anticipation stood firm. This was due largely to the man, the much respected, the right honourable Imam Adeel-Al-Bhukara.

Parvez was sat up against the back wall, his fingers moving quickly over prayer beads. Always happy to listen and learn and take orders from Al-Bhukara, who had been nothing short of a father figure to him. Not that his own father was lacking in that department. But this wasn't about playing catch in the park, or having an awkward conversation about the birds and the bees. Al-Bhukara was a different strain of father figure. He educated Parvez on Islam, the *real* Islam, on Jihadism, the *real* Jihadism. He educated him on politics, not the politics that we see on television and read about in the red tops.

He educated him on life.

Parvez was grateful. He owed his life to the esteemed Imam and, if ever called for, he would have given it. But, for the first time, he disagreed with Al-Bhukara – albeit in silence; there was too much respect to question or challenge him. But Parvez could not understand why out of the hundreds, no, *thousands* of young

Muslims that were available for selection, why the Imam was hell-bent on Jay. Ever since Jay started showing the first bit of interest in Islam, Al-Bhukara had been determined to meet him. To talk to him. To recruit him.

Was Javid at the Masjid today? How many prayers did he attend? I hear that he is attending Islamic classes after prayer? Tell me, again, about his bravery at Elmsleigh car park.

It was embarrassing for the great man. He must have had his reasons, but Parvez could not fathom what they could possibly be.

Yasir and his brother Irfan, younger by two years, sat at the front. Both local lads, both unemployed, both angry at the way the world had turned out for them. They had been tasked with writing a report, to choose any attack in the last twenty years and explore the motive, sacrifice and reward of it. How it had been planned and what they would have done to improve it. It was a heavy subject, but one that the brothers relished.

Stood at the window, looking carefully through the net curtains, was a pensive Amirah, her head covered with a shawl. She had done her part in trying to convince Jay to attend, though she wasn't sure he held the personality that was required. The Imam would be angry if she failed, and he would express that anger without restraint.

The door opened and in walked Kevin. He joined Amirah at the window and stood next to her, peering out, with his hands clasped behind his back.

'How did it go, Sister?' Kevin asked.

'It went!' Amirah replied.

'What does that mean?'

'I did what I had to do.'

'Did you manage to convince him?'

'I tried… God knows I tried. It shouldn't have to be this difficult.'

'We just have to get him here and Imam will do the rest.'

'What do you want me to say?' she asked, turning to him, her eyes wide and hands in the air. 'I… I *tried*, all right?'

She held back the profanity that was never far from her lips.

Kevin looked at his watch and nodded grimly. 'It's quarter past; he will not be pleased.'

'It's not on me.'

'I never said it was, Sister.'

The door creaked open and Amirah and Kevin immediately took their places on the floor. Parvez shifted forward from against the back wall, in amongst the others. Yasir and Irfan nervously placed their report on a small side table, ready to be scrutinised.

Even hobbling with the aid of a walking stick, Adeel-Al-Bhukara walked in confidently, larger than life, and sat down on the only chair in the room as though a king taking his throne.

Al-Bhukara had hurt his knee in the icy winter of 2007, when he'd slipped outside his house, landed on his backside and torn his tendons. However, the official line that he fed to his students was that he had been attacked whilst helping a young Muslim mother who was being pounced upon by baseball bat-wielding Kafirs. This version of the story added fire to the Cause, and it was better than telling everybody that he had fallen on his arse.

Adorned head to toe in black shalwar and kameez, slightly embroidered around the neck, Al-Bhukara ran his hand through his thick beard, which made him look older than his years. Behind the beard was hidden handsome features that, in the past, had attracted many suitors. But he was happy as a one-woman man. Happy with his one wife, Aaidah, in London. And happy with his one wife, Rani, in Bradford!

Aaidah lived with him, for the most part, here, in this house. Their two children, both now of age, had left for university and work. They never had any pressure to join him in jihad. It would have been deemed too dangerous for his own blood.

Rani, his stunning, go-to wife, lived alone in a two-bed flat, paid for by you and me. He would visit her as and when the fancy took him. She too wanted children, but he believed that a God-given body like that should not be spoiled by childbirth.

Al-Bhukara gave one last stroke of his beard and then tugged at the bottom of it, appearing to give it more length, and instead of any greeting or acknowledgement to his students, he went straight to the burning question.

'Where is Javid?'

Parvez bit his tongue at the mention of Jay's name, again. Yasir and Irfan twisted their bodies and looked at those that the question was aimed at – Kevin and Amirah. They looked hopelessly at each other and then at the Imam, whose dark eyes were like lasers, burning a hole through them.

Kevin smiled. 'We have done all we can.'

'Then why is he not sitting here? Amongst us? No, Kevin, you have not done all you can.'

'He's set in his ways,' Amirah said. 'He may just need some time and then—'

She was interrupted as the Imam loudly thumped the side table with the flat of his hand. It wobbled on two legs for a while, before deciding to descend and softly land on the carpet, taking Yasir and Irfan's reports along for the ride.

'Time is something that we can ill afford. *Time* is not on our side; have you not learned anything? There is a war waging out there, it is happening now, Muslims are dying *now*. I do not want to hear your excuses.'

That was it for Parvez. He couldn't just sit and listen to this anymore. He had to speak up and ask the question that was on everyone's mind. He refused to think of the consequences, as that would only serve to stop him. He had to say it. And he had to say it now.

'Why Javid? Why *him*?' he blurted out, fast and sharp. 'What is so special about him?'

The Imam stood up, appearing to his seated students about ten-feet tall. He opened his mouth and the room flinched. Then something happened that never happens.

The doorbell rang.

Aaidah, his London wife, the one with the children, could be heard walking calmly down the stairs.

Al-Bhukara motioned with his hands for everyone to stay calm. 'Start the cleaning process,' he instructed.

If the authorities had been looking at him, then Tuesdays and Thursdays, around two p.m, whilst his class was in full flow, would have been the perfect time to harass him. Yasir picked up both reports from the floor and looked aimlessly for a place to hide them. A report like that may not have been enough to press charges, but it would surely be enough to raise suspicion. Kevin slipped out the hard drive from the main PC, and from the bookcase grabbed the cordless drill, which was always fully charged and in place for such a situation. He drilled a hole into the centre of the drive, destroying all files and data on it. Files that included propaganda videos, explosive-constructing material, news reports on every terrorist attack over the last twenty years.

Again, nothing that would place you behind bars. But... where there's smoke, there is usually fire.

The bedroom door opened and everyone froze in their tracks. A smiling face popped around the corner.

41

I stepped into the room, nervous as hell. I was aiming for cool but I was coming across as a grinning idiot. My brain was screaming at me to rein it back a bit and keep my head down and wait for further instructions from the beardy bloke who looked to be in charge. But no, instead I sauntered around, working the room like Princess Diana, shaking hands with Kevin whilst simultaneously squeezing his shoulder, then moving smoothly onto a bemused-looking Parvez and giving him the same royal treatment. I spun on my heels and turned my attention to Amirah and gave her a wink! After completing the room with a formal introduction to my new Brothers, Yasir and Irfan, who I recognised as the Bus Stop Pakis, I stood facing the main man. His mouth was agape. I had the sudden urge to find my way through his beard to his chin and lift it shut for him. Instead I put forward my hand and he shook it warmly, sandwiching mine with both hands before respectfully lifting his hand to his heart.

'Javid Qasim,' he said. His voice caught; he smiled it away. 'I've been waiting for you.'

'You can call me Jay.'

I didn't quite know what I was expecting from him. His greeting was too warm, *too* gracious, as though I was the one to be shown respect to. It made me feel ill at ease, especially as I could feel the eyes of the rest of the group on us. He must have felt it too, as he cleared his throat and told me to find a place to sit.

He introduced himself as Adeel-Al-Bhukara, and now he had regained his composure there was an intimidating confidence about him; when he spoke, they listened. He seemed to demand a huge amount of respect, one born of fear. When the opportunity arose, I surreptitiously looked around the room, taking in every detail that may have been important, but it was tricky as Al-Bhukara was all over me, meeting my eye more often than I considered comfortable. There wasn't that much to take in anyway, really. A bedroom devoid of any bedroom furniture, questionably decorated. Flowery carpet *and* walls. A small side table that lay sadly on its side. Allah and Prophet Muhammad scribed in Arabic and framed on the wall. One chair, reserved for Al-Bhukara, whilst everyone else sat uneasily on the floor, presumably to hammer home the point that he really was The Man! I played along, afforded him the same respect and fear that he seemed to demand.

'Yasir, would you like to address the class and summarise on the subject of your report,' Al-Bhukara said. Yasir looked uneasily at him, concerned that a newcomer may not appreciate what he was about to say. 'We are amongst friends here, Yasir.'

'*Ameen*,' chorused the class.

'Yeah, Ameen,' came my clumsily late response.

Yasir stood up with his nose in his report.

'My subject for the report is the Boston Marathon bombings, which took place on April 2013, and in particular the actions, planning and poor execution of Tamerlan and Dzhokhar Tsarnaev. The death toll on the day was only three, out of a possible target of approximately two hundred and seventy people. Impact was low due to fundamental errors on the Brothers' part. Emailed to you all is my report, highlighting how and where this type of attack could be improved. You will find attached diagrams of vantage points that I would have selected, versus the actual vantage points. You will also see the type of explosive that was used, and how they could have been better built, concealed, and located for maximum impact. As always, please feel free to add your notes to further discuss at our next class.'

Al-Bhukara watched me, looking for a reaction, a sign, something, that would tell him where my loyalties lay. I felt sick to my stomach, my toes were curled tightly and my jaw set hard. I managed to control my breathing and adapt to my surroundings. I looked up at Yasir and said, 'Can you send me a copy of the report too, Brother? I would like to read it.'

'Inshallah,' Yasir said, smiling warmly at me.

I don't think I had ever wanted to hurt somebody so much as I did at that moment. He took his place back on the floor close to me and it took all my will not to move away.

Irfan stood up next, his report clutched in his hand, but Al-Bhukara put a hand up for him to sit back down. 'We have had enough excitement for one day, I think. Besides, I have a long drive to Luton today. We will reconvene on Thursday. Amirah, will you please brief Javid on the correct procedure when entering this house?'

*

I did not remember reaching into my pocket and taking out my cigarettes, but somehow one had made its way into my mouth and I was puffing away angrily at it with huge draws. Angry at what I had just heard and so fucking angry that Parvez was involved. Through the smoke I saw Amirah leave the house and stomp towards me. She didn't look too pleased. I couldn't care less, especially after witnessing this *place*, this hole of evil, that she had invited me to. I wanted to scream and shout at her, show her that I could stomp too. But I had to keep it together and make sure that I did everything in my power to shut this wicked place down.

I eased up on the cigarette and leaned against the car, crossing my legs at my ankles, and slowly relaxed my contorted features.

'Well. That was interesting,' I said.

'Are you out your bloody mind?'

'What did I do now?'

'One, you turn up almost twenty minutes late. Two, you ring the doorbell. Three, you walk around the room, chatting like it's a fucking social club.'

'Whoa. Hang on a minute, lady. I didn't know that. You didn't tell me about not ringing the bell. How the hell else am I supposed to make my presence known?'

'What did I say to you?' she spat, her anger rising a notch.

'You, um, you said to me, that... I don't actually know what you said to me.'

'Simple instruction, Jay. You couldn't follow one simple instruction. I said to *call me* if you are interested.'

'I'm sorry, truly. I didn't realise.' I *did* realise. My intention had been to catch them on the hop so I had something to bring to the table. As it turned out I didn't need to – it had fallen into my lap.

'Idiot,' she said, with a little less malice, a little less spite.

'Wanna lift somewhere?' I said, grinning.

Amirah sighed and jumped in the passenger seat of my Nova. I flicked my cigarette to the ground and got in too. I started my car and glanced sideways at her. The angry red in her face was disappearing as she took off her headscarf and let her locks loose. I couldn't help but think: *How could somebody so beautiful be involved in something so ugly?*

42

The ride to Amirah's place was filled with her voice. I barely spoke but I took it all in. She told me things about Al-Bhukara, things that I guess he, himself, wanted me to hear. They were very complimentary and painted him to be quite the freedom fighter.

After I had dropped her off, I texted Parker and requested that he call me. My phone rang within a minute and I pulled up in Tesco's car park and answered.

'How's it going, son?' That word and that voice, now all too familiar to me.

'Yeah, it's going all right. You?'

'What have you got for me?' he asked, never one for small talk.

'It's about number fifteen Jersey Way. I think I was right. There's all kinds of crazy taking place down there.' I waited for him to respond, to prompt me, ask me a leading question. He didn't.

'Hello, Parker?'

'I'm still here.'

'Oh, right... So, yeah, I'm in. I went to my first class today. It was bizarre, man. There were six of us plus the Imam. Check this, one of the students stood up, as cool as you like, and he spoke about how the Boston Marathon bombing could have been carried out with more efficiency. He said that the planning should have been better and the death toll should have been higher. He wrote a *fucking* report on it. He's going to email it to me to assess. I couldn't believe my ears. I was *freaking* out in there... But I kept my cool,' I added quickly.

'Okay, that's good, Jay. You did well.'

180

'Once I get that email through, I'll send it out to you and we can shut these bastards down, right?'

'It's not enough, we need more. A report, no matter how inflammatory, will not be enough to question and charge them. If it was a document about a forthcoming attack, with logistics, dates and personnel, then that would be a different prospect. However, I suspect that these guys are too careful to put something like that up on the airwaves.'

'So, what now? I mean, it's fairly obvious something very wrong is up. Can we at least keep tabs on them? Like, I don't know, bug the house or something?'

'We are keeping tabs on them.'

'Yeah? How?'

'You are.'

'I am what?'

'You, Jay, are keeping tabs; *you* are our eyes and ears.'

'Yeah… I guess,' I said. I felt a little dejected and I suddenly had an overwhelming feeling of what I was involved in, and what I had become. I stared out into Tesco's car park, watching shoppers walk in and out. Normal mundane chores seemed like a little piece of heaven. Just the thought of going back to that house and listening to that crap made me sick, and for the first time since this all began, I yearned for my old nickel-and-dime bullshit life.

But I couldn't go back, couldn't walk away. I may have just been some token Paki drafted in by MI5 to infiltrate other Pakis, but I was using my initiative and making things happen. I was in, I had made a breakthrough, all of my own doing. If it were up to Parker, I would still be wasting my time at the mosque rooting through suspicious beards. I like to think I was surprising them; I sure as hell was surprising myself.

It had been my idea to investigate that house and I was going to see it through.

'Tell me about the Imam,' Parker asked.

'His name is Adeel-Al-Bhukara. Um… Lives with his wife Aaidah. He has another wife in Bradford.' I tried to remember all that Amirah had told me in the car. 'Um… What else? Yeah, he has a limp, walks with the aid of a walking stick; apparently he was once battered by some white guys with baseball bats whilst trying to protect an attack on a young Muslim mother.'

181

Silence on the line. Do I carry on? Is he still there or had he dozed off? Then, after an extended beat, Parker said, 'Adeel-Al-Bhukara?'

'Yeah... You know of him?'

'I'm going to send you a photograph right now and I want you to confirm if it is the same person.'

There was some rustling around from his end. I put my phone on loud speaker, placed it on my lap and waited for the message to appear. I looked out through the windscreen just as Idris walked out of Tesco with a girl. He was all smiles as he carried a crate of beer, not a care in the world. New job, new friends. Old friends forgotten. I watched as he said something to her and she punched him playfully on the arm, and he pretended to almost drop the crate. They were approaching my direction and it was just fucking inevitable that I had parked my car next to theirs. Still a few metres away from my car, I considered ducking down in my seat, but I stood my ground. There was no way he would not recognise my car, the faded paint work, the number plate, the car where we'd sat so many times, chatting about everything and nothing.

It was obvious that there was going to be an interaction, even if it was studiously ignoring each other. I noticed him slow down a beat as he clocked my car, and I could see in his face that he was hoping desperately that it was unoccupied. Then there he was, walking past my car, right in front of me. The girl was chatting away merrily to him, oblivious to history.

Our eyes met. He offered me a canned smile and I returned it with a barely there nod. Maybe he noticed it, maybe he didn't. Maybe I didn't give a fuck.

But I did.

He turned away, but I kept my eyes fixed on him and, as soppy as this is going to sound, my heart broke a bit. I wanted desperately to get out and tell him everything. That like him, I was doing something worthwhile. He would have been so fucking proud.

They pulled away without another look and I turned my attention back to my phone.

I could still hear Parker rustling around, mixed with some incoherent mumbling and a few frustrated expletives. Eventually the message came through.

I quickly opened up the photo and there was no mistake as to who I was looking at. His body was partially covered by a huge rock and he was looking through the crosshairs of a rifle.

'That's him,' I said.

'Can you confirm?'

I just did!

'Yes, I confirm, that is Al-Bhukara, the same person I sat in front of today.'

'Interesting. That's very interesting.'

'Why is that interesting? How come you have a photo of him?'

'He has been on our radar since 2004.'

'Shit! No fucking way! How? *Why?*'

'In 2003, Al-Bhukara was partly involved in organising a bombing in Indonesia. They targeted churches across five cities. Eighteen killed.'

My hands clammed up, my heartbeat increased. I was in the same room as this guy just a minute ago. 'So why is he not in some hole in Guantanamo Bay or wherever it is you take them?'

'Let's meet. It's about time I told you about The Teacher.'

'The Teacher?'

'Same place as last time. Do you know how to get there?'

'The garage?'

'Yes. Do you know how to get there?'

'Um… Yeah. I think.'

'Tomorrow at ten hundred hours… Ten a.m.'

'Yeah, I know what ten hundred hours means,' I said, annoyed at his half-arsed explanation. But he had ended the call and I was speaking to dead air.

Every time I spoke with Parker, my life changed. And now it transpired that I had been in the company of a bona-fide terrorist. He had a past, he had his hand in an atrocity that I remember reading about and discussing with customers over a joint. Now I was acting undercover as his student, under orders from MI5.

What the fuck? I mean… What the *fuck?*

It wasn't that long ago that me and Mum were lounging around at home in tracksuits and odd socks, watching reruns of *Catchphrase* whilst drinking masala chai. My biggest problem then was… I don't know. I don't think I *had* a problem. But this…!

And as that thought cruised around in my head, the floodgates opened. It could have gone one of two ways.

I laughed.

First quietly to myself, nothing more than a reflective snigger, expelling air from my nose.

MI5!

A small snot bubble appeared and popped, and that only served to make me laugh some more.

The Teacher! What kind of dumb name is that?

It continued to grow louder and harder, my mouth wide open, cackling like a mentalist.

Undercover! Me?

As it reached a crescendo, I slapped the steering wheel. It must have been infectious as passers-by were watching me and laughing along.

They had no idea…

Eventually it died down and I wiped the tears from my eyes. I stepped out of my car and walked towards Tesco. I decided that whilst I was there I might as well buy some bread and milk, and that thought nearly set me off again.

It was time for a touch of much-needed normality.

43

'The Teacher,' Parker said. 'We don't know much about him.'

We were back inside the grimy garage, but with less grime. It had been tidied. Doors that had hung loose from the cabinets now tightened. The topless newspaper girls had been removed. The mannequin was dressed and stood modestly in the corner. I still wasn't quite sure the purpose of it. A shiny new kettle sat next to an unopened box of teabags. The table, clean. The floor, swept. Cheap air freshener lingered. Parker had walked around the room, nodding to himself, satisfied at the changes. I think he had been a bit embarrassed by it the last time we were there, and as a result he seemed to have exerted some clout. And voila. Still a shithole.

'What *do* we know?' I asked. Then I realised what I had just said. *We.* My subconscious had come to terms with the fact that I was part of MI5, whilst the rest of me watched from the sidelines.

'The Teacher is the founder and leader of a terrorist group called Ghurfat-al-Mudarris.'

'I've not heard of it.' I shrugged. 'Should I have?'

'No, they don't broadcast their intentions via media outlets such as Al-Jazeera, like other cells have done in the past. Though, if one was to go looking for it, they have a fair presence online, particularly heavy on social media.'

'All right, what else? Does The Teacher have a name?'

'Not that we know. No name, no description. We know he moves around frequently, mainly in Afghanistan and occasionally in Pakistan. His moniker has often been bounced around on the airwaves; there are hundreds of websites dedicated to him. Myths, mostly unfounded and probably untrue. However, what we do believe to be true is that he started off as a suicide bomber.'

'Hang on. How do you *start off* as a suicide bomber? It's not like he can work his way up from—'

His giant hand was in front of my face, blocking my view of him. Indication clear: shut up for a minute and I'll explain.

'1996, Yemen. A CIA training exercise went tragically wrong. A UAV—'

'Sorry. A what?'

'Unmanned Aerial Vehicle.'

'Oh,' I said. '*A drone!*' My tone suggestive.

'Yes. A drone.' I could tell that he was already regretting telling me this. 'It... It lost control. There was an accident and it struck a barn.' He blinked at me. I sat back in my chair, crossed my arms and blinked right back at him. 'The UAV was in the initial testing process, being flown around a wide open space, fields, for miles.'

'Apart from the barn?'

A pause. Pregnant. Overdue. Emergency Caesarean!

Then a slow nod to confirm.

'The barn wasn't empty... Was it?' I asked. He didn't answer. He didn't have to.

Yeah. He really did regret telling me this little heart-warmer.

'Go on then,' I said. 'You going to tell me about this Teacher fella or what?'

'As a direct retaliation, two weeks later, an attack took place. Three-man operation, outside the US Embassy in Madrid. All three vests went off, killing twenty-six. Two of the bombers died instantly but somehow *he* – The Teacher – walked away.'

'How is that possible?' I asked.

'According to eye witnesses, he was standing on the roof of a pharmacy, directly opposite the embassy. The first two bombers had already detonated, one inside the embassy and one at the entrance. But he had waited. As you can imagine, it was pandemonium, a crowd had gathered just outside the pharmacy. Up on that roof, he had with him a male hostage, a guard. He had removed his explosive vest and secured it around the guard. Using the guard's body as a shield between himself and the vest, he reached around and detonated whilst simultaneously pushing the guard off the roof and into the crowd below.' Parker studied me for a reaction. 'You asked me how it was possible. Well...

I cannot answer that. Even if he had extended the cord to the detonator, the speed and ferocity of the detonation should have ripped through him. Burned him alive.'

'But he walked away?'

'He walked away.'

Unable to find a meaningful word to say, I simply nodded. It seemed to satisfy him and he continued.

'This is where the line between myth and fact are blurred,' he continued. 'It has been said that he caught the eye of Osama Bin Laden.' I had wondered when his name would pop up, making an already surreal situation all the more so. 'The Teacher, by then, already had a small but fierce following. Men who believed in his methods, men who believed like he believed. To our knowledge he was never part of Al-Qaeda, but there are direct links between the two. They share the same facilities and ideologies as Al-Qaeda. However, The Teacher's method of attack is vastly different, and it's due to that very method that he's managed to grow and recruit so rapidly.'

'He doesn't use suicide bombers,' I said. He nodded. Gold star for me.

'Car bombs, timers, multiple gun attacks, IED's. You name it. But not once has he sacrificed one of his own.'

Parker stood up, filled the kettle and flicked it on. We waited for it to boil in silence.

I was quite surprised that I wasn't freaking the fuck out. It wasn't every day that you discuss Al-Qaeda and Osama Bin Laden as part of your job. The first class with Al-Bhukara had me so agitated, so fucking angry at their casual disregard for human life, all for a cause that I still did not fully understand. Now, I felt remarkably calm, *focused*. Eager to play a part in bringing down Ghurfat-al-Mudarris.

'How is this related to me?' I asked, as the kettle stopped whistling. 'I mean, I think I know what you're saying. This Teacher character is our main target, right? But how does that involve me, exactly?'

'Going back to Al-Bhukara.' Parker handed me a mug of tea and sat down. 'As I was saying to you over the phone, he has been on our radar since 2004. He is known to be a trusted associate to The Teacher. He has travelled to Afghanistan and

Pakistan close to the times when the attacks we believe The Teacher oversaw took place.'

'Have you not been following Al-Bhukara? He could have led you straight to him.'

'Not that simple, son. We had eyes on him twice. Once in 2007 on the Afghan–Pakistani border, and the last sighting to date was in 2011, in Islamabad.'

'Couldn't you have detained him?'

'We did… once. He didn't talk and we had nothing of substance on him. We leaned on him but it was clear that he had been trained and he played the game well. We had to let him go. After that he went dark.'

'Until I saw him yesterday.'

44

The drone attack and The Teacher were all that I could think about, even though Holly Willoughby was squirming on the *This Morning* sofa, wearing a tight, red dress, which in turn had men all over the country squirming on *their* sofas. I picked up the remote and absently channel-hopped, not stopping on any station long enough to determine whether it deserved my attention. I had new information fed to me by Parker, which I understood. But probably not in the same way he did.

I killed the noise of the television and rubbed my eyes with force, willing myself to go blind just for a minute. My phone buzzed and I removed my hands from my throbbing eyes.

A text message from Amirah.

> Before class later, we would like to welcome you to the group.
> Lunch today. 1pm. Ali's Diner. I know you know where that is. ;o)

Oh, leave me alone. Let me just have a day lounging around in my onesie. Be normal. Do normal things. Chores, even. I remembered that I needed to book in a service for my Nova as it was starting to misfire. A flickering light bulb in the hallway needed changing. I had to phone the insurance company and see if my policy covered stupidity damage, and then replace my television.

But, above all, I had a duty.

I picked up my phone and replied.

> Hey, Amirah. Sounds good. I'll be there. :o)

So much for *normal*.

*

I pulled up outside Ali's Diner at one on the nose. In fact, I had cruised past ten minutes earlier just to scope, make sure there was nothing untoward. The two brothers, Yasir and Irfan, were there already, sat at a round table. They had in front of them two tall multi-coloured milkshakes – it was hard to guess what flavour, maybe a mix of chocolate and vanilla topped with hundreds and thousands. Here's the thing with most Muslims who don't drink alcohol: they have to get creative in order to enjoy drinking in a social environment. An orange juice or lemonade would just not suffice.

I nodded my hello at them and they both nodded back simultaneously. They were the only two of the group who I didn't know very well. So we just avoided eye contact and made small talk, trying to get the awkwardness out of the way.

I ordered myself a cup of masala chai, knowing that as soon as I put my lips to it I would be comparing it negatively to the way Mum made it.

'I emailed the report to you, Brother Javid,' Yasir said. 'Did you read it?'

Yeah, I read it, you sick, twisted fuck.

'No.' I smiled. 'I will tonight... And please, you can call me Jay.'

'There is nothing wrong with your birth name,' Irfan piped up.

'Did I say there was?' I hissed at him.

Yasir discreetly elbowed his brother in the ribs as the bell sounded and the diner's door opened. In walked Amirah, with Kevin trailing close behind. The Brothers Grimm and I gave a sigh of relief at the much-needed addition. Kevin shook hands heartily all around and Amirah nodded coolly. I stood up and let her slide in, and quickly sat next to her before Kevin nabbed my place. He noticed what I was doing and smiled encouragingly as he took his place at the other end of the group, next to Irfan.

'No Parvez?' I asked.

'Running late. He had to... well, he's just running late,' Kevin replied.

'Oh, okay,' I said, not pushing for an explanation. I preferred it without him there. It was hard to play a role when someone knows you the way Parvez knew me.

They ordered – two sweet mango lassis and one pistachio kulfi with extra sprinkles of pistachio. Kevin stood up and raised his glass. 'I hope and I think I speak for all of the group when I say that we are delighted, just delighted to have you on board. Welcome, Jay. May your presence help us with our achievement.'

'*Inshallah*,' the table rang out, but not as enthusiastically as Kevin would have liked. He sat back down, smiled through a frown and addressed the lack of enthusiasm.

'Look,' Kevin started. 'We all come from different walks of life, yes? I know that better than anybody. And some of us here are a bit bemused by the way that Jay has been chosen.' Irfan shifted uncomfortably in his chair. 'It's not the way the Imam operates.' He turned to me. 'You see, Jay, we have all, one way or another, had to prove ourselves to the great man.'

'So have I,' I said defensively.

'Yes, you have. We are not saying any different. We know all about your bravery against the Kafirs. But more importantly it's your transition; you went from being a drug-dealing, alcohol-consuming lost soul, to a devout. That, my Brother, impressed,' he said, waving a finger in the air.

Parvez was standing over us. Nobody had noticed him enter, due to Kevin holding court.

'Salaam,' Parvez said moodily, and considered where he should place himself before sitting down next to Kevin, which made him directly in my eyeline. The side of his face was covered in black smudges.

'We were just talking about—' Kevin said.

'I heard,' Parvez snipped.

'You all right, Brother?' Yasir enquired.

Amirah spoke up. 'Whatever your problem is, leave it at the door. You've been a proper moody git recently.'

He ignored them both and concentrated on picking black muck out of his fingernails.

'Cheer up, mate,' I said, as a friend. 'What's that black stuff all over your hands and face?'

'It's nothing,' he said churlishly, whilst wiping the wrong side of his face.

'Come on, man. Something's wrong. What's up?'

'You! You're *what's up*!'

'Brother, this is not appropriate behaviour,' Kevin said. 'If you have a problem with Jay, we would all like to hear it.'

'He shouldn't be here,' Parvez said. 'He's not one of us.'

'If Imam believes he is good enough,' Amirah said, visibly bored of Parvez's whining, 'then that's good enough for me.'

'He is wrong this time,' Parvez countered. 'I've known Jay a long time and I know exactly what he is like, what his character is. Just because he started to attend the Masjid more often, it doesn't mean that he is one of us... Being Muslim is not enough. You need will and strength, and I am sorry, but he has neither.'

There was an uncomfortable silence as Parvez and Amirah eyed each other. Kevin broke it.

'Things change, *people* change,' he said, as if he had just coined the phrase. Yasir and Irfan, desperate not to get involved, stared at their milkshakes as if it could offer an escape route. Amirah tutted her annoyance loudly, just in case anybody wasn't aware of her obvious disdain. Kevin just smiled passively, to no one in particular.

Parvez got up and headed for the toilet.

'Jesus,' I said, and every eye shot towards me at my choice of words. 'What's his problem?'

'I understand what he's saying,' Irfan muttered from behind his milkshake. 'No offence to you, Javid. Sorry, *Jay*. We have all had to go through a process before we had the honour to sit and learn from Adeel-Al-Bhukara. He didn't request us the way he requested you. It's just strange.'

'What? What's strange?' I asked.

Irfan looked around at the others before he stopped at me. 'How much the Imam wants you.'

I let out a dismissive sigh, but I knew he was right. Parvez was right. Al-Bhukara didn't seem to be the type of man who would seek out somebody without good reason. From what I had heard he had hundreds vying for his attention. But he chose me. Insisted on it!

'And you want to know what else is a bit strange?' Yasir said, taking over from his Brother. 'He made me read out my report out loud, right in front of you. That suggests a very high level of trust in you, to let you hear straight off the bat what we are about. That kind of privilege has to be earned with time. How did he know how you would react?'

I nodded thoughtfully. All this attention was making my head spin. I knocked back my masala chai – it was nowhere near as good as Mum's – and stood up. I was done here. I said my goodbyes to everyone. Kevin's face fell. I think he was expecting a hearty gathering, where we all promised to stand tall, shoulder to shoulder, and take on the world. He stood up too and put an arm around me.

'Tell Parvez that...' I began. 'Tell him what you like, I couldn't care less. I'll see you in class.'

'Brother Parvez is just stressed out, is all. The reason he was late today was because the Imam punished him.'

'Punished him for what?' I asked.

'He dared to question him in class.'

'About me?'

Kevin nodded. 'The Imam does not like to be questioned.'

'What was the punishment?'

'He made him clear out his garage, mow his lawn and change a flat on his car.'

'That's harsh,' I said, wanting to say more. A lot more.

'Harsh? No. It builds character, Jay. It makes a Brother stronger.'

I nodded at him, appeased, but I was fuming inside at that fucking Al-Bhukara for throwing his weight around, and at Parvez for actually carrying it out. I shrugged his arm off my shoulder as politely as I could and he sat back down.

I walked away, crossing paths with Parvez, who had just walked out of the toilet. The dirt had been cleaned off his face. I stood in his way as he tried to walk past me back to the table. He looked up at me with red eyes and I stepped forward and surprised myself by embracing him tightly. It wasn't reciprocated. His hands hung down by his side. I don't know what it was about that fucking guy, but I had always felt protective over him. I clutched the back of his shirt as my embrace tightened and I whispered in his ear.

'I won't let you down, Parvez... I promise you. I won't let you down.'

He nodded in my chest and I let him go.

45

Three Months Later

Kafirs. Everywhere I look. Polluting my air with their dirty looks and deceiving thoughts. I see them now for what they are. What they always were. Bullies, oppressors, cowards. Making life hell for my Brothers and Sisters. Sat in their homes, using social media to reveal their true feelings, behind the safety of their keyboards, blindly spewing hatred towards my Deen, my religion. And for those who are brave enough to step to us, they do it in packs, and they do it to the weak, the elderly, the young, the women. Or they attack us with their billions of pounds worth of high-tech military hardware, and they dare do it in *our* land.

They do it because they are scared of us.

They fucking should be.

The Imam, the radicalised Imam Adeel-Al-Bhukara, was honourable in his words and in his teachings. He had taught me about life, about my life. The lies and the poison clear. Newsreaders, producers, journalists, scholars, experts, teachers, politicians, writers, actors, musicians, directors, all had a part to play. All had a share of the blame. You do and I do. Words are read and understood as gospel. For every atrocity, the word MUSLIM is emblazoned on the front of every newspaper and beamed on every channel. Mo Farah wins the gold medal at the Olympics and that word is replaced by BRITISH.

His words made me think. At times they made me angry. It wasn't hard to imagine how young Muslims could be so easily coerced, so easily brainwashed.

Al-Bhukara treated me like one of his own. It was clear to the rest of the group that we shared a connection. He would invite me to dinner once a week; his wife, Aunty Aaidah, would phone me the day before and insist that I request a meal of my choice.

Those last three months had been a life lesson. I grew close to my Brothers, Yasir, Irfan and Kevin. Amirah, well, she would never say, but there was something happening. A look, a smile, bodies brushing for a fraction of a second.

Then there was Parvez.

Our relationship, not quite strained, wasn't the same as it once had been. Gone was the annoying agitator. Replaced by a Paki I did not recognise, quiet, determined, focused.

On a mission.

*

I had completed a five-mile run, my eyes open, seeing everything. I felt strong. My mind sharp. The words of the Imam ringing in my head. *Allah gave you a tool, a vessel. It is your duty to keep it conditioned.* It had become a daily routine: a fruit breakfast followed by pounding the pavements of Hounslow.

I decided to warm down and walk the last mile to the alleyway behind Lampton Park where I was due to meet Parvez. We were going to attend Zohar prayers together at Sutton mosque. It was my idea. I had spent the best part of the last few months trying to convince a still-sceptical Parvez that I had the right to walk beside him. He wasn't suspicious about my intentions, he just didn't think I had it in me. He still saw me as Jay the fuck-about, the Jay that he had grown up with.

I slipped my headphones off as I reached the alleyway. I was a little early so, using the wall for support, I killed time stretching out cramp from my legs. From the corner of my eye I saw a young couple approaching. I recognised the girl, she lived a few streets away from me. Her name was Sabina or Saara, I couldn't quite remember. It was one of those white-sounding Paki names that parents like to call their kids so they don't get picked on at school. She was strolling without a care in the world with a skinny white boy. Hands entwined like they were ready to take on the world together.

I checked the time and grimaced. It was bang on twelve. I hoped hard that the ever-punctual Parvez would be running late.

But no. There he was.

Turning into the alley, a stone's throw behind the couple, and I knew he was looking at exactly what I was. *A Sister*, short skirt, bare legs, hand in hand with a Kafir. I couldn't make out his features, but I could just picture his face, eyebrows painfully narrowed and deep frown lines on his forehead. He would have been fucking livid.

I was going to let them pass, I *should* have let them pass, but I saw an opportunity to prove myself to him.

I cursed under my breath and sprung myself off the wall as love's young dream neared, all smiles and sweet talk, probably off to Lampton Park to eat each other's faces.

'Wotcha, Jay,' she said, smiling broadly.

I positioned myself so that my back was to Parvez. I didn't want him to know that I had clocked him.

I looked her up and down, all seventeen years of her. And then I looked down between them at their linked hands, before my eyes travelled to his. The look on my face made him immediately liberate his hand from hers. She looked at him disappointedly.

'This is Casey. Casey, this is Jay.'

He nervously snaked his hand out towards me, looking for a shake. He didn't get one. They looked at each other, embarrassed, the shift in dynamic obvious to all.

'We should go, Saara,' he said. 'We're going to be late.'

'What's your problem, Jay?' she said. 'Why you acting like a dickhead?'

I remembered her being such a sweet girl. It looked as though she had developed quite the feisty side. She grabbed Casey's hand tightly and lifted her chin up at me as a show of defiance.

'Why aren't you at school?' I said, like an overbearing big brother.

'Why don't you mind your own business, Jay? You obviously have a problem with this,' she said, lifting up her linked hand and taking his along for the ride.

'What happened to you, Saara? You used to be a bright girl. Why are you hanging around with Kafirs for?'

'Since when did you start using words like Kafir? Never mind what happened to me. What happened to *you*? Oh, I get it: you've joined the God Squad. Well, good for you. I heard that you were hanging around with those guys. That's your decision. But don't you *dare* try and tell *me* what I can or cannot do.'

Behind me I knew Parvez was rubbernecking, and with adrenaline still coursing through me from my run, and in the absence of an intelligent response, I dropped down to street mentality.

'Does your mum know she's raising a fucking slapper?'

The words sickened me.

It was at that moment Casey decided to grow some balls. He moved forward between us and dared to look me in the eye. His jaw set tight, his fists balled. I stepped into his face, ready to get into it.

'I feel sorry for you, Jay,' she said, grabbing his arm and moving him away.

They walked away and I kicked a discarded coke can towards them.

'You feel sorry for me?' I snorted to myself.

Then I started yelling. 'Don't feel sorry for me, I'm fine. It's *you* I feel sorry for.' I was hopping around now, ranting, the sound of my voice bouncing off the narrow walls in the alley. Snippets of what she had said to me were at the forefront of my mind. 'I'll tell you what happened to me: I opened my fucking eyes, yeah? It's time you opened yours. You are destined for hell, yeah? You hear me, Sister? *Hell!*'

I felt Parvez squeeze my shoulder, his fingers circling deep under my collar bone, calming me the fuck down.

'It's okay, Brother,' he said. 'Don't waste your energy. We must pick our battles carefully.'

Breathing hard, I bent down and placed my hands on my knees. I closed my eyes tightly and tried to justify my actions. I inhaled through my nose and exhaled deeply through my mouth. My temper calmed and my breathing relaxed, and with a clear mind I thought: *What the fuck have I become?*

46

Parker sat opposite me and stared. Those dead eyes that used to scare me no longer had that effect. I saw them for what they were. Dead. I stared back at him with my own glare, one that had hardened over time.

'You missed our last meeting,' he said.

'I was busy, man,' I said. 'Besides, I had nothing to report last week.'

'You haven't been answering your phone or texts.'

'You're starting to sound like a girl I used to go out with.'

Parker slowly nodded, a hint of disappointment in those dead eyes.

'Look, I told you, if there is anything worthwhile to report, I'll call you.'

'I'll decide whether or not your information is pertinent. From here on you turn up to meetings, you answer your phone and you respond to texts.'

'Call this a meeting?' I mumbled under my breath, as I looked around the same shitty garage we had been meeting at since it all started.

'Is everything all right with you, son?'

It had started to grate on me, that word. I'd found out recently that Parker had a family somewhere, a wife and children. Family that he did not see anymore, or, more accurately, family that did not want to see him anymore. So I'd let him get away with calling me son, but it had started to make me feel uncomfortable. He wasn't my dad, he wasn't my father figure.

'Everything is fine,' I said, dropping my eyes.

'Have you spoken to your... mother recently?'

'Yeah, spoke to her a couple of days ago.'

'And?'

'And what?' I said. 'What has that got to do with anything? What has that got to do with you?'

To his credit, he didn't rise to my outburst, which I regretted as soon as it flew out of my mouth. It wasn't my intention to be difficult but I was aware how I was coming across. I had a job, I know, a fucking duty, but it was becoming increasingly difficult. I was getting *too* close to them. In and out of class, bonding, forming *real* relationships, the environment *too* suffocating that it was squeezing the life out of me, and then coming here and unloading all that I was entrusted with. The Imam's words, at times, justifiable, making me realise, at times, that my duty as a Muslim was above and beyond my duty for anything else, but at other times, I knew... I knew what I had to do.

I stood up and boiled the kettle. I didn't offer Parker a drink but made one for him anyway.

'Sorry,' I mumbled as I handed him his coffee. 'I've just been a bit stressed out.'

He nodded his appreciation at the gesture.

'I was away,' I said. 'That's why I missed our last meeting.'

'Oh?' He waited for me to elaborate.

'I only got back yesterday.'

'Where did you go and who were you with?'

'Kevin Strauss and Al-Bukhara. Luton, Coventry and Bradford. I wasn't expecting to go away, it was a last-minute thing. That's why I couldn't get in touch. Whilst we were away, we stayed together, pretty much throughout. It would have been too risky to call you.'

'Okay, Jay. Tell me about this trip.'

'Three meetings in three cities. The first was in Luton, in what seemed like an unoccupied house. The second was in Bradford, sat in the back of a dark blue transit van in the middle of a forest. The third in Coventry, in an aeroplane hangar. This was, apparently, the most productive of the three. So much so that they arranged another meeting for the following night, at the same location. At that point money was exchanged.'

'Exchanged for...?' Parker asked.

'For guns,' I said. 'Ten sawn-off AK-47s. Ten Glock 19s. Clean, never fired. Boxes and boxes of ammo, I couldn't tell you how much, but more than necessary for a neighbourly dispute.'

'Sawn-off?'

'Yeah, around this size.' I spread my hands to indicate around eighteen inches.

Parker hmm'd and nodded and scratched his face. That particular information seemed to get him ticking.

'What is it?' I asked. 'The sawn-off?'

'Yes,' he said. 'A sawn-off is easy to conceal. It has no sight or stock. It's cut for close quarters, close destruction.'

'So, what? A public place. In amongst the crowd. A shopping mall, possibly.'

'Possibly... There are six of you in your class, right?'

'Seven if you count the Imam.'

'No, he wouldn't get his hands dirty. Any mention of location?'

I shook my head. 'No. And I didn't ask him. Al-Bhukara does not like to be questioned. But... on the trip back to London he was, I don't know... loose, relaxed. As though another piece of the puzzle had been placed. He spoke freely and openly, but it was like a riddle, it didn't make complete sense. But the intention was clear.'

'What did he say?'

I sat back in my chair, took a sip of my coffee, taking my time over what I was to reveal. I'd taken a risk: I had a recording on my phone, which if the Imam ever decided to carry out a random check, I would have been dealt with viciously and without question. But the risk was calculated; the way Al-Bhukara treated me, the respect and something close to love that he heaped on me, I didn't think that he would have ever checked my phone.

I selected the voice recorder app on my phone, placed it on the table and pressed play. Al-Bhukara's voice filled the room.

'Make no mistake, my young Brothers. Qayamat is coming. Judgement Day is almost upon us. The day of reckoning, the day when we must answer. It has been prophesised, written fourteen hundred years ago. Look around you and you will see the truth. Look around you and you will see the signs.

'Women are naked in spite of being fully dressed. Earthquakes have increased. The distance on Earth has become short. People are competing in constructing the tallest of buildings. Women lie with women and men lie with men. Trust is used to make a profit. Leaders of men cannot be trusted. Power and authority is in the wrong hands. The nations of Earth gather against the Muslims.

'*The predictions are coming true before our very eyes. We are duty-bound to be ready for Judgement Day. We must be prepared, stand our ground and give ourselves wholly to the Cause.*

'*No longer are we in a position to ignore these signs. We see them always in our everyday lives, we read about them and talk about them and we brush them off. No more. We refuse to be blinded by the sinners. We refuse to share the same oxygen as a man who speaks ill of us. A man who supports a war that only leads to the devastation and destruction of Muslims in every corner of the world. We are a hunted species no longer. Mark my words, Brothers.*

'*There will be much murder and killing.*'

47

Despite the high winds, I drove with my window down. I hadn't been sleeping too well and the biting air hitting my face helped me stay focused as I drove. I clocked myself in the rear-view mirror; tired as fucking hell stared back at me. The dark circles under my eyes had deepened and my stubble was days away from being a fully fledged beard. Mum would have been horrified. I had been speaking to her, or lying to her, once a week. She seemed so happy in her new life with Andrew, scoring herself a part-time job as a hotel receptionist, whilst Andrew was excelling at his job, teaching English at a local school. Yeah, man, she was pretty happy, especially happy with the lies I was feeding her about how fucking happy I was. She thought I had an office job! She thought I was in a steady relationship! I could hear in her voice how proud she was of herself that she had finally raised her boy into a man.

Yeah, I was a man all right. Just not the man that she had hoped for.

It had just turned half eleven, the threat of that fucked-up, sideways, windy rain looming. We had been summoned to the house for midnight. Al-Bhukara didn't give anything away apart from the time and date. I was close, and I was early by thirty minutes, so I parked my Nova near number fifteen and strolled down to the nearest Costcutters. A black Lexus slowly crept past me and away into the night. It was the same car that I'd seen on two other occasions over the last few weeks, once cruising menacingly down my road. I had a feeling who it was, and who had sent it. A typical Silas move, aimed to intimidate. It was obvious that he would by now have cottoned on to the fact that it was me who was responsible for him being locked up, and he was keen to illustrate his power from behind bars by sending the shivers up me. Even behind the tint on the windscreen, I knew it was probably Staples at the wheel, but even he wasn't dumb enough to try anything with so much heat around Silas and his crew. So I let them have their moment, not giving it too much thought.

I walked into Costcutters and picked up a bottle of water, a black coffee and some cigarettes. I still had around twenty minutes to kill so I decided to just walk from aisle to aisle, killing time. I spotted Parvez in the magazine section, engrossed in a movie magazine. Arnie on the front cover announcing that *he was back!* I slowed my pace and watched Parvez with interest. It was weird seeing somebody who was so against the West, reading something that embodied everything that the West was about.

He turned towards me and quickly placed the magazine back on the shelf, as though I had just caught him reading *Playboy*.

'Salaam, Brother,' he said.

'Walaikum-Salaam,' I said.

'You're early too.'

'Yeah.' I nodded. 'I'm going out for a smoke.'

'I'll join you, Brother.'

We stepped out and leaned against the wall at the side of the shop. I slipped out a cigarette and had some difficulty lighting it due to the wind. We waited for the clock to tick down in bouts of silence punctuated by the odd dialogue.

'You ever smoked, Parvez?' I asked.

'Yes,' he chuckled. 'Do you not remember? With you at your place, years back. We both had our heads out of your bedroom window.'

'Oh, man. Yeah, I remember,' I said, laughing at the memory. 'That's when your mum walked past and you crapped yourself.'

'That was the first and last time, Brother. Mum would have killed me.'

'You were convinced that she saw you. You were too scared to go home.'

'Petrified, Brother... Petrified.'

The chuckles died down and we were left with that stupid grin one wears on their face in the afterglow of laughter.

'I saw your mate,' Parvez said. 'Brother Idris. The policeman.'

'Yeah?' I said casually, wanting to ask more but not allowing myself to.

'He's doing well.'

'That's Idris. Always lands on his feet.'

'What happened between you? You two were like real Brothers.'

I shrugged, more to myself, and threw my cigarette down. 'We just drifted, you know. He's doing his own thing, and I'm doing mine.'

'Do you miss him?'

Like I've lost my right arm.

'What kind of a girly question is that? Course I don't miss him. We just drifted... Besides, I now got you to irritate me.'

'Do I irritate you?' he said, as if it was news to him.

'You're all right, Parvez,' I said, sidestepping the question. 'I've got a lot of time for you.' I smiled at him. 'Come on. Let's walk down.'

We walked at a snail's pace, despite the first signs of rain. 'Do you have any idea why the Imam requested us to meet tonight?' I asked.

'Yes, Brother, I do.'

'Well... Are you going to tell me?'

'You are going to find out very soon, but I don't think that it will concern you personally too much. I think you have only been invited to observe.'

'What does *that* mean?'

'Look, Jay. I stopped questioning the Imam's motives a long time ago. It was strange the way he demanded your presence a few months back, it's strange how he never raises an eyebrow at you, and it's particularly strange that he wants you here tonight. You have only been with us for a few months but he treats you as though you hold the same experience as the rest of the group.'

'Yeah, you've made your feelings clear about that already, Parvez,' I said, biting back my intended reply. 'But what's that got to do with tonight?'

He stopped in his tracks; the house was in view. We both looked at it and then at each other as the rain suddenly quickened and bounced off our heads.

'Don't you see?' he said, raising his voice, willing to be heard over the heavy downpour. 'This is what we have been waiting for, working towards for many months. Years.'

'What?' I said. I think I may have shouted. I wiped the rain off my face and it was replaced a second later. 'What have you been waiting for?'

'The final part of our education... For tonight we will be chosen.'

48

The electricity had gone out, due to the extreme weather, I guess. We were sat upstairs at number fifteen, surrounded by candles. The rain tried and failed to smash through the window and dampen their spirits. I felt left out, the only one in the room unaware of what was about to take place. The Imam was nowhere to be seen, but that in itself was expected; we all knew he liked to make an entrance.

Irfan and Yasir were at the window, counting down the seconds between the thunder and the lightning. Kevin was placing more candles around the room, and Parvez was just plain excited, rocking back and forth on the floor. Amirah was stealing glances at me and, when caught, a smile would play on her lips.

A flash of lightning brightened up the room for a heartbeat.

'That was four seconds this time,' Irfan bellowed excitedly. 'It's getting closer.'

'It's a sign from Allah,' Kevin said, but didn't go on to explain what the sign indicated.

'Get used to electricity cuts, guys,' Yasir said.

Everyone laughed along, apart from me. I didn't understand.

Another flash of lightning, followed by exaggerated screams and screeches. Whilst all attention was at the window, Al-Bhukara had walked into the room, Aunty Aaidah trailing behind holding a tray full of ladoos.

'Brothers,' he announced. 'And Sister.' He smiled. We all took our places on the floor in front of him as he got comfortable in his chair. Aunty Aaidah stood respectfully behind him. He had with him a brown envelope, which he placed on the side table.

'Many of you already know why you have been called upon,' he started.

'*Ameen*,' the room chanted back at him, followed by a monstrous roar of thunder.

'The final part of your education is upon us,' he continued. '*He* who gives will receive.'

'*Ameen*.' Louder.

I had no idea what the hell was going on; Al-Bhukara was talking in riddles again. I remembered what Parvez had said to me outside: I was there just to observe. So I mentally took myself out of the surroundings and watched it unfold.

'We have been here before but never again. For today you and I will go our separate ways. But always remember your names will forever be on my lips in prayer.'

'*Inshallah*.'

Al-Bhukara picked up the brown envelope and took out some documents.

'Yasir Ahmad,' he called.

Yasir stood up, walked to the Imam and collected his document.

'*Mashallah*,' boomed the room.

He looked humbled as Aunty Aaidah sweetened his mouth with a ladoo. He didn't take his place back on the floor.

'Irfan Ahmad.'

Irfan stood up, and I could see his hand visibly shaking as he collected his document and a ladoo.

'*Mashallah*.'

He stood proudly next to his brother. One by one, they were all called upon and handed a document and had their mouth stuffed and sweetened by Aunty Aaidah. They all looked like they had graduated, and in a way I guess they had. I was the only one left, feeling more than awkward by myself on the floor. Al-Bhukara looked at me, enjoying the confusion on my face.

'You see, young Javid, over the course of two years I have imparted all I can to your fellow students. I have seen them grow like flowers from concrete, and it has been a privilege and an honour.'

I nodded as if I understood, but I was desperate to know what the document was.

'But you, Javid...' He paused, toying with me. 'Eyebrows were raised, questions were asked. My decision challenged.

But in the last three months you have proved to be quite the student. Surpassing even my expectations, you have something that cannot be taught. You, Javid, have the heart of a warrior. So with that, I would like to call upon you... Javid Qasim.'

I looked up at Amirah and she motioned for me to get up. I approached Al-Bhukara and he handed me a document. I didn't get a chance to read it as a ladoo was being forced down my throat. I walked past the line of the others, who patted me on the back, apart from Parvez, who just looked at me with a face I could not discern. I stood at the end of the line and looked down at the document in my hands.

It was an E-ticket. A plane ticket.

Destination: Islamabad.

49

I texted Parker requesting an emergency meeting, and waited patiently for a reply for all of sixty seconds before calling him. He picked up straight away.

'I was just replying to your text,' he said, sounding alert despite it being past three in the morning.

'I need to see you, man,' I said, quick and desperate. 'I need to fucking see you, now.'

'Tell me where you are.'

'I'm... I'm at home. I just got in.'

'What's happened?'

'They want me to go to Islamabad. *Next week*. They want me to go to a training camp. In Islamabad, man. In *Islamabad*.'

'In Islamabad?'

No, in fucking Disneyland.

'Yeah, Parker,' I said wearily. 'In Islamabad.'

'I am going to have to inform Sinclair and work out the best move going forward.'

'Now?'

'Sorry?'

'Are you going to chat to Sinclair *now*?'

'First thing tomorrow, okay.'

'No, Parker, not okay. Not even close to okay. I am freaking out here. I need to see you right now.'

'Look, you need to stay focused, son. We—'

'I'm not your fucking son,' I snapped.

Shit... Fuck... Why did I say that? Why did I fucking have to go and say that? I slumped down on my armchair and rubbed my temple. I could hear him breathing and I knew I had marked him. Our relationship, as awkward and dysfunctional as it was, had shifted towards slightly more awkward and dysfunctional. I felt so small for making him feel like however the hell he was feeling. I wanted to apologise, but I didn't want to address it. Because addressing it would have meant addressing how he doesn't see his son anymore, and addressing how no one has a fucking right to call me that.

I waited it out.

'You said next week, right?' Parker said, after what seemed like an eternity. His voice softer than I had ever heard it.

'Yeah,' I said, matching his tone. 'Next week.'

'Okay, Jay,' he said, and I felt my stomach twist. 'It's late. We cannot achieve anything at this hour. I advise that you get some rest. I will speak with Sinclair in the morning and we will meet soon after. Same location. I'll text you the time.'

I wanted to say something, anything, just to keep the conversation going until things were back to normal between us. But he had terminated the call.

*

After the Imam had handed us the tickets, Kevin had suggested that we celebrate, but we couldn't exactly rock up at restaurant chanting *Allah hu Akbar!* So instead we'd decided to take a drive. Six of us bundled uncomfortably into one car. We could easily have taken a second, but everybody seemed too excited to split up, like they all had to be together to share and rejoice, like they were not willing to lose each other, not even for a minute. I'd volunteered to drive just so that I could regain a modicum of control in a situation that was fast spiralling out of control.

Amirah was in the passenger seat next to me, my hand on the gearstick, her hand placed on top of mine. I slipped my hand away and placed it on the steering wheel. I noticed her visibly bristle as she looked questioningly at me. From behind, unable to contain their excitement, voices overlapped, their breath hot in my ear.

I found that they had all attended training camps before. *Parvez, you dark horse.* The Parvez I once knew was lost. I wasn't altogether shocked that he had attended. Just disappointed.

It was clear that this particular visit to the camp was going to lead to something huge. Something extraordinary. They all alluded to it without spelling it out. Kevin said shit like: 'Our time is coming' and 'It will be an historic event'. In fact, that specific word, *history*, kept popping up. 'Our names will go down in history' or 'We will write history'. Whatever the hell it was that they'd been talking about, it was going to wake up the world.

And Parvez was in the middle of it all.

50

I arrived at the garage first and let myself in. A Cisco conference phone had been placed in the middle of the table and I just knew that it was for my benefit. The garage door lifted and in walked a new face. A face that I knew could only belong to Major General Stewart Sinclair. Parker had told me little about him, but what little he did impart was full of praise. According to Parker, the Major General was a man to be respected, listened to and, most importantly in this game, trusted. He took two long strides forward, letting the garage door close behind him, and took in his surroundings.

'I never did like this bloody place,' he announced. 'But, it serves a purpose.'

'Yeah,' I said, taking in his stripes above the breast pocket of his military uniform. 'That's exactly what Parker said.'

'It's very nice to meet you, Jay… Can I call you Jay?'

'I insist on it, Major General.'

'I've been hearing some sterling things about you.'

I nodded, not knowing how else to take the compliment.

'What do you say to a cuppa?'

'I say, yes please.' I watched him line up four mugs and I wondered who else, apart from Parker, would arrive. Plus there was the conference phone, which made five. It seemed like this whole training-camp situation had made some very important people sit up and take notice.

The garage door lifted and, with heavy footsteps, in walked Parker.

'Ah, Parker. Good timing. I just made you a cuppa.'

Parker nodded his thanks and turned around to shut the garage door when a voice said, 'Hang on a tick, I'm coming in.'

Lawrence. Just as I had remembered him from our one and only meeting. Slicker than slick and confident with it. A ridiculously tight suit, which he somehow managed to pull off. He walked in, closed the door behind him and looked around.

'Nice,' he said, looking at Parker. 'Classy.'

He walked over to me and patted me heartily on the back. 'Jay,' he said, stretching my name out as he sat opposite me. Sinclair placed a mug in front of Lawrence and offered him a canned smile, the factions clear.

'Right, let's not beat around the bush,' Sinclair said. 'Lawrence, if you will.'

Lawrence put the phone on loud speaker and dialled a number. A quick beat later a woman answered.

'Assistant Director Robinson, please,' Lawrence said.

'Right away,' she said, and the next voiced we heard was Robinson's.

Without preamble he asked, 'Is Qasim there?'

'Yes, Javid Qasim, Kingsley Parker, Teddy Lawrence and I are present,' Sinclair replied.

'Good, good,' the speaker bellowed. 'Good to finally make your acquaintance, Qasim. So, what have you got?'

All eyes fell on me and I opened my mouth to speak but my voice deserted me for a second. I took a sip of my tea, just to collect my thoughts and find my voice.

'I have been invited' – is that the right word, *invited*? – 'to attend a training camp with the rest of the group in Islamabad. The flight leaves next week, Wednesday. I have reason to believe that something... I don't know, something huge is being planned.'

'What makes you believe that this is the case?' Sinclair asked.

Suddenly, feeling overwhelmed at explaining myself, I looked at Parker for help.

'Jay was recently involved in a trip with Al-Bhukara,' Parker said, taking over. 'They visited an arms dealer and successfully made an acquisition of ten sawn-off AK-47s and ten Glock 19s. Coupled with the fact that the group is to fly out imminently for training...'

'So,' Robinson said. 'A gun attack.'

'It seems so,' Parker said. 'We have looked at known training camps in and around Islamabad but we have reason to believe that the camp in question is located about a five-hour drive south, in Khyber Pakhtunkhwa. There is a training camp that shares grounds with Al-Qaeda, which we know that Ghurfat-al-Mudarris is affiliated with. That is the likely location.'

'Are we positive, Parker?' Sinclair asked.

'It has to be,' Parker said.

'Okay, good,' Robinson said. 'Who will be in attendance? From the group?'

'Most of them,' I said as all eyes fell on me.

'And *they* are?' Robinson said, irritation emanating through the speaker.

I looked at Parker. I still hadn't told him about Parvez.

'Yasir and Irfan Ahmed,' I said. 'Kevin Strauss and Amirah Absar.' Saying their names out loud in this environment made me feel sick, a sense of betrayal creeping in. But I just could not bring myself to mention Parvez.

'And?' Lawrence asked.

'Hmm?' I replied.

'Parvez Ahmed?' Lawrence smiled. 'You forgot to mention Parvez Ahmed.'

'Yeah,' I said, eyes briefly on Parker. 'No, it's just that he… You know, I'm not certain that he will be attending.'

'Parvez has attended camp twice beforehand. Is there any reason why he would not attend a third time?' Lawrence asked, with something close to a fucking twinkle in his eyes.

'Until we can confirm,' Robinson crackled, 'we will assume he is to attend.'

It was naïve of me to have been surprised that they knew about Parvez. Just because I hadn't mentioned him before by name, it didn't mean that they couldn't find out. This was MI5. They probably knew everything about him, right down to the size of his Crocs.

It was time that I had a very difficult chat with Parvez, sussed him out and tried to get into his brain, see if I could somehow talk him out of it.

'I will confirm with you as to whether Parvez is attending, as soon as I know,' I stated. 'Until then we cannot *assume* anything.' I looked confidently at each of them, daring them to challenge me. Nobody said a word. I looked down at the phone and Robinson stayed quiet too. I knew that they were not in a position to test me. I held all the cards and without me they could go fucking whistle. I looked up at Parker. 'Tonight... I'll confirm by tonight, okay?'

He nodded. Robinson mumbled something unintelligible and was roundly ignored.

'And you, Jay?' Sinclair asked carefully. 'We would like you to attend too.'

'We'll provide you with a secure line so that you are still able to communicate with us,' Lawrence chimed, before I had a chance to respond. 'We are confident that your phone will not be taken away from you. Ghurfat-Al-Mudarris encourage the use of social media to raise awareness for the cause; it's a known method for recruitment.'

'It's imperative that we are able to keep in touch, Jay,' Parker added, his tone the opposite of Lawrence's. 'Otherwise, we would not be asking this of you.'

'Yes, of course, Jay,' Lawrence agreed, now warming to the subject. 'And just in case the situation allows, your phone will be set up with a built-in enhanced microphone, so that you are able to record directly onto an SD card and automatically send any conversations that may be perti—'

'I need time to think.' I had to cut him off, unable to get my head around secure lines and fucking training camps. I couldn't give them an answer until I had spoken to that idiot. 'I will also let you know about that tonight.'

A weird, heavy silence enveloped the room. Held back, as though they all wanted to grab me by the shoulders and shake me. Everything I had done for them to date was not enough, I knew that.

And then... Lawrence pulled out a carrot.

He stood up, smiling, cocksure. 'Jay, mate,' he said. 'Come with me.'

Lawrence lifted the garage door and we stepped out.

Now it was my turn to smile. I hadn't had much to smile about recently, and my facial muscles strained and my jaw hurt. But nevertheless I was beaming. Because there she was, sat right in front of me. I couldn't take my eyes off her. That beautiful body, slender and sleek and oozing sex appeal. God, how I had missed her.

My baby.

My BMW.

51

All I had been able to muster when I clapped eyes on my Beemer was, 'How?'

Lawrence had just replied smugly with, 'I pulled some strings!'

Yeah, whatever! I wouldn't have been surprised if they'd had it all along and were waiting for the right moment to dangle it. I was starting to understand how they worked, and how they would manipulate any given situation to fit in with their agenda. I swiped the keys hanging from Lawrence's hand and I was back in the hot seat. I started up the car and gunned the engine.

It. Sounded. Beautiful.

Lawrence appeared at my window and motioned for me to slide it down.

'Well,' he said. 'Happy?'

I looked around at my interior, my leather seats, my dashboard lit up with lights that I didn't understand and nodded coolly at him. 'Yeah,' I said.

'Good, good,' he said. 'So, this training camp... I think you should attend, Jay.'

'I said I'll confirm tonight.'

'Of course, tonight. Just remember, we've looked after you, gave you a job, got Silas Drakos off your back... I even got your car back. Time for you to repay the favour. Yes?'

I inserted a choice CD into the player and skipped to the harshest, most destructive battle tune ever recorded. Hit 'Em Up, by 2Pac. I opened up my glove compartment and slipped out my orange-tint aviator sunglasses and slid them on, just as the bass kicked in.

'*Yes?*' Lawrence asked me, again.

I put the handbrake down, dropped the gear into first and I looked at that sneaky fucker and simply shrugged. As shrugs go, it may have been my best.

The permanent smug look on that arrogant twat's face disappeared as I cranked up the volume. 'Pac started to spit out his message of intent, and I wheel-spun the fuck out of there, leaving Lawrence in my wake.

*

Once out of sight, I slipped my car to the side of the road and flipped open the boot, just in case the rucksack full of Silas' weed and cash was still there. Wishful thinking; it wasn't. In an evidence room somewhere, I guess, or possibly some bent coppers getting high on my supply. It didn't matter – with Silas locked up, I had nobody to hand it back too, anyway. There was no way I was trusting Staples with it.

I hit the motorway, wanting to open up the valves and feel the roar of the engine. I drove at high speeds, not quite able to believe that I had been reunited with my car, but at the same time I was fucking vexed at them for trying to bribe me. I kept the same tune on rotation and it did nothing but fuel my anger at their cheap trick. They thought I was that fucking easy. Well, in the spirit of my nigga 'Pac: *Fuck Lawrence. Fuck Sinclair. Fuck Parker, and fuck that fat motherfucker Robinson. And most of all fuck MI5.*

If I was going to go through with this, it was going to be on my own terms.

I slipped off the motorway into trustworthy old Hounslow, and made my way to Parvez's house. I parked in my drive, walked across the road and stood in front of his door. I had no idea what I was going to say to him. I purposely did not try to word or rehearse it in my head. It had to be a conversation that came naturally. But my objective was clear: talk him the fuck out of it.

I jabbed at the doorbell a couple of times and Parvez's mum opened the door. Her smile widened as she saw me and in turn made me grin stupidly. I felt like a child again, knocking on my neighbour's door, seeing if Parvez wanted to come out and play.

'Jay, Beta,' she screeched. 'It is so good to see you.'

'*Aslamalykum*, Aunty,' I said respectfully.

'You haven't been here in…'

'Ages,' I said. 'Years.'

'Well, don't just stand there, come inside. What can I get you? Chai? Samosa?'

'No, thanks. I'm fine… Is Parvez at home?'

'Yes, he is in his room, looking for a job on his computer. Go up and I will bring you chai and samosa in a minute.'

'No, Aunty, really. I am fine,' I said, making my way up the stairs as she disappeared into the kitchen.

I knocked on his door and, without waiting for a reply, I walked in. He was sitting on a swivel chair with his back to me, furiously closing windows on his computer. He swivelled around to me and his eyes widened.

'Oh, it's you,' he said, making me feel right at home.

'Yeah. It's me,' I said, taking in his room. It wasn't at all how I had remembered it. The posters had been removed. *Back to the Future*, *The Shawshank Redemption* and the cast of *Neighbours* had been replaced with framed Islamic art and religious signs. A prayer mat was sitting at the foot of his bed, with prayer beads placed respectfully on top. A slightly lopsided floating shelf, with some heavy-looking literature, hung above his desk. I tilted my head so that I could read the titles from the spine. *The Rise of Islamic State*, *The Book of Hadith*, *The Messenger* and a few editions of the Holy Quran.

This was going to be harder than I thought.

'Jay, you should have called first,' he said, looking annoyed.

I couldn't help but laugh. This coming from a guy who walked into my room on so many occasions without invitation. The intruder had finally become intruded upon!

'I was just at a loose end, so I thought I'd see what you're up to. So wha's crackin'?'

He narrowed his eyebrows. 'You know what's happening. I see you all the time, Jay. Why are you really here?'

'Man, you're difficult. I just wanted to see you outside of *that* environment. See what else is happening in your life.'

'That is my life, Jay… Just like it is yours.'

He swivelled around to his computer again and I was left facing the back of his head. After a beat he said: 'Mum's been on at me about getting married. She said that I am of age… I'm seeing a girl tomorrow.'

'No way. Really? I said, swivelling his chair back to me. 'A *girl... You*?'

'If you are going to make fun of me then—'

'Sorry, go ahead. Please.'

'Mum set me up with... You remember Aunty Kamila? She used to live on our road.'

'Aunty Kamila?' I said, smiling at the memory. 'Oh, man. Do I? She was all kinds of hot. Remember we used to call her Aunty Climax?'

'*You* used to call her that. Not me!' he chided. I pursed my lips to stop myself from grinning. 'Anyway, it's her daughter. Mum and Aunty arranged for us to meet tomorrow at Costa Coffee in Harrow.'

'That's great news. If her daughter looks anything like her then—' I didn't finish the sentence and further offend his sensibilities. 'Make sure you look the part, yeah? Dress nice. Don't turn up in your shalwar, kameez and Crocs. Make an effort.'

'I'm just going to be myself, Brother.'

'No. Don't,' I advised, somewhat harshly. His face reddened. 'Look, Parvez. People that say *I'm just going to be myself* always, always mess up. I'll tell you what being yourself is: it's picking your nose at a traffic light. You have all your life to be yourself. Listen, you're a good-looking guy and lurking somewhere in you is a half-decent personality. Go out there and impress the hell out of her.'

He nodded thoughtfully, as though he was actually taking my advice, and I could see him mentally going through his wardrobe, trying to figure out what he was going to dazzle her with. This was good, it was just what I needed. I could use this to make him think about his future and how different it could be. But then he shook his head, as if trying to clear away a mental picture of a happy life with a wife and a couple of little Parvez's running around.

'No, Brother,' he said, Parvez the Preacher reappearing. 'I cannot let anything pollute my mind. I have chosen a path. I am going to cancel my meeting with her. I have to stay focused, because next week, our life is going to change forever.'

Before I could reply, Aunty walked into the room armed with a tray full of savoury snacks and tea, even though I had twice declined her offer. I thanked her as she placed down the tray and ruffled my hair. Parvez rolled his eyes.

'So,' she said to me. 'Big trip for you both next week. Two weeks in sunny Turkey!'

Parvez's eyes widened. '*Mum!* Can you just go please?'

'Sorry, Beta,' she said, trying to kiss him on the head. He bobbed and weaved his head out of the way, but she was persistent and finally landed one.

'Seriously, Mum,' he tutted. '*Go!*'

She left the room, laughing to herself, and as the door shut I was on him straight away.

'Parvez, what the fuck, man?' I snapped. 'You have to tell me if you're going to use my name.'

'I had to tell her something.' He expelled air at the close call. 'I know I should have told you. I was *going* to tell you. How was I to know that you were going to pop around after *six years*?'

'What? What does that mean?'

'It doesn't mean anything.'

I let it slide. I knew what he was getting at. In his eyes, our relationship had always been one-sided.

'You said two weeks to her?' I said.

'Yes.'

'But surely we are going to be there for longer, right?'

'Probably.'

'Isn't she going to get suss when you're not back after two weeks?'

He fixed his eyes on me and blinked slowly. 'Brother, next week, just before I walk out of this house, I am going to embrace my mum tightly, because Allah knows that the way my life has been written, I will never be seeing her again.'

52

I walked back home in a daze. Head down, hands in my pocket, gently kicking a small stone along the way with me. I felt defeated, deflated. Even the sight of my Beemer could not get me out of my state. I hadn't even had the chance to talk Parvez out of it. It would have been a redundant discussion. His mind was firmly made up. He didn't care about his future, about getting married and having children. It was a shame – he would have made a good husband and father. His kids would have grown up to be just as irritating as him, and his wife would have walked all over him. And I think he needed that. It would have made him happy. But his head was somewhere else, cleansed of the thoughts that you and me would have, and replaced with ideas well beyond my understanding.

If he was willing to walk away from his family and knowingly break his mum's heart in the name of *jihad*, what chance did I have in changing his mind?

I fished my house keys out of my pocket and looked up at my front door, and the last person I expected to see was standing on my porch.

'You've changed the way you walk,' Idris said. 'What happened to your stupid I-have-a-limp, bad-man walk?'

I just shrugged sadly at him. I couldn't take anymore. My life was spiralling and this was the last thing that I needed.

'How've you been, Jay?'

'Good. I've been good,' I said, not convincing anyone. 'You?'

'You know?' *No, actually. I don't.* 'Just getting on with it.'

'New job treating you well?'

'You really want to know?' He smiled, knowingly.

'No,' I said. 'Not really.'

We stood, awkwardly regarding each other. I started to fidget and look around everywhere but at him. I saw Saara or Sabina or whatever her name was, across the road on her bicycle, and the incident with her and her boyfriend came back at me, and not for the first time I regretted acting like such a fool. I owed both of them an apology. Maybe I would buy her some flowers or treat them to a fancy dinner somewhere uptown. Anything to ease the fucking guilt I felt eating through me. She was eyeing me with suitable disdain. I put my hand up and waved at her, hoping that in that single gesture all would be forgotten and forgiven. She returned it with a wave of her own, one that involved a middle finger, whilst mouthing the words: *Fuck you!*

'Still have a way with the ladies.' Idris smirked.

'What's up, Idris?' I said, ignoring the remark. 'Why are you here?'

'Look, Jay. I'm not going to beat around the bush... I've been hearing things about you.'

'Have you really?' I waited for him to elaborate. 'So much for not beating around the bush!'

'I know what you're involved in.'

'I very much doubt it,' I said. As far as I was concerned, this conversation was over. He didn't know shit; he couldn't have. Yeah, he may know about my increased interest in Islam and my new so-called friends. But so what? I wasn't going to stand here and explain myself to him. He no longer had that right. I tried to step past him towards my front door but he side-stepped and stood in my way.

'Get out of my way, man,' I said. 'I'm not in the mood.' I tried to move past him again but he pushed me back.

'Not yet, Jay,' he said. 'I need to talk to you.'

I tried to push him back but he saw it coming and moved easily out of the way, causing me to clumsily stumble forward.

'Easy, Jay. I just want to talk.'

I spun on my heels and, before I knew it, I was nose to nose with him. Pent-up anger surfacing. He took a step back and put his hands out in a placatory manner. I swatted them out of the way and stepped back in his face.

'Let's not do this, eh, mate?'

'Get off my property. You're not welcome here.'

'Jay, listen, I just want a word. Then I'm with the wind.'

I attempted to push him again, and this time, if I am honest, he allowed me to, and he stumbled back against my Beemer.

I wanted to hurt him just like he'd hurt me. I wanted to show him how much I had changed. *Who the fuck was he to walk out of my life and wander coolly back in whenever he wanted to? No, I'm not having that.*

Before I knew it, one of my hands had gripped his jacket and the other was around his neck. He prised my fingers away from his neck without much effort and twisted my arm. I dropped to one knee, but my other hand was still gripping his jacket and he came down with me. We untangled and faced each other on the floor of my driveway. My neighbours were probably at their windows filming this! I was breathing hard and annoyingly he wasn't.

'Shit, Jay. You got some moves.'

I didn't think that he was taking this fight as seriously as I was, and that set me off again. I lunged at him. It was a slow and predictable move. He saw it coming; the fucking neighbours probably saw it coming; He moved out of the way and I went shoulder first into the back of my car. Before I could react, and swat away the stars orbiting my head, he had me in a headlock.

'Let go of me,' I screamed at him, as his bicep squeezed against my neck.

'Not until you listen to me.'

'Get the fuck off me.'

'Will you listen to me?'

Whilst we were on the floor bonding, we never noticed a mini-cab pull up in front of the driveway, or the car door open and close again. We never noticed her walk across the driveway and stand over us.

'That's enough,' she said, and Idris let go of me and we both looked up at her as though we were about nine years old and about to be grounded.

'Mum!' I said, expecting her to reach down and plant kisses all over my face and hug the crap out of me.

'Bring my bags in,' she said instead, and she let herself inside the house.

Me and Idris both got to our feet and brushed ourselves down.

'*That's* what I was trying to tell you, idiot,' he said.

'*What?*'

'Your mum,' he said. 'I called her back here.'

53

Qatar had been good to Mum. She appeared healthy, browner, her hair lighter, her face fuller. She looked like she had been having the time of her life until Idris called her back – for reasons as yet unknown to me. She carried a look on her face that I didn't want to believe was disappointment. But it was disappointment.

I stood in the living room in front of her. Idris had followed me in and was standing next to me. I watched my mum sitting in her armchair, taking in the room. My eyes followed her gaze and I saw the room through her eyes. Takeaway cartons, one for every day of the week, scattered across the battered and wonky coffee table. Pizza boxes, piled up on the carpet, one on top of another, creating a leaning tower, a telling narrative of my diet. Her eyes moved to where the television had lived, and it was time for me to open my mouth.

'Funny story, I—'

A stern finger was out before I had a chance to blag out an excuse, and a look flashed across her face. I was actually scared. Of Mum!

She looked at Idris.

'You were supposed to be his friend.'

'Aunty, you can't blame me,' Idris exclaimed.

'Yes, I can. You should have been keeping an eye on him.'

'Aunty, with all due respect, Jay's old and ugly enough to look after himself.'

'And how did that work out for him? Hmm? If that was the case, why did you phone me? Why didn't you just talk to him yourself?'

'We… Um… We haven't been in touch recently. That's why I went to you. Somebody has to talk some sense into him. There was no way he would listen to me.'

'Oh I get it,' I said. 'Is this, like, an intervention?' I said, half-joking.

Mum ignored me and I started to freak out a bit.

'Idris, you can go now. I need to speak with my son.' Mum looked at me. 'Alone.'

Idris said goodbye to Mum, which was largely ignored, walked out of the living room and into the hallway. I followed him out just as he was opening the front door.

'Idris,' I whispered. 'What the fuck did you do?'

'I'm sorry, Jay. I had to.'

I didn't press him. I was going to find out very soon what all this was about. He put his hand out and I stared at it for a second before shaking it.

'Catch you later?' He said it like a question.

The most honest answer I could give him was: 'Maybe.'

*

'You know,' Mum said softly, 'I don't know what happened to the TV, the coffee table or my plant pots, and I don't really care. I don't care that you have been pigging out on junk. I don't even care that you have been lying to me about getting yourself an office job. None of that worries me. Because I thought... You know what I thought? I thought, yes, he'll play up, destroy the house, live in the fast lane, and be downright self-destructive. I mean, you're young, I didn't expect you to run this house and live your life by the book. *But...* But I thought eventually, you'd come good... I thought you were your mother's son.' A tear slid out of her eye as she added: 'But you're not. You, Jay... are your father's son.'

'What does that mean?' It took all my might not to kneel down in front of her and wipe away her tears. She wiped her own tears and found some resolve.

'I lied to you about him.'

Lost for words, I waited for her to continue.

'I could have raised you as a good Muslim. But I let you be free of it. I never encouraged you to go the mosque, even though you did on Fridays, of your own accord, and it scared the life out of me.'

'Why?'

'Because I didn't want you to be like *him*,' she spat, full of venom and spite like I had never seen from her before. I let it sink in, and tried to establish what the common factor between my dad and me could have been. I drew a blank. She continued. 'I despised him for what he did to me, for what he did to us. I married him blindly, as was the way back then. I didn't know what he was or how he would turn out.'

'What was he?' I asked. 'How *did* he turn out?'

'I'll tell you what he wasn't. He wasn't a husband and he sure as hell wasn't a father. He... He was a fighter. A jihadi.'

The living room seemed to close in around me, squeezing the breath from me. My chest tightened and for a second I thought I was going to have a panic attack. I couldn't stand without aid, so I moved unstably to the nearest wall and leaned my back against it and slowly slid down to the floor.

'Why didn't you tell me?' I said weakly.

'Because it is my job to protect you, Jay. The only way *he* protected us was financially.'

'Three grand,' I filled in. 'I saw the pay-in book in the loft.'

'Yes, well, that was him. Father of the bloody year!'

'So, what? What are trying to tell me? He isn't dead?' I said, with hope.

'Oh no, Jay. He's dead, all right. But not when you think. He died twenty years ago.' She let that sink in before continuing, her tone now softer. 'He was involved in things that I... I couldn't get my head around. Things that I don't even know about. We had no contact for years. Just the cheques – *that* was our only communication. I didn't know where they came from, there was no stamp or postmark to indicate.'

'So how do you know that he's dead if there was no communication?'

'Adeel-Al-Bhukara.'

My eyes widened and in that very instant everything fell perfectly and without question into place. The insistence that I attend classes; treating me like a member of his family; the way that he afforded me a certain respect that was not apparent to the other students; the reason why, after three short months, he was ready to send me to Islamabad and prepare me for battle.

He treated me like the son of a jihadist.

I didn't realise that I was viciously scratching my forearm until Mum kneeled down in front of me and gently removed my hand. I looked down at my arm and the skin was red raw. I looked up at her.

'Did he love me?'

I think she had decided that it wasn't time to be pacifying me. She wanted me to know the truth, the whole truth and nothing but the fucking truth. She answered my question with silence and it near enough broke me. I forced myself to stand up, and I walked out of the room. I could hear her calling my name as I moved heavily up the stairs. I shut the door to my room, locked it and slid down against the door, determined not to cry. But the tears had found a way through and were flowing freely down my face.

It had been due for as long as I could remember.

A few seconds or a few minutes later, I heard her slowly come up the stairs, and I could tell by her movement that she was sitting with her back against my door. She didn't say anything but she made it clear that she was there. For me.

It took a while for me to find some strength in my voice. 'How did he die?'

'I don't know, Jay. Adeel, that leech, phoned me one day, telling me that he died for *the cause*. He refused to give me details, said he didn't know. But I could hear the lies in his voice. I received a cheque shortly after, raised from your father's estate.' She snorted. '*Estate!* I didn't even know my own husband had a bloody estate. You know something? I didn't shed a tear, not one tear. Me and you, we had got this far without him. We didn't need him.'

'I needed him,' I whispered. She didn't hear me; she wasn't meant to.

'Jay... I'm sorry, Beta. I wish there was another way. I wish I didn't have to tell you.'

I wiped my tears and fired at her: 'So, *why did you*? *Why did you tell me?*'

'Because I'm afraid... All right... I'm afraid that you have your father's blood running through you, and Al-Bhukara will move heaven and earth to take advantage of you.'

I opened my door and Mum got to her feet. We stood looking at each other, only the threshold between us. Her face mirrored mine in every way, the hurt, the anguish and the pain so evident.

'I promise, Mum. I swear. I won't follow in Dad's footsteps.'

'Can I come in?' she asked.

I nodded.

She stepped into my room and I into her arms, and we stayed like that forever.

54

I had around fifteen missed calls from Parker. I called him back.

'Sorry I didn't call,' I apologised before he had the opportunity to get all high and mighty. 'Mum came back yesterday. Things got a little heavy.'

'Okay,' he said, accepting my apology. 'Are you in a position to confirm whether Parvez Ahmed will be travelling?'

'Yes,' I said. 'He will be.'

'And you, Jay?' he asked hesitantly.

I promise, Mum. I swear. I won't follow in Dad's footsteps.

'Yeah,' I said. 'I'm in.'

Part Three

Islam is a way of life, not death.

– Anonymous

55

We landed at Benazir Bhutto International Airport, named after the Pakistani prime minister who served for two non-consecutive terms in the late eighties and mid-nineties. Oh, and by the way, she was female. For those who think that Muslim women are oppressed second-class citizens, this one was put in charge of a country widely regarded as backwards. Twice!

We collected our luggage in near silence. I could tell that the others were a little off with me for not making the effort to socialise during the flight. I should have, but the way things had escalated so quickly had made my head spin and I had trouble adjusting my mindset.

We walked out of the airport and stepped into the burn. Sweat coated us like a second skin. I slid on my sunglasses, looking for all the world like a holiday maker. Amid car horns, a mud-encrusted Toyota jeep jumped two lanes and pulled up in front of us.

'This is us,' Kevin said.

The driver jumped out, smirked at us by way of introduction, before literally flinging our bags into the back compartment.

'Is that our trainer?' I asked Kevin.

'That is Aslam. He's just the driver, amongst other things. He will prepare our meals, fetch our stuff, that kind of thing. But he is definitely *not* our trainer.'

Once Aslam finished destroying our luggage, he handed us unsealed bottles of water from an ice box. I smelled a whiff of cannabis coming from him; it was just a hint but it was unmistakeable. So, old Aslam was a puffer. I found that quite interesting. He had the beard but not the faith.

Kevin jumped into the front, before changing his mind and letting Amirah have that seat. It would have been too tight and awkward for her to be bundled in the back with four guys. Aslam's eyes lit up and his smile widened as she took her place in the front.

Amirah smiled back sweetly. 'You so much as look at me and I'll take your fucking eyes out.'

He didn't quite seem to understand her words, but he definitely got the message and didn't even attempt to glance at her once during the five-hour drive to the training camp.

*

Surrounded by intimidating rocky mountains, peaking high into the night sky, we stepped out of the jeep and stretched out the kinks in our necks and backs. I took in my surroundings. It was a large area of wilderness, with tall skeletal trees dotted sparsely around. Large, bright-eyed foxes watched us curiously as we followed Aslam into the camp. There were two medium-sized thatched huts, low and wide, next to each other. They were separated only by huge grey rock. Attached to the front of the rock was a gun rack filled with assault rifles.

We arrived just in time to see an episode unfolding. A young guy, probably in his late teens, stormed out of one of the thatched huts, a leather holdall gripped tightly in his hand, a mask of sheer determination on his face. He seemed very fucked-off about something.

Three guys followed him out and circled him, as though trying to block his path. There were raised voices aimed at him. Credit to the kid, he was giving it back, spit and venom flying out his mouth.

'Brother Iqbal, gather your thoughts,' one said. 'We have only been here for two days.'

'*No*,' this Iqbal kid cried. 'This *fucking* place…'

'Why don't you sleep on it and, *Inshallah*, tomorrow morning you will feel different.'

'I told you how I feel, now get out of my way. I'm going home, and if any of you had any sense you would join me.' Iqbal bustled himself past the three, and when he noticed us he started to spout some more. 'Listen to me, Brothers, turn back. Go back home. This place, it's… it's evil. Go back home to your loved ones. They will forgive you of anything. You don't belong here.'

I checked him out. He was a good-looking lad. White Adidas boots covered in reddish dirt, his jeans fashionably ripped at the knees and a Metallica T-shirt. He dressed similar to me, and from some of the things he was saying, I decided he thought like me. I wondered how he had fallen prey to the cause.

I wondered how I had fallen prey.

Kevin put his arm around Iqbal in an attempt to pacify him with words of Kevin-like wisdom.

'Man, get the fuck away from me,' Iqbal snapped, pushing him away.

'That's enough.' From a distance a deep, grizzly, authoritative voice cut him off.

Further down, away from the thatched huts, was a larger, wood-built hut. Attached front and centre above the entrance was a huge round clock that illustrated prayer times. A figure wearing army fatigues, right down to the boots, was standing at the door. Even from a distance it was clear that he was a hulk, easily clearing six-five and almost half as wide. He ducked his head low, stepped through the door and strode towards us.

Silence fell. All that could be heard was the heavy breathing coming from Iqbal. His eyes widened with fear and he took a step back.

The man approached and towered over Iqbal.

'*That's* the trainer,' Kevin whispered, with a touch of awe. 'Mustafa.'

'Iqbal,' Mustafa said, in an accent. 'Nobody is forcing you here, boy.' An American accent. 'We do not cater for cowards. This is a place to better yourself with belief, hard work and commitment. But don't you dare try and poison my students with what *you* think is right or wrong.'

He was talking directly to Iqbal but he was relaying the message loud and clear to us all.

Iqbal kept his head down. I wanted to put my arm around him and walk him away. From behind the large rock, Aslam staggered back into the mix. During the melee, nobody had noticed him disappear. Judging by his eyes and the dopey smile fixed on his face, he had evidently been smoking the good shit.

'Ah, Aslam,' Mustafa said. 'There you are. Will you run young Iqbal back to the city? Give him some money for a hotel and from there onwards he is on his own.'

Aslam nodded, not seeming to mind the five-hour trek back to Islamabad, just a few minutes after driving for five hours the other way.

As Iqbal and Aslam walked to the jeep, Mustafa boomed, 'If there is anybody else here who has any doubts, I urge you to join Iqbal right now. Because I warn you now, you will experience *Jahannam* before *Jaanat*.'

Hell before Heaven...

56

I've met some tough-looking guys in my time. Parker, Staples and Khan, to a certain extent. They all carried that look of menace, able to win a fight before a punch had been thrown. But this guy? Mustafa was a fucking man-mountain, built from the hardest of rocks. His body shaped in a way that disobeyed nature.

Mustafa had gathered us all after Iqbal and Aslam had departed. We were all exhausted from the trip and wanted to get our heads down – at least I did – but he obviously had something to say. He stood in front of us and tried to clasp his hands behind his back, but the shape and size of his body would not allow it, so he just let his arms drop by his side.

'For those of you that do not know me,' he said, looking at me before addressing the whole group, 'my name is Mustafa Mirza. Welcome to Ghurfat-al-Mudarris. For those who require translation – welcome to The Teacher's Quarters.'

Jackpot.

'I will be your trainer for the coming weeks. I was born and raised in Atlanta, USA. I joined the US Marines when I was nineteen so I could fight for my country, my people. I carried out two tours of Afghanistan and one tour of Iraq in five short years. And in that time I realised that I was not fighting for my people but fighting against them. I witnessed atrocities and attacks carried out by the US with very little justified intel. Families torn apart, villages devastated. Men and women tortured for a game. And I was part of that. Like a robot being programmed to carry out every instruction without question. It was in Iraq that you could say that this robot malfunctioned. One night I woke and, without thought, I made my way to the squadron leader's bed. I was possessed. My body moving on its own. It was with the strength of Allah that I placed my hands around his neck and strangled that murderous Kafir into a coma. It took seven marines to wrestle me away from him.' Mustafa took a long swig from a bottle of water and eyed us all in turn. He wiped his mouth with the back of his hand and continued. 'I was taken away and detained in military prison, but they could not break me, they could not break my faith. Even though I had been born a Muslim, it was on that day that I became one. I do not regret for one solitary second my time in the US Marines. Because to their detriment, they trained me extensively to be a killer. And with that knowledge and power, it is my humble duty to pass that on to you.'

We spent the night getting to know each other. Salman was the eldest of the other group and he instantly gelled with Kevin, who was the eldest in our group. They both had that sanctimonious bone in them, which made them naturally gravitate towards one another. Then we had Kamran, a family man who took great pleasure in passing around photos of his wife and twin girls and annoyingly gushing about them. It was truly frightening to me that somebody could feel more towards the cause than towards the family that he was evidently crazy about. Finally, there was Akhtar. Now, I may not be the brightest, but this guy did not have a clue. He didn't quite seem to know why he was here or what his purpose was. I mean, he had *some* idea, obviously, but behind his big eyes and blank expression something was amiss. He was just happy to tag along. I could see how somebody like that would have been coerced and groomed without much effort. Like a sheep, trying to fit in with the flock. All three of them were Luton-based and had attended classes exactly as we had done with Al-Bhukara. Now here we all were, ready to give our all in the name of Islam.

As for the other guy, Iqbal, the one who saw sense, he was London-based but was studying at Luton University. Previously a straight-A student and good Muslim, who one day walked into the wrong room and spoke to the wrong person and ended up here. Like myself, this was his first training camp, but he had been attending hard-line Islamic classes for the best part of three years, whilst his academic grades gradually slipped. Apparently, he showed great aptitude, especially in theoretical scenarios, and their Imam was more than impressed – enough to nominate and send him here. Iqbal quickly discovered the difference between theory and reality.

*

Amirah, being the only girl, had the run of her own hut. She said her goodnights and left. Exhausted, we all turned in.

I, somewhat predictably, couldn't sleep. I had learned to stop trying ages ago; if it came, it came. Instead I looked at the training schedule that Salman had handed out to us. It was printed on A5 laminated card.

SCHEDULE

04.30 – 05.00 FAJR PRAYERS
05.00 – 06.00 ISLAMIC STUDIES
06.00 – 08.00 PHYSICAL/COMBAT TRAINING
08.00 – 09.00 FREE TIME/SOCIAL MEDIA UPDATES
09.00 – 10.00 BREAKFAST/CLEANSING
10.00 – 12.00 MILITARY TRAINING
12.00 – 14.00 ZOHAR PRAYERS/LUNCH/FREE TIME
14.00 – 18.00 MILITARY TRAINING
18.00 – 19.00 ASAR PRAYERS/FREE TIME
19.00 – 21.00 ISLAMIC STUDIES
21.00 – 22.30 MAGHRIB PRAYERS/DINNER
22.30 – 23.30 BONDING/GROUP DISCUSSION
23.30 ISHA PRAYERS/LIGHTS OUT

Man, it was heavy.

I switched my phone on for the first time since we had arrived and noticed with relief that I had decent network coverage. Lawrence had been right, they had no intention of taking our phones away from us.

Mustafa had explained to us that extensive background checks had been carried out on us all before the Imam even entertained the idea of sending us to camp. We were trusted implicitly otherwise we would not have been here. Phones were a big part of our time here; we had been encouraged to take group photos, videos and selfies within the confines of the camp and post them onto social network sites, raising awareness amongst young Muslims and inspiring them to join the Cause.

I checked the time on my phone. It had just gone two, which meant that we had to be up in a couple of hours to start our day.

I thought about texting Parker to let him know that I had arrived safely, but I knew that they were tracking my phone anyway. I switched it off to preserve my battery, as there were only a limited amount of power sockets available, and I closed my eyes.

57

Not for long, though, as two short hours later I had been nudged, poked and prodded, and my cries of *five more minutes* had fallen on deaf ears. It wasn't until a bucket full of cold water nearly drowned me in my sleep that I woke up. I shot out of bed and stood, *seething*, toe to toe against the perpetrator. My eyes were level with two gigantic mounds covered by a faded, tight green T-shirt. My eyes travelled up. Then they travelled up some more, until I was craning my neck and looking up at Mustafa, who was looking down, smirking at me.

'Morning, Jihadi Jay,' he said, and placed the empty bucket over my head.

I kept it there for a bit, letting my temper simmer. I felt the bucket being gently lifted and Amirah was standing in front of me, looking as fresh as a daisy.

'Day one,' she said simply.

'Yeah,' I yawned. 'Day one.'

We walked out together into the stunning bright sunrise and I was immediately told to pray on my own, as everyone had already woken up and prayed as per schedule.

Islamic studies was next and Mustafa explained that it was up to us to take turns at leading the class. Kevin and Salman both volunteered, wanting to be the first to lead. A touch of rivalry was clear as they bickered about who was better suited. Then bizarrely, they offered it up to each other.

'Please, Brother, you teach. I insist.'

'No, no, you stood up first, you should do it, Brother.'

This went back and forth for a very long minute, before Kevin finally humbly accepted, much to Salman's annoyance. The classes weren't too different to what we had learned with Al-Bhukara, and I found myself drifting.

Physical training was next. I was in good shape due to my daily five-mile runs, and I always did excel at Physical Education at school. I was quite competitive in that manner. Mustafa started us off quite easily, some star jumps, which were a breeze, followed by some basic stretches to loosen up our muscles. It was a walk in the park and that's exactly what I found myself whispering to Parvez.

'Something you have to say, Jay?' Mustafa asked.

'No,' I replied, pushing my elbows through my shoulders. 'Nothing.'

'He said it's *a walk in the park*.' Parvez grinned at me.

Mustafa nodded thoughtfully, as he fingered his goatee. We continued to stretch for an obscene amount of time, punctuated with press-ups and sit-ups, but still easily manageable. We had a two-hour slot and I wondered how we would fill it.

'Right, soldiers,' Mustafa echoed. 'Relax yourself. Our friend Jihadi Jay here is under the impression that this camp is *a walk in the park*.'

'I didn't mean that exactly. I was just saying—'

Mustafa gesticulated a digging motion with his hands. I got the impression that he could actually dig a grave using his bare hands quicker than I could with a JCB.

'The next part of our physical training is one-on-one combat training. Jay, as you are evidently having the time of your life, please step forward.'

'Me?' I said, just as Parvez nudged me forward towards Mustafa. *What was up with him?* He seemed to have developed some confidence in this place, confidence that he had never expressed back home, as though he was in his element here. I looked up at Mustafa, balled my hands, put my dukes up and waited for him to kick the shit out of me.

'Please don't hurt me!' Mustafa mocked and the rest of the group sniggered. 'Turn around, Jay, you're not fighting me.'

I turned to face the group and sized them all up. Now, I ain't no slouch, I've been in a fair share of dust-ups in my life, and I could handle myself, and looking at these Pakis lined up in front of me I fancied my chances against any of them.

'Irfan. Please step up,' Mustafa instructed.

Irfan? *Irfan!* Please. Don't insult me. At least give me a challenge. He was shorter than me, skinnier than me and, in the time I had known him, slightly intimidated by me. He stepped up quite confidently. I looked at Mustafa and my open palms communicated to him how I was feeling about the mismatch. *Really. This guy*? I could see him pursing his lips, trying to contain a smile. Okay, so be it.

I started to play up to the audience, touching my fists together as I circled Irfan. He watched me curiously for a moment, before removing his kameez and standing topless in front of me.

The skinny bastard was *ripped*. Taut, wiry, *eight*-pack. Trust me, I counted.

I stopped showboating. He stepped forward and I instinctively stepped back. *Shit*. Not a punch had been thrown and he already had the upper hand. I threw a couple of quick air jabs at him, just inches away from his nose. On the second jab he grabbed my arm and dragged me forward whilst bringing his forehead down on my face. I went down on my haunches and put my hands up to my face and felt blood. Something was bleeding, maybe my nose or my lip, it was hard to tell as my whole fucking face hurt. The sneaky fucker went in for the kill just as I was getting warmed up. I was fuming. I bounced back up on my feet and charged at him, bent low, my head targeting his midsection. He sidestepped and locked my head in his arms by his waist and delivered a donkey kick to my already battered face. The kick wasn't hard and I knew that he had been holding back but my humiliation was complete. He removed his grip from around of my neck and I dropped face first into the dirt. I stayed rooted, letting my body rest. I could have actually fallen asleep right there and then, so exhausted was I.

'All right, guys. What did we just learn?' Mustafa asked.

'Always be ready to retaliate,' somebody answered. I think one of the Luton lot.

'Right,' Mustafa said. 'Two very significant words. *Ready* to *retaliate*. That is exactly what young Irfan demonstrated. This is what thousands of young Muslims around the world are demonstrating. Always be ready to retaliate.'

Irfan offered me a hand. I took it and got back up to my feet. I stood in front of him and patted down the dirt from my clothes and wiped the crap off my face. His face looked like it held a touch of arrogance, as though he had been waiting for a while to get one over on me.

So I kicked him as hard as I could in the nuts.

He grabbed at them before dropping in slow motion to the ground and curling up like a ball.

'So much for being *ready*,' I said, spitting blood from my mouth. 'Don't really see much of a *retaliation* coming anytime soon, either.'

58

Aslam had returned from the long drive back from Islamabad and, without missing a beat, he cooked us all lunch. I use the word *cooked* loosely. It was a soggy omelette and it was raw in places. I used the two pieces of bread provided to turn it into a sandwich, with a dash of Tabasco, which I'd had the foresight to pack, and washed it down quickly with a glass of what I hoped was water.

'What's next?' I asked, burping the meal away.

'Military training,' Amirah said. She was sitting closely next to me. It had not gone unnoticed by the rest of the group, but no one seemed to mind or think ill of it.

'What does that include?'

'Could be anything, Brother,' Kamran said. He had the photo of his wife and kids out again. It was leaning against his glass. Once again I mentally questioned his motive for being here. 'In the past we had sessions on building explosives. But I don't know what Mustafa has in mind.'

'In Jalalabad, Afghanistan, the training camp was tough,' Kevin said. 'The trainer would instruct us to make live bombs and then trap us in a cave with them. He would set the timer for sixty seconds in which we would have to disarm them.'

'Well, I'm not doing that!' I said, and immediately regretted it.

'I don't think this is that kind of training camp,' Parvez said. 'I, too, have had intensive bomb training: building, disarming and disposal.' He lifted his shalwar halfway up his leg to reveal... nothing. Just a hairy lower leg.

'Thanks for the leg tease, Parvez,' I said. 'Very titillating.'

He pointed to just below his knee and, past the wispy, curly black hairs, I could see tiny little holes, less than a millimetre wide and the same again deep. 'Nail bomb,' he said. 'I built it and I didn't connect the timer properly. I walked away confident, arrogant even, thinking that I had time. I was wrong; it went off sooner than anticipated. Thankfully I was far away enough from it to cause any real damage.' He smiled at the memory. 'It was a sure sign from Allah.'

'What do you mean, sign?' I asked.

'*He* was telling me to focus, to give my all to my *jihad*.'

Yeah, that or He was telling you not to fuck around with explosives.

'They didn't let me near the bomb-making kits,' Akhtar said sheepishly.

'Akhtar, Brother, there is a path set for you by the Almighty,' Salman said. 'And making bombs is not it.'

'Parvez, what did you mean that this isn't that kind of training camp?' I asked.

'Guns, Brother,' Kevin answered instead. 'Do you remember our trip with the Imam?' Parvez's face fell slightly. He had made it clear on more than one occasion that he should have been present for that trip.

'Yeah,' I said. 'I remember.'

'Well, it's a reasonable assumption that we're going to be heavily trained using those particular models. The AK-47 and Glock 19.'

'Any of you fired a gun before?' I asked. 'I haven't.'

'This is exactly what I mean.' Parvez sighed, excused himself, and walked off in a huff.

'What's his problem?' I asked.

'He doesn't mean anything by it,' Kevin said. 'You see, Jay, this is a very important part of our education. And you are, to some extent, not on the same level as us.'

'But here you are,' Irfan said, with a touch of antagonism.

'Yes, Brother, we have all, previously, had arms training,' Yasir said, gently touching his brother's arm in a calming gesture. 'This time it is not about how you handle a gun, it's how to inflict the most amount of damage with it.'

'You have a lot of catching up to do,' Irfan said. 'If you are going to walk with us we have to know that you are capable.'

Mustafa did not join us for breakfast. He probably had his eggs liquidised in the form of a protein shake, but he joined us after in the blistering morning sunshine. At each of our feet lay a Glock 19 and a sawn-off AK-47.

'Jihadi Jay.' I hated being called that, but I took it with the mocking humour that it was intended. 'I want you to pair up with somebody and observe carefully. Later, I want you to be able to do this by yourself.'

'Do what?' I asked, cradling my guns and standing next to Parvez.

'Brothers and, of course, Sister Amirah, apart from Jihadi Jay, you have all had levels of weapon training. For this exercise we are going to disassemble and check the Glock for any faults. You have ninety seconds starting…' Mustafa looked at his watch and smirked. 'Well, it started twenty seconds ago.'

Parvez was down like a shot, on one knee, hunched over the weapons. 'All right, Jay. I'm going to talk fast, so keep up.' He picked up the Glock. 'First remove the magazine.' He pressed a button and the magazine fell smoothly out of the handle. 'Retract the slide, check that there is no ammunition in the chamber. Then pull the trigger to its rear and retract the slide a touch, about a quarter of an inch, at the same time bringing the slide lock down on both sides.'

I was still trying to get my head around what he had pressed to make that magazine drop out like that.

'Once unlocked, remove slide, remove the recoil spring and barrel.' His hands were moving too fast and I could hear him explaining but the information wasn't getting past my eyes and into my brain. The gun was coming apart piece by piece easily in his hand, each part carefully inspected and placed by his side. 'I knew it,' he said, holding up a small spring. 'Look at the recoil spring: it's too short and it's too light. I did notice a difference when I retracted the slide.'

I nodded knowingly but I was lost.

I took the spring from his hand and studied it. I compressed it a few times before it bounced away out of my hands. Parvez shook his head and stood up. He nodded to Mustafa that he was complete, and looked pleased as he realised that he was the first. I stood next to him, hoping for some of the glory to fall on me. A few seconds later Akhtar stood up, wearing a lopsided grin on his face. Maybe bombs weren't his thing but guns certainly were.

'Twenty seconds,' Mustafa shouted.

Amirah was next, followed by Kamran, Yasir and Irfan.

'Ten seconds.'

Salman and Kevin were again competing with each other, not wanting to be the last.

'Time,' Mustafa announced, just as they finished disassembly. 'Okay, good job, guys. Now each of you tell me what you noticed.'

'Recoil spring was too short, causing friction in the slider,' Parvez said.

'Well done,' Mustafa said.

'The ejector pin was bent on my one,' Akhtar said carefully.

'Excellent, Akhtar, that's right, it was. Really good job,' Mustafa said, and Akhtar beamed at his achievement. 'And the rest of you guys?'

'Misfed ammunition. One jammed in the chamber.'

'Magazine extraction faulty.'

'The chamber was too small for the round.'

And on it went, one by one. Their attention to detail was frightening.

'*Mashallah*, you have all been taught very well,' Mustafa acknowledged. Then he said, 'Jay. Why don't you show us what you have learned?'

248

59

Under their judgemental glare and in just under twenty minutes I had managed to disassemble my Glock. There was a collective groan as I lost the spring again. Mustafa sent them all off for some shooting practice and left me to familiarise myself with my weapons in my room, so that I was on par with the rest of the psychos.

By myself, from the comfort of my sleeping bag, I seized the opportunity to drop Parker a quick text, trying to recall the quick-dash code training that I received before I had set off.

Hey Mum. Antalya is amazing. So damn hot, it nearly hit 40 degrees today and its around 19 at night. Made friends with a few locals. Not sure when or where we are heading to next. OOOXXXXXx

The mention of the temperature told Parker that it was, as assumed, AK-47's and Glock 19s. The number of kisses at the end confirmed the number of us that had flown out to camp; the small x represented me. The number of hugs represented those additional to us, preceding the kisses to indicate that they had arrived first. The not knowing when or where our next destination was expressed that no dates or plans had yet been revealed.

The clattering of gunshots rang out and I covered my ears with my pillow and closed my eyes tightly.

I didn't mean to fall asleep.

I woke up with a Glock in my face. I flinched and squirmed, trapped in my sleeping bag, trying to kick my way out of it. He pulled the trigger and I screamed, '*No!*'

Mustafa lobbed the Glock on my chest, followed by the magazine. Disappointment and anger blazed in his eyes. He walked out without saying a word.

'Salaam, Bruv.' Akhtar was sitting on his sleeping bag, his fingers moving quickly over prayer beads.

I unzipped myself out of the mine and stretched out. 'What's *his* problem?'

'You were sleeping. Mustafa was well vexed.'

'Yeah, I did notice.' I yawned. I was so fucking tired.

'You should have been practising. Like Brother Irfan said, if you are going to walk with us you need to be on the same level as us, innit?'

'What time is it?'

'About midday, bruv. Free time for a bit, then prayers and lunch. Probably chicken again.'

'The others?'

'Outside, chilling out in the sun. Taking group photos for Facebook and Twitter, encouraging the Brothers and Sisters around the world to join us,' Akhtar said. His words didn't fit. Didn't belong to him.

'What do you do in Luton, Akhtar?'

'Me, bruv? I don't do nothing.'

'You don't work, go to college, uni?'

'Uni?' He smiled. 'No, bruv. Just, you know, hang out with Brother Salman and Brother Kamran.'

'How do you know them?'

'From the mosque, innit? They looked after me, yeah. Helped me realise my path.'

'Which is what?'

'What?'

'Your path?'

'Death to all Kafirs, yeah?'

'Why?' I asked, curious to hear his personal reasons.

He just shrugged stupidly at me. 'It's just the way it is, bruv.'

*

Outside they were all posing. Parvez was sandwiched in between Yasir and Irfan. Arms around each other. Rifles hanging off their shoulder with chequered ghutrah scarves partially covering their faces. Kamran was clicking away, taking pictures with his phone. It was an unnerving sight. Amirah clocked me and jogged over.

'Jay. Are you all right?'

'Yeah, I'm fine.'

She glared at Akhtar, who eventually realised that she wanted him out of the way, and he walked off and joined the others. She grabbed my arm tightly and marched me out of earshot. We walked behind the large rock only to find Aslam there, getting high.

'Get lost, Aslam,' she said and he drifted away. 'Jay, what the fuck, man?'

'*What?*'

'Where are you, huh? What's going on in there?' she said, tapping her finger irritatingly on my head.

'Nah, it's cool.'

'From where I am standing it's pretty fucking far from cool.'

'Look, it was a long flight, then a long drive. I didn't get much sleep. I didn't think that we'd get into all this straight away. I was knackered.'

'We *all* were, Jay,' she hissed. 'This is not a holiday camp, this is serious. The others don't feel that you should be here. Mustafa too. It's only because of the Imam that you have been blessed to join us in the cause. Whatever it is he saw in you, we need to see that too. So get yourself together and sort yourself out.'

And before I could react with another lame excuse, she planted the softest kiss on my lips. I closed my eyes. It only lasted a second, but I kept them closed, savouring the taste, saving it to memory. When I opened them, she was gone.

I walked back, ready to throw myself in and integrate. Ready to prove that I was just as nuts as the rest of them. They were hostile, though.

'Here,' I said, with my hand out. 'Give me the phone, I'll take some photos of you guys.'

'No, it's okay,' Irfan said, without making eye contact. 'We're done here. Besides, it's meal time.'

Amirah disappeared for *Wudu,* and the others were all hanging out in twos and threes, face to face or in tight triangles, making it clear that I had some serious sucking up to do. Aslam walked out with empty plates and we all sat down and waited for our meal to arrive. It was some rank chicken, more bone than substance, but we were all too hungry to bitch about it, so it was wolfed down gratefully. I even offered my supply of Tabasco as a peace offering.

'Thanks, Brother,' Kevin said, as I watched in horror at his heavy-handed usage of it. 'After prayers we are marching.'

'Yeah, where we marching to?' I asked.

'Nowhere in particular, just around the camp. There's a lot more of it than what we see around us.'

'But it's baking, man.'

'That's why military training is between two and six. It's the hottest part of the day. Survive that and you can survive anything.'

'It's like forty degrees,' I moaned. As hard as I tried to fit in, my lazy nature would always reveal itself.

'Forty degrees is not hot, Brother Jay,' Salman said. '*Hellfire* is hotter. You'll do well to remember that.'

*

We all put on our hiking boots, or as close as we had to them. Yasir and Irfan had some serious military boots. Most of the others also had appropriate footwear. I brought with me some suede Timberlands. Cost me a hundred and twenty quid. They were bound to get ruined. In fact, they were already ruined, standing around in the dirty red earth. But the award for the stupidest footwear went to Parvez.

'You're not seriously wearing your Crocs, are you?' For once, I wasn't the weakest link.

'Don't mock me, these are the most comfortable shoes ever made.'

'All right, soldiers,' Mustafa declared, as he handed out bottles of water. 'I'll lead, columns of two behind me. Parvez, you take the back. I want to hear lots of encouragement, don't let your partner fall behind; if they do, you do. Keep up a medium-to-brisk pace.'

Not only did we have to do this hellish trek, we had to do it with our AK-47s strapped over our shoulder and across our chests. The only thing going for me was that Amirah was my walking partner, which would probably make the trek a touch more bearable.

It didn't.

Half an hour in and I was drenched in sweat. An hour and a half in and I couldn't stop myself from pouring the bottle of water over my head to cool down. Two hours in I was stumbling, and Amirah would tut and hoist me up by my arm. Every time I slowed down, that fucking Parvez would nudge me in my back with his rifle. The journey was punctuated by the group raising their guns over their heads and breaking into a chant in Arabic, over and over the same line.

'What are they saying?' I asked.

'*Life is a gift. Leave no man behind*,' Amirah answered.

'What does that mean?' I panted.

'It's the teachings of the Al-Mudarris.'

I wanted to press her but I could barely breathe, let alone converse anymore.

Just over the two-hour mark, and about eight miles later, we stopped. I removed the rifle from around my neck and slumped to the floor. I spread my legs and my arms out and looked up into the sun, which looked close enough to touch. The others stood around casually, taking small sips from their drinks, completely ignoring my melodramatics. I reached into my pocket and drained my drink, listening to the excited tones around me.

'Welcome to my playground,' Mustafa boomed.

I lifted my head and took in my surroundings. It was the assault course from hell. Amongst the obstacles there were high walls with ropes hanging off them, low nets entangled with barbed wire sitting over a muddy ditch, and high beams leading up to a ring of fucking *fire*.

I bit my tongue, afraid I was going to say something that I would regret.

'Today is your first day so I have gone lightly on you. But from tomorrow and every day that you are here, this is where you will be testing your will and your dedication. You will run, crawl, climb and jump until your body demands it. Craves for it.'

60

The first couple of weeks at camp were horrifying. I found myself becoming further isolated from the group. I watched them all complete the hellish assault course. I truly believed that each of them had been brainwashed to the extent of superior mental capacity to be able to crawl under barb wire and jump through rings of fire. The others encouraged me and Mustafa pushed me, but I would only disappoint them, disappoint *myself*. I just could not do it.

By the end of each day they were battered, bruised, bloodied and burned.

They were broken.

But every morning they would be up at half four for morning prayers, a smile on their face and faith in their hearts, ready to do it all again.

They were barely acknowledging me now, pissed off that I would not bleed for them, bleed for the cause. Amirah would sidle up to me once in a while, but I could tell that she too was frustrated with me. Akhtar would speak with me but only when nobody else was around. I think I was the only one who didn't treat him as though he was stupid.

One night, during Islamic Studies, Salman had been given the reins and he was holding court. He had posed a question to us and what a fucking question it was.

'What would be your ideal terrorist attack?'

Voices immediately overlapped, as everyone in their excitement wanted to get their idea in first. As though they had been given permission to reveal their innermost sick fantasies.

'Kamran,' Salman said. 'Why don't you go first and then we can work around from there.'

'Thank you, Brother.' Kamran addressed the group. 'I work as an IT consultant, and sometimes I work from home but mainly I like to plug in at a Starbucks. Now, when I am there and I fancy a smoke, I just pop out for five minutes, leaving my laptop on the table, then pop back again. Nobody bats an eyelid. Why should they? But what if I didn't come back? What if I had built a small explosive device, the size of a hard drive, and attached it inside the laptop? What *if...*' He smiled. 'What if we gathered, I don't know, say fifteen soldiers, fifteen laptops, fifteen built-in explosives, targeting fifteen of the busiest Starbucks across London, at the busiest time of the day. We all set the timer for the same time and five minutes before that we walk out nonchalantly, cigarette in hand, leaving our laptops behind. A Brother can cover a lot of ground in five minutes, so we'll be well out of the picture, and then we wait for the blasts, simultaneously and in perfect sync, fifteen explosions lighting up the skies of London.'

'That is sick, Bruv.' Akhtar was the first to react, after a few seconds of measured silence. 'We'll smash those over-charging, crap-coffee-making *Kafirs*, innit?' He put out a fist and was rewarded with a bump.

'Well, it doesn't have to be Starbucks, could be any popular coffee shop,' Kamran said.

'Or we could mix and match, bruv. We could do Burger King too or Mickey D's. But not Nandos, yeah?' Akhtar said.

'The size of an explosive that can slot into a laptop would be small,' Kevin pondered. 'I don't think it will be enough to cause maximum damage.'

'Coffee shops are small, everyone bunched in together. At a busy time there are, at the very least, twenty customers, *plus* staff. So say twenty-five,' Kamran countered. 'Multiply that by the number of locations. We are looking at... I don't know, I can't do the maths.'

'Three hundred and seventy-five potential casualties,' Yasir calculated instantly. 'If carried out properly, I think we are looking at fatalities in the region of a hundred, maybe a hundred and fifty.'

'I can just picture it,' Amirah said. 'They'll happily and obliviously be sitting on their high horse, dissecting whatever is the latest derogatory story about Islam, as if they have any fucking—'

255

'*Amirah!*' Parvez chided at her use of bad language.

'Let the Sister continue; her words are borne out of years of anger and frustration. Allah will forgive,' Salman said.

'Yeah, piss off, Parvez.' She sweetly smiled but didn't continue with her vision.

'And...' Kamran grinned. 'You know the beauty of it? It should be done on a Friday. At exactly one p.m.'

'Oh, that is genius,' Irfan contributed.

'I... I don't get it,' Akhtar said. 'Saturday is busier, yeah?'

'It's because,' I said, finding my voice, even though I was sickened to the core at what was so casually being discussed, 'on Friday, at one, many Muslims are at the mosque for prayers. Which means...'

'They won't be at the coffee shop,' Akhtar finally sussed.

'And those that are deserve to perish,' Amirah added. I couldn't believe the words that were coming from her lips. Those very same lips that had been attached to mine.

'I'm just going to pop out for a cigarette,' I announced. It wasn't the thing to do in the middle of a class, but I desperately needed to be away just for a moment.

I leaned against the rock, my trusty, go-to rock, and for the first time in months I craved a drink or a joint, anything to take the edge off. I couldn't do this anymore. I never could. I had let myself into this out of some misguided notion of friendship for Parvez. But he was as fucked up as the rest of them. I wanted to walk. Leave MI5 to figure out this mess. I had given them all that I could. I was fucking exhausted, man.

After I had smoked my third or fourth consecutive cigarette, I walked around the rock and narrowly avoided bumping into Mustafa.

'Why are you not in class?' he asked.

'Yeah, I'm going in now. I just came out for some fresh air,' I said.

He nodded. From behind me a sack was thrown over my head. I couldn't breathe and I fell back into the arms of whoever was behind me. He gripped me tightly by my arms and I thrashed out blindly with my legs. My arms were now being forced behind me and tied behind my back.

'*Mustafa, help me,*' I cried redundantly, as it was obviously his doing.

'Stay calm, Jihadi Jay, and stay still. Over your head is a hessian sack; it will allow you to breathe normally.'

'I... I don't know what's going on.' I stopped scrambling and forced my body to relax.

'Your Imam, Adeel-Al-Bhukara, holds you in very high esteem.' Mustafa's voice sounded distant. But I could feel his presence. 'But I feel as though his ordinarily good judgement has let him down. Your attitude, in particular, has let him and all your Brothers down.'

'*What?* I'm trying, man. Let me go... Please.'

'Aslam, take him.'

Aslam dragged me back. I dug my heels in, but he was surprisingly strong and had little trouble in moving me against my will.

'Where are you *fucking* taking me?' I shouted.

'You have been summoned, Jihadi Jay,' Mustafa declared. 'Al-Mudarris would like to see you.'

61

I felt what seemed like a hundred pair of coarse hands grabbing me by my shirt and lurching me out of the jeep. They loosened the string of the sack and roughly ripped it from over my head. I blinked rapidly, grateful when the sun hit me in the face, but that gratitude lasted all of about a second when my eyes landed on four bearded, hard-faced Afghani men pointing their rifles at me. They barked at me in Farsi, all at the same time, their hot breath in my face, their teeth crooked and stained. I didn't respond, in fear of saying the wrong thing and risking their wrath, but that seemed to rile them further, their voices rising as though I had offended them by not understanding the language. I threw my hands up to indicate surrender, and hoped that the body language would translate. One of them slapped some money into Aslam's hand and he jumped back in his jeep and left me in a strange land amongst strange men who looked ready to bite.

They formed tightly around me as I was frogmarched through the busy street. I could see the town folk glancing at me, but that was all, a glance, as though it was a normal occurrence. We crossed the road towards a line of fabric shops and small supermarkets. One of my captors entered one and returned with a six-pack of bottled water. I was poked with a rifle in my back and we continued to walk a little further until we were standing at a large metal gate. They unlocked it and we stepped through it. It was a small car park. I counted two white Ferraris, half a dozen jeeps with guns attached to the bars, one Mercedes and, if I wasn't mistaken, a tank.

We moved towards the white Mercedes. It was covered in dirt and earth but didn't look to be anything less than a year old. It had small little curtains in the back windows and a huge antenna sticking out of the back. They untied my hands and gave me some space. A bottle of water was handed to me and I drank it mercifully, letting the cold water drip from my mouth and down my T-shirt. I finished it in one go and was immediately handed another. They seemed more relaxed now that they were out of the public eye, as though my rough treatment was for appearances.

One pulled out a passport from his back pocket. It was burgundy with the coat of arms of the United Kingdom emblazoned on the front. He opened it and went to the back page and compared the photograph to the real thing. I smiled at him to help him make the match.

'Javid Qasim.' He smiled, warm and unnerving.

It wasn't the right time to say, *Call me Jay.* So I nodded.

He passed around the passport and they took turns to have a good look. As one does when looking at a passport photo, they laughed and mocked, patting me hard on the shoulder like an old friend. I joined in, laughing with them, keeping them on side.

Then the butt of the rifle cracked me in the back of the head and I saw black.

62

I had no idea how long I had been propped up on the chair. When I did eventually wake, from being rudely smacked on the head, it appeared that I was no longer in hostile territory. Gone were the four mean goons. I was sat at the head of a very long marble table. It could have easily sat twelve, on either side. On it was laid platter upon platter of goodness. Chicken wings, lamb chops, an assortment of rices and a variety of naan breads. I poured myself a glass of lassi and took a greedy, slurpy sip. I tore my eyes away from the food and looked around the room and realised that I wasn't in one. I was outside, with beautiful green rolling mountains acting as walls and the sky as a ceiling, so perfectly blue. The whole scene had a surreal, dreamlike quality. But the dull pain on the back of my head ensured that this was no dream.

I tentatively walked around the table, eyeing up every dish, making sure that I made the right choice. I wasn't sure that this was even laid out for me, but after my recent diet of rubbery chicken and dirty water, I didn't care. I was in enough trouble as it was. Might as well be in trouble on a full stomach.

I had to continuously swallow my saliva as my mouth was watering so much, waiting for my brain to make the right selection. *Damn*. It all looked so good. I couldn't wait any longer, I was hungrier now than I had ever been in Ramadan. I abandoned the careful approach and went hell for leather, topping up my plate blindly with whatever I could get my hands on. There was no way of telling when I would again have a meal this luxurious. With my plate precariously topped up and straining at my wrist, I started to stuff wings and lamb chops into my pockets.

'A man should act in accordance to his environment.' A voice came from somewhere behind me. I froze. A chicken wing fell out of my pocket.

Within a heartbeat of setting eyes on him, I lost all my appetite. I wanted desperately to tear my eyes away, but there was something about the way he held my focus that made it nearly impossible to. He walked closer towards me and with each step the revulsion on his face became more evident.

'I was once handsome,' he said. 'Just like you, Javid.' He sat down at the head of the table, just where I had woken up, and motioned for me to take a seat adjacent to him. I carried my plate and my bulging pockets and did as instructed. 'But that was a lifetime ago.' He smiled tightly, doing very little to improve his features.

The flesh on his face was seared, melted away, leaving a wrinkly, scabby burned layer where the skin had once lived. His eyes were set further back than they ought to have been, as if trying to escape the horror that was his face. He watched me watch him with interest as he took off his pashtun hat and revealed patches of his scalp the same consistency as his face.

He looked as though, once upon time, death had come calling.

There was no doubt whatsoever who I was staring at. I had, for reasons unknown to me, been granted an audience with the one they called The Teacher.

I tried to force myself to eat, but I knew I wouldn't be able to stomach it and it would ultimately come out the same way it had gone in. The quality of the food, and the fact that I was sitting with terrorist royalty, made it feel very much like the last meal afforded to a prisoner before his execution.

'You can eat it later, if you'd prefer. Back in your quarters,' he said. I released a much needed and pretty obvious sigh of relief.

'Do you mind?' I asked, making the briefest eye contact with him.

'Of course not, Javid. My appearance does not make for the perfect dinner companion.'

'No... It's not that. I'm just not very hungry.' He looked at the tower of meat on my plate and smiled. 'I... Um... Where am I?' I asked timidly.

'It doesn't matter,' he said. He glanced around at all the various beverages on the table and reached for the jug of lassi. And then, with a change of heart and seemingly without reason, he imparted: 'Afghanistan... In a place called Khost.' He poured himself a glass and topped mine.

I ran it around my head a few times, committing it to memory. At the same time, I couldn't help but wonder why he was openly telling me. Maybe because I would never have the opportunity to tell a soul. And now that he had started divulging he couldn't seem to stop.

'I bide my time on the border; we have locations in Parun, Asadabad and Gardez.'

I now knew enough about his movements to bring a lot of heat his way. If I'd been brought there because they had found out who I was working for, then they would never have let me leave with that knowledge. I briefly thought about jumping up and running for my life, past the mountains and into whatever lay beyond. I'm pretty fast, and he'd seen better days, so I was confident that I could outrun him. But a man like that was bound to have guards nearby, and getting caught would have been inevitable. So instead I conserved my energy and nodded accordingly, all the while making mental notes.

He stopped talking and sipped on his lassi. I picked up my drink and sipped along with him. We both placed our glasses down and simultaneously, using the back of our hand, wiped the milky moustaches off our faces.

'Have you any idea who I am?' he asked.

'Some.'

'My name is Abdullah Bin Jabbar,' he said. 'I am affectionately known as Al-Mudarris, or The Teacher.' He blinked.

'Are you going to kill me?' I blurted.

He laughed. *A familiar laugh.* Toothy and broad. It lit up his fucked-up face. 'Why would you think that, Javid?' He smiled, a hint of sarcasm present.

'I was kidnapped. Hit with a butt of a rifle and bundled into a car,' I said, seeing his sarcasm and raising it. There was something about him, and after every passing minute in his company, I started to feel a little comfortable, as though I didn't have to be on my guard with him. He had a certain way about him.

'Rest assured.' He placed his palms flat on the table and leaned in. At that moment it felt like he and I were the only people in the world. He lowered his tone. 'No further harm will come to you. My men are paranoid, they did not want to reveal my exact location to you.'

'But... you did,' I said.

'Because, Javid. I trust you.' He shrugged. It was a good shrug, nonchalant. Big enough to be noticed, without appearing overblown. It was natural. Fitting. It was...

I instantly broke out into a cold sweat. The colour drained from my face.

Once again my world tilted.

'Mustafa tells me that you have had some problems settling in with the exercises,' he continued obliviously. 'Tomorrow, you will accompany me to Nangarhar. I want to show you something, which I believe will help you to focus.'

I could hear him, but it was like he was talking very, very slowly, underwater, his words fading away before reaching me. My shoulders felt heavy, as though a small child was clinging onto my back, forcing me down into my chair. For the first time I looked past his spoiled face and saw him *properly*. My eyes travelled down to his feet: they were crossed at the ankles, like mine were. His palms flat against the table, as mine were; his physique, his posture, a mirror image. I recoiled back into my seat as if I had just taken a bullet.

The expert shrug. The toothy, broad smile.

All this time I had been wrong. *How could I have been so fucking wrong?*

Imam Adeel-Al-Bhukara did not send me to attend the training camp because he saw my father in me. He did so because Abdullah Bin Jabbar personally wanted me here.

The Teacher, AKA *Al-Mudarris*, AKA *Abdullah Bin Jabbar* was actually *Inzamam Qasim*.

AKA Dad.

63

I was led to my quarters for the night: a hastily built brick hut. It was cool, thanks to the table fan, and had enough amenities, including a half-decent rubber shower, to get me through my stay. I had taken a bottle of water out of the mini cooler and sat on the bed, looking out of the cracked plastic window, watching the sun dip and the moon rise, with only myself and my thoughts for company.

I hadn't divulged my revelation to Abdullah Bin Jabbar. It wasn't because I had any doubts, but because, really, what could I say?

Why did you leave us? We needed you.

Why did you choose this life over the life of being a dad, my dad?

I hate you, I love you, I have no feelings towards you.

Let's go play some catch, maybe kick a fucking ball about.

Hang on, Dad. Aren't you supposed to be dead?

Seriously, what? What the fuck could I have said? The synapses in my brain snapped, sending what felt like small electrical shocks through my mind. I wanted to throttle him; I wanted to embrace him. I wanted to kiss him; I wanted to spit in his face. Every thought contradicting, I threw my head in my hands and I used every ounce of strength not to cry. There was no way that I was going to shed a tear for that man. He was a terrorist, a fucking monster. He wasn't my dad.

Except he was.

After I had made that connection, he must have noticed the change in my demeanour, but he wasn't *Dad* enough to work out what it was – Mum would have sussed it straight away. Instead he said that I looked tired and that I should get some rest, maybe an early night.

How fucking paternal of him.

I woke up feeling strong, with a new resolve. I took a shower and looked around for my clothes. They had been taken and replaced by a green canvas bag, from which I fished out my passport, a wooden toothbrush and my worst nightmare, a brilliant white cotton shalwar and kameez. There was a harsh rap on my door, followed by a raspy voice.

'Wake, zohar prayers, five minoots.'

I did my business, uncomfortably, in a hole in the floor, and then I carried out Wudu and stepped outside into the blinding sun. There were lots of men milling about, all nonchalantly carrying rifles, just like you and I would carry our phones. One of them approached me. I recognised him as one of the four who had smacked my head with the rifle.

'Javid Qasim.' He beamed, checking out my outfit. 'Look like pure Afghani, Mashallah. My name Haqani. Come.'

He was there too. He had on mirrored aviator sunglasses that, coupled with the state of his face, made him look like a super villain straight out of a comic book. He acknowledged me with a nod of his dead head and continued to converse with two men. One held an umbrella over him to provide shade, and another took notes on an iPad.

Two rows of ten prayer mats were being laid out on the floor, and as the call for prayers rang out, everybody with a weapon removed them, placed them in a gun rack and observed the Azaan respectfully in silence.

Everybody took their places on the mat; the front centre was reserved for Bin Jabbar. I waited for everyone to take their place and I took position in the last available spot. Bin Jabbar looked back over his shoulder and spotted me. He whispered something to the man next to him, the one with the iPad. He looked crestfallen as he left his spot and approached me with a forced smile.

'Al-Mudarris has requested that you join him for prayer next to him,' he said, in a clipped English accent.

I weaved my way through the twenty-strong congregation and stood next to Bin Jabbar without acknowledging him. As the prayers started I found myself inching closer to him. Our elbows brushed and our shoulders touched as we bowed down to Allah.

Prayers finished and as the mats were being taken away, a white Mercedes pulled up – the same one that I had been brought in: I recognised the little window curtains. The door opened and the driver gave the keys to Haqani. The man with the umbrella escorted Bin Jabbar to the car and opened the door for him. Haqani motioned for me to jump into the front seat as iPad got into the back. Haqani started the car and the AC kicked in immediately, seeping some much needed cold air through my kameez. There was some discussion in Farsi coming from the back, followed by a tut and a sigh. Then iPad got out and opened my door. He inclined with his head for me to sit in the back, his frustration evident.

Little did he know that a father wanted to sit with his son.

Fuck, I had to stop thinking like that!

Haqani slipped the car into gear and spun off, driving like a man on a mission.

'Are you all right, Javid?' Bin Jabbar asked, concerned by the nauseated look on my face. 'Haqani, drive slowly.' Haqani slowed down a touch. 'You have to forgive him, he has somewhat of a manic disposition.' Bin Jabbar then said something else to him in Farsi; it sounded like an instruction.

'I very sorry, Javid,' Haqani said. 'I hit you on head with rifle very hard. Many sorry.'

'Yeah,' I said, rubbing the back of my head. 'It's all right, man. Don't worry about it.'

'Latif. The itinerary, please,' Bin Jabbar requested. He seemed to be enjoying showing me that he was in full charge.

Latif consulted his iPad. 'We should be arriving at Nangarhar in just over four hours. We are invited for a meal insisted on and provided by the Mehnaz family at their home at five p.m, after which you will have some down time. At eight p.m. a car will pick you up and take you to an airfield in Kabul, where a plane will be fuelled and ready to fly you to…' Latif turned in his seat and eyed me, before looking uncertainly at Bin Jabbar.

'It's okay, Latif. You may speak freely.'

Latif's eyes registered confusion, but he faced forward again and cleared his throat.

'You will fly north to Shebirghan to oversee the testing of remote explosive devices.'

64

It wasn't quite Beatle-mania, but it was close. As soon as Abdullah Bin Jabbar stepped out of the car, people seemed to gravitate towards him. Quickly building in momentum until he was surrounded by a crowd of fifty... sixty... seventy. They cried, they laughed, they begged for help. Haqani moved quickly to isolate him from the crowd. He seemed practised at it, but Bin Jabbar put a stop to it. I got the distinct feeling that he wanted me to witness the adulation.

I separated myself from it, not giving him the satisfaction, and took in the landscape. It was a sight to behold. In front of me a large lake led up to a sequence of breathtaking, snow-topped limestone mountains, disappearing into the skies. They looked too beautiful to be here, as if they had been picked up by a giant hand and mistakenly positioned in this place. Because behind me, all I saw was devastation.

'I once lived in those mountains,' Bin Jabbar said, now standing next to me. 'It was home for me for a while.'

Yeah, so was Hounslow.

'But I had to keep moving. The Americans had located me.'

'What happened?' I turned to face him.

'This happened.' He spread out his arms to indicate the destruction around him. 'Last month, two drone strikes hit the Nangarhar province. I and thirty of my men were the target,' he said, pointing at the mountains. 'Two of my men were crushed by falling rock. The rest of them, they managed to escape by boat, here. In this small village called Hisarak.'

'You weren't here,' I said, without question.

'No.' Guilt crossed his face. 'I was in Jalalabad.'

'You knew it was coming.'

He nodded grimly. 'The information that I received was not reliable. The dates were incorrect. I didn't have sufficient time to organise evacuation.'

'You said there were two strikes.'

'Yes, right here, where we are standing. The Americans were not aware that I had escaped. Or... maybe they were aware.' He shrugged. I looked away. 'They released another drone, a direct hit into the village. Forty-seven lives perished. Fifteen of my men. The rest—'

'Civilians.'

'That's a very cold term, Javid. They are not civilians, they are not numbers or statistics. They were residents, with homes, families, livelihoods. They had plans for the future. Not big plans, like Mr and Mrs America; they had small plans. Getting through the day with enough to feed their family or to buy their child shoes and a third-class education. You see, Javid, this was always a poor village, which moved at a slow pace. This is not like Kabul, which could and has, to an extent, recovered from such an attack. Here the unintelligent lead the uneducated. I, we, helped fund this town.' He pointed at a once-white, once-formed building, sliced and diced but still attempting to stand proudly amongst the rubble. 'That was once a hospital. We enlisted good local men to build it, and we provided capable staff to run it. And when these good people needed a hospital the most...'

*

We headed towards what had been formerly known as the hospital. Haqani and Latif followed behind us, keeping their distance, reading the mood correctly and giving us room. We walked past homes in various states of disrepair, subsiding into the earth, windows smashed, front doors hanging off their frames.

But the force of the impact had been felt most at the hospital.

I carefully stepped amongst the rubble and gently touched what was left standing of the structure, scared that if I applied too much pressure it would come down around me. It felt cold to my skin as my palm moved across the surface. I could hear a thousand desperate screams piercing through my mind, visions of failed escape and trapped souls, wanting nothing more than to die instantly.

'For most, death was immediate,' Bin Jabbar said, reading my thoughts. 'For others it would have been a slow journey.' He put his hand out and I couldn't think of a reason to not take it. I placed my hand in his and he pulled me out of the ruins. 'Times have changed. We live in a world filled with lies and hate.' He continued as we moved slowly around the wreckage towards the back of the hospital. 'There was a time where we would fight chest to chest, with nothing but guns and knives. Setting traps and seeking out the enemy. But those days are no longer. Now bullets are replaced by drones, manned from beyond sight, behind the luxury of a remote control, and *they* have the nerve to say that *we* don't fight fairly.'

We rounded a corner and what I saw then will haunt me for the rest of my life.

Bodies laid out neatly, in two rows of six, covered in white sheets.

'Their rules of war, invented to serve their purpose, and give them the advantage. It is the fight of a coward. We put our bodies and lives on the line and they just flick a switch.' There was a rise and a tremor in his voice. 'What they have in weaponry, we have twice that in heart.'

He moved towards the smallest body, kneeled down and slowly removed the white sheet. A little girl. Eyes closed, lips parted, face smashed. A small skinny arm had been placed next to her shoulder, like a broken piece of a jigsaw that did not quite fit. I placed the white sheet carefully back over the body.

I remembered, from what seemed like a lifetime ago, Khan telling Idris that he had *picked the wrong side*. The destruction of the hospital, the bodies, that dismembered young girl – I wanted to strike out with all my might. I had sick thoughts and fantasies fuelled by revenge. Every part of me wanted to wreak havoc, to turn my own body into a weapon and wage war against the Kafirs responsible. I wanted to hurt them and then move onto their fucking families and eat their children.

These thoughts, they... they soon go. And I'm me again. Rational. I vomited.

Gently, Dad rubbed my back.

65

We ate like kings. Kings in squalor. The Mehnaz family had welcomed us into their broken home with God-like worship for Al-Mudarris. They didn't seem to think they had the right to sit or eat with him, so they just stood around aimlessly, not quite knowing what to say or do. They fussed around him, topping up his plate and glass without request and smiling stupidly and gratefully whenever gratitude came their way. After the meal, Bin Jabbar requested the room. It was a demand wrapped up in the guise of a respectful request, and everyone vanished. Apart from me and him and two cups of masala chai.

'I am sorry you had to see that,' Bin Jabbar said.

I shrugged, then felt overly paranoid at the gesture.

'You said it happened about a month ago,' I said.

'Just under, yes. You are wondering why the bodies are still there?'

'Yeah.'

'Most of them have been buried. The remaining are waiting to be claimed.' He took his cup and poured some tea into his saucer. 'We wait twenty-eight days and then they will be taken away.' He lifted the saucer to his lips and drank straight from it. 'If there is no family to claim the bodies then it is up to the people of Hisarak to pull together and give them a respectful burial. They died as martyrs; a place in Jannat is waiting.'

We sipped on our tea in a bout of silence. My eyes everywhere but on him. His eyes only on me.

'Before Ghurfat-al-Mudarris, were you part of Al-Qaeda?' I said, leaping recklessly into a cop question.

'For a short while I fought for them. But I didn't agree with their methods.'

'Is that a result of it?' I said, inclining my head towards his face.

He nodded, as he filled his saucer with more tea.

'One thing that I never agreed with was the sacrifice of life for the cause. But regardless, I was sent on a mission, strapped to an explosive vest. I never intended to give my life on that mission. I wanted to live to fight another day.'

'Did you... detonate?'

Another nod.

'So... How did you escape?'

Bin Jabbar leaned in close to me. His face, lit up by the harsh light from the bare bulb, emphasising every cut, burn and sear. He smiled and said, 'Does it look like I escaped?'

I averted my eyes and sipped on my tea. He leaned back and looked at me with amusement. Sizing up his son, probably wondering if I had it in me to walk in his shoes.

'We still have a relationship with Al-Qaeda. We use their groundwork, their infrastructure. But we do things a little differently. We do not broadcast ourselves or send out recorded messages to Al-Jazeera or the media, sitting in a cave, brandishing guns and claiming responsibility. They, the West, the infidels know what we want; we do not need to spell it out. They can stop all the bloodshed, the deaths of innocents, whenever they want. Until then we are standing firm and we are here to catch whatever is thrown at us, and throw it back at them with the might of Allah.'

He looked at his watch. I looked at his watch. It looked expensive and it looked to be saying a few minutes to eight. I knew our time was coming to an end. A thought shook through me as I realised that I wanted to spend a little longer with him. A lot longer.

There was a knock on the kitchen door, one that indicated that our time was up. It was hard to discern from his face what he was feeling, but I saw regret, or maybe I just saw whatever I wanted to.

'Adeel-Al-Bhukara is a dear friend of mine, a friend whose opinion I value highly,' he said. 'He has put in a great deal of faith in you. I want you to go back to the training camp, Javid. Mustafa is a good man – let him guide you, build you. I do not want to hear that you haven't been trying. You have seen with your very eyes what we are up against. Use it.' He pressed his finger to my chest. 'I know better than you that you are capable.'

The kitchen door opened and Latif sheepishly popped his head around.

'The car is waiting, sir,' he said nervously.

'Let it wait,' Bin Jabbar said calmly.

'But, the itinerary.'

'I don't care about the itinerary,' he yelled. 'I am talking with my...' My eyes widened and the hairs on my back of my neck stood. 'I am talking with Javid. I will be out when I am out.'

Latif's head disappeared and the door closed. Bin Jabbar motioned for me to get up.

'Walk with me, Javid.'

We walked out into the evening and said our goodbyes to the Mehnaz family. They were handed a wad of cash by Latif, which they declined at first but then took willingly. Haqani was waiting inside the Mercedes as Latif held the car door open.

We stood facing each other, both firm in the knowledge of what we were to each other but neither willing to admit it.

'Aslam has been sent to pick you up. He will drive you back to the camp,' Bin Jabbar said.

It was all too brief. Two days in the company of a man who I had no feelings for, but I wanted more. I wanted him to acknowledge the *fact*. Behind his tortured face, behind his sick beliefs, behind the monster was my father and I wanted him to say it.

Just fucking say it.

I looked down at his outstretched hand and blinked. They were my hands...

I shook it, my grip tight as though to prove a point. His thumb ever so gently brushed against my knuckles and my breath caught. I immediately dropped my hand from his. With the slightest of nods I walked away without giving him a second look.

Determined that one day, somehow, it would be me that would take him down.

66

I arrived back at camp around seven in the morning, and the troops, as per schedule, were being put through their paces by Mustafa with some hand-to-hand combat training. They eyed me curiously, but I kept my head down and walked past them to my room. My intention was not to ignore them, but it probably came across that way. I sat up on my sleeping bag, tea in one hand, phone in the other, fully aware that I had to send a message to Parker, informing him of my dalliance with The Teacher, but I... I just couldn't do it. Not yet. I had to get my head together first. I heard multiple footsteps approaching and the group all bundled in and stood around me. There were no handshakes or *salaams*. Amirah moved to hug me, but something in my face stopped her. The rest didn't say anything, unsure where to start, until Parvez asked, 'Why are you drinking your tea like that?'

'You should try it,' I said, sipping tea from the saucer.

'Where did you go?'

'Across the border. Afghanistan,' I said coolly.

'Jalalabad?' Kevin asked.

'Yeah, amongst other places.'

'What did they do with you?' Parvez approached me, and sat cross-legged at the foot of my sleeping bag, invading my private space as always. It made me smile. 'Why are you smiling?' he asked.

'How are you, Parvez?' I said.

'Aren't you going to tell us what happened?'

'Nothing happened. I've had a lot of time to think and I just want to apologise to you all. I wasn't there with you, not fully. I was scared, but not anymore. You don't have to worry about me. I've got your backs and I hope that you have mine.'

'We shall see,' Irfan said sharply and walked out. Yasir followed, embarrassed by his hot-headed younger brother.

'I hope so, Brother,' Kevin said, uncertainty etched in his face. 'Rest, for now. After breakfast we have military training. Today we will be climbing the highest of mountains, where we will break for lunch and prayers and continue well into the evening. *Inshallah*.'

'He shall not be participating.' Mustafa entered the room. 'Jay will be spending some time training by himself.'

Questions clear on all their faces, but not on their lips.

I nodded to myself. I knew this was coming. I wasn't like the others; I was different. I was the son of Al-Mudarris.

'It's not my decision,' Mustafa continued. 'It has come from higher authority, one which cannot be questioned. However, I must clarify, this is not a punishment. There is no doubt that Jihadi Jay' – he winked at me – 'has the same intention and passion as everybody here; do not be fooled into thinking any different. But he will progress quicker and faster working on his own. You will still be able to see him during meal times and free time, and he will still pray with you, so you will have plenty of time to bond, to create that trust.' Mustafa clapped his hands. 'Okay. That's enough for now. Give him some space and the rest of you reconvene outside in fifteen minutes.' He grinned. 'We have a mountain to conquer.'

They all bundled out except Amirah and Akhtar. Akhtar sat on his bed and Amirah stood over me. We eyed each other quietly for a moment.

'Amirah,' I said. 'Whatever this is… Between us. It has to stop.'

She nodded. I think that she was relieved. I looked at Akhtar. He was busying himself, pretending not to listen.

'I need to focus,' I continued. 'Maybe after we—'

'What happened to you out there, Jay?'

'Remember you once told me to open my eyes,' I said. She smiled sweetly at the memory and I almost fell back in love right there. 'Well, they're open.'

She leaned down, kissed me on the cheek and walked out.

Akhtar seemed relieved when she had left. 'Wanna hear a joke, bruv?'

No, not really.

'Yeah, go on then.'

'Where do suicide bombers go when they die?'

'I don't know. Where do suicide bombers go when they die?'

'Everywhere!' He started to chuckle.

'Not bad, Akhtar. You really put the "fun" into "fundamentalist".'

'I'm glad I'm not a suicide bomber,' he said. 'I mean, I'd do it if I was asked… But I really don't want to die.'

'You all right, Akhtar?' I said, pouring some more tea onto the saucer.

'Yeah, Bruv. I'm good.' His drooped shoulders told me something different.

'What's up, man? You know you can talk to me.'

67

I had set off around three in the morning and arrived at the assault course around two hours, three cigarettes and two bottles of water later. I looked at the hellish course in front of me. The sweat, effort and traces of blood of the group still lingered. I had no idea how long we had left at the camp, but I knew with conviction that I had to beat this thing. I had to show *him* that I was strong. As strong as the others. As strong as him.

I climbed onto the high beam and sat in the middle of it, slipped out my phone and composed a coded text to Parker, stating everything I knew about The Teacher. Not quite everything. I wasn't ready to tell him about our relationship.

My finger hovered over the send button as I read and reread the message. It was enough to give them enough intel to track his movements and possibly lead to capture. If Dad ever found out that it was me, he would probably ground me for a very long time!

I smiled sadly at the thought and pressed send.

Sorry, Dad.

*

From a distance, through the dusty haze, I could see a jeep approaching. I pocketed my phone as the jeep pulled up and Mustafa stepped out.

'I thought I might find you here, Jihadi Jay,' Mustafa said, looking up at me perched on the beam.

'Do you have to call me that?'

'Yes.' He smiled. 'I can't work you out.'

'What's to work out?' I said, sparking up.

'Not everybody is granted an audience with Al-Mudarris.'

'Well, I must be the lucky one then, eh?'

'There is something about you. People seem to believe in you, though you don't believe in yourself.'

'I get by.' I shrugged.

'Okay, Jihadi Jay. This is how it will be. You have free run of the camp. I will join you as and when I can. We'll go through some hand-to-hand combat training and we'll get you out for some shooting practice.' He eyed up the course. 'But this course… it's broken many men. I am going to leave it up to you how you wish to tackle it.'

*

It became routine. At four o'clock each morning, I would wake up, cleanse, pray and head to the camp. I would walk at pace for almost two hours to the assault course, that time shortening each day, until I could do it in under ninety minutes. Upon arrival I would run several laps of the running track around the assault course, keeping one eye on the course at all times, beating it mentally, trying to build up the strength to tackle it. Mustafa would drive down and join me daily whenever the group had free time. I took in all I could from him.

I could disassemble, check, clean and reassemble a Glock as easy as tying my shoelaces. I could, from a running position, duck and roll, landing onto one knee in perfect shooting position, with the sawn-off AK-47 gripped firmly in both hands, my finger on the trigger, ready to take out the enemy. My hands, which had never before felt the effort of a hard day's work, developed thick callouses. The smell of cordite warmed me and filled me with the kind of comfort that only a gun could provide.

As for the assault course, well, that turned out to be my kryptonite. Mustafa mentioned that he would soon be communicating with Al-Mudarris on our progress. My dedication and work rate had already improved, but I wanted him to know that I could do it all. I didn't have the blind faith that the others had, that divine mental strength. I was just a son trying to impress his dad.

I stretched out on the floor and closed my eyes, trying to picture myself beating it. I was rudely poked in the chest by the muzzle of a rifle.

'Salaam, Brother.'

I opened my eyes. The sun bounced off his head, giving the impression of a halo. His AK-47, as though a natural extension of his arm, pointing at me. His eyes were unwavering and he was chewing on a toothpick. A far cry from the fool I had grown up with.

'Man, get that thing out of my face,' I said, slapping the gun away. 'What are you doing here, Parvez?'

'Mustafa sent me. Said you might need a friendly face.' He smiled to indicate how friendly his face could be. 'Have you completed it yet? The course?'

'I was just thinking about it.'

'It's going to have to wait, Brother. Mustafa has called a meeting.'

68

Parvez and I walked back to base at a snail's pace. It was the ideal opportunity to talk with him and see if I could find a chink in this jihadist's armour. I had to be careful not to give the game away. But it was no good; he was at his militant, preacher best.

'What happens after?' I asked him. 'You know... after?'

'We go on. We fight. Another target, another location.'

'What if you get caught?'

'I won't get caught. Even if I get caught, I won't get caught.'

'Parvez, c'mon man, I'm shattered. Stop talking in riddles.'

'They can catch me physically but they will never get inside here,' he said, tapping his head.

'You know you'll be locked up for the rest of your life, right.'

'So?' He shrugged. 'There are a million Brothers ready to step up and take my place.'

'But *the rest of your life*. That's a long time.'

'The afterlife is longer, Jay.'

'You know they'll torture you,' I said. He yawned. 'Are you listening to me, man? They'll *torture* you.'

'Yes, I heard you. I'm ready, Brother. I have been ready for many years. I have prayed, begged Allah to give me this chance. I have got on my knees and cried for the opportunity to make a change, to give a voice to Muslims. I don't think about being caught or tortured or never seeing my family. I have chosen a path, the same as you, to fight, to kill, to deliver a message from Allah.'

Shit.

'I'm not going to ask you the same question,' he said. 'I know if you were to ever get caught you would do the same.'

I put my head down and kicked a small rock, watching its journey.

'Goes without saying, Parvez,' I said.

*

The meeting took place within Mustafa's quarters. There were nine small wooden desks laid out in rows of three, a pencil and a pad sitting on top. The others in the group had already taken their places. Irfan turned from his position in the front row and motioned for Parvez to join him. I sat at the back. Next to me was Akhtar and next to him, Amirah. Mustafa stood at the front, facing us. He had a small remote control in his hand and his chest muscles seemed to be dancing of their own accord as he waited for us to settle in. Behind him was a large white screen. He clicked a button on the remote control and the projector above me woke up. It whirred for a minute and then it shot out an image onto the white screen.

My blood ran cold. I was looking at an aerial view of a street. A street that I had been down many times. Where I had shopped and eaten and got drunk. A place where, even though you were surrounded by thousands, you were invisible.

'This is Oxford Street,' Mustafa said, his voice low and measured. '*This...* is our target.'

The room erupted with an '*Inshallah*' back at him and it frightened me to death. I glanced across at Akhtar and saw fear in his eyes.

This was it, this was the moment that I had been selected for. There was no way I was going to remember all the details to report back to Parker, but it was imperative that I did not miss anything out. Masked by the excitement of the noise around me, I slipped my hands in my pocket and held down the home button on my phone.

My phone had been set up so that a long press of the home button would record audio straight onto a micro SD card, which would automatically send itself as a message to Parker's phone. I hadn't used this function for previous communication because I'd wanted the SD card to stay clean. Even if after the card was formatted, it would still be possible to recover data from it. My instructions were clear: use it and lose it.

Mustafa gestured for the room to calm and I casually removed my hands from my pocket.

'It was supposed to be a ten-man operation, but as you all are aware, young Iqbal decided it wasn't for him. It's okay, what I see in front of me is more than enough.' Mustafa moved his eyes over each one of us. 'You will work in pairs, apart from one group of three. Now pay attention and take notes.' He waited for everybody to pick up a pencil and open up their pad before he continued.

'Your starting point will be Park Royal, West London.' A click of the remote, the slide changed to a nondescript mid-size industrial unit. 'Kamran and Akhtar: you are to travel by Tube and step off at Oxford Circus. You will come up at ground level at the Nike shop. That is where you will hold your ground.

'Parvez and Jay: a car will be provided. You are to drive to Cavendish Square. From there you will walk to Oxford Street, towards Oxford Circus tube station, directly across the road from Kamran and Akhtar. I want you to split up into two locations. Jay, you will hold position at the mouth of Argyll Street, facing Oxford Street. Parvez, next to the station there is a fashion shop called Tezenis. A Brother who works for a lettings agent will be waiting for you with a key for an empty apartment directly above Tezenis. Let yourself in and make your way through to the living area. You wait there until it is time and then walk through the French doors that lead to a balcony. That balcony looks down on Oxford Street.'

'Kevin, Salman and Amirah,' he continued, calmly laying down his instruction. He spoke slowly and clearly, loosening his American drawl, giving us the opportunity to take down detailed notes. At every point of instruction, he would click the remote and change the slide, and point to exactly where each person should be holding position.

Around me I could hear the frantic scrabble of pencil on paper. I knew that I too should be taking notes. The intention was there. My pencil had made contact with the pad but all I could accomplish was a grey dot, which grew darker and bigger as I applied pressure on it. My hand was rooted. It wouldn't move, paralysed at the overload of information that was flying towards me and the knowledge of the target.

'The time: one p.m,' Mustafa said. 'The date: one of the busiest days of the year. January first. New Year's Day.'

The pencil snapped in my hand.

Salman stood up and smacked the table with the palm of his hand. Kevin, not to be outdone, stood up and thumped his chest. Both screaming 'Inshallah'. Yasir and Irfan embraced, whilst Parvez started to repeatedly yell 'Allah hu Akbar'. Amirah stood on the table and joined in with the chant. Kamran stood up and screamed at the top of his lungs, 'Leave no man behind!.'

Akhtar was the last to stand. He did so hesitantly, eyes darting around the room. He lightly patted his chest, inaudibly mouthed something, trying so hard to believe, wanting to believe, but not quite fully understanding the enormity of what was happening around him.

But I did. I understood.

As I watched them manically bouncing off the walls, shouting and screaming words that were never meant to be used in this context, an emotion that could never be articulated burning brightly into their twisted faces, I truly understood.

They were angry.

Angry at being seen as second-class citizens. Angry at being seen as an evil religion, when at the heart of Islam lies peace. *Angry* because one soldier is beheaded in broad daylight in the streets of London and it is milked by the media, and by those who consume the media, and they carry the flame as they watch documentaries condemning the actions on *every* fucking anniversary, refusing to let the flames die – but are happy to turn a blind eye to those very soldiers in their pristine uniforms, with their expensive weaponry, walking into our communities, our villages, our homes and murdering, pilfering, raping, shattering thousands of innocent lives. A small girl, an innocent child, blown to pieces by a remote-controlled bomb whilst she sheltered in a hospital, her body still unclaimed – does she get the time of day, a fleeting moment's thought, column inches, *a fucking documentary*?

Those conflicting thoughts that had besieged me of late hit me like a speeding train. I stood up and screamed at the top of my lungs.

'Allah hu Akbar!'

69

They all spilled out amongst the mountains, dancing, shouting and shooting the sun from the sky. Mustafa approached each of them, one at a time, a small holdall in his hand. He requested that everybody drop their phones inside. We wouldn't be needing them any longer. He reasoned that the time for relaying our message on social media was over for now, and it was time to focus solely on the mission ahead. Truth was, Mustafa did not trust a single motherfucker regardless of the importance that he regularly put upon it.

My hand slid into my jean pocket, index finger chipping desperately away at the slot in my phone, trying to blindly remove the SD card. I saw him striding towards me just as the card dislodged. I slipped out my phone and dropped it in the holdall.

I was absolutely petrified, my right leg was trembling and I was worried that the card would pop out of my pocket. I forced my leg to stop and I smiled at him.

'Hard work starts tomorrow,' he said. 'Today you have the day to yourself. Go celebrate. You have the run of the camp.'

'Oh, okay. Thanks,' I said, just because I had to say something.

'And Jay... You have done well. I may not show it but I am proud of you.'

I beamed as though his words meant everything to me. He slapped me hard on my back and then moved away, only to be replaced by Akhtar.

'What you up to, Bruv?' Akhtar asked. 'Why are you not celebrating?' His smile could not have been any weaker.

'You go ahead, I'll catch up with you later,' I said, as the guns cracked around me. 'I'm gonna go for a walk. Take it all in.'

'Can I come with you?'

I inhaled deeply. I needed time to think. I needed time to myself, to get away from the anger and the excitement.

'Akhtar, listen, Brother. Why don't you join in the celebrations? I'll be back soon.'

He looked around at the spectacle and swallowed. 'Please can I come with you?'

'Fuck's sake,' I snapped. He flinched. 'Just leave me alone for a minute.'

He looked at me as if he had just been slapped. He tried to compose himself quickly but I had hurt him, and it showed. He moved away and picked out a rifle from the gun rack and shot holes into the sky with the rest of the jihadis.

*

It wasn't my intention, consciously anyway, but I had ended up back at the assault course. It was reaching mid-afternoon and the sun was at its hottest. I looked up at the skies for some divine intervention, some inspiration. Nothing!

But I did it anyway.

Now, a better story would tell you that I had completed it. Beaten it. Scaled the wall, crawled through the barbed wire net, swished across the high beam and jumped through the ring of fire amongst all the other obstacles. And the rest of the group had gathered, watching me, cheering me on. Willing me across the finishing line, where they would carry me up on their shoulders, shouting my name, accepting me. Trusting me to walk side by side with them in battle.

Well, this isn't that kind of story.

I set off. The barbed wire net was the first obstacle. I laid on my stomach as low to the muddy ground as possible. I crawled, letting my midsection and my arms inch me forward, my legs remaining passive. I crept slowly, *slowly* through the net and about halfway through, when I dared to think that I could make it unscathed, a metal wire grazed my back. It didn't break the skin, it barely scratched it. But it served as the final straw.

With my face in the dirt I started to bawl uncontrollably.

I cried for my mum. I cried for my dad. I cried for Parvez. I cried for all the Muslims around the world who had to pick up a weapon and resort to jihadism because they truly believed that there was no other way. But most of all, I cried for myself. Knowing that my actions, from here onwards, were going to hurt a lot of people.

It seemed like an eternity before I got through to the other side of the net. I didn't even bother entertaining the idea of the rest of the obstacles. I was done.

It had beaten me.

70

Christmas Eve

We had spent those last few weeks sticking close with our
allocated team members. Encouraged to spend as much time
as possible together, to fully trust and understand each other,
bucking one up if the other tired. We studied the material
comprehensively. We discussed what we would wear, what the
traffic would be like, best route to the holding point. I had spent
hours in close proximity to Parvez and in that time I did not once
attempt to question his motive, talk him out of it. I knew that he
could not be reasoned with; his brain had been cleansed to the
extent of no possible return. All he could see was the *jihad*.

It was the night before Christmas and I was staring into the
dark from my sleeping bag, the furthest away from the festive
feeling that I had ever been.

'From your position on Argyll Street, Brother,' Parvez said
through the darkness, 'you'll be fully mobile, able to move in
any direction. As will the rest of you.'

'Yeah,' I said. 'I know that already.'

'But me, I'll be on the balcony. Stationary.' He hesitated. 'My
target from that height will be far and wide. I can take out as
many *Kafirs* as the bullets I have. And, Brother, I intend to make
every bullet count. I have been granted the most effective position
and I am grateful for Mustafa to have that faith in me. But...'

'But what?' I hated hearing him talk like that, although that
kind of language had become second nature to me.

'It means that escape for me will be less likely.'

Even though he couldn't see me in the dark, I nodded.

'If I get caught, I swear to Allah I will never ever give up my
Brothers.' He sniffled. 'No matter what they throw at me.'

286

I didn't want to patronise him. Tell him that everything was going to turn out just fucking wonderful. I knew that he would be arrested as soon as he set foot back in London. That plans were probably being put in place as we spoke. He was going to be locked up somewhere dark and dingy and horrific, and tortured until he broke. And it would all be my doing. But it was easy to justify to myself. Somebody like Parvez, no matter how I felt about him, the best place for him, for all of them, was under lock and key.

'Goodnight, Parvez.' It was the only thing I could say.

'Goodnight, Brother.'

71

The whirring sound of a washing machine woke me up. It was loud and rude and abrupt, as though it was spinning rocks. And it sounded like it was getting closer. I sat up on my sleeping bag. Everybody else was awake and sat up too, scratching their heads and rubbing their eyes as they tried to determine where the offending sound was coming from. It grew louder and louder still and the room felt cold, as though a huge breeze was blowing in.

'What *is* that?' Salman asked, stepping out of his sleeping bag.

We were all standing now, frightened to leave the solace of our room. Amirah's head popped around the doorway.

'Come,' she shouted over the noise. 'Come quickly.' Then she dashed.

We all pegged it after her, and looked tentatively outside at the black helicopter approaching to land in the enclave between the mountains.

'It's a helicopter.' Akhtar stated the obvious.

Shit! It's on. I tried to step back and find a quiet place to keep my head down. This was about to get really messy and I didn't want any part of it. Any second now, some pretty pissed off soldiers were going to leap out of that helicopter and rain hell. I felt a sudden surge of guilt overwhelm me.

'They found us. Tool up!' Kamran said.

'No. That's not military,' Irfan shouted over the noise. 'Look, there's another one.'

A second helicopter, a white one, was making its way down to land. I surprised myself by breathing a sigh of relief.

As they landed, loose earth blew hard, causing a giant cloud of dust to travel towards us, covering us in dirt. Through the dust cloud Mustafa came jogging towards us, taking us by surprise, which made us all scramble back into our room.

He entered our room. 'Apologies for the rude awakening, soldiers.' Mustafa raised his voice over the thunderous roar of the two helicopters. Immediately questions flew at him.

He put up two meaty hands and the room quietened.

'By the mighty grace of Allah, I believe that every one of you is ready.' There was no *Inshallah* or *Mashallah* booming back at him. Instead just a fear of the unknown. 'I have watched you all grow into fighters, into jihadis. *Now* is the time to prove your faith. *Now* is the time for you to take that step.'

What?

'The attack will no longer take place on New Year's Day,' Mustafa said, handing out new passports. Fake passports. 'It will take place the day after tomorrow. On Boxing Day.'

Part Four

Ballad of a Dead Soulja

– Tupac Shakur

72

Unit 71, Park Royal, London, Christmas Day

The two helicopters had flown us from the training camp in Khyber Pakhtunkhwa to Kabul, where we were driven to Hamid Karzai International Airport. To my disappointment the fake passports held up and we were able to board the plane and fly thirteen hours direct to Amsterdam Airport Schiphol, after which we stepped on a Eurostar to take us from Amsterdam to St Pancras, London. Four prepaid minicabs had been waiting for us to take us to Unit 71, Park Royal.

Throughout the journey, we were split into our designated teams, dotted around the airplane or on different carriages so not to attract suspicion. We were not allowed to leave each other's side for a second, to the extent that we had to accompany each other for toilet breaks and wait outside the cubicle. This had made it impossible, as was the intention, to raise a call for help.

It was an exhausting passage from Pakistan to London, but the guys had buzzed with anticipation throughout, fuelled by adrenaline and untapped aggression.

It was approaching midday as we arrived at Unit 71. About three hundred square feet of floor space, with eight no-nonsense single beds on the near side and one on the far side, with partitions around it, for Amirah. A large steel safe with a digital numerical security pad loomed menacingly by the far wall. Its shape and design was that of a wardrobe. Two wide drawers at the bottom and two tall doors at the top.

Kamran walked confidently up to it. From his pocket he slipped out an envelope and calmly punched in four digits. The safe clicked and he took a step back.

'What is it?' Irfan asked. 'What's inside it?'

'I don't know yet, I haven't looked, have I?' Kamran replied.

'Well, what are you waiting for?' Irfan joined him, kneeled down and opened one of the drawers. He pulled out a brown paper package, tied with string. 'Jay. This has your name on it.'

I stood rooted.

'*Jay*,' Irfan hissed. 'It's yours, take it. There's one here for all of us.'

We all stepped forward as Irfan handed out the packages.

'It's clothes,' Akhtar said, as he ripped open the package. 'Oh, that is sick. This is designer gear, bruv. I got a Tommy H shirt and Levi's. And a long coat...' He looked at the label. 'Ben Sherman.' He laughed. 'Trainers, socks, toothbrush, digital watch. They even got CK chaddis!'

I carefully opened my package. It was similar. In mine I had a full black Adidas tracksuit, with Nike kicks, and a chunky black puffer jacket.

'They want us to blend in,' I said to myself.

'Of course they do,' Kevin said, patting me on the shoulder. 'We can't exactly walk around looking like...' He searched for the right word.

'Terrorists,' I said, quietly.

Kevin scoped the room, looking to see if anybody heard. 'Brother, don't ever make that mistake again.'

'I was only—'

'Just don't,' he said. The conversation was over.

'Hey.' Irfan opened the tall safe doors. 'Look at this.'

We all gathered around and there was a collective sharp intake of breath as we set eyes on nine neatly lined-up sawn-off AK-47s and nine shiny Glock 19s.

'Take your guns,' Irfan said. 'They are your responsibility. Put them by your beds, get used to having them close to you.' Irfan carefully handed out the weapons. 'They look unused but check and clean them anyway.'

'What's in the bottom drawer?' Yasir asked. Irfan opened the last remaining section and there sat a small black plastic box. We all hovered over his shoulder as he carefully flipped open the lid. After a while of staring at it, and nobody wanting to spell out exactly what it was we were looking at, Salman said, 'It's there for those who need it.'

'Why would we need cocaine?' Akhtar said.

'Because it speeds up the way your mind and body works,' I said, reaching into my past. I pulled one of the small zip lock plastic bags out of the box and prised it open. My little finger dipped in and I sampled the gear, just a touch but enough for it to take immediate effect on my heart rate.

It was strong. It was required. It was forbidden in Islam.

'At your own discretion,' Irfan said quietly, handing out the bags to the group.

Nobody, not any one of those high and mighty, fundamentalist, religious, Allah-fearing, zealotry-preaching *Muslims* said anything.

Hypocrites. Dipping in and out of the laws of Islam to suit their agenda.

73

The knock on the door was jaunty. Jauntier than Parker was used to. Jaunty enough to irritate him, and just enough jaunty to warrant him putting down his shop-bought tuna pasta, getting up off his armchair and peeking through the blinds. It was the last person he would have expected to see at his home on Christmas Day. Curious, Parker put on his cargo pants and answered the door. He would deal with it as quickly and efficiently as possible, and send him along on his merry way.

He opened the door and there was a bottle of something in his face. Parker inclined his head slightly to see Teddy Lawrence beaming from behind it, with teeth that Parker had often fantasised about knocking into the back of his throat.

'I know you don't drink, old chap. So I found this non-alcoholic wine from a quaint little off-licence down this delightful little road that I was surprised to find that *you* lived on,' Lawrence said. He might as well have sung it. He placed the bottle in Parker's hand, declaring 'Merry Christmas!' and let himself in.

Parker stood at the door, looking at the spot where Lawrence had just been standing, and wondered how he had slipped past. He shut the door and attempted to prepare himself for whatever this was. He walked into his living room to see Lawrence walking around the room, whistling appreciatively at his surroundings.

'What is this, Victorian?'

'Edwardian.' Parker looked at his living room through Lawrence's eyes. After his wife and family had left him, he decided on a whim to buy the three-bedroom semi, on a leafy street in a green part of London. He had hoped that it would help build bridges with his wife and children, show them that he had changed. They were yet to visit.

'Yes.' Lawrence clicked his fingers. 'Edwardian, of course, the symmetry.'

Parker just nodded. He didn't quite understand what Lawrence had meant by *the symmetry*.

'Shouldn't you be with your family, Lawrence?'

'Shouldn't you be?' Lawrence replied, all too quickly. 'And call me Teddy. We're not at Thames House.' He smiled, parking himself in Parker's armchair.

'What do you want, Teddy?' It sounded wrong but he went with it.

'What's this?' Lawrence said, picking up the ready meal. 'Pasta?' He sniffed it. 'Tuna pasta? Not very festive.'

Parker took it from him and placed it back on the coffee table. It didn't look like Lawrence was in a big hurry to leave, and it wasn't like Parker had anything planned, so he sat himself down on the sofa adjacent to *his* armchair and asked again.

'What do you want?'

'Susan, my wife, is in the kitchen preparing a feast for a small army. Her mum and sister too. I sensed that they wanted to have a bitch about me, so I left them to it for a couple of hours. Told 'em that I'm off to see my good mate.' He smiled. 'But he wasn't at home so I thought I'd come and see you.'

'What do you want?' Parker asked for a third time.

'Ah, yes, I know what we need.' Lawrence stood up and wandered out of the living room without explanation.

Parker thought... Well, he didn't actually know what to think. Lawrence had let himself in, made himself at home, and was now wandering around somewhere in his house. He eyed up his armchair and knew that it would be beyond childish to get up from the sofa and reclaim it.

Lawrence walked in brandishing two wine glasses and stopped in his tracks at the sight of Parker comfortably back in his armchair. He looked at Parker in mock annoyance. Parker looked back defiantly. And then they both started to laugh.

The ice slowly but surely started to melt.

'It's Christmas,' Lawrence said, finally answering the question, as he poured and handed a drink to Parker. 'I thought it was as good a time as any to apologise.'

'Well.'

'Well what?'

'Apologise then,' Parker said, setting them both off again.

'I've been a shit. You've had your moments too, but I know I pressed your buttons hard... And,' Lawrence smiled, 'I've just become a father very recently. An event like that gives you... I don't know... clarity. So, yeah. Sorry, Chalk. Truly.'

It was quite the turn of events, but he appreciated the gesture, especially on Christmas Day. They clinked glasses and Parker congratulated him on fatherhood.

'You think we're ready?' Lawrence's tone now down to business.

Parker sighed. 'From the intel, yes, I think we are.'

'I agree. I've heard the message from Qasim over and over. The fucking nerve of these guys. The *audacity*. On the busiest day, at one of the busiest times.'

'It's a good plan,' Parker conceded.

'You think? It screams hatchet job to me.'

'I think the effectiveness is in its simplicity. Nine men, split into four groups. Two groups of two at one end of Oxford Street, the busiest end. One group of two at the other end. With the final group of three entering Oxford Street around the halfway mark via Poland Street. It's a variation of the pincer movement. Full control with thousands of shoppers blocked in.'

'And throw some AK-47s and Glocks into the mix...'

'Carnage.' Parker nodded.

'Yeah.' Lawrence mirrored him. 'Carnage.'

'Thankfully, it won't come to that. As soon as they set foot into the country they will be detained. The relevant authorities will be on alert from the twenty-seventh.'

Lawrence frowned, 'I think the twenty-seventh is too late.'

'We have to rely on the intel. According to Jay, they will be arriving at Heathrow on the thirtieth. Even if they change from that location, we will, by then, have every entry into the country under heavy surveillance.'

'What if they change the date?' Lawrence said, as he refilled the empties.

'We have to rely on the intel,' Parker said again and sat back in his chair, deep in thought.

If the date, location or plan had changed, Jay would have found a way to get that information to him. He had been efficient and detailed in his communication so far.

There was no reason to think anything had changed.

74

Unable to sleep, this time with good reason, I padded quietly to the bathroom. I gently placed the seat down on the toilet and sat. My head in my hands, palms pressed hard into my eyes. I was lost. I didn't know where or who to turn to. There was nobody in that room who would or could help. They were ready to fight, willing to take whatever their bleak future threw at them for a piece of history, for a cause. For a belief that only a few could understand.

I had to get in touch with Parker. Desperately. I had to find a way. Mustafa knew what he was doing when he took our fucking phones away. He went on and on about bonding and trusting your Brother, but he didn't trust a fucking soul.

I had already tried once to escape from the unit, but the door was heavy-duty and locked from inside, secured with three large padlocks. The three keys were currently with Salman, Kevin and Parvez. There were no windows that I could hop from. I looked up at the bathroom ceiling and there was a large vent, large enough for me to fit through. If I somehow managed to get the vent open without waking up eight angry terrorists, then what? Was I going to crawl around blindly through the spider-infested tunnels like an action hero, hoping it led me out to the outside world?

I was running out of options. My only chance was that very small window of time when we leave the unit to travel to Oxford Street. And by then, it may be too late.

A knock on the bathroom door shook me.

Resigned to the fact that I wasn't about to escape from the vent, I opened the door.

'You've been in there ages, Bruv,' Akhtar said.

'Yeah.' I shrugged. 'The mirror is very flattering.'

'What?' he said, not getting it.

'Nothing,' I said, not explaining it. 'Can't you sleep?'

He shook his head. 'Do you remember what we talked about? At the camp?'

I grabbed him by the arm, pulled him into the bathroom and locked the door.

'*Fuck's sake*, Akhtar,' I whispered. 'Do you want the whole room to know?'

'Sorry, bruv.'

'Yeah, I remember. What about it?'

'Nothing. Just want to say thanks for understanding. I don't think anybody else would have.'

'That's all right, man. That's absolutely fine. Just remember what I said.'

'I don't need to, bruv. I've made my mind up.' He smiled, big and forced. 'I'm going to go out there tomorrow to kill as many Kafirs as I can, Bruv. Do Allah's work, yeah?'

I nodded whilst my heart broke. 'Just remember, you can change your mind. You won't be letting anybody down, I swear.'

'What about you, bruv. You ready?'

'As I will ever be,' I said, knowing that I had lost him.

75

Boxing Day – 5.00 a.m.

Fajr – morning prayers – were at six a.m. The alarm went off an hour earlier. In turn we all showered. The typical-looking Pakis amongst us changed their appearance as much as possible. Shaving off their beards, styling their hair to fit in with the West, leaving no reason to be *randomly* pulled over and searched. We got into our new clothes, and complimented each other on how different we all looked.

We then stood side by side and prayed together for the final time.

It was emotional for them. It was emotional for me. After prayers we all embraced each other tightly. The tears that came were inevitable.

Still with a few hours to kill, some tried on their long coats, getting used to having the bulk of an AK-47 strapped under their arm and a Glock in the side pocket. Others sat silently on their beds checking and cleaning their weapons. Nobody really conversed, everything that needed to be said had been. Decisions made, minds made up.

I watched it all from my bed. Serene expressions all around me. Cool, calm, collected, even with the knowledge that they were about to unleash bloody hell on hundreds.

'Any way I can get some fresh air?' I asked to whoever was listening.

'I don't see why not,' Kevin said, glancing at his watch. 'I could do with some too.'

'You know that's not such a bad idea,' Kamran joined in. 'We can go out as intended, like a dress rehearsal. Get used to the idea of walking around with the AK-47 strapped to our shoulders.'

I sat forward on my bed in anticipation of a possible escape. Make that call to Parker. Get the fuck outta dodge.

'No.' The voice of reason. Salman.

'Why not?' I asked.

'You'll get all the fresh air you need in due course, Brother. For the meantime, let's just stay put. Keep in mind we are not far from the A40. A police car sees a bunch of Pakis walking out of a unit, it is going to raise suspicions.'

'We can go one at a time,' I countered weakly.

'I said no,' he snapped. 'Please, Brother,' he added.

I looked at Kamran, who just shrugged it off, and then at Kevin, who seemed to have lost interest in the venture. I sat back in bed, rejected. I looked at my watch: just over four hours until one.

302

76

Kingsley Parker had woken to find a smile on his face. He had a well deserved day off from work, and the visit from Teddy Lawrence on Christmas Day had affected him more than he thought it would. They had finished off the bottle of non-alcoholic wine, and exchanged some friendly conversation. He didn't misunderstand, though; despite the friendly exchange, they were never going to be actual friends, not really. But it was nice knowing that he didn't have to worry about Lawrence tripping him up at every turn, just so that he could make himself look good and climb the ladder to wherever it took him. Especially with such an important result looking to go their way.

Thanks to Jay, they had the known locations and compounds of The Teacher. A team had been dispatched promptly to Afghanistan to locate and capture Abdullah Bin Jabbar. It's funny that even with all the resources MI5 had at their disposal, they had to rely on a Muslim drug dealer from Hounslow, snatched off the streets to work undercover as a spy, just to find out his real name. It had always been a long shot, scouting Javid Qasim as a possible asset, though it looked to have worked. Parker, though, couldn't take all the credit for Jay. It was at a meeting twelve months ago that Major General Stewart Sinclair had insisted on Javid Qasim.

'It has to be Qasim,' the Major had said. 'I want you to make sure he has no choice but to work with us.'

Parker had countered against it. 'With all due respect, Major, he is an unknown quantity. And it's going to take up a lot of resources. We have many Muslim agents who can infiltrate The Teacher's network.'

'They'll see our guys coming a mile off, regardless of their religion. Qasim fits the profile.' Inevitably, the Major had his way.

Parker had wondered at the time, and wondered again now, as he recalled the conversation, if Sinclair knew more than he was letting on. Either way, it didn't matter. Very soon, months of hard work – work that wasn't natural to Parker, who was better suited to the battlefield – would pay off. The Teacher would be located and eight of his disciples would be locked up in a hole for the rest of their lives.

Parker reached for the bottle of vodka on his bedside table and stared at it, surprised at the lack of an urge to break the seal. He opened the drawer of his side table and stuffed the bottle inside. That comfort blanket was no longer required.

77

10.30 a.m.

'Kamran, Yasir, Irfan, Parvez, Jay, Akhtar, Kevin and Sister Amirah,' Salman said, standing in front of us. We were fully dressed, AK-47s hanging from our shoulders, hidden under our coats, each with a Glock slipped in a side pocket and a rucksack full of ammunition. Plus the small bag of cocaine. 'Each team will arrive at their destination at varying times, dependent on their mode of transport. According to the schedule, we should be in position well before one o'clock. Keep yourself busy, window shop, have a bite to eat, but stay low-key. Make sure you are not far from your allocated position. Our watches have been synchronised to the second and our alarms set for one o'clock, where we will have a window of around ten minutes before we are set upon. When your bullets have been embedded into as many Kafirs as possible, lose your weapon and lose yourself in the crowd. Oxford Street will be heaving, so escape shouldn't pose too much of a threat. We meet back here, Unit seventy-one. We still have it for another seventy-two hours.' He watched us, one by one, relishing the position that he had seemingly given himself. He cleared his throat at the awkwardness of what he was going to say next. 'The cocaine.' His face fell. 'As Jay pointed out, it increases the way your mind and body functions. Instincts will be quicker, reactions sharper. I will not advise one way or another upon the consumption, but it is there if you need it....' Salman's words trailed off.

Kevin stepped in. 'Too much can be dangerous, too little may be ineffective.' He slipped the ziplock bag out of his pocket and pried it open. 'I'd like to give a small demonstration for those who haven't used before.'

Using a small plastic straw and a small flat plate that was provided, Kevin sensibly advised the best way to consume. I looked around at the reactions of the others; they seemed uncomfortable at it being discussed, I could tell that they did not want it to be addressed. God forbid that they take some fucking coke, but taking lives, well, that's just fucking acceptable in Islam! I was fuming inside at the sanctimonious hypocrisy of it all, and if Salman hadn't continued with his *motivational* bullshit speech, I swear I may have fucking lost it.

'This is not the end of our journey, this is but the beginning. Inshallah we will carry out our work with the efficiency and ruthlessness that is demanded of us. We have come a long way and we will not *fail*.'

'Inshallah,' Kevin said.

'We will not fall.'

'Inshallah,' Parvez joined him.

'We will take out as many as our body and our bullets allow us to. Do not let some misguided notion of guilt enter your mind. Be strong and you will be rewarded.'

The chants grew louder as the rest of us chorused along.

'We get through this and we live to fight another day and, most importantly, as according to the teachings of Al-Mudarris, *we leave no man behind*.'

The room went into overdrive.

78

10.45 a.m.

Kamran and Akhtar were the first to leave. They were to take
the 487 bus to Hanger Lane station and then a tube on the
Central line to Oxford Circus station, where they would step out
at the business end of Oxford Street, just under the Nike flagship
store. They looked ready, game-face on. Even Akhtar looked in
the zone. They left quietly with the silent promise of returning as
heroes.

11.02 a.m.

Salman, Kevin and Amirah were next. Amirah stalled, she
dithered with her outfit, not quite comfortable. She complained
that her trainers were too tight and her hoody too constricting
around her neck, resulting in a touch of claustrophobia. Her
coat, a beige mac, was too big for her and the strap from the rifle
kept slipping off her slender shoulder and getting caught in the
arm of her coat.

'Shit, this coat is too big, it's not keeping the gun in place,' she
moaned. 'And this *fucking* hoody... I can't breathe in this thing.'

Salman was stood by the door, impatiently tapping his foot on
the floor, casting glances at his watch. Kevin walked calmly to
Amirah and put his hands around her waist. Her eyes widened
at the intimate gesture as he moved in closer and tightened the
hanging belt on the mac around her waist. 'That should keep
your gun in place, Sister. Keep your coat buttoned and belted up
until it's time.' He loosened the tie string around the hoody and

stretched it away from her neck. 'Is that better?' She nodded. 'Just keep breathing, okay? In through your nose, slowly out through your mouth, right?' Amirah managed a nervy smile.

'Ready?' Salman snapped. Amirah shot daggers at him.

'Yes, Brother,' Kevin said.

They turned and nodded at us, Amirah's eyes catching and holding mine. I had to look away and when I looked back they had gone. They had a short walk to the minicab office, where a cab had been booked to take them to Soho Square, where they then would walk to Poland Street and hold position before descending into the middle of Oxford Street.

11.15 a.m.

The two brothers, Yasir and Irfan, stood in front of each other, both hands placed on the other's shoulders, heads down, foreheads touching. Their eyes were closed as they said a hushed prayer.

They opened the door and walked out. A silver Transit van, which hadn't been there when we arrived last night, was waiting for them. On the side was a logo: *Mohsin's Electrics. Our prices won't shock you.* Parvez and I watched them get in. The keys were hidden in the sun-visor. Yasir started the van and they drove off without looking back. Destination Centre Point, where they would park in the nearest NCP car park and make their way on foot to Tottenham Court Road tube station. Opposite end of Oxford Street to Kamran and Akhtar. The objective to box in the shoppers.

11.30 a.m.

The last two left standing. Me and my childhood friend, Parvez Ahmed. The irritant, the agitator, now standing with me, an AK-47 strapped to his shoulder, a Glock 19 in his pocket and a rucksack full of ammunition. I looked at him for what he was, what he had become; he was no longer that guy that I knew and loved. Something, someone, had screwed with his head and I was looking at a soldier, a jihadi. Ready to go to war without regard for his own safety and without regard for the lives of others. He truly believed in the cause and it was that belief that gave him that air of invincibility.

'Jay,' he said. 'Are you ready?'

'Yeah,' I said, with as much confidence as I could muster, and I opened the door.

A midnight blue Ford Mondeo was sitting outside.

'I'll take the wheel,' I said, walking towards the driver's side. I placed my rucksack in the back seat. Parvez buckled up, cradling his rucksack in his lap. I adjusted the seat to give me some leg room and fixed the rear-view mirror. I looked towards Parvez, who was staring blankly in front of him. My mouth opened to say something but there was nothing left to say. So I started the car, put it into first and we were on our way to Oxford Street.

79

11.47 a.m.

Akhtar had never travelled by Tube. The smell, the juddering movements and constant battle for a seat maddened him. Every time the Tube stopped he would hustle and bustle through the crowd of those trying to step off, only to find that somebody quicker, smarter than him had beaten him to a seat. He was frustrated and tired, really very tired. It seemed like he had been constantly on the go. The demanding schedule of the training camp, the rigorous assault course, the long walks in the soaring heat, and the long journey from Pakistan to London. What was in front of him didn't seem too relaxing either. On his feet, shooting, running, escaping. He just wanted to rest, sit down, even just for a minute.

He had lost Kamran somewhere in the carriage, but that had always been the plan. Kamran had said it wasn't clever for two Pakis to be sitting together, especially with their long coats and rucksacks; it was bound to raise a few eyebrows regardless of how much they tried to fit in. You can't disguise brown skin.

Akhtar started to feel queasy. The coat was making him sweat; the temperature inside the Tube was the extreme opposite of the December weather. He held on tightly with his left hand to the overhead rail. His shoulder started to hurt and he wanted to change arms. However, his rifle was sure to slip if he held onto the rail with his other hand. He looked around the carriage through the bodies for Kamran and spotted him in the far corner. He had only managed to get himself a seat!

The train slowed and the doors opened. He looked out of the window and saw a sign for Marble Arch. A fair few stepped off the train and two seats became available. The trouble was that the seats were next to Kamran and he wasn't supposed to be seen with him. But his body moved without engaging his brain. As he scrambled through the aisle towards his goal, he could see Kamran give him the eye before looking down to the ground in ignorance. The empty seat furthest from him was taken quickly by a sprightly pregnant woman, leaving only the seat directly next to Kamran available. Akhtar hesitated for the briefest of moments, but then decided to sit his backside down. He figured if Kamran didn't like it, then he could go and stand somewhere.

Akhtar rested his rucksack between his legs and discreetly positioned his AK-47 so it sat across his chest for comfort. He gave a sigh of relief and stared up at the complicated web-like map of the London Underground. He frowned when he realised that they had to be off in two more stops. He had hoped for a longer stint in the seat. He sat back, exhaled deeply and closed his eyes as he thought about how many *Kafirs* were going to fall. It concerned him that he'd had doubts at the training camp. Not anymore. He still didn't quite understand the reason for carrying out such a vicious attack, even though he had been told over and over by Kamran and Salman. Akhtar would walk away with renewed vigour after speaking with them, but when he found himself alone, he would find holes in the logic. Maybe he wasn't clever enough to understand politics or jihadism or whatever this was, but he owed it to his Brothers to stand by them and have their backs. He opened his eyes and a little Oriental girl was smiling mischievously at him. He put his thumb to his nose and wiggled his fingers and her smile turned to laughter. Her parents looked to see what she was laughing at and in turn smiled pleasantly at him. Cute family, Akhtar thought. He glanced over his shoulder at the pregnant woman, who was reading a baby-names book. He wondered what she would choose.

He looked around the carriage some more. A young couple were holding hands and brazenly stealing kisses, typical Kafir behaviour, but Akhtar found it kind of sweet. A group of tourists stood at the far corner, with expensive-looking cameras around their necks. A huge Russian-looking, heavily tattooed man, engrossed in his phone.

His eyes started to move quicker now, darting from face to face. Making snapshot associations. A young boy with his granddad. An Indian family of four. A group of friends discussing what shops they were going to visit.

It hit Akhtar like a long overdue slap in the face. These people, they were all going where he was going; these very people that he had made relationships with, albeit just the brief smile or nod of fellow passengers, were the very same people that *he* had to put down.

What had they done to him, again?

The Tube slowed down and the doors opened at Bond Street. He silently willed for them all to step off the Tube. He could feel sweat dripping down his forehead. His eyes travelled back to the Oriental girl and she was no longer smiling at him. She looked concerned by his demeanour.

The doors closed. Next stop Oxford Circus.

'Bruv,' Akhtar whispered. '*Bruv.*' But Kamran's eyes remained focused on his shoe laces. So Akhtar nudged him softly with his elbow.

'*What?*' Kamran hissed, then nervously looked around the carriage.

'I want to go home.'

'*What?*' Kamran said, in disbelief. '*No!*'

'I really, really want to go home, bruv.'

'Get yourself together, Akhtar.' But it was too late, Akhtar was already standing up. '*Sit down. Will you please sit down?*'

'I'm really sorry, Bruv.' Akhtar stood up. 'I know you looked out for me and that. But I don't want to do this anymore.'

Then to Kamran's horror, Akhtar slipped his hand into his coat pocket, removed and placed the Glock 19 on the seat in front of him. He then took off his coat and slipped the AK-47 off his shoulder and placed that on the seat too. Kamran was up like a shot, walking backwards through the carriage, his fingers working quickly over the buttons of his coat.

He knew for certain that his jihad was going to begin here and now.

As the pregnant lady turned the page of her baby-names book, her eyes landed on the weapons laid out on the seat next to her. She screamed. Then everybody else screamed.

Kamran's coat was fully open and his AK-47 was in shooting position.

He shouted: '*Allah hu Akbar!*' and pressed the trigger.

The father of the cute little Oriental girl went down, with a shot to his back, trying to protect his daughter. The pregnant woman ran screaming towards the opposite end of the carriage, another deafening shot as Akhtar watched as her right ear flew off, the impact spinning her around. Everyone was on their feet, trampling over each other, trying to get away.

After the first two shots there was a pause. Akhtar knew that Kamran was hitting the selector, switching it from semi-automatic to automatic firing. There would be no escaping the sharp, relentless burst that would spray death every which way.

Akhtar stepped forward towards Kamran, but there was no chance that he could beat the quick flick of a switch. Then two huge tattooed arms tightly bear-hugged Kamran from behind, the Russian passenger squeezing the life out of him.

'Kamran,' Akhtar shouted, but there was no way his voice would be heard over the screams. 'It's over, Bruv. Can we go home, please?' Their eyes were locked and Akhtar was aware of the flash of disappointment in Kamran's eyes.

The Tube started to slow down on approach to Oxford Circus. Passengers frantically slammed the doors with the palms of their hands. Kamran, one hand just about mobile against the tight grip, reached into the side pocket of his coat and managed to grab his Glock.

'*Brother, I beg you,*' Akhtar shouted.

Kamran's hand gripped the handle and pointed his Glock towards the slowly opening door and the masses of people leaning against it. Akhtar went down on one knee, picked up his own Glock from the seat, smoothly flicked it off safety and shot his friend in the face.

Kamran's body slackened in the Russian's arm and he slipped to the floor.

The doors fully opened and the passengers fell forward, making a mountain of bodies on the platform.

The screams started to die down, replaced with the sounds of heavy boots entering the carriage, shouting an angry and repetitive message.

Put down the weapon, put down the weapon, put down the weapon.

Akhtar placed the Glock back on the seat and felt a boot in his back pushing him down, his face making hard contact with the floor so that he tasted blood. He was handcuffed and they went through his pockets, finding only the small bag of cocaine. They spun him around and he looked up to see eight, nine, ten armed transport police officers with guns trained at him.

He chewed on something in his mouth and spat out a bloody, broken tooth.

Then he said the two words that Jay had told him to remember.

'*Kingsley Parker.*'

80

The cabbie had spent the best part of the journey eyeing up Amirah from the rear-view mirror. Amirah wished that she could have shot him in the back of the head, or at least thrown a few choice expletives his way.

'This is Soho Square,' the cabbie announced. 'Anywhere in particular?' He raised his eyebrows. 'You want to see a show? I can take you.'

'No,' Salman replied from the front seat. He looked at his watch: they had over an hour before history was made. 'Pull up next to that Lebanese restaurant, on your left.'

'As you wish.' The cabbie pulled up and Salman paid the fare with a crisp fifty and the three bundled out of the cab.

'Let me shoot him,' Amirah said, half jokingly, as she discreetly adjusted her rifle and tightened the belt on her mac.

'It's good to see you back again, Sister,' Kevin said, as the minicab pulled away. 'For a minute, I thought you were going to fall apart on me back at the unit.'

'I just freaked out a little. I'm okay now. I promise.'

'Let's eat,' Salman said, leading the way into the small Lebanese restaurant.

They waited to be seated but the only two waiters were otherwise occupied. Not with customers; they were gathered around a small television. They decided to seat themselves, choosing a Formica table for four next to a window, giving them a clear view of the passers-by.

'Order something that can be made quickly, nothing too heavy,' Salman said. 'Maybe a salad for you, Amirah?'

'Why don't you order your own food, eh?' she said, picking up the menu.

'I'm getting a lamb roll,' Kevin decided, as he put down the menu and looked outside. There was a hard-faced woman, mid-thirties, sitting on a bench just outside Soho Square. She was well dressed, in a sharp trouser suit, clearly not a Boxing Day bargain hunter. But her disposition did not match her attire. Her feet were flat on the floor, pointing inwards, one hand was gripping a clump of hair tightly as she cried hysterically on her phone.

Salman tried to get the waiters' attention, but they hadn't even realised that they had customers, so engrossed were they in whatever programme they were watching. He tutted his annoyance loudly and went back to the menu.

Kevin shifted his eyes from the woman to the green of Soho Square. In the centre of it sat the famous Tudor house. There were some shoppers, if their bags were anything to go by, animatedly talking to each other. One was slumped down, head in her hands, and judging by her rhythmic shoulder movements she seemed to be crying too. Everyone, in fact, on the little green square seemed to be acting strangely. Anxious, scared faces. Some on their phones, walking around in small circles, gesticulating, frustration apparent.

Kevin blinked and moved his eyes back to his companions. They were both still concentrating on the menu. He looked towards the two waiters, and the chef who had now joined them. They had their arms around one another, still glued to the box that was obscured from Kevin's vision.

He expected the worst, even before he had got to his feet and walked across the restaurant. He approached the waiters and stood behind them, watching the television over their shoulders.

He watched for a minute and then calmly walked back to the table and took his seat.

'I've decided,' Amirah announced. 'I'm going for the chicken sandwich.'

'Did you manage to get the waiters' attention?' Salman asked.

'Kevin, your face has turned white,' Amirah said. 'Even more than usual.'

'I want you both to listen to me very carefully. No sudden movements and no reactions,' Kevin said slowly. 'Nod if you understand.'

Salman and Amirah glanced at each other, turned their attention back to Kevin and nodded.

'Something really bad has happened.'

81

12.06 p.m.

Parker was feeling uncharacteristically upbeat. He finally got out of his bed, feeling as if a weight had been lifted from his shoulders. He never sought glory, but he knew it was close and it gave him a sense of satisfaction that had long been missing.

He opened his wardrobe and took out grey tracksuit bottoms and a grey sweatshirt. He put them on, along with a pair of black running shoes that he had bought with good intentions, but had never quite found the motivation to put them through their paces. Today, though, he was going to run. It was Boxing Day, and he figured that half of London was sleeping off a hangover, while the other half were knee-deep in sales, shoving and pushing for a marked-down microwave. He looked out of his bedroom window and his quiet neighbourhood seemed like the perfect place for a run. He stretched his neck far to his right, enjoying the crack.

His mobile phone started to ring.

He continued to look outside at the pleasant view that he had never really noticed as he stretched his neck far to his left.

His landline started to ring, too.

Parker turned slowly away from the window, with a creeping feeling that his run would end before it even began. He walked to the landline. That feeling of lightness had been all too brief; his footsteps felt heavier and that weight slowly returned around his shoulders. He picked up the landline, ignoring the incessant tinny ring from his mobile phone.

'Parker,' he said.

'I've got through,' a voice said, but not to him. To him it said, 'Answer your mobile phone, right now. Answer your mobile!'

Parker didn't bother to ask who it was, but kept the phone to his ear. He reached across to his ringing mobile, but before he could answer he heard the sound of someone relentlessly pounding on his front door.

He put his mobile to his free ear.

'Hello,' he said tentatively.

'Please hold for Major General Sinclair,' a voice said as the person on the landline cut him off, leaving him with a dial tone. He placed it back in its cradle and moved the mobile to his favoured ear.

'Parker,' Sinclair suddenly boomed.

'Major.'

'Two shooters armed with sawn-off AK-47 and Glock 19s.' Sinclair went straight into it. 'One opened fire on a tube on the Central Line, between Bond Street and Oxford Circus. One fatality, many casualties. The shooter was then inexplicably shot and killed by his partner, who we have detained. Both parties presumed Muslim.' The pounding at the front door continued as Parker tried to digest the information. He walked downstairs with Sinclair in his ear. 'Get yourself down to Oxford Circus station. A room has been secured in the premises for you to question the suspect.'

'Is there nobody on site that can question him? It will take me some time,' Parker replied, opening the front door. A man in black motorbike leathers handed him a helmet.

'Negative, Parker. He is not talking to anybody, not a soul. He won't even tell us his name.'

'Why do you think that he's going to tell me?'

'Because he specifically asked for you by name!'

Parker took a moment to let that settle in and Sinclair afforded him that moment.

'Our intel was wrong.'

'Yes, Parker,' Sinclair replied. 'We think it was.'

*

With the help of the motorcyclist, Parker switched on the Bluetooth on his phone and connected it to the headset within the crash helmet. A call came through instantly.

'Parker? Lawrence.'

'Lawrence.' A brief hesitation as his mind cast back to the previous day's conversation. 'What's your position?'

'Oxford Circus tube station. I've met with the suspect. He's not talking; he wants you.'

'I'm en route. ETA fifteen.'

'The suspect asked me if I was Kingsley Parker, so it's clear that he doesn't know you personally. Therefore, Qasim must have talked. It looks like just the date has been moved forward. Judging by the time and location of the arrest, I don't think anything else has changed. If we work on that basis, then the attack is to take place in fifty minutes. We have to assume that it will be at the planned locations and that there will still be two teams of two coming in from either end of Oxford Street and one team of three coming in from Poland Street. The forth team has been neutralised. One man down and the other arrested.'

'One of the teams includes Jay,' Parker pointed out.

'I know,' Lawrence sighed. 'Look, Parker, we are going to have armed cops all over the street; they don't know about Qasim. I don't know to what extent he is playing terrorist, but if they see him waving a gun around, he's going down.'

'We need to start the evacuation.' Parker moved away from the subject. He wanted to argue, to put measures in place so that the police were aware of Jay, but it was a losing battle, a battle he didn't have time for.

'Already on it, evac is underway as we speak. But there are approximately fifty thousand shoppers and we have less than an hour. It's going to be full-blown pandemonium.'

Parker closed his eyes and visualised a mass stampede, shoppers trampling over each other to get to safety.

'They won't get out in time.'

'Armed police are gearing up, we have neighbouring police stations releasing bodies, we're going to flood the street.'

'Okay, good work, Lawrence.'

'Look, Parker. We could be completely wrong with the times and locations. But until you have spoken to the suspect, we won't know.'

82

12.12 p.m.

'I can see the car park,' Irfan said.

'Where?' Yasir asked, frustrated as he looked through the windscreen at the standstill in front of him on Upper St Martin's Lane.

'Far right, yellow sign, NCP in big, black writing.'

'Yes, I see it, Irfan.' Yasir released some frustration, but not all.

'We are one step closer to our goal. Just have to park the van, a short walk and maybe a ten-, fifteen-minute wait.' Irfan smiled at the thought. 'It's happening, Brother. All our hard work and dedication is about to be realised.'

'I wish I shared your enthusiasm,' Yasir said, looking at the traffic. 'We haven't moved in a long while.'

'It's just Boxing Day traffic, it will move. We have time on our side.'

'I don't know.' Yasir frowned. 'This is something else. I think there has been an accident. That traffic light has changed to green over a dozen times and not one car has passed through.'

'What do you suggest?'

Yasir looked at his watch. 'We're not going to make it for one.'

'We must. We will, *Inshallah.*'

They could hear the wail of the emergency services getting louder but they could not determine the emergency. The lights turned green. Yasir, hopefully, slipped the van into first, even though they were fifteen cars away from the lights. The car at the front did not move. The lights turned amber, then back to red.

'We have to adapt and improvise,' Yasir said.

'Yes... How?'

'I want you to go to the holding point.'

'No. We go together, Brother. Allah will get us there on time.'

Yasir smiled. 'Even the mighty Allah has no power over the unpredictable London traffic.'

'I don't understand. What about you?' Irfan suddenly seemed daunted, carrying out the attack without his big brother by his side.

'I am going to turn the van around. There was a pay-and-display about a mile back, I will try my luck there. If not, I will park on a double yellow if I have to and join you.'

'Let's just leave the van here in traffic. Then we can go together.'

Yasir shook his head. 'It's too risky. It will be noticed. We will be noticed.'

'I'm not going without you, Brother.'

Yasir reached across past Irfan and opened the passenger side door.

'I'll be there. I promise. Now go.'

83

12.15 p.m.

'Jay,' Parvez said. 'You're taking too long.'

'What the hell do you want me to do?' I snapped at him, as if the fucking traffic was my fault. 'Anyway, we're only down the road from Oxford Street.'

'Do you have an A to Z?'

'Yes, Parvez, I have an A to Z. In fact, I have a whole set of encyclopaedias up my arse.'

'Why do you have to be so crass?'

'Well, don't ask me stupid questions. No, I do not have an A to Z.'

'We need to find somewhere to dump the car.'

We had been inching through Regent Street. I looked out of the driver's-side window at Hamleys toy store. It was rammed full of kids and overwhelmed parents. There were Christmas green elves lined up outside, showcasing the latest toys. Imagine having to wear that outfit to work. Imagine dying in it.

We were supposed to park in the NCP on Cavendish Square, but on approach we noticed a lot of police presence, so we moved right on past it. I was tempted to jump out of the car and spill my guts to the cops, but that would have unhinged Parvez, and with his current mindset, he was capable of doing anything. I had only one option and that was to phone Parker, somehow. I had looked out for phone boxes throughout our journey from the unit, but thanks to the mobile phone era, they seemed to be few and far between. The ones that I did see were not easily accessible without going off track and raising suspicion. I still had over thirty minutes before it kicked off and to my relief I noticed a phone box across the road from Hamleys.

I had to be very careful with how I was going to present this to Parvez.

'You know, Parvez,' I said, 'I'm glad that I am doing this with you.'

'I am too, Jay. I had my doubts about you. But the way that you have proved yourself in the face of—'

'Listen, I want to do something,' I interrupted before he went off on one. Time was of the essence.

'What?' he said, looking slightly aggrieved at being cut short.

'I want to phone my mum.'

'There's no way.'

'Parvez, listen, we have over thirty minutes, and we're just down the road from our destination. There's a phone box just across the road.' I pointed over his shoulder. He didn't even bother to look. 'Look, man, I don't know where we will be after this is over, or what is next for us. You've had a chance to say goodbye to your mum; I want to do the same.'

He didn't respond. I took off my seatbelt. His head darted towards me, his eyes questioning me.

'Just take over the wheel. I'm going to nip across the road, make a quick call to Mum and I'll meet you back in traffic. Two minutes, three tops.'

'I'm sorry,' he said, looking anything but sorry. 'I can't allow that.'

'What the fuck's that supposed to mean?' I snapped. 'Who put you in charge? I'm going to phone my mum,' I said, reaching for the door handle.

'I said, I can't allow that.' His Glock rested just under my ribs.

I released the handle and put both my hands back on the steering wheel.

'Put your seatbelt on,' he instructed.

'Fuck off,' I hissed. The Glock dug deeper into me. I put my seatbelt on. 'Unbelievable, Parvez. *Brother!* Truly un-fucking-believable. This is how you going to play me, huh? You pull a fucking piece on *me*?'

'Be quiet.'

'What you going to do? Shoot me?'

'Yes,' he said coldly. 'Take this next left. Do it now.' I pointed the car out of traffic and turned into a quiet side road. 'Park the car.'

'It's a double yellow,' I said weakly. I parked the car and killed the engine. He kept his eyes and gun trained on me as he fished out the cocaine from his pocket. He tried, unsuccessfully, to pry open the zip-lock bag with one hand. He handed it over to me.

'Open it,' he said.

'You don't have to do this, Parvez,' I said, opening the bag and handing it back to him.

'It will help me stay sharp. Allah will forgive.' And then, like the complete fuckwit that he is, he stuck his nose in the opening of the bag and sniffed the contents, through both nostrils, at the same time.

'That's not what I meant. We can walk away,' I said softly, finally giving away my hand.

We locked eyes, and in that moment I watched as his eyes narrowed. A small, righteous *I knew it* smile appeared on his face.

'Get in the back.'

'Seriously, Parvez. Let's not do this. You have your whole life—'

'You didn't notice, Jay. But you know what I just did?'

'What?'

'I just flicked the safety off the Glock.' He sniffed. 'Now get in the back.'

I took off my seatbelt and climbed into the backseat. He turned his body to face me, his Glock steady, his eyes wild. His smile bigger than I had ever seen.

'I always knew you were weak, Jay. I *always* knew. The problem is you don't care, not enough, not like I do, *Brother*. You may have fooled the Imam into believing that you were destined to become some sort of great *jihadi*. You almost fooled me. But in my heart, I knew.'

'You didn't know shit, you twisted fuck.'

He lifted his gun so that it was pointing at my head. I flinched.

'You know how I feel about your language, Jay.' The coke had taken over him fully. 'There's a latch in the back seat. Lift it, pull the back seat down and get in the boot.'

84

Parker walked through Oxford Circus station, into an area normally closed off to anyone but staff. He glanced into a large room, which was brimming with MI5 and Met personnel, waiting impatiently as the IT guys set up workstations and network points. He didn't enter and was instead led to a room with two armed guards waiting outside and Lawrence pacing in front of them.

'Thank Christ!' Lawrence exclaimed. 'Go.'

Parker flashed his credentials at the two agents guarding the room and they stepped to one side. Parker entered the room alone. The suspect had his head down, resting on his cuffed hands on the table. Parker shut the door behind him. The suspect lifted his head.

'Kingsley Parker?' he asked tiredly. As though he had asked that question a hundred times.

'Yes.'

'Prove it.'

'I believe we have a mutual friend. Javid Qasim.'

Akhtar straightened up in his chair and beamed at him. 'What's happening, bruv?'

Parker did not know how to answer that, so he answered the question with a question of his own.

'What's your name?'

'Akhtar,' Akhtar answered. Parker didn't have to know his full name. Jay had already provided full names of the group.

'Right, Akhtar. I don't wish to appear rude, but I am going to ask you some questions – questions which will require very short answers. Understand?'

'Yes.' Akhtar smiled, passing the first test.

'Is the attack going to take place today instead of New Year's Day?'

'How do you know about New Year's—'

'Just answer the question, Akhtar.'

'*Jay…*' It dawned on Akhtar. 'That Brother was undercover, yeah? I *knew* there was something about him. Something different.'

'Akhtar. Look at me. Focus and just answer the damn questions.'

Akhtar nodded. Parker waited.

'What was the question again?'

Parker was a heartbeat away from beating the hell out of this guy.

'Is the attack going to take place today instead of New Year's Day?'

'Yes.'

'What time?'

'One p.m.'

'Are the holding points the same as they would have been on—'

'Look, Bruv. Everything is the same: the time, the location, the holding points. Just the dates have changed, yeah?'

That was all the confirmation that Parker required. He spun on his heels and turned the door handle, but before opening the door he turned back to Akhtar and asked, 'Why did you shoot your partner?'

'He wasn't my partner, he was my Brother, yeah?'

'Why did you shoot him, Akhtar?'

'Because I didn't want him to kill any more people.'

Parker nodded and walked out of the room.

'And?' Lawrence was on him.

'It's confirmed.'

Lawrence took out his mobile and made the call.

'We have confirmation; relay message to all teams, we have confirmation. Seven targets will be in place as briefed,' he said.

Six targets, Parker thought.

Lawrence killed the call and wiped the sweat off his forehead. 'Let's go.'

'Where?'

'They've set up an operations room; we'll have live updates. There's nothing more we can do.'

'I need a vest and a gun,' Parker said. 'I'm going out there.'

85

12.30 p.m.

I was tempted, if I'm honest. Just to curl up into a ball in the boot of the Ford Mondeo and rest. Let the good guys, whoever they were, fight the bad guys, whoever they were, and leave me the fuck be.

All I had to do was close my eyes and wish the world away.

Though, you know me by now. I've changed a bit. A lot. No longer was I that ignorant drug dealer from the happy streets of Hounslow. What I was now was something that I would have never contemplated. I was a… I don't know, but something, someone. Able to make a difference, do something right.

I had to make my move.

Parvez had taken too much coke for a first-timer, and I could tell from his muffled voice, from my position in the boot, that he was hopped up and raring to go. But in that state he was bound to make mistakes. Which he had. He had left me in possession of both my Glock and AK-47, in the boot of a car that was less than two years old. Most new cars, as a safety precaution, have an internal latch inside the boot, just in case your mate traps you in there whilst he goes out on a killing spree.

I waited for him to leave. I figured that I could have pulled the latch at any point and escaped, but that would have unsettled him further. I listened to him pray loudly, as if he wanted me to hear. He repeatedly asked Allah for forgiveness and strength. The car door opened and shut. I heard the *click* of the central locking. I was ready. Then another click of the central locking, the car door opening again, some rustling around, a loud sniff. Then the car door shut and then another *click*. I counted sixty seconds in my head and felt my way around the inside of the boot for the latch. I pulled it towards me and the boot door lifted. A middle-aged man watched me rise up, a half-smoked cigarette wastefully dropping from his lips. I stepped out.

'I need to borrow your phone,' I said.

He didn't indicate a yes or a no and I didn't have time to waste, so I reached into my pocket and pulled out the Glock and trained it on him.

'I need to borrow your phone, mate,' I said, and as an afterthought, 'please.' He stood frozen, and what had seemed like a good idea at the time just ended up delaying things. So I slipped the Glock back in my coat pocket and went through his coat, searching for his phone.

I took out his iPhone and swiped the home screen, only to be confronted with a pin code.

'Oh, for fuck's sake,' I snapped. 'Pin number? I need your pin number.'

He mouthed it at me. Sirens blared somewhere close behind me and it seemed to shake him out of his state.

'One two three four,' he said again. I wanted to tell him off for having such a lax security code, but I didn't have time. I tapped the code then dialled Parker's number.

'Mate, really sorry, but I gotta take your phone. Take my advice: get as far away as possible. Tell everyone, get the hell out of here. Some serious shit is about to go down.'

I removed my puffer jacket and flung it in a rubbish skip along with both weapons, and walked away towards Regents Street. Parker answered the phone.

'Parker.'

'Jay.'

'It's happening today. Not New Year's Day. *Today.* At one p.m. Parker? *Parker?*'

'Jay, we know. I am here on location. Tell me yours.'

'I'm approaching Regents Street, then making my way onto Oxford Street. I have to stop Parvez.'

'That's a negative, Jay. Do not approach Parvez or any of the other targets. Turn ar... head towards Piccadilly Cir... Oxford Street is be... vacuated. We have men...'

'Parker, you're breaking up. Parker? *Shit. Parker?*' The line went dead and I pocketed the phone. I didn't quite understand

328

what he wanted to say, but I'd heard enough. I was beyond relieved that help was here and I just knew that Akhtar must have had a change of heart. I punched the air in delight like a sap.

Fucking legend. I love that guy.

I hoped that they were treating him like a hero rather than a terrorist.

I picked up the pace, brushing past anxious shoppers. Traffic that I had been stuck in only minutes ago was all but gone. Whatever was left was carrying out three-point turns and getting as far away as possible from Oxford Street. I should have turned on my heel and followed suit – Parker had warned me as much – but I still had one more person to pull out of the fire.

I started to run.

86

12.43 p.m.

Salman trudged to the men's toilet, dejected. The news had shocked him; it had shocked them all. They discussed the possibility of walking away, starting again, a new target, a new location at a different time. That discussion lasted less than a minute as they all quickly agreed to stick with the plan, regardless of losing two men. Salman's return from the toilet was in stark contrast to his departure; he was nearly bouncing back to the table. The chef, from behind the counter, was looking at him curiously and had a fair idea of what had occurred in the toilet.

Salman sat down and Kevin pointed discreetly at his nose. Salman wiped the residue of cocaine from his nostrils.

'Amirah?' Kevin said.

Amirah stood up and headed to the ladies' toilet.

Kevin waited a moment and then he made his way to the men's. With his colourful, drug-fuelled past, he knew how much he should take to keep him alert and focused. Unlike Salman, who seemed agitated and excited, with crazy eyes darting all over the place.

Kevin did what he had to do. As he sat in the cubicle, those familiar feelings started to return and he remembered why he had easily become addicted to it. He relaxed his breathing and felt his heart rate slow down. The toilet door flew open and he could hear heavy breathing and the scrambling of feet. He wiped his nose, got up and walked out of the cubicle, not expecting to see a female in the men's toilet. Especially one waving around a Glock 19.

'It's Salman. He's freaking out. He's freaking the fuck out,' Amirah blurted.

'Sister, slow down. Breathe.' He recognised the effects of the cocaine.

'Fuck breathing, Kevin.'

'Tell me.'

'I don't know, I... I...' She rubbed her head with the same hand that was holding the Glock. 'Just come with me.'

Kevin nodded, and they walked out. Kevin led and Amirah walked too close behind him, clipping the back of his heels.

Cocaine was a bad idea.

Kevin entered the restaurant floor and stopped in his tracks. Amirah bumped into his back. He evenly took in the scene before he could make a considered decision.

The two waiters and a very distraught and tearful chef were lined up against the counter, hands clasped atop of their heads. Salman was standing in front of them, his long coat in a puddle on the floor at his feet, as he brandished his AK-47. The Glock was tucked into his jeans in the small of his back.

Kevin looked out of the large window. Thankfully no passers-by had yet clocked the fact that there was a gun-wielding lunatic inside. But it was only a matter of time.

'What shall we do?' Amirah asked, her hot breath in his ear, annoying him.

'Stay here. Don't move. Don't do anything.' Kevin walked calmly towards the door and turned the sign so it read *Closed for Business*, and then locked the door from inside.

'Salman,' Kevin said, walking carefully towards him.

'We got a problem, Brother,' Salman said.

'I can see that.' Kevin tried so hard to keep his cool, when all he wanted to do was snatch the gun away and beat Salman around the head with it. 'Tell me what happened.'

'The chef, he... he... he was on the phone. To the police—'

'I swear,' the chef blubbed, 'I wasn't calling the police. I was on the phone to our supplier. Why... Why would I call the police?'

'He kept taking sneaky looks at me, Kevin,' Salman countered. 'He was talking in hushed tones. The bastard is lying to us. He's called the police. I know he has.'

'No... Please. I—'

'Shut up.' Salman held the AK-47 up, his finger flirting with the trigger. The chef flinched and wet himself. The waiters took a small step away from him in disgust.

'*Wait*. Just wait. Let me think for a second.' Kevin was fast losing his cool. But he kept it together. Somebody had to. He looked around the restaurant, at the table where an elderly couple had been sitting. 'Where did the customers go?'

'They left,' Salman said.

'When?'

'When *what*?'

'When did they leave? Did they leave before you decided to sabotage the mission or after?'

'I don't know, I... I don't know. Maybe before.'

'They left before.' Amirah was back at his shoulder. 'When I came out of the toilet they were gone, and Salman is right, that chef *was* on the phone.' She started to again rub her head anxiously with the cold barrel of the Glock. 'That's when Salman lost the plot.'

'Amirah. Will you please put that gun away? I beg you,' Kevin pleaded.

Yes, cocaine was a really bad fucking idea.

87

12.46 p.m.

Lawrence sat slumped in an uncomfortable plastic chair in the makeshift conference room watching live CCTV footage from various different vantage points on Oxford Street. There were desks set up around him, the heavy clacking of fingers on laptops, a variety of ringtones blaring around him. He was satisfied with his part, at least, in gathering the troops and starting the evacuation. He had his iPad in front of him and he had it on Sky News. The press had been quick to report the shooting on the Central line with a high level of accurate detail.

A heavyset policewoman walked into the conference room. Lawrence had not been introduced to her and frowned that she should walk in without challenge.

He looked her up and down. 'Excuse me, lady. You can't be in here. It's packed enough as it is.'

She either ignored or didn't understand the cutting remark.

'Special Constable Cooper,' she announced. 'I need to speak to somebody in charge.'

They both looked around the packed room; everyone looked to be equally in charge and equally in need of direction.

'What is it? I can help,' he said, ushering her out of the room and the noise.

'An emergency call has just come in. It was from a Lebanese restaurant in Soho Square. The head chef, a Siddiqui Raheem, reported suspicious behaviour from three of their customers.'

'Go on.'

'He'd been watching the news, and he knew about the shoot-out on the Tube. He knew that the shooter was dressed in a long coat, and that he was concealing a gun and a small bag of cocaine.'

'The *bloody* press. How did they get that information?' Lawrence shook his head ruefully. 'And?'

'According to Raheem, the three customers in the restaurant are all wearing long coats, still buttoned up, even though the heat is on inside. He also saw one walk out of the toilet with white powder on his nostrils and upper lip.'

'How far is Soho Square to Poland Street?' Lawrence said, as he unlocked the screen on his mobile phone.

'About a seven-minute walk.'

Lawrence put the phone to his ear. 'Take two four-man teams out of Poland Street and send them to Soho Square. Three possible targets sighted.' He covered the mouthpiece of the phone and asked Special Constable Cooper, 'What's the name of that restaurant?'

88

Amirah sat back at the table, chewing slowly on her sandwich. The food helped with the effects of the cocaine and it slowly started to wear off. She glanced at her watch and realised that they were going to be late if they didn't leave in the next few minutes, and even then they would have to run to their location.

Kevin was still trying to pacify a very agitated Salman. Amirah watched impatiently, deciding that if these two could not come to a resolution then she was walking out regardless, with or without them.

'This is not our *jihad*, Brother,' Kevin said.

Amirah was impressed at the level of calm that he exhibited; she would have shot Salman in the head if it meant that she could carry out her God-given mission. Yes, she had also seen the chef making a phone call, but she now conceded that really it could have been to anyone. The coke was making everybody paranoid, and now that she was coming down off it, she could see that all they were doing was wasting time.

'Please put down the gun,' Kevin continued. 'If you shoot them, this place will be crawling with police and our jihad will be over. Is that what you want, Brother? All our hard work going to waste? Please, think with a clear mind.'

Amirah saw Salman's gun waver, the craziness in his eyes seemed to dissipate as the effects of the drugs started to wear off and realisation hit him.

'We have to go, Brother,' Kevin said, putting his hand on the gun and slowly lowering it. 'We have to be quick. Let's tie them up and secure them in the back room.'

Amirah stood up and buttoned up her coat. This was it. It was all that she had wanted since her husband who she no longer spoke about had perished, along with her brother, in a mindless act of violence in her village in Kashmir, carried out by British soldiers. It boiled inside her, every day.

'I'm sorry, Kevin,' Salman said, as he straightened up. 'I lost my mind. I don't know what I was thinking.'

Idiot.

Once this was over, Amirah would have some severe words with Salman, but at this moment her head was back in the game. She reached into her coat pocket and enjoyed the cold feel of the Glock. She tightened the belt around her coat and placed the rucksack on her back. She looked over at Kevin and smiled internally that she had a Brother in him that her own brother would have been proud to stand with. She peered through the window, mentally trying to figure out the quickest way to Poland Street. A raindrop appeared at the window and she lifted her head towards the heavens.

Before her eyes could reach the sky, they stopped halfway up the building across the road. Fourth floor, open window, her eyes locked on a figure dressed in black, elbows on the window frame, pointing a rifle at her.

Salman was right.

'Kevin,' she said calmly. 'There's a sniper up on—'

A muffled shot slammed into her chest and dropped her where she stood. Kevin turned towards her and watched helplessly as her dull beige mac started to turn a beautiful, deep red. He reached into his coat pocket and in a smooth motion flicked off the safety and shot the chef in the head.

A second shot made its way into the back of Kevin's shoulder, the impact spinning him around so that he was facing the window as the third shot found his heart. He fell at Salman's feet, his dead eyes open, staring up at him. Both waiters climbed up and dropped behind the counter, until Salman was the only one standing on the restaurant floor.

He had a fraction of a second to decide his next move. Any moment now, some pretty pissed-off-looking armed *Kafir* cops were going to come in looking for any excuse to rip him in half with bullets. He could take down as many pigs as he could and go out in a blaze of glory. Like a martyr.

The trouble was, he wasn't ready to die.

He was scared.

Salman lifted his arms above his head and dropped to his knees in surrender.

89

12.55 p.m.

Parker had never been comfortable in his role at MI5. He could not get his head around the constant battle, factions that should have shared the same objectives but were too busy furthering their own agendas and careers. Back on tour of duty he had been in charge of millions of pounds' worth of equipment, but here he had trouble sending out a fucking attachment on a fucking smart phone. Hated it. He fucking hated it. Having to dress a certain way in an office environment. He missed the uniform, the weight of it, the blandness working around him like a second skin. Most of all he missed one thing, the one thing that brought so much misery to others but made him carry out his job with ruthless efficiency. It made him feel whole, it made him despise himself. But it made him feel like a soldier again.

He felt the weight of the Browning strapped to his thigh and another strapped to his back. For one day only he had to become that man again, that killer. Coldblooded and merciless.

He would become Chalk.

*

Regular updates were being fed to him through his earpiece. The reports he was receiving were positive. The planned attack looked to be coming apart at the seams. Two of the four teams were now out of play, two terrorists dead, one female critically injured, and two captured alive.

Word had spread quickly to the public that there had been a shooting at Oxford Circus station, but that it had ended quickly and that the evacuation was just a precaution. The shoppers were being directed into the middle of Oxford Street and in batches down the side roads. Some impatiently, of their own accord, found sanctuary in large retailers and shopping malls. The large stores were starting to become packed with bodies, so all fire exits and back doors had to be opened, allowing them to spill out into the safety of the back streets.

Parker could see worry and excitement on their faces. Joking, laughing nervously, filming the organised pandemonium on their handheld devices. Savouring every moment for the stories they would be recounting for the rest of their lives. The police were doing a good job. The public too. Information had not reached them yet on the second shooting at a nearby Lebanese restaurant. It was only a matter of time until it did, and that's when, inevitably, they would lose the plot.

The earpiece vibrated and Lawrence's voice came through.

'Parker. We're doing well.'

'We're not there yet,' Parker said.

'No, no, we're not. But signs are looking promising. South side of Oxford Street has been cleared. I can't see shooters turning up there without a target. If they do, they'll be dropped.' Lawrence sighed. 'The problem is this end. We have a huge amount of civilians gathered outside Oxford Circus station. They're calm at the moment but I can't see them getting clear in the next eight minutes... Hang on, Parker, I've got something coming through.'

Lawrence was right, they were doing well. Of the nine attackers, five had been nullified.

Which left four.

One of the four was Jay.

Which left three.

Of the three, two were heading to a redundant location; it had been evacuated apart from a strong police presence.

Which left the lone gunman.

Parvez Ahmed.

Parker looked up towards the apartment above Tezenis. The grand French doors leading to the balcony just above Oxford Street. Below the balcony there were masses of bodies stuck in a human traffic jam, not quite knowing which direction to move in. He pushed through the bodies, gently at first, mumbling his apologies. Any force in his movement would only serve to panic the public.

'Parker.' Lawrence was back in his ear, voice higher, on edge. 'Somebody matching Parvez's description has been spotted. He was seen letting himself into a narrow walkway next to Tezenis. He's heading into the apartment above.'

Parker moved quickly towards the apartment, more forceful now, his body abruptly shouldering shoppers out of the way.

'If he does make it out onto that balcony, he'll be taken out by snipers,' Lawrence said.

'We cannot let it get to that stage. As soon as a shot is fired, it's going to cause a mass stampede. We'll lose lives from that alone. Tell them to hold fire. I'm going in. I won't let Parvez step on that balcony.'

90

12.56 p.m.

Irfan needed his elder brother more than he ever had before. Even more than when his teacher at high school, Mr Miller, had stood back and watched young Irfan have the shit kicked out of him by a group of bullies. When he had got home that day and told his brother, it was the teacher that took the brunt of Yasir's violent revenge, not the bullies. Mr Miller had never again returned to the school. Mr Miller had never again walked without aid of a walking stick.

Irfan was hidden inside an abandoned Royal Mail truck. On his knees amongst the mail sacks on the cold floor, praying that he could make the right decision, a decision worthy of a jihadi. He could not fathom what had happened; the streets should have been packed full of Kafirs, but they had disappeared before his very eyes only to be replaced with more cops than he could count. He had to adapt to his surroundings. Improvise. He thought hard about an alternative target. Centre Point, a thirty-three-storey office block, was an option. A central London landmark. He could easily walk in, guns blazing, taking out whoever he set his sights on. He pushed the rear door of the truck open slightly and peeked towards the structure. He couldn't see from his vantage point, but he pictured the faces of hundreds of office workers staring curiously out of the windows. His mind was made up.

Irfan stepped out of the truck. His target was no more than sixty metres away. If he could make that distance without getting shot then his jihad was still very much on. He moved slowly, bent at the waist, using cars as cover, fifty metres away, forty. He unbuttoned the top two buttons of his coat and picked up the pace. One more car to get past and then he would have a ten-metre clear run into the building. He crouched low behind the last car, breathing hard, and undid the last few buttons. He rested his head on the number plate and willed his breathing to slow. He dismissed the idea of consuming cocaine, as he was already buzzing with anticipation.

Irfan stood up, faced his target and whispered, '*Allah hu Akbar.*' He took a step forward. A hand grabbed him by the scruff of the neck and pulled him back down onto the ground.

'Stay down,' Yasir hissed.

'*Yasir?*' The words soundlessly rushed from his lips as a tear escaped from his eye.

'Just stay down, all right?'

'I don't know what happened. They knew... They knew we were coming,' Irfan said, tears freely running down his face.

'I know.' Yasir nodded solemnly.

'I have an idea, Brother.' Irfan wiped the tears from his eyes. 'We hit Centre Point. There must be a thousand *Kafirs* in there.'

'Centre Point is a shell. It's empty. Has been for the last two years.'

Irfan leaned his head against the back of the car and closed his eyes tightly. Yasir opend his mouth to speak but Irfan's eyes shot open. They were alive with hope.

'Across the road, there's a Garfunkel's,' Irfan said excitedly. 'There has to be at least fifty diners in there, plus staff. Adapt and improvise. We do it, we do it now.' His eyes travelled over Yasir. 'Where's your coat? Your guns?'

'It's over, Irfan. This is not what we planned. It's a suicide mission. You walk in there, you're coming out in a body bag. There are cops everywhere.'

Anger and disappointment flashed across Irfan's face.

'I'm going in without you.'

'We are not martyrs, Irfan. We are soldiers. We walk away from here and start planning our next attack. You are no good to me dead. There is no way that I am letting you go in there. Remember the words of Al-Mudarris.'

Irfan nodded.

'Leave no man behind.'

91

It took me the best part of thirty minutes to get through the crowd and onto the corner of Oxford Street. I could see the entrance that led up to the apartment above Tezenis and I knew if I approached it I was bound to get stopped, captured or shot. I rounded the corner unchallenged and stood with the crowd. The balcony above Tezenis was empty, but Parvez was sure to be in the apartment already. A police van had climbed the kerb and was parked just under the balcony, and I thought briefly about climbing onto the roof of it so I could get closer to the balcony. But two things were against me. One was that the balcony would still have been out of reach by about seven foot, and secondly, how the hell would I climb onto the roof of a police van without getting nabbed? I discounted that thought and tried to look for a way in, within the means of my limited skillset.

Amongst the crowd in front of me, a head stood out above the rest. I pushed and squeezed through until I was by his side.

'You have to get me in, Parker.'

'Jay, get away from here,' he said, marching on.

'Let me talk to him. I can help,' I said, matching him for pace.

'Get away, Jay.'

'Parker, will you fucking listen? You're going to go up and kill him without question and without thought.' He stopped outside the entrance to the apartment. Two men in suits, trying to fit in but clearly MI5, nodded at Parker. I grabbed his arm. '*Please.*'

He shook his head and made his way up to the apartment.

92

12.59 p.m.

Parker let himself into the apartment and into the large marble hallway. Fixing the suppressor onto his Browning, he held it up in shooting position. He expected it to feel natural, as though an extension of his arm, but his hand shook. Using his foot, he slowly pushed the door open and stole a quick glance into the living room. Parvez was standing at the tall French doors, looking out towards the balcony, cradling an AK-47 in his arms. A Glock 19 was tucked into the back of his jeans. Parker took a breath and entered the room, his gun trained on Parvez's back.

'Parvez Ahmed.'

'It's too late,' Parvez said, without turning around.

'Drop your weapon and turn around slowly, now.'

'It's almost time.'

The alarm on Parvez's digital watch went off.

93

The alarm on my digital watch started to sound. I looked up at the balcony and through the net curtains of the French doors I saw a flash of light, quickly followed by another. Red dots speckled the otherwise white net curtains and my heart took a dive.

The double doors opened and Parvez staggered out onto the balcony. The AK-47 was hanging freely around his neck, swinging side to side as he struggled to place one foot in front of the other. He winced as he reached behind and produced the Glock, struggling to lift it into shooting position, as though it was too heavy for him.

I shouted his name and I know he didn't hear me, but his eyes locked onto mine. He smiled weakly at me and found the strength to lift the gun.

Another shot rang out from behind him and the impact sent my friend tumbling over the balcony, landing flat out on his back on the roof of the police van, the back of his head smashing the rooftop lights.

That's when a wall of screams deafened me and I found myself being knocked to the ground as panic kicked in and there was an almighty charge. I didn't have time to understand what had just happened on the balcony, as I was struggling for breath. On my hands and knees in a crowd of legs, trying to get myself up on my feet, a knee smashed into my ribs, sending me onto my side and smashing my head against the pavement. I forced myself to keep consciousness, as heavy footsteps clambered over my beaten body. I curled myself up into a small ball, as kicks rained down on my head, my arms and my legs. As the knocks slowed I got back onto my hands and knees and inched onto the pavement, managing to hang onto a lamppost for support. Slowly, I lifted myself up and took in the scene in front of me.

It was hell.

I watched as men, women and children pushed, pulled, elbowed and trampled their way to safety – without any clue as to where safety lay. My head throbbed and I felt blood trickle down my face. My body screamed at me in pain. I steeled myself and screamed back at it. I moved like a bull with my head down as I forced my way to the entrance of the apartment. It was no longer guarded.

Using both hands on the bannister, I took two steps at a time. The effort made me lightheaded. I pushed open the front door and made my way into the living room. The room was empty apart from one of Parvez's Crocs laying sadly on its side in front of the blood-splattered net curtains on the French doors.

I pushed the doors open and stepped out onto the balcony.

Parker was there, looking down at the manic scenes below him.

I stood next to him.

'Are you all right?' he asked.

I looked down at the roof of the police van. Parvez, on his back, motionless, staring up at me. Glock in his dead hand and the AK-47 hanging uselessly off his neck.

Was I all right?

I didn't think that needed answering. So instead, finding my voice, my eyes fixed on Parvez, I said, 'The Teacher. He's my father.'

Parker nodded.

I removed my eyes from my friend and looked at Parker.

'You knew?' I said.

'Sinclair,' he said.

I punched him in the chest with everything I had, but I was tired, and it was weak. I punched him again. 'Why didn't you tell me?' My punches grew with strength as I started to howl and tears flooded my face. Pounding him over and over. He stepped forward and held me tightly in his arms as I screamed for him to let me go.

'It's okay,' he said, as snowflakes started to fall and dissolve. 'I've got you, son.'

346

Epilogue

I've seen some things that I know will be scarred into my consciousness until my dying day. The pictures form in my brain like a reel from a movie, telling a story that nobody wants to hear. The devastation of the drone attacks in a small village amongst the mountains called Hisarak. The small bodies covered in white sheets. The burned face of a man who I loved and loathed. The face of the Shaitan.

My friend, Parvez, splayed out, dead on the roof of a police van.

That image did the fucking rounds, man. It was captured and celebrated by the media and was just as recognisable as that blown-up London bus a decade ago.

It had taken three months of bullshit therapy for me to realise that whatever was in my head was not leaving anytime soon. They say time is a great healer. Yeah, well. We'll see about that.

I was no longer MI5, they told me. I laughed in their faces when they said that.

As if I ever was.

I was never a spy. I was a fucking pawn in their sick game. They knew, *Sinclair knew* that the Teacher was my father from the very start and they used me to get close to him. But the dumb fucks that they are, and after all the information I have given them, they still haven't managed to catch my dad.

I wasn't the only one that had parted company with those leeches. Parker resigned from his post too. He was a broken man after that fateful day. His decision to not let me up to talk Parvez down ate him up. His inability to stop Parvez from getting onto the balcony, which led to a further shooting, which in turn *led* to a fucking stampede so brutal that it took the lives of six. He blamed himself.

Rightly fucking so.

I tried to move forward the best way that I could. I cut out any semblance of that period of my life like cancer.

Akhtar reached out to me. If it wasn't for him, God knows what kind of massacre would have taken place that day. But I couldn't, wouldn't, let myself reach back to him. I didn't need a person like that in my life, a constant reminder of the horror my life had been.

'We haven't done that in ages,' Idris said.

'Hmm,' I said, as my automatic wipers came to life at the first sign of rain. 'Done what?'

'Sat in silence.'

'Yeah, I guess.' I turned onto his road.

I had been spending a lot of time with Idris. I hadn't wanted to but he was annoyingly insistent and manoeuvred his way back into my life. He turned up at my house at the start of the year, armed with a holdall, and announced that he would be staying with me for a few days. I still hadn't fully told him everything, and he never asked, but like a good friend, he was there when I needed him most.

'Five-a-side tonight, don't forget.'

'I can't tonight.'

'I expect you to pick me up at quarter to eight,' he said, ignoring me.

'Why am I always picking your ass up and dropping your ass home?' I said, as I pulled up outside his house and killed the engine.

'Cos you got the motor,' he said, gesticulating his hands around my car like a magician. 'Don't be late!'

'Seriously, I can't play tonight. I've got a flight to catch tomorrow.'

'Oh shit, Qatar! Is that tomorrow?' Make sure you give your mum a kiss from me.'

'I'll tell her you said hello,' I said, making a face.

'When are you back?'

'Fourteen nights and fifteen days.'

'Why couldn't you just say two weeks?'

I shrugged, reached into the back seat and brought forward a plastic bag. I pulled out a maroon silk shawl.

'I got this for Mum. What do you think?'

'Yeah, very nice. Will you tell her it's from both of us?

'No.'

He let himself out of the car. I started the engine. He knocked on the passenger-side window. I slid it down.

'What now?' I said. I could tell from the expression on his face that he wanted to say something soppy and meaningful, like: *after all you've been through, you deserve a holiday*. But he knew better.

'Send me a postcard.'

'Not going to happen.'

'I'm gonna miss you.' He grinned.

'Fuck off!'

'Call me the moment you land otherwise I won't be able to sleep.'

I slid the window up, hoping to catch his head in the frame. He moved his head back and gave me the finger.

I drove off, smiling.

It was small normalities that I once took for granted, slowly creeping their way back into my life. The back and forth with Idris reminded me just how nice it was to be regular, even if it was a fleeting feeling. But that's what my life demanded, more moments like that. I'd had my car serviced and valeted earlier, whilst I went shopping in Southall for a gift to take for my mum. It was bland, it was uneventful. It was perfect.

I pulled up in my driveway and that sense of normality was ripped away from me once again, and my mind went to that dark place as I looked at the *For Sale* sign erected outside Parvez's house. His parents had moved out soon after his funeral. A funeral that I had not been invited to. The intense media scrutiny, and a regular brick through their windows, was too much for them to take. I knew that they had held me responsible, and forever would.

I closed my eyes tightly and let the cool breeze coming from my window wash over me. Tomorrow, I'd try for normal again.

I opened my eyes at the sound of a car door closing, and standing at my window was Silas.

'Hello, old chum,' he said, beaming. 'I haven't seen you in ages.' I caught a glint of something as his arm snaked through my window and sliced my throat from ear to ear.

I blinked rapidly as both of my hands flew to my neck, blood seeping through my fingers and onto my mum's silk shawl.

They say you see your life flash before your eyes in those precious last moments.

Not for me.

Instead, I wondered how I would be remembered.

As a drug dealer, a jihadist, a spy?

Or just another Muslim, who died struggling to find his place in the world.

Acknowledgements

I have to start by thanking God, for kicking me out of the slow lane and pushing me to my limit. To my amazing wife, who tried and failed to get a line in the book and share the credit. Thanks, sweetheart, I could not have done it without you. My two beautiful boys, who inspired me and continue to do so more than they will ever know.

To my mum, my dad, for constantly telling me how great I am. I'll never tire of hearing that! To my brother, for taking an obscene amount of time reading the first draft and advising me.

A huge thanks to Julian Alexander – agent extraordinaire! Even at its worst, you saw something special in my writing. For that I will always be grateful. Also Ben Clark, Niamh O'Grady and all at LAW literary agency.

To my amazing editor, Clio Cornish, you have been fantastic throughout. Thank you for guiding me through the process with your distinctive vision and helping shape my book. I hope we are on the same team for many books to come. To Lily Capewell, you made me feel brave when I wanted to hide. To Lisa Milton, and the wider team at HQ/HarperCollins for all your help and support. For those involved, who I have missed out or not had the pleasure to yet meet, you are appreciated.

A special mention to Ben Aaronovitch and BA Paris. Your support made me believe.

I guess I should shout out to my friends, otherwise I won't hear the end of it. Look closely: there are parts of all of you in this story.

Last but not even close to least, I must give a huge thanks to one of our finest authors, Stephen Leather, for taking the time out to read a very early piece of work that I almost chickened out of sending to you. Hitting send was the best move I have ever made and it was thanks to you that I found myself in Julian's office and subsequently signing a book deal.

These are just a few names that have helped me achieve my dream, and I am truly and forever thankful.